DREAMS OF LILACS

LYNN KURLAND

JOVE BOOKS, NEW YORK

THE BERKLEY PUBLISHING GROUP
Published by the Penguin Group
Penguin Group (USA) LLC
375 Hudson Street, New York, New York 10014

USA • Canada • UK • Ireland • Australia • New Zealand • India • South Africa • China

penguin.com

A Penguin Random House Company

DREAMS OF LILACS

A Jove Book / published by arrangement with Kurland Book Productions, Inc.

Jove Books are published by The Berkley Publishing Group.
JOVE® is a registered trademark of Penguin Group (USA) LLC.
The "J" design is a trademark of Penguin Group (USA) LLC.

For information, address: The Berkley Publishing Group,
a division of Penguin Group (USA) LLC,
375 Hudson Street, New York, New York 10014.

ISBN: 978-0-515-15347-7

PUBLISHING HISTORY
Jove mass-market edition / May 2014

PRINTED IN THE UNITED STATES OF AMERICA

10 9 8 7 6 5 4 3 2 1

Cover art by Jim Griffin.
Cover design by George Long.

"Clearly one of romance's finest writers."   —*The Oakland Press*

"Both powerful and sensitive . . . a wonderfully rich and rewarding book."
                    —#1 *New York Times* bestselling author Susan Wiggs

"A sweet, tenderhearted time travel romance."
                                        —*Joyfully Reviewed*

"A story on an epic scale . . . Kurland has written another time travel marvel . . . Perfect for those looking for a happily ever after."   —*RT Book Reviews*

"[A] triumphant romance."   —*Fresh Fiction*

"A perfect blend of medieval intrigue and time travel romance. I was totally enthralled from the beginning to the end."
                                        —*Once Upon a Romance*

"Woven with magic, handsome heroes, lovely heroines, oodles of fun, and plenty of romance . . . just plain wonderful."
                                        —*Romance Reviews Today*

"Spellbinding and lovely, this is one story readers won't want to miss."   —*Romance Reader at Heart*

"Breathtaking in its magnificent scope."   —*Night Owl Romance*

"Sweetly romantic and thoroughly satisfying."   —*Booklist*

Chapter 1

Isabelle de Piaget leaned against the wall of her father's great hall, out of the torchlight, and wondered if it were possible for a woman to hide her almost unbearable urge to panic so her family wouldn't notice.

It wasn't something she considered very often. In fact, she supposed she had never once in her score and three years of life considered such a thing. Her life, she would be the first to admit, was so near to perfection as to be indistinguishable from it. Her parents were kind and loving, her siblings very tolerable, and her surroundings magnificent. She had never once been beaten, never not had enough to eat or warm things to wear, never had anything terrible happen to her. Her life had been substantially less pleasant when she'd been sent to market for fathers of potential husbands to look over, but that hadn't been her family's fault. In truth, she could have expected nothing less.

What she hadn't expected, however, was what a messenger had handed her but a handful of hours earlier, a missive she had the very unpleasant feeling would completely change the course of her life—

"You're thinking very hard."

She closed her eyes briefly when she realized her twin brother, Miles, was standing next to her. She wondered if she'd said anything aloud in her distress, then decided the best thing to do was attack before Miles thought too much about what she might or might not have said.

"'Tis good for the faculties to engage in robust thought now and again," she said briskly. "You might give it a try."

He only leaned back against the wall casually. "I would, but don't want to hurt myself. You, however, seem to have little fear of the same. Would you care to divulge what strengthens your robust faculties at the moment?"

As if she would trust him with her current thoughts! Miles was a vault when it came to the hearing of secrets guaranteed to produce a swoon in those with a less sturdy stomach, true, but to reveal the contents of the missive she had just received would be too much for his ironclad belly.

She glanced at him to find that he was still studying her with undue scrutiny.

"I wasn't thinking about anything," she protested.

He shot her a skeptical look.

"Very well," she said, desperate to get him to go away. "I was thinking about how much I love my family. Why don't you go sit with them over by the fire and allow me to think kind thoughts about you as well?"

He shrugged slightly. "You looked as though you might need aid in your latest plot. How could I not offer my services?"

"Plot," she repeated, wishing she'd been able to add to that what might sound more like a careless laugh than a sick sort of quack better suited to a duck preparing to have a final waddle before winding up on a spit. "I'm not plotting."

Miles only lifted an eyebrow briefly, then smiled and leaned his head back against the wall. Isabelle attempted to imitate his pose, but the best she could do was wrap her arms around herself and try not to shiver as she looked out at the group of souls clustered there in front of her. She could bring innumerable evenings to mind where the family had either gathered where they were currently in the great hall or in a more intimate setting in their sire's solar. If anything happened to them . . .

She pulled herself away from that thought before it got away from her and blossomed into a panic she truly couldn't control.

She took a deep breath, then considered her family in a measured, detached fashion.

Robin was there with his wife, Anne, and their two spawn. Amanda was there as well with her husband, Jackson the Fourth, along with their daughter and newborn son, Jackson the Fifth. She herself was there with Miles, of course, which was perhaps rarer than she would have cared for. Miles tended to have itchy feet, which kept him always looking for the next adventure.

Her younger brothers, John and Montgomery, were also there, freshly knighted and looking particularly happy to be sitting sprawled in chairs before the fire. Well, Montgomery looked happy. John looked as if he might be plotting something. Then again, of late John always looked as if he were considering things he shouldn't have been. Dangerous things.

She understood that, as it happened.

The only ones missing were Nicholas and Jennifer, who were currently at Nicholas's keep in France, Beauvois, awaiting the birth of their second son. Her mother planned to travel to France soon to be of use to her daughter-in-law. Robin would stay at Artane with his family, no doubt, to see to their father's affairs, but it was very likely that the rest of the family would find itself in France to celebrate Nicky and Jennifer's new child. All in close proximity.

An interesting coincidence, that, to be sure.

"You're wheezing."

"I spent too much time in the stables today," Isabelle answered without hesitation. "It's entirely possible I sniffed too much hay."

It was also possible that the thought of her family being together in France in the near future was enough to leave her unable to breathe. How much easier life had been when she and her siblings had been young and innocent and heedless of any potential danger. She sighed.

"Why must things change?"

She wished she could take the words back the moment she said them, but it was too late. She looked reluctantly at Miles to find him studying her too closely for her comfort. Indeed, he had turned to face her, leaning his shoulder against the stone.

"Time is a river you cannot stop," he said. "All you can do is navigate it as best you can."

"I might have an opinion on where my boat is going."

He didn't look at all surprised, which made her wonder if perhaps she should be more discreet about allowing her thoughts to show on her face.

"And are you considering manning the tiller?"

"Of course not," she said, trying to put just the right amount of firmness in her tone. "I'm just babbling. Besides, where would I go?"

"Perhaps a better question is, where would you go if you could filch a horse and be on your way without having to ask permission?"

"My only destination is the fire across the hall where I might sit with my family and enjoy the evening."

He didn't seem inclined to lead the way. "You know I won't say anything to anyone," he remarked mildly. "If you cared to unburden yourself."

Which, she had to concede, was the absolute truth. If there were anyone alive she could trust with her most appalling secrets, it would be Miles. She suppressed the urge to look around her to see if she were being eavesdropped on, paused, then gave in to the impulse. She glanced about her whilst trying not to look as if she were glancing about herself. Then she looked at her brother, just to see if he looked at all queasy.

He didn't, damn him anyway.

She, however, felt profoundly ill. It wasn't that she wasn't used to a fair amount of scheming. She was a de Piaget lass, after all, and her mother and older sister were famous for their plots and schemes, things that were discussed regularly and with great enthusiasm. By the ladies of the hall, at least. Her father tended to close his eyes briefly, breathe carefully a time or two, then find something requiring his immediate attention elsewhere when faced with a retelling of those tales. Her brothers simply shook their heads, as if they were unequal to expressing their admiration for deeds accomplished.

She paused. Well, perhaps that wasn't entirely accurate. Her eldest brother, Robin, tended to roll his eyes and summarily dismiss any of the truly noteworthy pieces of mischief his female relatives had combined. Her next oldest brother, Nicholas, was wont to simply walk away without comment. Miles generally smiled indulgently, whilst her next youngest brother, John, would never stand still long enough to hear the successful resolution of the adventure. Her youngest brother, Montgomery, was the one who shivered violently at any retelling, though she had the feeling that it was less out of admiration than it was sheer terror. Then again, he had been in the thick of more of their plots than he likely cared to think on.

That was definitely something to remember, should the need for a willing participant in a plot arise.

"Iz?"

She took a deep breath. "I'm thinking about an adventure."

There, that sounded reasonable. It sounded a far sight more reasonable than telling him that she'd received a missive addressed to her specifically that instructed her to find a way to present herself immediately at a particular abbey in France or her grandparents' lives would be the forfeit. She'd been so stunned first by the fact that anyone would know her name that she'd hardly had the presence of mind to ask who had engaged the messenger. The man had said he'd simply been handed the missive by someone in York who had paid him very handsomely for his services—

"Does this adventure involve a boat?"

She looked at her brother to find him smiling faintly at her, as if he thought to tease her for her plans. She took a deep breath.

"It might, actually."

His smile faded abruptly. "You cannot be serious."

"I thought you were merely listening, not commenting."

He shut his mouth that had fallen open. "So I was. Go ahead."

Isabelle suppressed the urge to shift. Miles would notice that and know that she was being slightly less than frank.

"I was thinking I might make a little journey," she said. "To see a relative or two." She paused. "Not in England."

"I see," he said, and no doubt he did. "Whilst I'm always eager to make a journey, I wonder why—if you're seeking an adventure not in England—you don't wait and be about your business with Mother and her enormous guard?" He looked at her pointedly. "She'll be going to France in a month, as I'm sure you already know."

"Oh, I don't know," Isabelle said, waving her hand about in what she hoped was an airy, careless fashion. "I thought it might be interesting to make a journey alone."

"To France," he said carefully.

"It has been done before."

He looked almost . . . unsettled, which for Miles was rather unsettling indeed. "Isabelle," he said, using her entire name, which for him was also rather unusual, "you cannot simply traipse about the wilds of England and France by yourself."

"Why not?" she asked. "You do."

"I am not the stunning youngest daughter of Rhys de Piaget."

"You aren't ugly, Miles," she said. "Not entirely."

He smiled and even she, who had more than ample memories of just how awful he'd been as a lad of ten, had to admit he was quite possibly the most handsome of her parents' sons, damn him anyway.

"I have a sword," he noted.

"I could find a sword."

"I know how to use mine."

"And you think I couldn't manage the same?" she said archly.

He turned, leaned his back against the wall, and rubbed his hands over his face. "Iz, I don't doubt there are many things you could do if you set your mind to it," he said with a sigh, "but hefting a sword isn't one of them."

"I've watched you lads in the lists often enough. And Amanda can use a sword. Why can't I?"

He shot her a look. "Because you haven't the temperament of your older sister who would just as soon stab me as to look at me if I vexed her."

"I won't need a sword," she said confidently. "I thought I would go in disguise."

"Of course you did."

"As a lad."

"What else?"

"I don't think anyone will notice me."

Miles looked at her, then laughed. "Believe that if you want."

"A little dirt here, a smudge there, and *voilà*," she said firmly. "A lad too uninteresting to bother with."

He shook his head. "I imagine it would take a bit more than dirt to hide who you are to any but the most witless of men, but we'll argue that point later. I still don't understand why you can't simply wait for Mother and go in her company."

"I need an adventure."

"Then cast caution to the wind and ride to the shore when it threatens rain."

She would have glared at him, but the missive she'd shoved down the front of her gown was burning her like a handful of live coals. If she didn't do what she'd been instructed to do, her entire family would die. Wasn't that what had been said? She was to present herself in France, at the abbey at Caours, and not tell anyone why she was doing so. Her family would perish, or so the missive said, if any but she arrived. Details about her parents and siblings had been provided, details that could have only come from someone who had either observed her family closely or knew someone who had.

She looked down her nose at her brother. "I require a journey of slightly more substance than a trip to the shore. And I have it very well thought out, thank you very much."

His mouth worked for a moment or two, then he resorted to blinking at her as if he'd never seen her before. "But why?"

Well, that was something at least that she absolutely couldn't tell him. She cast about for something plausible to say, which wasn't all that difficult. The truth was, she had been longing to have a change of locale for some time, for very particular reasons. She turned to face him.

"Because I'm tired of being merely the one who's left."

He frowned. "What are you talking about?"

"It's what they call me," she said. "The fathers who come here looking for a wife for their sons. They come for Amanda, apparently unable to reconcile themselves to the fact that she's been wed for four years. Once they can no longer deny that Amanda is not for sale, they look around in consternation. After that—without fail—they announce that they'll settle for the one who's left." She lifted her chin. "They don't even know my name."

He winced. "Oh, Iz—"

"And that, Miles, is why I want to make a journey on my own. So someone at some point in the future will know my name, even if it's merely to associate it with an ill-advised adventure."

He reached out, slung his arm around her shoulders, and pulled her into a quick embrace. Then he pulled away, put both hands on her shoulders, and looked at her seriously.

"The ones who matter know who you are."

"Unfortunately, they are not the ones presenting themselves at the gates and offering to take my dowry."

"Father isn't forcing you to wed, is he?" Miles asked.

"You know he isn't, but that hardly matters. I'm a score and three. Too old to be home and a burden to my parents."

He shot her a look of disbelief. "You can't believe they feel that way."

"I feel that way." She shrugged his hands off her shoulders and wrapped her arms around herself. "I know I'll have to wed eventually, and I suppose I must needs wed someone who doesn't know my name, but perhaps I could have at least a few days to myself." She looked at him. "Before I give up my freedom."

He shook his head. "I'm enormously glad I'm not a woman."

"So am I. I wouldn't be able to filch your clothes otherwise."

He scowled at her briefly, then laughed apparently in spite of himself. "My clothes are far too big for you. I think even Montgomery's wouldn't fit you."

"Which is why I set things of his aside several years ago."

"You, Isabelle de Piaget, are a remarkable woman."

"Desperate, rather." She looked at him. "You won't give me away, will you?"

He sighed deeply. "Fool that I am, nay. But," he added, suddenly serious, "I will insist on coming with you."

"But—"

"I must away to Wyckham for a day or two to see to business for Nick, but I will return as quickly as possible. I insist that you wait for me, then I will take you south myself. Without a guard—well, not much of one at any rate—and we'll both go as a pair of lads. I guarantee you'll have adventure enough."

It was an offer she never would have expected and knew she shouldn't spurn.

If only—

"Very well," she said, wondering how much time she would need to spend in the chapel, repenting of her lies, by the end of her quest. "I'll wait for you."

"Vow it," he insisted, "or I march across the floor and tell Father all right now." He held out his hand. "Vow it."

She sighed, rolled her eyes, then linked thumbs with him as they'd been doing since they were small. Foolish, perhaps, but it had been their sealing of secret bargains from the time they'd first hit upon the idea whilst about the goodly work of repaying Robin for some indignity perpetrated on their very young selves.

"Satisfied?" she muttered.

"I suppose I have no reason not to be," he said, looking at her closely, "though I daresay your heart wasn't in that last bit."

"I'm tired."

"Good," he said. "Stay tired until I return. I'll leave before dawn tomorrow, then return as quickly as I may." He kissed her forehead, then put his hands on her shoulders. "Don't do anything foolish, Iz. I'm in earnest."

"Me?" she said, finding that she couldn't put a decent amount of scoffing in her tone. "Why would I do anything foolish?"

He pursed his lips, then released her and walked away. She resumed her place against the wall and watched him go. Men. Impossible creatures who were, she had to admit, quite often baffled by things they couldn't possibly understand, such as the necessity of leaving on a quest to save one's family.

She could only hope Miles wouldn't kill her when he found her after realizing she had sailed for France without him.

Four days later, she stood in an inn, fully prepared to take a ship to France at dusk, and hoped that she hadn't killed a different brother.

Montgomery lay at her feet, senseless and drooling.

It was her doing, of course. After Miles and John had left for Wyckham, she had convinced him to come south with her by telling her father she wished to see her mother's mother, Joanna of Segrave, before she spent the summer in France aiding Jennifer with her new babe. She and Montgomery had been sent with a large guard, which she hadn't considered an impediment to her plans. Surely no one would notice a lad slipping out the window and trotting off to the docks by way of the garden, would one?

She had presented her true plan to Montgomery and been utterly unsurprised by his unwillingness to participate in it. She had walked over to the window to rethink her strategy only to have Fate step in and offer aid where she'd least expected it.

Montgomery, always susceptible to even the possibility of feminine tears, had sighed deeply, then approached to see how she fared, no doubt thinking that she was on the verge of a decent bout of the former. He had apparently seen something on the floor he'd assumed was hers and bent to retrieve it.

She had turned, then spotted something herself, which was the trajectory Montgomery's head would take when he straightened, and how easing the shutters open just a bit more might lead to an abrupt encounter for her very chivalrous if not stubborn brother. Her father had, as it happened, insisted she learn to cipher and do the odd calculation right along with her siblings. Who could have predicted it might serve her at just the moment when her straits were most dire?

She had swung the shutter open, shrieked for her brother to look out the window, then watched as he had caught the top of his head against the wood. He had gasped out a particularly unknightlike curse, fallen to his knees, then continued on his way down. She supposed it could be debated later, but she'd been fairly sure that hitting his head on the edge of a trunk on his way to the floor had contributed substantially to his state of senselessness.

Moving him had been impossible, so she'd draped her gown over his inert, manly form, then arranged her hair she'd cut off and fashioned into a makeshift wig over his head.

All of which had left her where she was, standing near the window and preparing to make her escape.

Montgomery groaned, then opened his eyes and looked at her blearily.

"Iz?"

She leaned over and patted his head. "Sleep, brother. You're very tired."

He frowned, but he apparently couldn't fight the relentless closing of his eyelids. He began to snore.

She supposed he would survive.

She stood, had a final look at Montgomery to make sure he was still alive, then took her courage in hand and slipped out the window.

She carefully tiptoed along the roof of the floor below. It was more difficult than she'd suspected it would be, but she pressed on. She had spent her fair share of time listening breathlessly to her brothers' most exciting tales, most of which had seemed to include daring escapes, so she'd known what to expect. A pity she hadn't spent just as much time actually sliding down slippery wooden roofs and thereafter hanging from the edge of them as she had listening to tales recounting that sort of thing.

She wasn't altogether certain she hadn't made an unwholesome noise of some sort, but that couldn't be helped. She looked below her, saw that only a well-rotting compost pile lay there, and let go of wood that seemed quite content to see the last of her. She landed ungracefully—flat on her back, actually—but quickly scrambled up to her feet. She brushed her cloak off, rather wished she hadn't cut her hair with her dagger upstairs so it could have prevented a few things she didn't care to identify winding up down her back, then put her shoulders back and continued on her way.

The streets were rather more populous than she would have expected, but 'twas a port town after all and there were seamen coming and going about what she assumed was their usual business. She walked down the way quickly, as if she were truly in a great hurry to be off and doing. She supposed the manly swagger could be saved for another time, when she had more experience with feigning an identity and a sex not her own.

The ship she'd selected for her journey was where she'd seen it earlier in the day, but it was obviously preparing to make sail. Isabelle felt a thrill of something go through her. It wasn't fear, surely. It was excitement mixed with purpose. She would have preferred that excitement come with less of a desire to heave what little supper she'd managed earlier onto the nearest empty spot, but she supposed she would learn to manage that in time as well.

She looked about her for the only part of her plan she supposed Miles would have approved of: Arthur of Harwych, her chosen companion on the voyage south. She supposed she might pay a price eventually for ruthlessly using the affection of a would-be suitor for her own purposes, but she would pay that price later. She hadn't been foolish enough to think she should cross the seas without someone to guard her back. Perhaps it was sheer good fortune that Arthur had appeared at her father's gates—and only at the gates given that he was never allowed inside—the morning Miles had left for Wyckham. A quick conversation with him out of earshot of her father's guards had resulted in his promise to meet her in her current locale and accompany her to France. He would likely spend more of the journey puking over the railing than being of any use to her, but that couldn't be helped.

She supposed at some point she would need to tell him what she was about, but her plan was to simply insist that he return on the same boat to England and tell her family that she was safe. She had no doubt he would do whatever she asked of him, poor lad.

Unfortunately, at the moment it looked as if he wouldn't be doing anything at all for her given that he was nowhere to be found. She muttered a curse under her breath. If the man arrived on time to his own burying, she would be thoroughly surprised. Obviously, she would have to see to her business on her own. She had no other choice.

She saw the captain standing on the dock, looking over his craft with a critical eye. He bellowed an order or two, then folded his beefy arms over his chest and frowned fiercely as he watched those orders be carried out without hesitation. A man not to be trifled with, obviously.

But he was no doubt a businessman and would be just as glad as the next man for a bit of gold in his purse. She walked up to him as if she had every right to, then stopped and waited for him to acknowledge her. She cleared her throat for good measure, then folded her arms over her chest as she'd watched her brother Robin do countless times when preparing to intimidate those less intimidating than himself.

The captain turned his head and looked at her with one eyebrow raised. "Aye, lad?"

"I seek passage," Isabelle said in her manliest tones. "I've the coin to pay for it."

"Let me see."

She had a handful of gold sovereigns in a small sack she'd kept separate from the bulk of her funds, lest she reveal all she had at once and find herself without it. She held the sack up where the captain could see it.

"I'll open it on deck," she said firmly.

He scowled at her. "You'd best be sure those aren't rocks or you'll be swimming back to shore."

"I'm sure."

The captain nodded briskly toward his ship. "Keep your sword loose in its sheath and stay out of the way," he advised. "Oy, there, damn ye, Ralf! I said lash that bloody barrel to the larboard side, ye fool!"

Isabelle hurried up the gangplank whilst the offer still stood, handed the captain her gold once she was on board, then watched him count it. He nodded shortly, pocketed the coins, then turned to do a bit more shouting.

She had to admit that there was a moment or two as the ropes were being hauled back onto the ship when she wondered if she'd made a terrible mistake.

Those moments passed quickly enough. She stayed out of the way and concentrated on keeping her hood up around her face. Not a lock of her hair reached past her chin, her face was liberally covered in soot, and she had no bloody choice but to present herself at her grandmother's abbey in France and satisfy whoever it was who had summoned her.

And hope he didn't kill her for her trouble.

She contemplated that for quite some time, until she could no longer see even the torchlight from the shore and suspected they were fairly far out to sea. The moon was useful enough, she supposed, though even it looked as if it might soon be obscured by clouds.

She jumped a little when she realized the captain was standing next to her. She smiled, then realized she was a lad and likely should have been scowling, so she attempted that. The captain merely pursed his lips.

"Heard we've a bit of a blow coming our way," he said mildly.

"Indeed?" Isabelle asked, then she coughed and attempted a response that sounded less like a squeak. "I suspected as much."

"You're welcome to shelter in my poor quarters if you like, my lady."

She looked at him quickly, but he was only watching her with an assessing gaze. She supposed she could have protested a bit more, but there was little point.

"Was the gold not enough?" she asked grimly.

"Oh, 'twas more than generous," the captain said, though he looked as if he wished it hadn't been. "I'm as willing as the next lad to take gold and keep my mouth shut. I just have to wonder if your sire knows what you're about."

She felt her mouth go dry. "My father?"

"If I had the sense of a turnip, I'd turn the ship around," the man said frankly, "for I've no desire to tangle with Lord Rhys."

Isabelle felt her mouth fall open. "How did you know who I was?"

"Didn't," he said easily, "until we were well on our way and by then I couldn't turn back. A few of my lads are more observant than I. Since your sister is wed, that makes you the youngest, doesn't it?"

She supposed it did, but there was obviously no point in saying as much.

The captain shrugged. "There's a storm bearing down from the north and I've no mind to fight it. We'll make for France and I'll see you safely to wherever you're going."

Isabelle sighed. "Thank you."

He studied her briefly. "I can't help but think you've a good reason to be where you are."

"Several of them, actually."

He shook his head slowly. "Your father won't be pleased, but I imagine you've already considered that. Now, do you care for one of my lads to keep you safe, or is your dagger deterrent enough? I'm assuming since you're carrying one that you're a fair hand with a blade."

"Well," she admitted, "my brothers wouldn't actually cross blades with me, but I've made notes of all their most lethal movements should I find myself in a tight place and need inspiration."

The captain's mouth had fallen open.

"I have held a blade," she said crossly. "I'm not completely without skill." Never mind that she'd only fought imaginary opponents in the privacy of her own bedchamber. Her siblings had done the same thing in their youth.

"As you say," the captain managed. He eyed the horizon behind her. "You might want to review your skills in a safe spot until the storm blows over."

"I love a good storm."

And that was the last thing she said for quite a while. She finally resorted to finding herself a place where she could wedge herself between a pair of barrels lashed to the railing. It seemed as good a place as any to contemplate her straits and wonder if a few prayers might not be called for.

Miles de Piaget strode into the inn, wishing he'd been able to savor the smell of the sea air outside. He supposed with as much of his life as he'd spent on the edge of the sea he should have been weary of it, but he wasn't. Unfortunately, at the moment he was far too preoccupied with trying to find his sister to notice anything but his own panic.

He'd spent two days at Wyckham, then returned to Artane to find that Isabelle had already gone south with Montgomery, supposedly to visit their grandmother Joanna. He'd cursed her thoroughly—out of earshot of his unsuspecting parents—then run up the stairs at the back of the hall to waste no time in rifling through the contents of her bedchamber. He hadn't been surprised to find her diary with all manner of notes made about doings in the lists.

He had, however, been very surprised to find a bit of stone that had obviously been chipped away and refitted over a place to secret the saints only knew what. He'd anticipated finding a collection of her most romantic thoughts. What he hadn't expected was to find a missive from someone threatening to kill her family if she didn't present herself as quickly as possible at a particular French abbey they were all rather familiar with.

He had stood in the middle of her chamber and tried to decide if he felt worse for her that she had shouldered such a burden herself or worse for the lad who had written the missive, for when Miles found him, his death would not be a quick and easy one.

He had gone back downstairs, kissed his mother, embraced his father, then poached his father's fastest horse and immediately headed south, under absolutely no illusions about what his sister intended to do.

And he was at least four days behind her.

It took only a brief word at present with the innkeeper to learn where his youngest brother was lingering. He took the stairs three at a time and strode down the passageway. He threw open the last door available, quickly determined that just Montgomery was inside, then shut the door behind him.

"Where is she?" he said without preamble.

Montgomery didn't look well. That, Miles supposed, could have been the result of several things. Having lost their sister was one. The way his brother was holding a damp cloth to the top of his head might have been another. Miles strode across the room and pulled Montgomery's hand away. The cut was fairly large as was the bump underneath it, but at least the cut was healing. Montgomery would be sporting that bump for another fortnight at least.

"What befell you?"

"What befell me?" Montgomery echoed incredulously. "She hit me over the head, that's what befell me!"

Miles shot him a look of disbelief.

"Well, she did," Montgomery said stubbornly. "I was leaning over to rescue some ridiculous bit of feminine frippery, then the next thing I know she's clunked me over the head with a heavy stone." He paused. "Or a brick." He considered a bit more. "Or perhaps she simply heaved the trunk up and dropped it on me."

Miles looked about the chamber for a likely tool and saw the shutters. He walked over to them, pulled them open, then ran a finger along their lower edges. There was blood there, though it was thoroughly dried. He sighed, then leaned out the window to see what was below. Nothing but garden, but a garden that could easily be used as a path to the docks.

"I've been looking for her," Montgomery said, sounding for the first time very young and very frightened. "I vow I have."

Miles looked at his brother and smiled. "I don't doubt it, Montgomery. Izzy's headstrong."

"Father will kill me—"

"Nay, he won't," Miles said, praying that would be the case. He should likely say a prayer for himself that he would escape a similar fate. "Did she say anything to you about what she intended to do?"

"She said she was meeting Arthur of Harwych and sailing to France on business of her own," Montgomery said, sitting down on the end of the bed and putting his face in his hands. "Of course I forbade her."

"And of course she ignored you. Have you seen Arthur?"

Montgomery shook his head gingerly. "I'm guessing he took the ship with her." He looked at Miles. "Tell me she isn't going to wed with him there."

"Not unless she's had a terrible blow to the head and lost all her wits," Miles said. "My guess is she intends that he guard her back whilst she's about her quest."

Montgomery's mouth fell open. "Quest?"

Miles decided that if Isabelle hadn't been willing to tell their youngest brother what she was about in truth, he had no right to pass on those details himself. Well, that and he had no reason to disbelieve the author of the missive who had threatened to kill the entire de Piaget family if Isabelle spoke of her errand.

"But why France?" Montgomery said in disbelief.

Miles shrugged. "Who knows what goes on in the mind of a wench?"

Montgomery looked at him earnestly. "I tried to frighten her off the idea, Miles, truly I did. I spoke of the perils of the food, the feistiness of the peasants, the endless forests full of ghosts and bogles." He shivered. "Terrible things, all."

"Could you dredge up nothing more menacing?"

Montgomery threw up his hands, then put his hand to his head when apparently the motion was more than he should have indulged in. "I resorted to something I thought would convince her to put her hair back atop her head and that was tales of the lord of Monsaert—"

"Gervase de Seger?" Miles asked with a laugh. "That was the best you could do?"

"Miles, he's a demon," Montgomery said with feeling. "You know what happened to him in the fall."

Miles would have attempted to enlighten his brother about the particulars, but Montgomery had warmed to his topic and was obviously beyond hearing him.

"He was attacked by something foul and turned into something fouler. His people haven't seen him since that time unless he gathers darkness around him and steps outside his gates to terrify his peasants."

"Rubbish—"

"It isn't," Montgomery insisted. "How do you know he won't find Isabelle traipsing about the countryside, abduct her, and toss her into his dungeon where he might torment her at his leisure?"

"Because, unlike you, I don't believe in faeries," Miles said, "which leaves me with powers of reasoning you don't have." He pushed away from the wall he'd been leaning against, then walked to the door. "I'll do some investigating, then return. Don't go anywhere."

Montgomery only groaned in answer, which Miles supposed was answer enough.

He left the inn and made his way to the docks, hoping without any confidence at all that he might find his sister loitering there. She wasn't, of course, nor was that useless youngest son of Henry of Harwych. Miles milled about, trying to see who was preparing to go and who was arriving. He found several lads, finally, who had obviously just arrived and were off for a meal and something decent to drink. He stopped one and put on his most pleasant smile.

"Good journey?"

The lad shivered. "Fortunately for us."

"Where did you sail from?"

"Calais, and we're bloody lucky to be here," the lad said. "A handful of days earlier and we would have gone down like Captain Allard's crew."

Miles felt something slither down his spine. "How many days ago?"

The lad considered, then shrugged. "Two, my lord, perhaps three. Begging your pardon?"

Miles let him go catch up to his mates, then looked out over the sea. It looked fairly calm, but he had grown to manhood on its edge and he knew very well how quickly things could change.

It wasn't possible that Isabelle could have been on that doomed ship, was it?

He considered. He had always had a bond with Isabelle, a strange sort of something that brought her to mind at times when he wouldn't have suspected it. He'd had the occasional curse thrown at him because he'd been her twin brother which apparently made him some sort of demon. He wasn't sure why that had seemingly never applied to his sister, but he had to admit that at the time he'd happily accepted any sort of unsavoury reputation he'd been able to acquire. Along the way, he had quite often had flashes of what he supposed might have been termed intuition. If she'd been in danger. If she'd been about to do something foolish. If she'd needed him. He stood there, unmoving, for so long that his back began to plague him.

He felt nothing.

He didn't stop to consider what to do. He found a ship, booked himself passage, then returned to the inn to tell Montgomery what to do and which horse to see to.

He would sail for France.

He could only hope he would find his sister there, alive.

Chapter 2

Gervase de Seger rode like a demon from Hell.

Or he would have, had he been equal to it. It galled him to the very depths of his soul that all he could manage was a very anemic shuffle on a nag that was better suited to carrying a statuesque and unskilled ladies' maid. But simply getting atop his ancient, faithful steed had taken the better part of a quarter hour, so he supposed he should simply be grateful for what he was able to accomplish and leave the blistering speed to those better suited to it.

By the saints, he felt old.

He wasn't, of course, but that didn't change the fact that he would rather have been in bed than out in the bloody driving rain. It had been raining for the better part of three days, something that likely should have given him pause as he'd made a decision to leave his hall. In fact, he couldn't remember the last time he'd seen a storm so fierce. At least he'd been at home in front of a hot fire for most of it. He pitied any lad with the unfortunate necessity of traveling by either land or sea. Why he'd chosen to join the ranks of those poor fools, he surely didn't know.

He sighed. The truth was, he'd left his comfortable roost

because if he'd had to spend another day haunting the inside of a hall so bleak it bothered even him, he would have done damage to someone. To spare any innocents that fate, he had instead reached for his cloak and decided to seek out a bit of air. He'd driven himself out the front door, down the steps, and across the courtyard to the stables where he'd frowned so fiercely that not a word had been spoken by anyone as the oldest horse in his stables had been saddled for him. At least most of the lads had had the good sense to turn away while he'd struggled to get himself up into the saddle. The one lad who'd been fool enough to watch had earned the full force of Gervase's glare and gone scampering off to no doubt tell more tales about darkness and terror and things that the lord of the hall was apparently responsible for.

He supposed he should have been happy for the addition of unsavoury items to his reputation. His father, after all, had been known as the Griffin of Seger, though perhaps he hadn't merited a title so fierce. Gervase knew that the cheekier lads in his own employ—as well as a few of the more vocal lads down in the village—had taken to referring to him as the Crow of Monsaert, damn them all to Hell. If he could have repaid them for the slight, he would have. Unfortunately, the best he could do was keep to his castle, let the gloom ooze out the windows and front door to infect the lands surrounding his estate, and hope that it would be enough to keep enemies at bay until he was more himself. If he ever again became what he had once been—

He dragged his hand through his hair and lifted his face to the sky, pushing aside thoughts that didn't serve him. The rain was freezing, but he relished it. He needed clarity and 'twas a certainty he wouldn't find it at home. The chaos there was unrelenting and worsening by the day. His brothers were in desperate need of things he hadn't a clue how to give them, his coffers were emptying at an alarming rate, and he wasn't healing as quickly as he should have been.

That made it a bit difficult to protect himself against whomever was trying to kill him.

At least he'd managed to get himself to the stables today. He'd shuffled out his front gates a se'nnight ago in an ill-advised attempt to be about his business and the effort had left him practically crawling back to bed for the rest of the day. Today not only had he managed to get himself to the stables, he'd managed to get atop a horse and ride out the front gates. A feat worthy of song, to be sure.

He would have laughed at the absurdity of it all, but he couldn't. He was a score and eight, but he might as well have been four score and eight for all the strength he had. He should have been at the height of his vigor and prowess. He'd been there a year ago, undefeated in over a decade of jousting, heir to a vast estate, betrothed to the most beautiful woman in all of France. He had occasionally looked at the state of his life and been a little envious of how marvelous it all was. Of course, his father had been dead, which had grieved him, and his mother— or his stepmother, rather—had been without any redeeming qualities at all, which had vexed him, but those were simply things given to him to remind him that life was never perfect. No matter how the rest of his life had spoken to the contrary.

It had all changed in the blink of an eye—

His horse stumbled and caught itself heavily on one leg, almost sending him pitching over the poor beast's head. He managed to stay in the saddle only because he'd spent every day there since he'd been able to sit up on his own.

Well, save the past four months, but that was time better left rotting in the past where it belonged.

"Help!"

He had to shield his eyes against not only the driving rain but the wind that seemed determined to blind him. He saw finally what would have been not even a ripple in his life before but was now a situation he could honestly say he wanted no part of.

A young lad was being tossed about by a trio of men who it seemed hadn't been content to merely rob him. One held one of his boots aloft, one held a bag of what Gervase could only assume was coins, and a third satisfied himself with giving the lad a little lesson in the harsh realities of the world. Just the sight of that was enough to leave Gervase wishing he'd stayed at home.

But he was first and foremost a knight, and he could not fail to render aid when called upon.

His steed seemed to feel the same obligation, for he picked himself up into a respectable trot that almost bounced Gervase from the saddle. Perhaps together they made a more terrifying sight than Gervase had supposed, what with him swathed in a black cloak and his horse an enormous black warhorse who had struck fear into enemies a score of years earlier. The ruffians fell back in terror, then ran off with a speed Gervase was forced to admire. They did however, in true ruffian fashion, taunt their victim with the loss of his purse, his dagger, and apparently his only remaining boot as they went. Gervase didn't bother to give chase. The dagger couldn't have been worth anything and the purse was likely of no value, either. The lad now kneeling in the mud wore clothing that was serviceable but not overly fine, but no cloak. He was soaked to the skin with his shorn hair plastered to his head. He was also gasping for breath, as if he'd never once taken a decent blow to the gut.

Gervase shook his head. The current crop of lads France produced was disappointing, to say the least.

He was tempted to leave the boy there on the side of the road, but something stopped him. He couldn't credit it to any altruistic motive, so he decided that he would blame a vile meal and a sour stomach for the fact that he couldn't bring himself to turn his horse away and head for home. Any desire he'd had to ride over his land had disappeared abruptly at the sight of three lads he could have bested with a steely glance a year ago. He couldn't bring himself to admit that without the advantage of a horse, he would have been at their mercy. Better to credit the weather for his change of heart.

He scowled down at the boy. "Up on your feet like a man, you woman, or have you no pride?"

In answer, the boy threw up. Well, at least he'd had the manners to turn away and vomit into the weeds. Perhaps the manners of peasants had improved whilst he'd been riding all over France, ridding those peasants' masters of their horses, armor, and whatever other gear could be used as ransom at tourney. There, that was a pleasant thought. Gervase concentrated on that while he waited for the peasant before him to finish with his business.

The boy wiped his mouth finally with a trembling hand, then looked up.

Gervase almost fell off his horse.

That was, he admitted freely, the most beautiful boy he had ever seen, the poor little bugger. He'd obviously had a rough go of it. Blood from a cut over his eye had coursed down his face and somehow dried in spite of the wet, matching perfectly the new blood dripping down his chin from where he'd obviously just been struck in the mouth. Blackened eyes or dirt? Difficult to tell, but the dazed look in those eyes made Gervase suspect foul play. He might have pitied the boy, if he'd had any pity left.

"Where's your home?" he asked briskly.

The lad shook his head, then clutched that head quickly in his hands.

Gervase frowned. Perhaps the lad had run away. "Your master's name, then," he demanded.

"I . . . I don't remember."

Gervase would have pressed him a bit harder, but he didn't suppose he was going to have any decent answer whilst the lad was again puking up what was left of his guts. He put his hand over his own belly protectively, then decided his hand was of better use over his mouth. He would have stuck his fingers in his ears, but that would have shown an appalling lack of control.

The lad looked up at him with a truly lovely pair of aqua eyes, gurgled, then those eyes rolled back in his head and he pitched forward into the mud, quite obviously senseless.

Damn it anyway.

Gervase cursed viciously. He started to ride on only to realize he was still sitting in the same bloody place, still cursing in a way that would have singed the ears of any of the nuns up the way at the abbey at Caours. He was tempted to ride there and send them out for a rescue, but that would mean leaving the lad facedown in a puddle. By the time the sisters arrived, the boy would have drowned.

Gervase tried to shrug. One less peasant to feed. France would have been better off that way.

He cursed a bit more.

He went so far as to insist his horse walk on, which it did, in a grand, sweeping circle that led him right back to where he'd started from. He looked down at the boy now on his left and cursed a bit more. To say he didn't want to become involved in another's misery was understating it badly. The very thought of it sent unpleasant sensations down his spine to curl up quite unhappily in the pit of his stomach. He was quite content to go on with his own miserable life and leave the rescuing to those more inclined.

But if not you, then who?

"Any number of fools," he ground out.

Unfortunately, Fate seemed not to be listening. And he knew

it was Fate nudging him. Fate or another of her vile sisters,
Responsibility, Honor, or perhaps even Charity. He had more
than a nodding acquaintance with all four of them, even going
so far at one point to be quite proud of that fact.

He now only stuck his fingers in his ears to drown out their
incessant yapping.

Even singing quite loudly the raunchiest of pub doggerels
didn't drown out that insistent and quite annoying prodding. It
just left him looking no doubt as mad as everyone thought him
to be. Mad and evil and ruined in both body and mind. He
looked up at the sky that was now dark gray in spite of the fact
that it was near noon and supposed the weather wasn't going to
improve any. He was already soaked to the skin. His mount's
mane was plastered to his neck and his forelock dripping down
the length of his nose. They weren't going to get any wetter by
doing a good deed.

He swung down out of the saddle.

Well, in truth, he fell out of the saddle, twisted on his way
down, and landed full upon his victim—er, his peasant in need
of a decent rescue, rather. He had one good arm left, but that
was of little use when his right leg was so damaged. He did
manage to get himself up to his knees, but he had to remain
there for far longer than he wanted to think about simply trying
to ride out the waves of shattering agony that washed over him.
He finally sat back on his heels with a gasp, then shook the boy,
hoping he hadn't wasted a good deed by killing the poor lad.

The boy finally lifted his head.

Unsurprisingly, he began to weep.

Gervase would have clapped his hand to his head, but
thought it might be best that at least one of the two players in the
current drama not be covered in mud. He would execute the rescue, because he was already in the mud, then he would do the
lad a further good turn and instill a bit of manliness in him
before he turned him loose. By the saints, the sound issuing
forth from the whelp in front of him couldn't even have been
called a decent howl. It was more of a whimper, as if the boy
simply couldn't take any more that day.

Gervase had a particular distaste for whimpers, though he
chose not to examine why.

"Can you rise?" he growled.

The noise, blessedly, ceased and the lad nodded.

"What's your name?"

"I . . . don't . . . know."

"Why not?"

The boy looked about him from eyes that were definitely blackened and seemed to be actually a little baffled in general.

"I . . ."

"Whence do you hail?" Gervase asked impatiently.

"Um . . ."

Perfect. No name, no village, and obviously no ability to defend himself. Gervase supposed he could kneel there all day in the rain and the lad still wouldn't have a decent answer for anything. He suppressed the urge to roll his eyes and instead studied the lad for a moment or two. Perhaps he should at least give the lad a name before they attempted any more noteworthy acts.

"I shall call you Parsival," Gervase announced. Parsival had been his favorite horse in the days when he'd had a horse worthy of that sort of name.

Parsival the lad didn't seem as grateful as he should have to be wearing such a grand alias, but Gervase supposed he might grow to appreciate it. He thought perhaps enlightening the lad about the numerous and marvelous qualities of his favorite jousting horse while about the happy work of getting the lad onto the back of his current horse, who was not so marvelous, would keep him from dwelling on how difficult it was to even get himself to his feet, much less himself and someone else to that place. Especially since that someone else was as weak as a gel.

Pitiful. No wonder the boy had fled his home. The looks of disappointment from his sire had likely become too numerous to bear.

Gervase had to pause and simply struggle for breath for a moment or two once he'd managed to stand. That and fight such enormous waves of dizziness that he greatly feared he might have to use Pars's weeds as a place to deposit his own vile morning meal. He waited until he thought he could remain standing with some success, then reached down and pulled his shivering peasant to his feet.

He then exhausted his descriptions of Parsival the horse, which left him too exhausted himself to do anything but stand there and watch numbly as the boy struggled to get into the saddle. At least the lad had that much skill. Unfortunately, even the effort of watching left him unable to do anything but stand there with his arm over his horse's withers and lean his head against the patient beast's neck.

The saints preserve them from anyone who might have been bent on mischief. 'Twas a damned certainty it wouldn't be him doing the saving.

Walking, after he was able to manage it, was an agony he would have happily foregone, but there was nothing to be done about it. He had made his bed—or his road, rather—and he could only lie in it.

He wasn't sure how long it was before he saw the stump of a felled tree just off the rutted path he was taking. He hobbled over to it, then stood there for several minutes simply breathing. Once the pain was manageable, he availed himself of the steadiness of his ancient steed and used the poor beast as a means of heaving himself up onto that stump. Without allowing himself to consider the price he would pay, he put his foot in the stirrup and swung himself up behind his barely conscious passenger. The lad had had the good sense to wrap his hands in fistfuls of mane, so perhaps he wasn't as useless as Gervase had initially feared. The manliness, though, was definitely a problem.

And one he had no intention of solving, to be sure. He took the reins and encouraged his mount forward with a few feeble clicks. He had other things to be seeing to besides a stray he'd found on the side of the road. Important things. Things that required his personal attention.

He made a list, but it wasn't a very long one. He had long since driven off any friends he might once have possessed and the reputed blackness of his temper had seen to acquaintances and neighbors. In truth, all that was left for him to do was shout at his steward a time or two each se'nnight to make certain the man stayed fixed upon his tasks, then retreat to his bedchamber and cast spells, or torment small animals, or whatever it was the local populace suspected he was doing. They might have boasted that his wings were clipped, but he knew better. If he'd actually presented himself down at the village inn in all his gloomy glory, the whole of the tavern would have soiled themselves and prayed for mercy.

Which was why he remained at home. Altruistic, truly, but that was one of his nobler virtues.

The rain continued to drench him until he was within half a league of his hall. It relented then, only enough for the clouds to huddle about the towers of his castle as if they had secrets to tell the guards there, secrets they didn't want him to hear. He would have protested, but he supposed the weather was a bit beyond his purview. He settled for scowling just as a matter of principle lest anyone think he was overcome by the sight of his hall in its current state of neglect, and continued on, muttering the odd curse under his breath to keep himself company.

The portcullis was up, which would have infuriated him a year ago. Now, he was merely grateful he didn't have to waste breath to call to his guardsmen to raise it. He rode through his gates and stopped in front of the stables. A stable boy appeared immediately at his side, trembling so badly he would have spooked Gervase's horse if the poor tired steed had had any verve left in him. As it was, the beast simply reached out and nosed the boy's tunic, no doubt looking for some sort of afternoon delicacy. Gervase tossed his reins at the boy, then considered his situation. He could shove his new acquisition off the saddle first, of course, then get down himself in the confusion, but that didn't seem particularly sporting.

He sighed, then gritted his teeth as he wiggled his boots free of his stirrups. He was more careful that time when he slid to the ground, but still it was breathtakingly painful. He clutched his saddle for several moments, struggling to breathe without gasping, then looked at the prize he'd brought home.

He looked around him for aid and found it in the person of the captain of his guard. Sir Aubert was simply standing there with his arms across his chest, watching silently. Actually, Aubert did everything silently, everything from killing foes to expressing opinions on Gervase's recovery from the attack that had left him half dead. If Gervase hadn't known the man for the better part of his life, he might have suspected him of foul deeds. He was quiet yet all the more terrifying because of it. The saints be praised he was trustworthy.

He had obviously been out for a ride himself, which told Gervase that he perhaps hadn't had as much privacy as he'd thought. Unsurprising, but somewhat comforting, truth be told.

Aubert uncrossed his arms, then walked over to Gervase and made him a slight bow. He looked at the lad draped over the horse's withers and merely raised an eyebrow.

"A lad in need of a rescue," Gervase said shortly, "as you likely already know. Dump him in the kitchens."

Aubert lifted Parsival's head up by his hair, then froze. Gervase understood. A burden for the poor wretch to be so fair of face. He watched Aubert consider, glance his way briefly, then shrug. The man lifted the lad out of the saddle with surprising gentleness. Gervase would have asked his captain why he didn't just heave the lad over his shoulder and trot off with him, but perhaps the blood on the lad's face and the bump on his head that even Gervase could now see gave him pause.

"The wounds were acquired at two different times," Aubert offered mildly.

"Think you?" Gervase asked.

"One's crusted over, the others are still bleeding."

How that man had managed to observe that in such a short time, Gervase couldn't have said. Then again, he'd won more than one tournament thanks to those unwholesome powers of observation. If Aubert said it was so, he was happy to believe it.

"Take him to the infirmary, then."

"Until he's healed?"

"When else? But *then* dump him in the kitchens. I've no need for yet another lad to coddle."

Aubert nodded, then walked away with his burden. Gervase watched him go for a moment or two, more to give himself a chance to catch his breath than because he was curious as to why his captain, who had absolutely no patience for lads who showed the slightest sign of weakness, would be so carefully carrying a boy who still should have been huddled behind his mother's skirts.

It was odd, though, wasn't it?

He shook his head, leaving things he couldn't fathom to the realm in which they belonged, then turned his attentions to the next monumental task of the day, which was to get himself back inside his great hall where he could collapse in front of the fire and hopefully be fed something decent. He held on to his horse for another moment or two, then nodded to the master of his stables, who had stopped a lad from removing Gervase's buttress too soon. His faithful steed was led off to his oats and his napping. Gervase wished he could have enjoyed the same attentions.

Help arrived, happily, in the person of a half brother he could tolerate for more than a quarter hour. Heaven knew he had a robust selection to choose from. Joscelin was the second of six lads Gaspard of Monsaert had sired on a woman he'd wed not a month after Gervase's own dam had perished. Why the pair of them hadn't managed a girl or two to leaven the loaf, Gervase couldn't have said. All he knew was that for the past year he'd been mother and father both to that collection of spawn and he hadn't been equal to the task.

Joscelin said nothing. He simply offered his shoulder as a handy place for Gervase to rest his hand as they started back toward the hall. If he had done less resting and more clutching, Joscelin didn't seem to notice. Then again, Joscelin tended to listen more than he spoke, a trait Gervase appreciated given the endless babbling of the rest of his siblings.

"Wet out," was his only comment.

"Very," Gervase agreed.

Joscelin said nothing more. He merely walked alongside Gervase, as slowly as if he were some species of nobleman who was making a procession through his village and feared someone might miss a particular bit of fine embroidery on his surcoat if he walked too quickly. If he paused now and again to apparently study a bit of stone out of place in the pavement, or dig about something else with his toe, Gervase made no comment. He was too busy being grateful for the chance to pause and catch his breath.

It was truly a miracle he wasn't dead.

At times, he wondered if he might have been better—

"Who's the lad?" Joscelin asked.

"Don't know," Gervase wheezed, grateful for the distraction. "I came upon him as he was being robbed. It seemed only sporting to at least trot over and see what could be done."

Joscelin smiled faintly. "Damnable chivalry."

"Isn't that the truth," Gervase said grimly. "Always cropping up when you least expect it."

Joscelin laughed a little. "I daresay. What are you going to do with him?"

"I have absolutely no idea. Want him?"

"Me? And what would I do with a lad?"

"Make him your squire?"

"Thank you, but nay. I had one, sent especially to me to curry favor with you, who I sent back because he wasn't yet weaned. I don't need another useless lad to train."

Gervase stopped and looked at his younger half brother. "I'm sorry," he said simply.

"Don't be daft," Joscelin said. "You'll regain your strength and be what you were before. I suspect you've spent all this time abed not healing but rather lazing about with an endless succession of handsome wenches."

That wasn't even worth a response, so Gervase merely pursed his lips and continued on his way. He heartily wished he had never left the hall that morning, but what else had he been able to do? He had spent three months abed with one leg so broken and the other wrenched about so badly that he'd wished it *had* been broken. His right arm had been broken as well and his hand crushed under a weight so immense he was surprised he managed to grasp anything at all. The memory of how he'd come by his wounds was sketchy at best and something he didn't like to dwell on if he could help it.

In truth, he couldn't quite remember anything past seeing one fire near his stables and more smoke coming from his great hall. He'd set lads to attend to his horseflesh while he'd run back inside the hall to make certain the whole bloody place didn't go up in flames. He'd hardly been able to see for the smoke, but he'd heard a horrendous crack echo in what had been a very elegant chamber full of fine carving and delicate stonework. He'd thought the roof was caving in only to realize that snapping sound had been his thigh bone. He'd realized that only because his leg had collapsed beneath him and he'd seen the bolt sticking out of his flesh along with what surely couldn't have been bone. If it hadn't been for his brothers and his captain finding him to carry him outside—

He took a deep breath and walked back into his hall. He patted Joscelin's shoulder, then forced himself to make his way across the floor without aid. He heard his younger brothers come tumbling inside from the direction of the kitchens, but he couldn't bring himself to even attempt to greet them, much less name them. All he knew was that there were six of them and they deserved better than he was able to give them. He cast himself down into a chair in front of the fire and closed his eyes. Joscelin did him the favor of removing the offenders with a promise of training in the lists if the lads fetched their gear quickly. Cries of joy ensued.

Gervase sighed, then opened his eyes. He jumped a little in

spite of himself at realizing he wasn't alone. His next youngest half brother, Guy, was sitting across from him, watching him with a faint smile.

"Nice ride?"

"Delightful," Gervase muttered. "What news while I was away on my errand of mercy?"

"The Duke of Coucy wants to make a visit."

Gervase realized his mouth was hanging open, so he shut it with a snap. "You cannot be serious."

"I believe I am."

Gervase rubbed his left hand over his face because that was the hand that functioned as it should. "Hell."

"Not this time. I understand he's not bringing his eldest daughter."

The eldest daughter who would allow her father to skewer her on the end of his sword before she would be forced to see what had become of her erstwhile affianced lord. Gervase supposed he wouldn't have been any happier to see her. That he had once found himself set to wed the harpy—no matter her admittedly staggering beauty—was something that continued to beggar belief. He'd obviously allowed his late father to convince him of the desirability of the match as he'd been fully into his cups.

Of course, those happy tidings of not having to see her again any time soon didn't do anything to solve the problem of how he was going to feed anyone, much less house them. The greater part of his castle was undamaged, but the great hall still looked a bit scorched about the edges where his servants hadn't been able to remove the soot. He supposed a tapestry or two or a bit of whitewash would have solved that, but he hadn't had the heart to see to either.

"He's only staying one night, if that eases you," Guy continued. "He wants to see for himself that you're still alive, I suppose."

"I can't imagine why," Gervase said, sighing deeply. The bloody floors were going to have to be cleaned, at least. "When?"

"In a handful of days, or so I hear."

Gervase didn't bother to wonder how it was that Guy heard these sorts of things and he didn't. 'Twas common knowledge that Guy had been the one to keep things running while Gervase had been abed, trying to keep himself from dying. Perhaps it would have been better—

He blew out his breath. He refused to entertain that thought, no matter how often it clamored for his attention. The hall was his and he would hold it as long as he had breath. He would undo the damage his father had done to it because his grandfather, Abelard of Monsaert, had made him swear an oath he would do so. Never mind that he'd been a green lad of a score and two when he'd put his hands in his grandfather's and, in a truly subversive act, given his fealty to his grandfather, not his father.

Nay, the hall was his as was the burden of seeing to it and the souls attached to it.

"You're fortunate to be alive."

"Tell me something I don't know," Gervase said wearily. He looked at his brother. "Send Cook to me, would you? I'd best think about our guests sooner rather than later."

Guy nodded, then rose and went to do his liege lord's bidding. Gervase watched him go, then leaned his head back against the chair. No more do-gooding. A single morning of it and now look what he was faced with. It was tempting to simply go back to bed and hope that—

He rolled his eyes, pushed himself out of his chair, and moved to stand with his backside against the fire. He'd healed as much as he was going to heal. It was far past time he ceased coddling himself. He would simply march forward boldly and ignore the things he couldn't solve at present.

Such as who had tried to kill him.

And why.

Chapter 3

S*he* woke.

She lay still because she found that even breathing hurt her head. Moving was beyond her, for even the slightest motion left her feeling as if her head were being cleaved in twain. So, instead of inflicting more pain upon herself, she chose to simply lie there and breathe as gingerly as possible.

Time wore on in a particularly uncomfortable way, much like a fever that wouldn't break no matter how much she willed it to. She wasn't entirely sure that she didn't sleep, though her dreams were unpleasant ones full of noise and confusion and fighting a raging storm in the midst of the sea. If she hadn't been in such pain, she supposed she might have feared she was dead.

She woke finally and realized two things immediately: she had no idea where she was, and, worse still, she had no idea *who* she was.

She froze, because that's what a lad in a spot of trouble did.

Where had she heard that before?

Ah, she remembered. It was what her father had always instructed her brothers to do when finding themselves hard up against a clutch of enemies with no easy way to escape. She frowned. She had a father, that much was clear, and apparently brothers as well. It bothered her quite a bit that she couldn't remember their names, but perhaps those would come to her as well in time. She could see her father's face . . . and then she couldn't. She frowned, but supposed that would clear up with time as well.

"I don't care for this," a voice said with a huff.

"Be that as it may," another voice said evenly, "this is what His Grace requires."

"I am not a tender of sodden orphans who were better sent home to their mothers!"

She wanted to tell the voices that she wasn't an orphan, that she had a father at least and presumably a mother, but she made the mistake of shifting and the pain in her head was so blinding that all she could do was seek refuge in senselessness.

The next time she woke, she found she could at least move her head without blinding pain. She had no idea how much time had passed and still couldn't remember her name, but she thought she might attempt the opening of her eyes without too much trouble. She looked at the ceiling above her and was surprised to find that it was made of rather lovely wood, not thatch. Perhaps she found herself not out in the wilds but in a proper castle, though why that should have made any difference to her, she couldn't have said.

"I refuse to tend this . . . this creature!"

Another voice responded. She recognized it, which led her to suspect that she'd heard it before, perhaps in her dreams. She didn't dare attempt to turn her head, so she simply lay there and listened.

"His Grace requires this—and here is his brother to no doubt say as much."

"Lord Joscelin," said the first voice, sounding as if it were coming from a throat on the verge of closing up entirely.

"I thought perhaps I would come and see what my brother brought home."

She decided there was no reason not to at least look to her right and see who stood there. Moving her head was out of the question, but a look, aye, that was possible.

Three men stood there. The one closest to her was the oldest of the lot, his pate covered with wisps of white hair and his face adorned with a ferocious scowl. She scowled back at him, then looked at the second man. He was tall and solemn, wearing a sword. At least he wasn't scowling at her.

The third man was younger still, and he had no sword. She would have checked for a dagger in his boot, which made her wonder why that thought had occurred to her, but she found she could scarce look at them as they stood there, much less look anywhere else. She took a careful breath.

"Who are you?" she croaked.

The white-haired one drew himself up. "I am Master Paquier," he said. "I am His Grace's personal surgeon, so I suggest you accord me the respect due me."

The third one there, the youngest, drew up a stool next to where she lay and sat down. He seemed the most cheerful of the lot, which was pleasing. He smiled at her in a friendly fashion.

"I am Joscelin—"

"Lord Joscelin," the man with the sword corrected mildly.

Lord Joscelin shrugged. "Joscelin is enough, I think." He smiled again. "This canny warrior standing behind me is Sir Aubert. He's the captain of my brother's guard."

She considered that for quite some time. If the man sitting down was a lord and his brother had a guard, then he was obviously a lord himself. She congratulated herself on that sterling piece of logical thinking, then took a few more moments to let her head clear a bit longer.

"Who," she managed, "is your brother?"

"Gervase de Seger," Joscelin said. "Do you know him?"

She attempted to put that name with anything useful, but failed. She couldn't even shake her head, but she did wiggle her fingers in a way she hoped would speak for her.

"I take it not," Lord Joscelin said.

"I don't know . . . anything."

The surgeon made noises of disbelief. "How is it possible that she—"

"He," Joscelin corrected Master Paquier quickly. "*He* says he doesn't know anything."

She wanted to tell him that she was most certainly not a he, but something stopped her. *'Tis always best to be underestimated.* The words washed over her mind like a wave, then receded, leaving her wondering where she'd heard them. If they wanted to think she was a boy, they were welcome to. Perhaps that was for the best and would buy her a bit of safety where admitting to what she was might not. Of course, she knew differently. She also knew her name, which was . . .

On the tip of her tongue, she was certain, but no closer. She frowned, then looked at Joscelin.

"Who is he? Your brother, I mean."

"The lord of Monsaert," Joscelin said.

'Tis said Gervase de Seger, the lord of Monsaert, goes about in demon form. Very dangerous . . .

The words came at her from an unknown direction, but washed over her just the same, filling her with terror. She sat up with a gasp, then realized quite suddenly that that had been a very bad idea indeed.

Darkness descended.

She woke to the feeling of someone shaking her. She pushed the hands away and realized to her surprise that she was able to manage it. She opened her eyes and found that whilst it wasn't particularly pleasant, at least her head didn't feel as if she'd been volunteering it as an anvil for the castle's blacksmith.

She managed to sit up without the world spinning uncontrollably, which she supposed was progress. She put her hands to her head just as a precaution, waited until she thought she could look around herself with success, then opened her eyes and looked at the person standing next to her bed. It was someone she hadn't seen before, which she had to admit was slightly unnerving.

"What do you want?" she said hoarsely.

The woman—and it was a woman, it appeared—put her hands on her ample hips and glared. "You, in the kitchens right now. My lord told me he would give you a se'nnight to recover from that wee knock on your head and then you were mine. Get yourself out of bed, you lazy whelp, and follow me. Important guests have been sighted and I'm short a pair of hands."

Before she could protest, the woman had ripped aside her coverlet and thrown a pair of boots at her.

"Put those on, *now*. I've no time to waste coddling runaway lads."

Whatever she was, she was fairly sure she wasn't a runaway, though what did she know? She wasn't a lad, that was for certain, but it didn't seem as if the woman in front of her was interested in that fact. Perhaps the best she could do was do as she'd been ordered to and hopefully investigate her surroundings in the bargain. It was best, when planning an escape, to be familiar with the lay of the land.

She frowned thoughtfully. Her father again, obviously.

Before she could put on her boots, her hands were taken and examined. The woman frowned.

"I don't think you've done a decent day's labor in your life."

"That, my good woman, is rather offensive."

The cook raised her hand, then reconsidered. "I should slap you for your cheek, but I will admit that you look as if you've had enough of that recently to suit you." She took a step back and put her hands on her hips again. "You'll probably be useless, but I'm in a tight spot. Perhaps you'll learn quickly."

There was that. She put on boots that were definitely not hers and had a hole in the sole of one, then stood. She swayed. The cook caught her, which she greatly appreciated. When the stars cleared, she realized the good woman was staring at her intently.

"Lord Gervase bade me take you to the kitchens," she said with a frown, "and I don't dare gainsay him, but I can't imagine what I dare do with you." She started to speak again, then shook her head. "Wrap that cloak around you and let's be off. Best not to run afoul of his temper."

Gervase of Monsaert. She shivered at the very name, though at the moment she was too dizzy to wonder why. She had vague memories of hearing about terrible things he'd done, but she honestly couldn't bring any of them to mind at present.

She took the cloak she was handed, put it around herself, and followed the cook from where she'd been. The healer's house, perhaps. She walked with the cook across the courtyard, unsure if she were more surprised by the number of people there or the fact that she was able to walk—mostly—without fainting. She only ventured one look at anything but her feet, but quickly discovered that was a very bad idea indeed. She was immediately on her knees without knowing quite how she'd gotten there.

"Oh, by all the blessed—"

"Allow me, Mistress Jehanne."

She recognized that voice. It belonged to Joscelin—or, rather, Lord Joscelin. She felt a hand on her head.

"Can you stand?" he asked.

The cook snorted loudly. "And what good does it do if he can? Just what am I supposed to do with this one? A useless—"

"Perhaps, Mistress Jehanne, but let's remember that he's been through quite an adventure. Why don't you go on ahead and I'll see him to the hall safely?"

"Don't know why you'd bother," the woman muttered, then strode away.

She held out her hand and instantly an arm was there for her use. She used that arm as a means of getting to her feet, then wished with particular fervor that she hadn't bothered. She stood there for several minutes, just breathing in and out, wondering how she might make her escape before the lord of the hall used her for his nefarious purposes.

Then again, demons likely didn't visit their kitchens very often, so perhaps that was the place for her. She would do what work was required, sleep when she could, and determine where she was. Her liberty likely wouldn't come easily, but it would come eventually if she were canny. She could pick any lock set before her because . . . because Jake had taught her to do so.

Jake? Who was Jake?

She looked up at Lord Joscelin. She had to admit he was extremely handsome and she was not unaccustomed to extremely handsome men. She wasn't sure why that was, but it rang true in her mind so she accepted it as fact. She attempted a smile.

"I've lost my memory."

"So I see," he agreed.

"It's a terrible bother."

He laughed a little. "I daresay it is, la—*lad*. Can you remember nothing?"

"Nothing that makes any sense."

"Time will cure that, I daresay. Until then, I imagine the kitchen is the safest place for you. We're due to be overrun by the Duke of Coucy and his entourage tonight."

"I don't know them."

He smiled again. "I do and there's little to recommend them, trust me. Shall we go? I'll make certain you have a spot well out of the way."

She nodded, though she supposed the cook would have a far different opinion once Lord Joscelin was out of earshot. But she

wasn't particularly comfortable with the thought of having to
entertain a duke, so perhaps he was right and the kitchens were
the safest place for her. She happily let him tuck her hand in the
crook of his elbow and lead her where she supposed she needed
to go.

The kitchens were a familiar place, she had to admit, and the
bustle there was soothing somehow. She was assessed quickly
and put to scrubbing pots. She had obviously washed several
things over the course of her life, but she had to admit after a
pair of hours with her hands in extremely hot water with harsh
soap that she could safely say that it was not what she was
accustomed to doing for long periods of time.

"Useless lump!" the cook shouted at her. "Find something
else to do!"

The floors needed scrubbing apparently, despite how many
muddy feet were tromping over them or how much grease and
leavings from the cooking fire were spilled on them. She
scrubbed until her hands were burning after which she was put
to fetching water from the well. That lasted perhaps the least
amount of time because she simply was not equal to the labor
of hauling heavy buckets of water. Cook finally simply bellowed
at her to stay out of the way, which she was happy to do. She
chose a handy wall to lean against and hoped her head would
soon stop spinning. Once she thought she could manage it, she
opened her eyes and looked about her. The kitchens were, she
had to admit, very nice. Not that the kitchens of her father's hall
weren't equally fine—

She froze, because the memory was just beyond her finger-
tips. She was certain if she could simply stretch her hand out a
bit more, she would find it there. The kitchens in her father's
keep were large and staffed with not only an excellent cook but
hardworking and contented helpers. She had been in those connected chambers countless times not only to filch apples for her
horse but for her brothers as well because Cook had been particularly susceptible to her entreaties. The kitchens at . . .

"And who do we have here?"

She looked at the young man standing in front of her, grin-
ning. He wasn't particularly handsome but he was obviously
quite impressed by his own sorry self. She sent him a look she
had seen her sister send to countless lads who had come seeking
her hand. Her sister whose name was—

"You're a pretty thing."

She realized the young man's hands were on her waist and moving upward at an alarming rate. Her father would have slain him for that, of that she was sure, so she felt no hesitation in putting her hands in the middle of his chest and giving him a hearty shove.

"Surely you jest, sir," she said in her best imitation of Amanda.

Amanda.

Amanda de Piaget.

Her sister, Amanda, which made her Isabelle de Piaget and the lad in front of her about to find himself in the sights of Rhys de Piaget, who would likely beat him to a bloody pulp before he bothered to run him through.

She felt memory rush back to her. She was Isabelle.

But what in the hell was she doing in France?

Obviously she was still missing several important memories, memories she would have to acquire later. For the moment, she was facing a very angry lad who obviously seemed to think that being thwarted in his desire to kiss her was a grave insult to his pride. His face was very red. She was fairly sure that if he didn't take a breath soon, he would experience an unpleasant bit of business with his poor form.

"Breathe," she suggested.

"You stupid—"

She held up her hand. "Language, sir. I doubt your mother would approve of your behavior."

"My mother *definitely* wouldn't approve of what I'm about to do to you," he snarled.

Well, there was no time like the present to dispense a little instruction for the betterment of men in general. She was fairly sure she'd heard that either from her mother or her sister. Perhaps the both of them. She watched as the lad reached out to take hold of her with his right hand. She was fairly sure she'd never had to defend herself against such an aggressor before, but what she did remember was a brief lesson on what to do in such straits given by some exasperated older brother or another. It was almost without thought that she grasped the lad's right hand with her left, wrenched that hand, then took the heel of her right hand and slammed it with all her strength into his nose.

His head snapped back, which she found somewhat gratifying.

Unfortunately, it only seemed to enrage him the more.

She looked around her for aid, but there seemed to be none forthcoming. She sighed. Obviously she would have to take matters into her own hands. She took the lad by the shoulders and kneed him quite firmly in the privates. Whilst he was about a fair bit of gasping, she took the opportunity to draw his sword.

It was quite a bit heavier than she'd counted on, which gave her pause. She wished her memories had come back in less of a patchwork fashion. She was fairly sure she'd watched her brothers—whose names she still couldn't bring to mind—in the lists, but she was equally sure they had never allowed her on the field with them. She would certainly have something to say about that when next they met.

But first, the challenge before her.

Because she was a de Piaget and even de Piaget women didn't shy away from the difficult.

Apparently.

She took a firmer grip on her filched sword and prepared herself to defend her own honor.

Chapter 4

Gervase sat at the table and contemplated the nearness of his escape from a life of absolute hell.

That hell had nothing to do with his supper, which was surprisingly edible, or the fact that his leg was throbbing so badly that there was no possible way for him to be comfortable, which was nothing out of the ordinary. It had, unfortunately, everything to do with his guests, the exalted and very impressive Duke of Coucy, his lovely wife, and the conspicuous absence of their eldest daughter, Evelyne. The other daughters had come along, of course, but the one Gervase had once been betrothed to had apparently had other things to do.

He wasn't nearly as devastated by the slight as he was sure Evelyne had intended he be. Indeed, he wasn't feeling slighted at all. Instead, he was sipping his wine while holding the cup with his left hand and marveling at the blessed fact that he was still unwed. That he ever should have found himself bound in any way to the souls around him was enough to send shivers down his spine.

The young misses weren't without their redeeming qualities, he had to admit. They would grow up to be absolute beauties like their eldest sister, which would no doubt guarantee them a long string of suitors their father would examine like rare pearls on a string before choosing just the right one to complement their lovely faces. They would also, poor things, learn at their mother's knee how to manage the intrigues of court and castle. He wasn't sure he wanted to think too much about what sort of women they would end up being, but that was, he supposed, something he wouldn't have to witness. He had already seen it in their sister and didn't care to see any more of it.

Ah, for a woman who didn't relish that sort of sparring.

He made polite conversation with the duke and duchess, because that skill at least remained with him, though he had the feeling that taking the time to do so would cost him his ability to walk easily. Sitting in the same place for too long, he had learned by painful experience, never served him—

"You have to come witness this."

He jumped a little when he realized Joscelin was whispering in his ear. Truly he had to get hold of himself. He never would have been taken thus unawares before his accident. Obviously he was spending too much time ruminating on his aches and pains as if he'd been a hoary-headed soldier holding court in front of the warmest spot in the pub. He looked at his half brother with a frown.

"Witness what?"

"A pitched battle in the kitchens."

Gervase swore. "Can't you see to it?"

"I could, but I think you might like to have a look first."

"I have the feeling this is going to ruin my evening."

"I think you might be surprised."

Gervase managed to push his chair away from the table, but he suspected that might be the extent of his successes at the moment. He was appropriately grateful when Joscelin stepped into the duke's line of sight and peppered the man with questions about his supper. Guy did the same for Her Grace, which left him the chance to heave himself up, clutch the table for a moment, then sling his arm around Joscelin in a comradely fashion.

"Guy, come sit in my chair," Gervase said expansively, hoping his smile came out as more a smile and less a gritting of his teeth. "Domestic troubles, apparently."

Guy took over so smoothly, it was as if he'd been born to do just that. Gervase thought a kind thought or two about his brother, then continued on to the kitchens, trying not to lean so hard on Joscelin that he brought him to his knees.

"A hint?" he asked.

"Oh, nay," Joscelin said with a half laugh, "I wouldn't think to spoil your pleasure at what awaits you."

Gervase hardly dared speculate. He simply walked along the passageway silently. Well, silently except for the occasional catching of his breath he couldn't quite muffle when he made a misstep.

He came to the door of his kitchens and stopped so suddenly, he almost pulled Joscelin off his feet. He could scarce believe what he was seeing, but there was no denying it. There was a lad there he didn't recognize, but he was sporting Coucy's colors so perhaps it was safe to assume he belonged to the duke. That knight, and Gervase used that term advisedly, was currently trying to retrieve his sword from a slip of a thing who was wielding the sword in question with, ah, absolutely no skill at all but a fair amount of enthusiasm. He had no doubt that at some point, she actually might manage to do damage to someone, most likely herself.

Gervase leaned closer to Joscelin. "And just who," he managed, "is that?"

"The lad you rescued on the road."

Gervase realized two things right off. One, the lad was definitely not a lad—a reassuring realization, actually; and two, the lad was going to kill the kitchen staff if someone didn't get that sword away from him—er, her.

"Very lovely for a lad," Joscelin murmured.

Gervase shot him a glare, then released him and stepped forward with as much grace as he could manage.

"Enough!" he bellowed.

Coucy's guardsman leaped back as if he'd been burned. Gervase took note of the man's bloodied nose and realized that perhaps there had been more going on than he'd suspected at first. He sauntered over to the guardsman with as much swagger as he could manage—which wasn't much, as it happened— stopped, and wished he could fold his arms over his chest without wincing. He settled for a silent study of what that lad—er, *girl*, rather—had left of the young man in front of him. Actually, he suspected Coucy's guardsman wasn't all that much younger than he himself was, which told him everything he needed to know about the fool's judgment.

"Assaulting my servants, are you?" Gervase asked politely.

The man looked at him with fury. "She's just a serving wench—"

"Who belongs to *me*, which you should have had the wit to remember."

"She has my sword!"

"I'd say you were fortunate she hasn't managed to use it on you," Gervase snapped. He walked forward until he was standing almost toe-to-toe with the other man. "If you move, I'll use it on you myself."

"As if you could—"

The lad stopped speaking for two reasons. The first was that Gervase hadn't hesitated before plowing his fist into the other's mouth. He suppressed the urge to faint from the pain of that. The only thing that kept him on his feet was sheer feistiness, something that had come in handy over the past few months more often than not.

His own labors might have only silenced the other for a moment or two, but Aubert had caught the miscreant as he stumbled backward, turned him around, and invited him to place his face very ungently against the stone surrounding the enormous hearth that found itself conveniently within reach. Coucy's lad slumped to the ground with a groan, then was still. Gervase smiled pleasantly at his captain, then turned to look at the other player involved in the evening's entertainment.

He felt the eyes of all his servants on him, but he didn't bother to check for looks of disdain or horror. It wasn't as if they hadn't seen him in all his ruined glory before. None of them would miss his right hand that was a web of scars from flames that had burned him. At least someone had possessed the charity to put out the flames on his smoldering self before his face had been burned as well. Then again, he supposed his foul humors made up for any saving of his visage.

He ignored his servants and concentrated instead on the girl standing there holding aloft a sword that she couldn't possibly manage.

He felt as if she'd just taken that sword and stabbed him through his damned belly.

What had he been thinking? Honestly, he just didn't know.

Perhaps the wet had rotted his brain to the point where he would have mistaken his horse for a lad. Perhaps he'd been so damned preoccupied with his own sorry life that he hadn't been capable of looking beyond it at what lay ahead. Perhaps he had never seen a woman that beautiful before and his instinct for self-preservation had taken over and rendered him not only blind but daft.

It was indicative of how his life was progressing that such a wench as that one should be a servant.

He took the sword out of her unresisting hands and tossed it in the direction of its proper owner. He turned back to her, then decided abruptly that looking any closer at what was before him was a very bad idea indeed.

Again, he was without a doubt one of the dimmest men in France.

Then again, perhaps he could be forgiven for mistaking her for a lad given the circumstances of their meeting. It had been pouring with rain, he had been indulging in a substantial amount of self-pity, and she had been puking her guts out into the weeds. The only thing he could say with certainty was that if he ever had the chance to do a little damage to her attackers, he might just have to linger at the task.

He considered her appearance and thought that perhaps he couldn't be blamed for having failed to properly identify what she was. She was dressed in lad's clothes, her hair was short almost to her chin, and her face was slightly worse for the wear. Obviously she was in disguise.

Why was the question he supposed he would have to find an answer to sooner rather than later.

He folded his arms over his chest and suppressed a wince at the pain that caused him. It made it easier to dredge up a scowl, which he supposed could only serve him at present.

"Who are you?"

She didn't lower her eyes, which gave him pause. Rather cheeky for a mere serving girl, to his mind.

"I don't remember," she said.

"He's lost his memories," Joscelin said helpfully.

Gervase shot him a look that had him holding up his hands in surrender.

"Very well, *she* has lost her memories. That's inconvenient, wouldn't you say?"

Gervase had many things he thought he could say, beginning and ending with questioning aloud what in the hell he was going to do with a woman of that beauty in his kitchens. She would be a beacon to any and all rogues in the area and he would likely be hearing soon that she was with child, which wouldn't allow her to scrub his floors.

"Her hands are blistered," Cook offered helpfully from his right. "Can't manage a proper day's labor, that one."

"And this is my affair?" Gervase said, stepping back because he had no choice in the matter. If he caught another sight of those aqua eyes in that face of absolute perfection—

Well, he would have drawn his hand over his eyes. If he'd been prone to exhibiting weakness, which he most certainly was not. Failing that, he supposed he could have invited his captain to help him also place his face rather ungently against the stone of the hearth until good sense was dislodged.

By the saints, he was lusting after a serving wench. What next? He scowled at his cook.

"Put her to sewing then, or something useful."

"If you say so, my lord," Cook said doubtfully.

"I do. And supper was delightful."

Cook harrumphed a bit in pleasure, then sent her kitchen staff scattering with bellows and judicious wieldings of her spoon.

"Not her," Gervase said before he thought better of it.

Cook shot him a look he gave her back accompanied by his fiercest frown before he turned and made his way from the kitchen without looking at his . . . well, whatever she now was. Not quite a scullery maid, but perhaps close. The saints only knew what Cook would set her to doing. Whatever that was, it was no longer his affair. He had important things to be seeing to and no time to concern himself with a lass who should have been home where her mother could have watched over her.

What in the hell had she been doing out in the rain masquerading as a lad?

He was tempted to gnaw on that mystery for a bit, but, as he had said to his cook, supper had been delightful and he didn't want to ruin it by speculation that would no doubt leave him with indigestion.

He stopped midway up the passageway, then looked at his brother.

"Take a message for me."

"Of course."

"Tell Cook privately to keep that wench out of sight until this rabble leaves."

"Should she have a guard?" Joscelin asked mildly.

"Aubert will see to that."

"You didn't say anything to him."

"You know I didn't need to." Gervase shrugged. "We don't talk much."

Joscelin smiled faintly, then turned and walked back down the passageway. Gervase continued on his way, then stopped before he reached his great hall. He waited until his captain, who had been walking ten paces behind him, caught him up. He considered, then looked at the older man.

"Did I need to say anything?"

Aubert merely shook his head.

"Did you know he was a she?"

The look his captain sent him almost made him smile. He pursed his lips in an effort to keep himself from it.

"Very well, I'm an idiot. It was raining and my wits were soggy. It was also no mean feat to get that one up on my horse, not that she weighs more than a boy."

"I haven't said anything, my lord."

"Aubert, my friend, you never need to."

Aubert made him a solemn bow, then waited until Gervase had walked on ahead. Gervase supposed that left him on his own, which was a place he had to admit he didn't particularly care for of late. It was ridiculous, of course, because no respectable warrior allowed something as trivial as lack of company to unsettle him. Never mind that he'd been alone when he'd been attacked—or so he thought. The precise details of the encounter continued to elude him.

He thought he just might have a bit of sympathy for that poor daft wench in his kitchens.

Daft, stunning wench that she was.

He walked back to the table, booted Guy from his chair, then sat down with as much grace as he could muster. It took quite a bit of effort, as it happened, to sit without groaning, but he managed it because if he had learned nothing over his score-and-eight years, he had learned to never show weakness.

"So, Gervase," Frédéric of Coucy said slowly, "how is your investigating coming?"

"Investigating?" Gervase echoed politely.

"Into the accident," Frédéric said, frowning slightly, as if he couldn't understand why the subject wasn't a clear one. "Surely you wonder how it all came about."

Gervase lifted his shoulder in a half shrug. "Occasionally." Aye, every single moment of every single bloody day. If an accident it had been and not a planned assault.

"But aren't you afraid it might happen again?"

He was, every day, all day every day until there were days he was so caught up in a maze of his own damned thoughts, he feared he might never emerge from them again. He looked at Evelyne's father and shrugged carelessly.

"I'll find the perpetrator eventually, I imagine."

Frédéric looked slightly uncomfortable, if such a thing were possible for the pompous arse sitting there. "Of course, the betrothal . . . "

Gervase waved away the man's words before he could finish spewing them out, mostly because there also hadn't been a day since he'd regained consciousness that he hadn't rejoiced that he wasn't going to be wed to Frédéric's eldest daughter. Blessings came from unexpected places, apparently.

"No need to discuss it, of course," he said.

"Well, your face was spared, but—"

"Let us speak of more cheerful things," Gervase interrupted. "How are things at court these days? The boy king's mother is still wielding her influence, I assume?"

Coucy's conversation tended to be limited first to his own dazzling self, then his equally fascinating adventures at court. Gervase was happy to sit in front of a hot fire where the heat seemed to do his body good, sip wine that he was fairly sure wasn't poisoned, and let Frédéric carry the conversation without any help from him. There was something to be said for entertaining insufferable noblemen.

It was nothing he'd cared to do in his youth, to be sure, no matter his place in his father's house. His sire had adored that rot, the endless parleys with other nobles, the long suppers where affairs of the realm were discussed until the less-interested diners were falling asleep onto their trenchers, the endless machinations of court and castle. If there was a bargain to be made, a treaty to be signed, the mending of a broken alliance to be seen to, his father had been there, fair breathless with enthusiasm over yet another opportunity to sit and chew on the intricacies of the same.

He would have rather been shoveling out the cesspit.

Which was why he had spent as much time as possible and in any guise possible on the battlefield, mock or real. It wasn't that he *couldn't* sit and discuss things that bored him to tears; he simply didn't care for it. As he was not caring for it at present. He was, however, as capable as the next lad with mud and dung on his boots at keeping his countenance, so he pasted a polite smile on his face and listened to the long-winded fool in front of him go on about things Gervase supposed he might be sorry he hadn't listened to.

Why had a girl of that beauty run away from her family?

He sipped his wine and allowed himself the pleasure of thinking on a mystery that was slightly more palatable than the one that concerned his sorry self. The bumps and bruises he could easily attribute to her unfortunate encounter with ruffians. He hadn't paid any heed to the bump on her head, though he supposed he could ask Master Paquier about it easily enough. Had she simply been out for a walk and found herself clouted over the head?

Perhaps the better question was, why had she been out for a walk dressed as a lad?

Determining those answers seemed like handy enough sport for the next few days and heaven knew he needed a bit of sport in his life. He couldn't remember the last time he'd done something simply for the distraction of it. He'd spent his youth preparing to be a knight, then his majority, such as it was, driving himself in tournament after tournament, pausing only to engage in the flirtations expected of a young man with a heavy title awaiting him.

Only his life had taken an abrupt turn in a different direction when his father had died suddenly, his stepmother had decamped for points more exclusive, and he had been left with not only the care of a duchy but six brothers, several of whom had certainly not been able to carry on by themselves.

Perhaps the world wouldn't end if he indulged himself in a little investigation. It would be a pleasant diversion from the absolute hell that was his life at present. Perhaps she was a lost serving girl. A lady's maid. The daughter of a very minor lord who had wanted to wed her to an unsavoury suitor. Until he discovered what she was, he would give her a marginally safe place to sleep and goodly work to do. What else could she possibly expect? A better name than Parsival, surely, but that was something else to think on at his leisure.

The only thing he knew for sure was that in spite of whatever else he did with her, he was never, *ever* going to look at her again. He'd already had enough of his flesh burned over the past few months. He wasn't about to subject his eyes to the same fate.

"And of course there are the usual troubles with England—"

Gervase forced himself to pay heed to his guest. Coucy would, he knew, eventually tire of listening to himself talk and want to go to bed. And then he would have peace to retire to his solar, sit in front of his fire, and contemplate the mystery of a young woman with eyes like the sea who he vowed he was never going to look at again.

He supposed if he reminded himself often enough of that, he might actually manage to believe it.

Chapter 5

Isabelle straightened and put her hands against her back. Of all the things she'd expected to be doing with her life, working for a demon lord as his servant was the very last.

She had been in the kitchens for three days, doing anything that didn't require her to put her hands in water. She might have protested the common labor, but she had hesitated to do so. She was, she had to admit, having an opportunity she never would have been afforded in England. Her father was very good to his people—that much she remembered—but having his daughters attending to menial kitchen labor was something he would have balked at. That wasn't to say she couldn't feed herself if need be. Even her brothers weren't above making their own porridge or fetching fruit from the larder. Her sister, Amanda, rarely made an appearance in the kitchens, but then again, she was notorious for burning everything she touched.

It was very comforting to have those memories returned to her.

Her memories were less reliable the closer she got to her present location. She remembered waking in the healer's house, she was fairly clear about what had been occurring since then, but she had no idea how she'd come to be in France in the first place.

She had to admit that was the most perplexing thing of all. Why would she have left England to begin with? Her life had been perfect in England. Artane was a spectacular hall, her family warm and loving if not a bit in the habit of patting her head and sending her off to the solar to do something safe, and her collection of suitors—

Well, the last was perhaps nothing to boast of. Unfortunately she had very clear memories of the lads who had come to court her, perhaps because she had yet to meet a prospective groom whose father hadn't been far more concerned about her dowry than her name. Actually, she couldn't bring a one to mind who had even known her name. They had come seeking Amanda. It was only after being assured that Amanda was most definitely wed that they had been forced to ask for the one who was left.

She had to admit she had—she thought—grown tired of no one taking the trouble to find out her name.

She paused with her hand on her broom and frowned. There was something else in her past, something she couldn't lay her finger on, a conversation that nagged at her, as if it had been terribly important. She sighed, then relinquished it to the blackness that seemed to contain far too many of her memories.

She brushed her hair out of her eyes, still slightly shocked by the fact that she hardly had any left. Then there was the large bump on the side of her head that still pained her greatly. It wasn't possible that someone had abducted her, clunked her over the head with a rock, then cut her hair and deposited her in France, was it? It surely wasn't possible that she had decamped for France of her own volition.

Was it?

She couldn't imagine her father had allowed her out of the great hall much less the front gates without some sort of guard in tow and perhaps even a brother or two. 'Twas extremely unlikely that she would have been out on her own alone.

She sighed. The truth was, she simply didn't know. She had difficulty remembering what had happened to her a quarter hour ago, much less anything farther in her past, though she had quite vivid recollections of her recent adventures in the kitchens. Her encounter with that cheeky guardsman who had been plunged into unconsciousness by Monsaert's lord and one of his men had somehow been enough to earn her a pair of guardsmen who loitered about the kitchens unless she ventured forth to draw water from the well at which point they followed her. She might have been without critical memories, but she was no fool. They were there to shadow her, though for what reason she couldn't have said.

Did Lord Gervase perhaps know who she was?

She didn't think so. The cook called her *girl* and the guardsmen called her nothing. She was still holding to her intention to divulge nothing until absolutely necessary, though she wasn't exactly sure what she feared might happen. Would she be held for ransom? Monsaert's great hall looked to need a bit of tidying, but it was obviously a very rich holding. Not even Artane's woodwork was so fine—

"Girl!"

Isabelle jumped in spite of herself and looked at the cook. "Aye?"

Cook nodded toward the passageway. "Go sweep the great hall."

Isabelle frowned. "Are they changing the rushes today?"

"*They* are *you* and nay, *you* are not changing rushes because we have none. Go sweep the dirt from the floor."

"No rushes?"

"Master doesn't care for them. Now go before I take my spoon to you!"

Perhaps the master didn't care for them because he was afraid he would lose his implements of torture and other sundry devilish devices in them. Isabelle shrugged to herself, then picked up her broom and walked across the kitchen, smiling at the lads and lasses there who smiled in return. There were several who didn't smile, but those were the ones who looked as if they were one misstep from plunging into the pit of Hell. She supposed with enough time she might befriend them, but she wasn't sure how much time she would have at her current locale.

Though why she wasn't running screaming into the night at just the thought of where she found herself, she didn't know. She never would have admitted to believing in ghosts and bogles and demons who roamed their ruined castles at night, howling over the injustices heaped upon them, but she couldn't deny there were strange happenings in the world. She had seen things she couldn't explain. Why not warlocks as well?

The fact that the servants in the kitchen had been particularly unwilling to talk about the master of the house had given her pause, true. Either Lord Gervase was never there and they had imagined up in their fevered imaginations what he might be like, or he was there consistently and they knew of what they spoke in whispers behind their hands.

Neither boded well for her, actually.

She glanced over her shoulder to find her usual two guardsmen there. She considered, then stopped suddenly and turned around to face them.

"What are you doing?" she demanded imperiously. Best to unsettle them into telling her the truth about their instructions.

They both had come to a teetering halt. The one on the left was simply staring at her with a frown, but the one on her right was gaping at her. She focused her attentions on him because she suspected he might be more amenable to a bit of pointed questioning.

"Your name, sir knight?"

"Denis—"

"Shut up, you fool," said the other.

Sir Denis shut his mouth, but his eyes were still wide.

"Sir Denis," Isabelle said, leaning closer to use a more conspiratorial tone, "you do your family credit with your diligence. Why are you guarding me?"

"Don't answer her."

Isabelle considered, then turned to look at the lad on the left. She gave him her most dazzling smile. To her surprise, he took a step backward. She'd seen her sister Amanda do the like countless times when needing to charm this lad or that, but she'd never attempted it herself. Well, not that she remembered. That it worked as it should was particularly gratifying.

"Your name, good sir?"

"Ah—"

"His name is Lucas, my lady," Denis supplied.

"I think she is no lady," Lucas said in a low voice.

"Are you blind? Of course she is!"

"She's sweeping the bloody floors, you fool."

"Why else would he have set us to guarding her?"

Isabelle watched them go at each other for another moment or two, then decided that perhaps slipping in a question or two whilst they were otherwise distracted might yield interesting things.

"Why did he set you to guarding me," she asked. "Whoever *he* is."

Lucas looked at her in surprise. "'Twas His Grace, of course."

"Nay, 'twas Sir Aubert in particular to set us to the task," Denis said, shaking his head, "though I'm quite sure it was Lord Gervase to insist upon it. And he did so that there might not be a repeat of the other night."

"Ah," Isabelle said slowly, "I see."

"Not that you didn't defend yourself like a right proper lad," Denis added, "which I only saw because I happened to be there in the kitchens fetching something to drink. And then His Grace came and took the lad's sword from you and Sir Aubert commanded us—"

"To keep our bloody mouths shut," Lucas said, elbowing Denis quite firmly in the ribs. "Which we will do, *demoiselle*, if you'll permit us."

Isabelle nodded thoughtfully, then turned and walked up the passageway. Obviously Lord Gervase had his men intimidated, which she understood. Her father's men served him because there was a certain amount of boasting that accompanied the privilege of serving the finest swordsman in England. Robin's men vied with her father's men for the title, but it was a friendly rivalry. If the lord of Monsaert could manage to instill that sort of loyalty in his men, perhaps he wasn't a demon after all.

Though it was entirely possible they served him out of sheer terror that he would use them in his spells if they didn't do what they were told.

She walked out into the great hall and paused to admire it. One of the clearer memories she had was of her father's hall, which she had to admit was spectacular. This was not so much spectacular as it was elegant and somehow very, well, French.

That wasn't to say it wasn't enormous, because it was. It was simply finer than anything she'd seen outside of London. There was an enormous hearth to her right, built of obviously very fine stone that no doubt required all sorts of scrubbing to keep it as lovely as it looked at the moment. The floor was laid with more fine, smooth stone, and the ceiling above her was made of very fine wood.

She paused. It looked as if a part of that ceiling had been recently replaced, for the wood was not as seasoned as the rest, but what did she know? Perhaps the rains had wrought damage she couldn't account for.

The floor was indeed bare, which she supposed should have surprised her, but Nicholas's floor was also bare in his French keep at—

Beauvois. Her brother had a keep in France called Beauvois. She put her hand out against the wall and closed her eyes as memories washed over her. Her brother Nicholas was lord of Beauvois, which wasn't all that far from where she was at present if her map-reading skills weren't failing her.

Had she come to France intending to go to Beauvois? But if that were the case, why did she now find herself in Monsaert instead? And, more to the point, why did she find herself at Monsaert posing as a servant instead of at Beauvois lingering as a pampered guest?

She paused. Was she on a quest?

She started to sweep as she turned that over in her mind. Obviously her plans had gone awry at some point, apparently taking her memories with them, but when? Had she boarded a ship, reached Calais, then somehow been diverted on her way along the coast? She supposed the possibility of that was fairly reasonable, but there were only so many reasons for that sort of diverting. Given the state of the bump on her head and the fact that she had no gold in her purse—much less a purse to start with—perhaps she had been waylaid, robbed, and clouted into insensibility. Perhaps she had been brought to Monsaert and Lord Gervase hadn't known what to do with her. Perhaps he had seen her and decided it might be good sport to ransom her. She couldn't quite believe that, but until she had proof perhaps it was best not to discount anything.

What did trouble her was what had potentially happened to her traveling companions. If anything had befallen her brothers—

"Ha."

She looked down to find that her rather substantial pile of dirt had been attacked by a small boy who was obviously quite eager to be noticed for the deed. She pursed her lips at him, then recaptured her dust and moved it away from him.

He followed and kicked again.

She reswept and shot him a warning look.

He pulled back and applied himself so forcefully to his task that the bulk of her work flew up into her face and made her sneeze.

"Yves, leave him to his work," a voice said from behind her.

Isabelle looked over her shoulder and wondered how she had failed to noticed the table there under a rather lovely window. She had no idea what it overlooked, but it seemed to provide a decent bit of light for lads who were obviously about some scholarly bit of labor.

There were two of them sitting there with their chins on their fists, watching with the joy of lads who had suddenly found something to do besides conjugate Latin verbs. Another lad of perhaps ten-and-eight was leaning negligently against the wall, watching with a bit of a smirk. She saw a movement to her left and realized that Lord Joscelin had walked into the hall, then come to an abrupt halt. He lifted an eyebrow at her, then went to lean against the wall next to who had to have been one of his brothers.

"Yves, what are you doing?" Joscelin asked politely.

"I'm showing *him* who's lord here," the boy said, looking quite fierce.

Isabelle considered the little lad standing in front of her, considered the pile of dirt he'd disturbed not once but thrice, and decided that perhaps a brief lesson in manners couldn't go awry. She poked him in the belly with her broom.

"Move," she suggested.

Yves the Fierce and Terrible spluttered as if the assault to his dignity was simply too much for him to bear. He stepped back and drew his wooden sword with a flourish.

"You," he said distinctly, "shall pay for that slight."

"Sword!" someone bellowed from behind her.

Isabelle looked and saw another wooden sword flying her way. She decided she would question where it had come from later. She caught it, then turned to look at who she could only assume was a lad belonging to the de Seger family. He engaged in a bit of parrying with the air, then rested his sword against his shoulder.

"Do you yield?" he demanded.

She suppressed the urge to smile. "I don't think we've begun the battle," she pointed out, "though I do appreciate the extra time you've allowed me to prepare for it."

"You sound like a girl," he said, beginning to frown.

"Is that an impediment?"

He drew himself up. "I didn't say you *was* a girl, I just said you *sounded* like one. Now, defend yourself, you knave, if you dare."

Isabelle tossed her broom aside, then wished she'd spent even ten minutes with Robin in the lists, but perhaps all those years of observing from afar hadn't gone to waste. Admittedly, she was fighting a lad who couldn't have been more than five or six, but at least she was managing to keep him from putting her eye out with his stick.

"Yves, real knights don't fight girls," a voice taunted.

"She's not a girl," Yves said, panting.

"Actually," Joscelin said mildly, "she is."

Yves stopped in mid-lunge, drew back, then looked at her in horror.

"Is you a girl?" he squeaked.

"*Am* I a girl?" she said. "Well, of course I am."

"Then why didn't you say so?"

"You didn't ask."

He looked terribly offended, as if she had dealt the killing blow to his pride. He resheathed his wooden sword into his belt with a hearty and disgusted thrust, then glared at her.

"I don't fight girls."

"Perhaps you should stop stepping in their dirt as well," she advised, "lest you find you have no say in the matter."

He puffed out his chest. "I *always* have a say in the matter—"

"And just what in the *hell* is going on here?" a voice thundered from the shadows.

Lads scurried. Isabelle found herself with not only Yves, but one of the other lads hiding behind her skirt—er, well not her skirts, but the trousers she had been given. She held on to her wooden sword and felt completely ridiculous.

Then again, Robin had always instructed those fortunate enough to train with him to use whatever weapons they had to hand when in a tight spot. Of course, she had never been recipient of that training because he had apparently thought the only thing she needed to hear was, "go back to the house and stitch in safety, Iz." Little had he known that all her eavesdropping on his tales of prowess and his complaints about the failures of knights of the realm would serve her so well.

She lifted her chin to face her doom, then felt her mouth fall open. She was fairly sure the point of her sword met the ground abruptly as well. She could feel one of the boys behind her trying to bump it back up where it might have served her, but she was too stunned by the man she was looking at to do anything but gape.

Perhaps she had temporarily lost not only her memories but her ability to appreciate an exceptionally handsome man. She knew he had rescued her in the kitchens a handful of days before, but perhaps she had been more distracted by the feel of steel in her hands than she'd realized at the time. Surely that was the only reason she hadn't spent just as much time then staring at the man in front of her as she was at present. To call him merely handsome was truly to do him an injustice. He was absolutely—

Well, she was tempted to sit down until she had better control over herself, and she couldn't remember ever having had the sight of a man render her that unfit.

To her surprise, she realized that he was wounded. His angry stride across the great hall was less of a stride than it was a limp, as if his right leg especially plagued him. His right hand he held clenched in a fist, as if it didn't open very easily. At least she assumed that was the reason and not because he intended to come and strike her.

She raised her sword on the off chance that she was wrong.

A soft gasp came from behind her, but that was all. She was too far into it to back away now, so she put her shoulders back, lifted her chin, and decided that if he was going to attempt an insult to her person, she would make sure it took a bit of effort.

He stopped and looked at her as if he couldn't believe what he was seeing.

"Surely you jest, *demoiselle*."

She pointed her sword at him. "You do not find me defenseless, sir."

He looked almost as offended as Yves the Ferocious had. "I do not strike women," he said curtly.

"And if I were a lad?"

"Then I would take you out into the lists and beat you senseless for daring to lift a blade against me," he said. "If that makes your decision for you."

She propped her sword up against her shoulder as she'd seen her brothers do more times than she could count, then looked at her opponent coolly.

"Then I shall be what I am and rely on your chivalry to carry the day."

He folded his arms over his chest, no doubt in an attempt to intimidate her, but she was immune. She'd seen it done too many times in her own home to be impressed. That, and his hand hadn't strayed to his sword hilt, which boded well for her. He also still held his right hand in a fist, which intrigued her.

"And if I have no chivalry?" he asked.

"You'll notice that I kept the sword, just in case. Splinters can be troublesome in the right spot, you know."

Someone from behind her guffawed but choked on his laughter at a look from the lord of the hall. He schooled his features into less of a scowl, then looked at her.

"My youngest brother should not have raised a sword against you."

"He kicked her dust as well," the other lad behind her said helpfully.

A scuffle ensued. She turned around, caught the littlest lad by the arm and pulled him to his feet.

"Go sit down and behave," she said sternly.

He hesitated, looked around her at his older brother, then bolted. The next lad up in age made her a brief bow, then followed his brother to safety. She now found herself alone, facing Gervase de Seger, demon lord of Monsaert.

It was surprising just how handsome a warlock could be.

"What is your name?" he asked shortly.

She considered, then decided there was no reason to be honest. Her father wouldn't have been in like circumstances, she was sure of it.

"I don't remember," she said.

"Where are you from?"

"I don't remember that, either," she lied. It bothered her, that little lie, but what else was she to do? Even if proper knights didn't lie to save their necks, women were permitted a bit of leeway when using what assets they possessed. The truth was, she had several questions about her current straits and she wasn't sure she wanted to admit more than she had to before she'd discovered those answers. She attempted a pleasant smile. "I don't believe we've been properly introduced."

His eyes narrowed. "Why would I give my name to a serving wench?"

She blinked, then realized that as far as he was concerned, that was exactly what she was. She inclined her head, then picked her broom up from where she'd dropped it. She walked over to the table and set the wooden sword down very carefully, then went back to her sweeping.

There was absolute silence in the chamber except for the brush of the straw against the stone. She swept around the boots of the lord of Monsaert, then continued on her way, not looking at anything but where she was going.

It took a bit, but finally those boots scuffed against the stone and took the lord of the hall away. She would have ignored the hitch in his step, but it was difficult to do so. She watched him casually as he limped back across the hall and slammed his way out of the front door.

Interesting.

There were murmurs behind her, but she didn't attempt to sort them out. She simply continued with her work.

She looked up at one point to find Joscelin in her way. He moved aside, his hands clasped behind his back.

"Forgive my brother his vile humors."

"He's hurt."

"Have you heard that or did you divine that by looking at him?"

"The latter, assuredly."

"I don't think he intended to be so rude."

She stopped her sweeping and looked at him. "I am a lowly serving wench in a high lord's house. Why would he favor me with anything but what I deserve?"

"Well," he began slowly, "whatever you might or might not be, I can assure you 'tis his pain that speaks, not his cheery nature."

She smiled. "Cheery? If I were to listen to the rumors, I would think he was instead grimly plying his dark arts on unsuspecting scullery maids after supper simply to entertain himself."

Joscelin laughed a little. "Considering the state of his temper over the past half year, I daresay not even plying a lute and fine wine would convince unsuspecting scullery maids to tolerate him for more than a heartbeat or two." He hesitated. "Forgive Yves as well. He has been without the gentling influence of a woman for too long. My dam found us too taxing a burden and decamped for court last year, or perhaps the year before. I don't remember exactly when it was."

Isabelle sighed. "The poor lads."

Joscelin glanced at the lads collected around the table. "It was difficult for them," he conceded. "I didn't care, because I've been away from home for many years and it wasn't as if she was particularly fond of me while I was home. For the others, though?" He shook his head. "It was hardest on Yves, of course, because he's merely five—"

"Six a fortnight ago!" Yves bellowed.

"Six, a fortnight ago," Joscelin corrected. "Fabien is ten, Pierre ten-and-four, and Lucien ten-and-eight. Lucien should be seeking his spurs, but our father is dead and my oldest brother Gervase—" He took a deep breath. "Well, he's had the hall to see to, of course."

"Of course," she said. "And how old are you?"

"A score and three," he said. "How old are you?"

"I don't know," she said, because it wouldn't do to tell him more than she needed to. "Old enough, I suppose."

"Are you wed?"

"Saints, nay," she said with a laugh, then she realized that perhaps she shouldn't be volunteering things so readily. Unfortunately, Joscelin reminded her quite a bit of Miles, which she supposed might be a very dangerous thing, indeed. She would be telling him things she hadn't intended to very readily if she didn't watch herself.

It was somewhat comforting, though, to realize that she might have an ally where she hadn't looked for one.

She thanked Joscelin for the pleasant conversation, then continued to sweep, slowly moving across the hall where she might concentrate her efforts around Yves, who was not a quiet scholar. He seemed particularly unhappy about the sums he'd been set to do. She leaned over and whispered at him.

"Are there pebbles in your garden?"

He looked up at her, his eyes swimming with tears. "Suppose so. Why?"

"Go find me two score of them."

"So you can chuck them at me?"

She smiled. "Of course not. You are far too fierce for me to even think such a thing. I thought simply to teach you maths the way my father taught them to me."

"Girls can't add."

"Indeed?" she said easily. "Are you willing, Lord Yves, to find out if that might not be true?"

He smiled suddenly, a sunny little smile that smote her to the heart. "Lord Yves," he said with a whisper of a laugh. "No one calls me that."

"I shall, for 'tis your birthright, isn't it?" She reached out and ruffled his hair. "Fetch me pebbles, my lord."

He bounded up out of his chair and bolted for the kitchens. Isabelle watched him go, then continued to sweep until she heard rocks being deposited with enthusiasm onto the table where the boys were laboring. She found a hand suddenly on the handle of her broom and looked up to see Lord Joscelin standing there.

"What do you want?" she asked.

"I'm trading you one disagreeable task for another," he said with a smile. "I'll sweep; you teach sums."

"Your brother will be furious."

"My brother is always furious." He took the broom away from her and nodded. "Go on with you, wench, and work your magic over there."

She would have chastised him for referring to her so commonly, but that was what she was at present and he had said it in the same affectionate tone Miles always used, so she left him to her work and happily walked over to the table. She was immediately provided with a chair, so she sat down next to Yves and smiled.

"Shall we begin?"

"Will you parry with me if I say aye?" he asked solemnly.

She laughed. "I just might. Gather up your pebbles, Lord Yves, and let's see how you fare."

Within moments, she had the bulk of Gervase's brothers either sitting at or on the table, keeping her company during her labors. It took her a bit to understand why she couldn't stop smiling.

She felt as if she were at home.

In Monsaert, of all places, with its lord who was full of vile humors and his collection of brothers who weren't.

She was obviously on a quest, her quest had obviously gone awry, but perhaps for the moment she could be content with attending to Yves de Seger's sums. The rest would no doubt sort itself out as it would.

Surely nothing terrible would come of a bit of delay in her plans.

Chapter 6

Gervase looked out the window in his bedchamber and was rather grateful he was at least able to stand to do so. There had been many fortnights during which even that simple accomplishment had been beyond him.

He wasn't sure at the moment that he was all that grateful for it, unfortunately. The fields that made up his view still looked as barren as they had four months earlier. Perhaps leaving things to lie fallow every now and again was good for them. Heaven knew he had little choice in the matter at present.

Obviously it was far past time he made a brief journey to the village to speak with his *prévôt* to see about routing his peasants out of bed to see to spring planting. Master Humbert had served his father for years, which Gervase supposed would stand him in good stead at present. It was for damned sure he hadn't had much of a relationship with the man before.

Besides, who knew what sort of gossip he might overhear at the local inn?

He drew on a cloak, belted a useless sword about his hips out of habit, then rubbed his right thigh for a moment or two to try to ease some of the discomfort. It served him as well as it did every morning, which was to say not at all. 'Twas little wonder his temper was as black as night. If he ever had another day where he wasn't in pain even in his sleep, he might manage something other than a snarl when he spoke. Unfortunately, he didn't hold out much hope for it.

He could walk, though, which was definitely an improvement. Whether his bones had been set properly in his leg and arm, he couldn't have said.

He opened the door, then walked out into the passageway. Two of his men were standing there, looking impossibly grim. At least things there were as they should have been. He smiled pleasantly at them.

"Where is Sir Aubert?" he asked.

"Training the men, Lord Gervase."

Gervase nodded. "One of you tell him I'm riding to the village to seek out Master Humbert. I'm leaving in half an hour."

The man nodded briskly and hurried off to deliver the tidings. Gervase made his way to the hall, trailed by his remaining guardsman. He would break his fast, hopefully without seeing anyone he didn't want to see, then force himself to get on a horse and get himself to the village. He couldn't say he felt any stronger than he had the day he'd brought home that stray wench, but perhaps he was. He'd forced himself to walk to the stables and back each day for the past several days. He supposed he wasn't managing it in any less time, but at least after the journey he wasn't retreating immediately to his solar to give vent to a very large collection of vile curses for the rest of the day. He could only hope a small journey out of the keep wouldn't finish what was left of him.

He limped into the great hall, then came to an abrupt halt. That was painful enough that he had to put his hand out to the nearest wall and simply breathe for a moment or two. Once he could manage that, he had another look at the madness going on in front of him.

His orphan who had started out as a lad, then become a lass, had now apparently decided she was a scholar.

"She's helping Lucien with his Latin."

Gervase scowled at Joscelin who had seemingly recently taken up the very annoying habit of popping up where he was least expected. "She's doing *what*?"

"You heard me."

"I heard you," Gervase agreed, "but I didn't believe you." He looked back at his newly acquired serving wench who was currently shaking her head and instructing his younger brother to repeat what he was doing. "I still don't believe it."

"Come and listen, then."

"I don't have time," Gervase lied. "Things to do."

Joscelin didn't move. "Have you considered that she might not be just a serving wench?"

"I've been too busy to consider anything save my usual business."

Joscelin only continued to regard him with far too much discernment. "Of course. Why would you be curious about a girl who looks like that?"

"She's a runaway servant," Gervase said, because that sounded like a reasonable thing to say. "I'm being excessively generous by giving her food and a place to lay her head."

"And two of your own guardsmen. *Very* generous."

Gervase looked at his brother coolly. "I believe I'm finished with this conversation."

Joscelin only continued to watch him, a smile playing around his mouth. Gervase was heartily tempted to wipe that smirk off his brother's face, but Joscelin was, damn him to Hell, at the height of his prowess. That was saying something because the lad had been formidable at ten-and-six when Gervase had first begun to take him along tourneying. That decision had been easily made. Joscelin was the only one of his half brothers he had known well enough to trust. He wasn't sure if that said more about him or about his stepmother, who hadn't trusted him around her sainted spawn.

He took a deep breath. Perhaps it was just better not to think at all.

"I think I would be careful with her," Joscelin said with a shrug as he walked away.

Gervase was tempted to beat a few details out of the lad, but Joscelin had already trotted lithely out of reach and Gervase had no desire to bellow after him. He scowled. The wench was nothing more than she seemed, which was a servant. Perhaps she'd been a servant to a lord with sons and she'd eavesdropped on their lessons as she'd been scrubbing the floors. Perhaps she'd been cleaning ashes out of the fire as the lord himself had furthered his learning. The reasons why a lowly serving wench with such astonishing beauty might have skills that most scullery maids did not possess were many and varied. He was just certain he would be giving them a proper examination the first chance he had.

Fortunately for him, that opportunity was not presenting itself at present. He turned his back on the spectacle of his brothers sitting happily around the table, waiting breathlessly for that angel of a girl to help them with their studies, and stomped toward the front door with as much enthusiasm as he could muster.

That vigor lasted until he'd gotten out to the courtyard. He had to stop for a moment or two, then lean over and catch his breath until the pain in his leg receded a bit.

Damn her, who *was* she?

An hour and many curses later, he walked into the village hall and looked for a seat that he could get back up from comfortably. He wasn't surprised to watch villagers scatter before him like leaves before a fall wind. He rolled his eyes, then took the first seat he found. Aubert sat down with him, then had a casual look about. Gervase had no doubts he could simply ask his captain for the number and kind of everyone in the common chamber and have an accurate account. It wouldn't have surprised him to know Aubert had marked not only what everyone was wearing, but what they were eating as well.

He looked up as his forester swept into the tavern and strode over to him. He was bowed to, then Master Humbert took the third seat.

"A good morning to you, *monseigneur le duc*," he said with a smile.

Gervase attempted a smile. "And to you, Master Humbert. What tidings from the village?"

"The usual," Humbert said with a shrug. "Tales of your fierceness, speculation about what you do in the keep at night, questions about spring planting."

"No worries that I won't be able to defend them if necessary?" Gervase asked lightly.

Humbert's smile faded. "That, too, my lord, if you must know. Though 'tis cheering to see you here, isn't it?"

It was a damned sight more cheering that being limited to

looking at the canopy of his bed, though he supposed he would do well to keep that thought to himself.

"It is," he agreed simply.

"Though I am curious as to why you wanted to meet here and not in your hall."

"Breath of fresh air," Gervase said succinctly. And fewer ears listening from the shadows, which was something he supposed he didn't need to say. "Anything I should know?"

Master Humbert proceeded to give him a list he tried to pay appropriate heed to. Truly, he did. Could he be faulted if he found it difficult to concentrate on the pedestrian task of running an estate the size of a small country when he had other things that puzzled him?

Who *was* she?

He wasn't entirely sure Master Humbert wasn't still talking when he set aside his cup and prepared to leave.

"Lord Gervase?"

He blinked. "What?"

"Shall I bring you the rest of the tidings later? To the keep?"

Gervase nodded, then paused. He wasn't sure how to ask the question without attaching more significance to it than he wanted to, but he had to know before the woman in his hall made him daft.

"A final question," he said.

"Of course, my lord."

Gervase chewed on his words for a moment or two. "Have you heard of anyone missing a servant?"

Humbert blinked. "I beg your pardon?"

"A servant, man. A wench who goes about the kitchen scrubbing floors and making sausage."

Humbert laughed a little. "Aye, I knew what they did. I just wondered why you were curious. Did you lose one?"

"Nay, I didn't," Gervase said. "I was just curious."

"I haven't heard of anyone having lost a serving girl, but I could ask, if you like."

Gervase shook his head. "I'm not *that* curious. 'Twas nothing more than idle talk in the kitchens, you know." He rose and put his right hand down on the back of his chair to steady himself without thinking beforehand what it would cost him. He gritted his teeth for a moment or two, then smiled at his forester.

"I've business back at the hall. Come to me on the morrow, perhaps."

"As you wish, my lord. Safe home, as always."

Gervase ignored that, because things like that made him feel as if Fate were watching him far too closely. He wasn't altogether certain that Joscelin hadn't said the same thing to him at some point before his accident. It would have been convenient if he could have remembered the events leading up to it, but he couldn't and there was nothing to be done about that. He was perhaps in his own way missing as many memories as that poor daft wench back in the castle, sweeping his floors and helping his brothers with sums that even he had to think about for a moment or two.

He nodded to Master Humbert, then turned and left the common room with as much confidence in his step as he could muster. He supposed he couldn't be blamed if he had to pause several times between the door of the hall and the village stables. His meal had been hard on his belly—

Only he hadn't eaten anything, he supposed.

He swung up onto his horse—that poor old horse who seemed not to feel the indignity of being all Gervase could manage—then nodded for Aubert and the lads to begin the journey home. He would have far preferred to sit still and try to manage his pain before he wept, but he knew from experience that it wasn't going to get any better. There was something to be said for simply riding into the storm, as it were.

He wasn't sure how long it took them to reach the keep. He was simply glad to see it rising up in the distance. That hadn't always been his reaction to the sight of his home, to be sure. He'd been scarce three winters when his mother had died and his father remarried with unseemly haste. A large succession of half siblings had then arrived. The boys had never treated him as anything but a brother, but he couldn't say the same for his stepmother. She had barely tolerated him, though he couldn't have said why. Perhaps she resented not only his father's affection for him, but his own place in the house of Seger. At least her lads hadn't possessed any of her less desirable traits. After all, 'twas Joscelin and Guy who had put out the flames and saved not only him but their hall. He wasn't sure he could ask for more loyal siblings than that.

He dismounted in the stables, handed his reins to the same

stable lad he'd relinquished his horse to almost a se'nnight ago
after rescuing his scullery maid—and had it been that long?—
and was pleased to see the lad looked hardly troubled at all by
Gervase's presence. Perhaps things were improving.

He left the stables and walked back up the way to the great
hall.

Or at least he did for a score of difficult paces before he saw
something that forced him into a stumbling run before he knew
what his body intended.

He managed to remove the offending man from the woman
the bastard had just slapped before the brute could hit her again.
He overbalanced and fell against the wall of his keep thanks to
the effort, but he supposed that was a happy bit of good fortune
because he took the man with him.

It was Coucy's man, the one who had assaulted his rescued
gel in the kitchens.

He stepped away, then backhanded the fool with his good
hand. The rather heavy sound of cheek against stone was particularly satisfying.

Coucy's guardsman's hand was on his sword, but it fell away
when he realized whom he was facing. Gervase looked at Aubert.

"Take him to the dungeon."

Aubert nodded and two of the lads took the offender away
with as much gentleness as Gervase would have used himself in
their place, which was exactly none. He looked at the woman in
front of him to judge the damage.

She was clutching the front of her gown together, which told
him two things. First, someone had obviously found her something womanly to wear. Second, based on the red handprint on
her cheek and the tears standing in her eyes, she had spent more
time in the company of a knave than he might have preferred.
He took off his cloak, then pulled her away from the wall and
swept it around her shoulders. He helped her lean back against
the wall where he thought she might be more comfortable while
he shouted at her.

"Where," he asked as calmly as possible, "are your guardsmen?"

"I told them to stay inside," she said, her voice trembling
badly.

"Why?" he asked. It was such a reasonable question and he
asked it with hardly a raising of his voice. Hardly.

"Because I was just coming outside to see if there were any flowers blooming in that patch of dirt there outside the hall door. It seemed a poor use of their time, don't you think?"

He had to admit that a year ago he would have thought the same thing, though he was hardly going to say as much to the trembling woman in front of him.

"That lad was lying in wait for me, I believe," she continued. "In the shadows there outside the door."

Gervase exchanged a look with Aubert, who stepped back a pace or two to impart an edifying suggestion to a man who then ran off quickly toward the hall. Perhaps Coucy's man's journey to the dungeon would meet with a few unexpected bumps along the way. That was always a bit difficult to predict in these circumstances.

He turned back to the woman in question and felt fury sweep through him again. That someone should have laid a hand on—

"You will not strike me."

He blinked. "What?"

She lifted her chin. "You *will* not strike me, sir."

"Strike you," he mouthed, then he cleared his throat. "*Strike* you? Daft wench, I've a mind to take my *blade* to you!"

He said that with enthusiasm. It was entirely possible that he shouted it. He was so turned about and his leg so on fire, he honestly couldn't have said what he'd done. He curled his right fist into a ball and rested it against the stone, leaning on it to take some of the pressure off his leg.

Two of his younger guardsmen came rushing out of the hall, men that should have known better than to be led about by a wench, no matter how beautiful she might be. He supposed those were apologies on their lips, but he cut them off with a sharp motion of his good hand. He looked at Aubert.

"Take them into the lists and kill them."

"What?" his servant who couldn't possibly be that exclaimed. "You cannot be serious!"

He glared at her. "You, mistress," he said in a low voice, "are one word from finding yourself sharing their fate."

"But I *told* them to stay behind!"

"And for that, they will die—"

She put her hand on his arm. It was only because he was already in pain that it fair brought him to his knees, no other reason. By the saints, he was a score and eight. He could boast of conquests all over France. Whether or not he had actually made those conquests was perhaps beside the point. His reputation for wenching, his desirability as a lover, his bloody endless coffers of gold that hadn't mattered a damn bit because his face and form had taken the day, every day, for as long as he could remember—

And now to be undone by a scullery maid?

He pushed away from the wall and pointed a withered finger at her.

"You, be silent."

She stepped in front of her guardsmen. "I will not let you slay them."

He took her by the arm and pulled her close where he could bend his head and whisper in her ear.

"If you have any sense at all," he murmured, "you will cease this instant with making me look weak in front of my men."

She looked up at him.

He suppressed the urge to clap his hand over his eyes to spare what was left of his wits any further destruction. If he did nothing else that day—or perhaps over the next fortnight, perhaps longer if it seemed necessary—he had to get her out of his hall. He might have to find a name for her first, but, aye, she had to go. If not, she was going to be the death of something. Him, his good sense, his ability to move from one end of the day to the other without spending the bulk of that day wondering how in the hell a serving wench could be so damned beautiful.

Perhaps she was a faery. He didn't believe in faeries as a general rule, but he thought he might have to revisit the possibility of them very soon. It seemed a far better use of his time than to fight the urge to pull the woman standing so close to him he could feel her breath on his neck close, wrap his arms around her, and keep her safe.

By the saints, he didn't even know the girl. She could have been full of shrewish and nasty humors, spreading grief and destruction wherever she went. She had obviously cast some sort of unholy spell over her guardsmen.

That brought him back to where he had been, industriously chastising her for making him look weak in front of men who were obviously just as overcome by the fairness of her face as he was.

"I'm sorry," she said very quietly. "That was badly done."

"Harrumph," he said, because it was all he could manage.

She stepped away from his hand on her arm, which he didn't care for particularly, then turned and looked at the young knights who were standing there looking as if the blades had already gone into their bellies.

"I apologize to you both," she said without hesitation. "I shouldn't have asked you to ignore the task you were given."

"And they were fools to listen to a mere serving wench," Gervase added, because the two fools quaking in front of him were directly responsible for the terror he'd felt at the sight of Coucy's little sod assaulting the woman in front of him. He looked at Aubert. "Help them understand to whom they will be listening from now on. Don't spare any effort in your instruction."

Aubert merely walked away without comment. The two young knights hastened after him, which Gervase supposed said something about their characters. He had the feeling they would be spending the next fortnight in the infirmary, recovering from their instruction, which was likely too kind a fate for them.

He had to simply look up at the sky for several minutes until he had control over himself. What he wanted to do was first do damage to the two fools who had allowed themselves to be led about by a ring through their noses, then he wanted to take Coucy's man and beat him to a bloody pulp. Unfortunately, he wasn't in any shape to do either.

"I apologize, Lord Gervase."

He looked at the girl in front of him. Obviously she thought his fury burned brightly toward her still. He supposed it wouldn't do him any good to admit what he was thinking, so he frowned a bit more at her lest she think she had the upper hand.

Frowning was a good way to keep from gaping, he supposed. He also suppressed the urge to shake his head in wonder. Was it possible this one was a servant? If it had been merely the fairness of her face that was so unusual, perhaps he would have assumed she was an oddity, a rare flower planted in common ground, a girl whose father must have lost many nights' sleep fretting over what would become of her, but she was canny, intelligent, and unintimidated by his sour self. Remarkable.

"Did he hurt you?" he asked.

She shook her head.

"Did he touch you?"

She hesitated. "He tried to kiss me, but I avoided that. And most everything else."

He started to shout at her, but he realized that she was on the verge of some sort of womanly something. He did his best to suppress his alarm. He was accustomed to ladies of breeding and their schemes. The truth was, there wasn't a lady of breeding that he'd encountered more than once who hadn't been as ruthless in her own sphere as he was in his.

But a tenderhearted serving wench?

The saints preserve him, he was in trouble. Perhaps 'twas time he put her back to work and escaped to hide in his solar.

He nodded as curtly as possible—which wasn't much—toward the hall. "Come with me."

She didn't move. "And if I say you nay and rely on the merits of your chivalry?"

"And what makes you believe I have a smidgen of chivalry?"

"I have a nose for that sort of thing."

He almost smiled. It took him a moment or two to recapture his frown. He didn't want to like her. He nodded to himself over that, congratulating himself on a thought that surely made more sense than any other he'd ever entertained. She wasn't a boy, which should have given him pause. He had the feeling she wasn't a scullery maid, either, which *did* give him pause. He couldn't remember the last time he'd met a serving wench who could speak Latin and do sums, which led him to believe that she couldn't possibly be a servant.

Who the hell was she?

"I'm taking you to my solar," he said, grasping for the first thing that made sense to him, "where I will lock you in to help you learn to suppress your less sensible impulses. I will then accompany Cook as she brings you endless baskets of mending and sewing. You will remain in my solar until I give you permission to leave it."

"Does it have a window?"

He shot her a dark look and had a faint smile in return. "None that you'll be using," he muttered.

"And my guardsmen?"

"They will be cleaning the cesspit for the foreseeable future, assuming there is something left of them after Sir Aubert finishes with his labors. They can thank you for that. Do you care to cause anyone else any grief?"

She lifted her eyebrows briefly but said nothing.

"Then let's go."

He wanted to stride angrily, but all he could manage was an anemic amble. If the *demoiselle* of a place she couldn't remember noticed, she said nothing. She simply walked next to him, silent and grave.

It took him longer to reach his solar than he would have liked, but once there, he pointed to a chair near the fire.

"Sit."

She shook her head. "I'll build up the fire, my lord. You sit."

"I do not need to be coddled," he said before he thought better of it.

She turned and put her hands on her hips. "I wasn't coddling you, Your Grace, I was trying to be of some use."

He merely pointed at a chair and waited until she'd sighed, then walked over to cast herself down into it. She looked at him, clear-eyed and unrepentant. He had the feeling she was only barely keeping herself from sending a crisp *satisfied?* his way.

He ignored her, then went to fetch wood. He carried an armful over to the fire, dropped a piece, then leaned over to pick it up from where it had almost landed on her toes. He would have thought that living with his broken body for so long would have taught him something, but obviously he had learned nothing so far. He overbalanced, his right leg gave way, and he landed hard upon his knees. The wood spilled out of his arms and half into the fire, sending sparks shooting out from the hearth onto them both.

His companion said nothing. She merely stomped out what was live, then quickly piled the wood onto the fire as if she'd done it countless times before. All that was left for him to do was put out a single smoldering spot on his hose, then attempt to salvage his pride. He trotted out a selection of curses for inspection, gave vent to a handful of them, then wondered why it was they didn't soothe him as they should have.

She moved a heavy chair where he could reach it. He used it to get to his feet, then collapsed into it with a groan. She sat down in the chair facing him, then looked at him with a polite smile, as if she hadn't just witnessed him making a fool of himself.

"Shall I read to you?"

He looked at her in surprise. "What?"

She started to speak, but a knock interrupted her. She looked at him.

"May I?"

"Best take my sword."

She smiled. He realized then that he was in a fair bit of peril where she was concerned, which had to have been the most ridiculous thing he had ever thought over a lifetime of ridiculous thoughts. She was a simple wench, he was lord of a vast estate—

She pulled the dagger from his boot without comment. Poor fool that he was, he simply had no energy to protest. He listened to her open the door and greet his second-eldest half brother.

"Lovely cloak," Joscelin said politely. "Are you cold or off on a journey?"

"Neither now that your brother has made such a nice fire."

"That wouldn't be the first time," Joscelin said.

Gervase cursed him as thoroughly as he had breath for, then glared at him for good measure when he came within view. "What do *you* want?" he snarled. "And your humor is, as always, sadly misplaced."

"You need me to bring sunlight into your gloomy life," Joscelin said, sitting down across from him.

"That's her chair, you fool. Get up."

Joscelin paused, then stood up and turned his back to the fire, waving their wench expansively back to where she'd started.

"My apologies, *demoiselle*. But you still haven't told me why you're wearing a cloak. Seems passing pleasant in here to me."

"She is wearing my cloak, you idiot, because *you* didn't stop her from leaving the hall and she was accosted in the midst of the courtyard!" Gervase bellowed.

Joscelin's mouth fell open. "By whom?"

"Coucy's man. The one whose nose she bloodied earlier."

Joscelin turned to her. "Forgive me. I had no idea."

She shook her head. "It was my fault. I told my guardsmen to remain inside."

"And they listened to you?" Joscelin asked in surprise.

"I can be very persuasive under the right circumstances."

"Aye, when you're breathing," Gervase muttered. He started to say something else, then realized they were both staring at him in surprise. "Well," he said defensively, "she's not precisely ugly, is she?"

"Hardly," Joscelin agreed.

"She needs a new gown," Gervase said shortly. "Take her to your mother's solar and find her something suitable. Do *not* remain inside while she changes into it." He shot the girl he couldn't possibly call Parsival a look. "You can attempt to repair what you're wearing. I'll go find you other things to mend, then you will remain here seeing to womanly things until I give you other instructions, is that understood?"

She looked at him for several moments in silence, then nodded. Gervase shot Joscelin a dark look.

"I would see you in the lists if I could."

"You have often enough in the past," Joscelin said easily. "I daresay you'll be there again in the future."

He said nothing because there was nothing to say. But after Joscelin and his charge had departed for safer ground, he did send a page to Cook for as much mending as she could find, then he paced in agony until a knock sounded on his door. He opened it, expecting to see Joscelin there, but it was Guy. He opened to his brother, then realized Joscelin and their servant who wasn't a servant were hard on his heels. Guy gave way to their serving wench and Gervase ignored how the look of admiration his next youngest brother gave her irritated him. She was a servant, nothing more. What did he care how his brothers looked at her?

"You look as if you need an afternoon in the lists," Guy said easily. "I've offered several times, brother, to aid you."

"I don't think I could stand two minutes against you," Gervase said, though it cost him a great deal to admit as much. "I'll begin with a much lesser swordsman. Perhaps that lesser swordsman there," he said, glaring at Joscelin.

Joscelin only smiled. Guy shrugged and made Gervase a bow.

"I'll be off to see to what is needful, then."

Gervase nodded, because the words of gratitude he should have been uttering were simply beyond him at the moment. Guy merely smiled and left the chamber, no doubt to see to things Gervase should have been attending to himself.

He stood aside as Cook arrived with two enormous baskets of mending and the tools necessary to see to them. He watched Joscelin treat that exquisite serving wench with far more deference than he would have a servant he merely wanted to bed. He waited until she was settled, then he took his brother by the back of the tunic and walked him over to the door. He pushed him out into the passageway, then joined him there, pulling the door shut behind him.

"You know something," Gervase said bluntly.

Joscelin looked at him innocently. "I know many things—"

Gervase growled at him. "Don't be an ass. Who is she?"

"That depends on what you intend to do with her."

"She's a serving wench. What can I possibly intend to do with her?"

"If she's that," Joscelin said slowly, "then why are you asking me anything?"

"Because she's terribly outspoken for a mere serving wench," Gervase whispered angrily.

"Why don't you ask her who she is?"

"She can't remember."

"Then why would you think I would know anything?"

"Because you're smirking."

"I'm not. I'm admiring."

Gervase gritted his teeth. "Admire something else."

Joscelin only smiled and walked away. "You're awfully possessive of a mere serving wench."

"I want to know what you're thinking!" Gervase shouted.

"I don't think you do," Joscelin called back cheerfully, "though I would find out who she is before I did something stupid if I were you."

Well, of course he intended to find out who she was. It was what he'd started out to do that day. He'd been interrupted by arriving back at the keep to find her almost overcome. Obviously, he was going to have to keep a better watch over her. If that required him to remain near her for a goodly part of the day, each day that she remained in his hall, so be it.

Altruistic to the last, that's what he was.

He could only hope he wouldn't pay a steep price for the exercising of that virtue.

Chapter 7

Isabelle sat in a chair near the fire and thought she might like to forget the events of the morning.

It was odd, wishing she could trade the memories she had for ones she no longer had, but being pulled into a relatively deserted part of the courtyard by a man with less-than-chivalrous intentions was something she would have preferred not to remember. Knowing she was responsible for the saints only knew what where Gervase's guardsmen were concerned was worse.

She'd spent the rest of the day in Gervase's solar, mending and being quite grateful for a gown that fit and didn't sport a rent down its front. She'd had her meals brought to her, been escorted to the garderobe as often as she cared to be, and passed the rest of the time doing something she didn't mind doing. It gave her ample time to watch the goings-on around her.

Brothers had arrived singly or in pairs as seemed to suit them until she had all of them in the solar with her. Even Guy had joined them after supper, having been prevailed upon by his younger brothers to read them something. Isabelle could scarce believe anyone was wealthy enough to own so many folios, but she couldn't deny what she'd seen.

It was a gathering she was accustomed to, which gave her a strange sort of comfort. It also wasn't as if she wouldn't have been sitting at home, stitching as well, which also gave her comfort. Yves had spent the past hour sitting on a stool in front of the fire, moving that stool progressively closer to her until he was leaning against the front of her chair. She ruffled his hair at one point and had a sweet smile in return. It was enough like being with her nieces and nephews that she felt her heart be eased.

Fabien was lying on the rug at her feet, contemplating soldiers someone had carved out of wood. Lucien and Pierre were engaged in chess and Joscelin was sitting to her left, staring thoughtfully into the fire.

Guy set aside the book suddenly and sighed. "Enough for the moment." He looked at her. "*Demoiselle*, you needn't continue to ply your needle. Take your ease."

She smiled, though she did set down the sheet she was hemming. "I thank you for your concern, but I don't consider this taxing work. I've done it at home often enough."

Joscelin looked at her carefully. "Are your memories returning, then?"

"I remember how to stitch," she hedged. "Is that not enough for the day?"

He smiled pleasantly. "I suppose so, for it means my hose perhaps might cease to have holes in the toes. But let's stretch ourselves to choose a name for you." He looked at his brothers. "Lads?"

"Marie," Yves said promptly. "I like that name."

"Something more elegant," Fabien said.

"Hildegard," Joscelin said.

Isabelle shot him a look, but he only laughed.

"Something else, perhaps. Imogen or Catherine or Isolde." He looked at her. "What do you think?"

"I think I don't have an opinion," she said promptly. Actually, she did have an opinion and that was that Joscelin was thinking on a few too many names similar to her own for her taste. Perhaps it made no difference if he did know who she was, but obviously her father's injunctions about secrecy were too ingrained in her to ignore.

"I won't pester you," Joscelin said pleasantly. "Instead, why don't you pester us? Ask us anything you like and we'll give you the complete truth."

She looked at the collection of Gervase's brothers and wondered why he wasn't there with him. "Where is your brother?" she asked, before she thought better of it.

Guy laughed a bit. "He is the most interesting of us, to be sure. And I imagine he's off doing lord-of-the-manor things. I'm happy to see him take over the task, though I was willing to see to it in his stead for a bit."

"Guy is too modest," Joscelin said. "The keep would have gone to ruin without him. He is also the one who pulled Gervase from the fire and saved the hall."

Isabelle shifted to look at Joscelin. "Is the entire tale tellable or would that be asking too much to know it?"

"'Tis freely told as long as Gervase isn't within earshot," Joscelin said seriously. "'Twas last fall when the harvest was full on—"

"Nay, you must go farther back than that," Guy said. "He wouldn't have been here if Father had been alive, which would have changed the entire sequence of events." He looked at Isabelle. "Our father died almost a year ago, you see, and our mother—well, let's say she wanted to pursue her interests elsewhere. At court, as it happens."

Isabelle had seen the clothing the woman had left behind and even that small glimpse into her trunk had told her perhaps all she needed to know. Things were assuredly more refined in France when it came to fashion, but even the woman's leavings were sumptuous, far beyond anything her own mother would have thought to have made up. Far too costly.

"Is she still there?" Isabelle ventured.

Guy nodded. "She writes now and again, just to see how we fare."

"To describe her lavish life," Lucien said in disgust, "and remind us to see her kept firmly in it."

Guy shot him a look. "Hold your tongue, brother." He looked at Isabelle and smiled. "My mother's family was not wealthy and my father was good enough over the course of his lifetime to see to their needs. Gervase has made a few changes."

"Be honest about it," Joscelin said with a frown. "Gervase sees to the care of our mother's family without hesitation. Our uncles he has cut off, but you must admit they deserve as much."

Guy conceded the point with a nod. "They are a fine collection of wastrels, true. At least our aunt is seen to along with

Mother and Grandmère, so I don't suppose they have any reason to complain."

"Nay, they do not," Joscelin said pointedly.

Isabelle assumed, based on the looks they were exchanging, that they had had this conversation more than once.

Joscelin turned to her. "As Guy was saying, our Father died a year and a half ago. Gervase and I were off tourneying—"

"Again," Guy grumbled.

"'Tis hardly our fault you don't care for it," Joscelin said with a shrug. "You were invited to come along, more than once."

"I had other things to do," Guy said quietly. "Here, as it happens."

"Which was your choice." Joscelin turned back to Isabelle. "As I was saying, Ger and I were off razing the countryside and plunging cheeky knights into poverty by ransoming them for ridiculous sums when we received word that our father was dead. We hurried—"

Guy sighed but said nothing.

"We *hurried*," Joscelin said, "but we were quite far away and by the time we returned, Father was already buried. The only reason the hall wasn't in complete chaos was because our good Guy here took charge. Very capably done."

"Thank you," Guy said dryly. He looked at Isabelle. "Once my brother returned, he of course took his rightful place. He named the day of harvest as was custom, though he has unusual ideas about how that should be accomplished—"

"What Guy means is that Ger went out in the fields and actually picked things off vines," Joscelin said with a snort, "which Guy finds slightly beneath him."

"It is good to maintain the boundaries of rank," Guy said mildly.

Isabelle supposed they had had that conversation more than once as well. It was odd, she had to admit, to watch the men of another family discuss things they had obviously had a lifetime's worth of discussion over. She could have sat in her father's solar at Artane, brought up a simple topic, and predicted exactly what her family would say about it. Here, there were undercurrents she didn't expect and couldn't anticipate. She wondered what Gervase would say about any of it, if anything.

"He has his reasons to associate with the peasantry," Joscelin said.

"And see you how those reasons have served him!"

"Guy, he wasn't in the fields when he was attacked, he was in the hall."

"Attacked?" Isabelle asked.

Joscelin nodded. "Though there is a bit of confusion surrounding that. Guy isn't completely wrong when he suggests that Gervase being in the fields contributed to the disaster. The last time I saw my brother that day, he was speaking to his forester. I was distracted by an exceedingly handsome wench who I fear I thought might enjoy a tour of the stables—"

"And did she?"

Joscelin smiled faintly. "I don't remember, actually. By the time we'd examined the very fine qualities of my brother's horseflesh, I could smell smoke. I fear I left her behind. I ran to the hall, meeting Guy along the way, and we came inside to find Gervase lying on the floor and the hall on fire around him. If Guy hadn't been there, we wouldn't have saved him."

"How terrible," she murmured.

"It was Fate," Guy said. "I found my brother on the floor, unconscious, a bolt sticking out of his leg and a heavy stone from the mantel crushing his right arm. Joscelin arrived just in time and we managed to pull Gervase to safety." He shot Joscelin a look. "I still say something must have happened to him in the fields."

"So he could drag himself back to the hall by himself, then set the whole damned place on fire?" Joscelin asked. "Help me understand how that is possible."

"Men can be carried, you half-wit."

"Why not let him simply rot in the field—"

Joscelin stopped speaking abruptly. Isabelle looked up and understood why. Gervase stood at the doorway, looking less than pleased. He walked into the solar and shut the door behind him. Guy rose without having been asked and vacated what was obviously Gervase's chair.

The lord of the hall limped over, then lowered himself with obvious effort into the chair. He leaned his head back against the wood and closed his eyes. Isabelle had no trouble discerning that he was in obvious pain.

If he had been caught in a fire, he was very fortunate it hadn't touched his face. As for the rest of him, he didn't look overly damaged save his right hand, which looked as if he'd thrust it into a cooking fire. She supposed it was too late to heal it, though she wasn't above considering a thing or two. Not that he would have allowed it, likely. If his brothers fell silent about his accident when he entered a chamber, he certainly wasn't going to want to discuss it with her.

She considered, then looked at Joscelin. "Have you a lute?"

Gervase opened his eyes and looked at her in surprise. "You can play?"

"Ah," she managed, stalling as best she could. "Can't everyone?"

"Perhaps she is a jongleur," Yves said from where he sat in front of her. He twisted around and looked at her. "Are you, mistress?"

"I suppose anything is possible," she said, "though I'm sure my skills are paltry compared to any of yours."

"Does anyone in your family play?" Joscelin asked.

"My—" She shut her mouth. "I don't think I remember."

"Don't torment the girl, Jos," Guy said with a snort. He walked over to a trunk and pulled out a lute. "I'll entertain you with my paltry skills."

His skills were hardly that, though Isabelle supposed her brother John was the far superior lutenist. She closed her eyes and found she could bring to mind numerous times when she had sat in her father's solar, listening in just such a way to her younger brother trot out the songs he had learned from the extremely expensive master he'd studied with. Their grandmother had paid for those lessons and Isabelle had taken her share, so she supposed the gold had been well spent.

She realized almost immediately that playing for anyone would be a very bad idea indeed. Whilst she recognized many of the songs Guy played, she found there were many she didn't know. If she were to play the things she knew, it was entirely possible someone might make note of them and divine where she had learned them.

"Bed, lads," Gervase said suddenly, interrupting Guy during a song. "Guy, give Joscelin your lute and see the lads safely to where they belong."

Guy rose willingly enough and handed his lute to Joscelin. "Put that away," he commanded.

Joscelin nodded and merely watched his brother gather up the rest of the brothers and leave the solar. Isabelle reached for her stitching, but Gervase shook his head.

"Play for me."

She bit back half a dozen retorts that came immediately to mind. Indeed, all that time she'd spent writing down her brothers' most stinging replies had obviously not been wasted. But the man was feeding her, he had rescued her not once but twice. And she had the feeling that he was baiting her for what were no doubt his own perverse reasons. She looked at him narrowly, lest he mistake compliance for acquiescence, then took the lute from Joscelin.

"Anything in particular your commanding self would care to hear?"

"Something in tune, hopefully."

It was on the tip of her tongue to tell Gervase to go to Hell, but she thought that might be ill-advised. She took the lute, retuned it, then sat and thought for a moment or two before she chose something that John had claimed to have heard the last time he'd been in London. She didn't watch either of the brothers as she played, preferring to watch the fire so she didn't have to see their reactions. She was hardly her brother's equal, but she had sung with him often enough and she could certainly tell when she was out of tune.

She finished and hazarded a glance at her audience. Joscelin was simply watching her with a small smile on his face.

Gervase, however, was gaping at her.

"Out of tune?" she asked sweetly.

He shut his mouth. "Another." He paused. "If you please."

"Do you know this?" Joscelin asked and hummed a tune. "I'll sing it with you, if you like."

She was surprised not by the offer, but by how it caught her about the heart. How many times had she and John done the same thing to entertain their family in the evenings? It wasn't so much that which grieved her as it was the fact that she couldn't remember the last time she'd done the like. After Michelmas? In the dead of winter? She closed her eyes briefly and tried to bring to mind the last thing she could remember. She could see Arthur's face and felt a sense of urgency about the conversation, but she had no idea what the conversation had been about. It had been at her father's gates, which wasn't a surprise given that her father never allowed him inside.

She took a deep breath and ignored her unease. At the very least, she had to get word to someone that she was well, though she supposed she could just as easily walk out the front gates and trudge to Beauvois. She supposed the easiest thing to do would have been to simply tell Gervase who she was and ask for an escort, but something stopped her. For all she knew, she had come to France with the express purpose of accomplishing something at Monsaert, though what that could have been save proving to herself that Gervase de Seger did indeed not have horns, she couldn't have said.

But word, at least, would have to be sent.

Guy was the most likely choice. He was always leaving the keep for one reason or another. Perhaps he wouldn't be opposed to a little errand of mercy to the abbey at Caours.

"My lady?"

She looked at Joscelin and smiled. "Sorry. I was lost in thought."

"Finding any memories in the weeds there?"

She realized what he'd called her, but assumed that was just Joscelin being polite. She shook her head. "Nothing useful. Let's sing."

Joscelin had a lovely voice. She was slightly surprised to find there was a third voice as well, humming the occasional octave below where she was, then occasionally adding a more complicated harmony. She finished the last note, then looked at Gervase.

"Very lovely, my lord."

He took a deep breath, then put his hands on his knees. "You may play again tomorrow night."

"Very gracious of you, my lord."

He shot her a look, then looked at Joscelin. "She'll sleep in my chamber—"

"But, Ger," Joscelin said in surprise, "she cannot."

"I wasn't suggesting she sleep *with* me," Gervase said stiffly, shooting his brother a murderous look. "She will take my bed because the chamber is the most secure. I will sleep here."

"On the floor?" Isabelle said in surprise. "But you cannot."

Gervase shot her a look. "I do believe, *demoiselle*, that you, being a servant, are not in a position to tell me what to do. And haven't we had this discussion before?"

Isabelle considered what remained in her arsenal of feminine wiles. That thought felt very familiar, which left her wondering if perhaps she had considered the same quite recently. She struggled to latch on to the memory, but finally had to simply let it slip away. At least she remembered what she had to use in getting her way, not that she'd had to use that collection of levers very often. The truth was, she had never asked for very much which left her father granting her whatever small request she made of him without hesitation.

She suspected, though, that coming to France without a dozen of his fiercest guardsmen had been something she hadn't dared even approach him about, which led her to wonder just how she'd managed it and who had come with her.

And where they were at present.

She rose, returned the lute to its place, then walked back to the fire and looked at Gervase.

"My lord, it is not coddling to insist that you use common sense. If you sleep on the floor, you will not be able to rise in the morning and then where will you be? Your people depend on you to protect them. How will you do it if you cannot move?"

He cursed, then heaved himself to his feet. He glared at her, seemingly on the off chance she had misinterpreted his first look, then walked out of the solar without speaking further. Isabelle looked at Joscelin.

"That went well," she said.

"He's touchy."

"He has reason, I daresay."

Joscelin rose and smiled. "He does, but don't let him trouble you. If I had said the same thing, he would have acquainted my mouth with his fist. Repeatedly."

"I can't believe that."

He laughed a little. "Very well, he has never struck me. I won't say, however, how often he has repaid me for some imagined slight in the lists." He tilted his head sideways a bit and studied her. "What do you know of him?"

"That he's a warlock who sacrifices small animals when the moon is full."

"Is that so?" Joscelin asked, his eyes twinkling.

She nodded. "I didn't believe it, of course, because I don't believe in ghosts and bogles and warlocks, but his reputation extends . . ."

"Where?" Joscelin asked. "To where does it extend?"

She shut her mouth and glared at him.

"Your memory fails you, I see."

"When I least expect it, it seems."

He shot her a skeptical look, but started toward the door. "You'll be safe here if you don't mind the floor. I'll find you a pallet and blankets. Bolt the door until I return, lady, if you would."

She followed him to the door, then bolted it. She turned and looked over Gervase's solar. She had the feeling it looked much as it had during his father's time.

She rummaged about until she found a quill, ink, and a piece of parchment. She had selected the smallest one she could find, so perhaps it wouldn't be missed. She had just sat down at Gervase's table when a banging at the door almost sent her pitching forward onto the pot of ink. She took a deep breath, then went to answer the door.

Gervase stood there with a servant behind him, both of them carrying blankets. Isabelle stood back and watched as the servant laid out a pallet for her in front of the fire, spread a blanket on it, then built up the fire for her. He made Gervase a low bow, then fled the chamber with the alacrity of a man who thought remaining might spell his doom. Isabelle looked at Gervase to find him staring at the things atop his table. She stepped to block his view as unobtrusively as possible.

"What," he asked, gesturing behind her, "do you think you're doing?"

"Ah," she said, because lying did not come readily to her, something she was obviously going to have to address sooner rather than later. "I was thinking that if a name came to me, I should write it down," she attempted. "Because I can't seem to hold on to the memories I have currently. Perhaps if I study the list, I might piece my past together."

He studied her for a moment or two in silence, then shrugged. "Make free with my things, then."

"I will repay you—"

He waved aside her words. "Nay, the offer was genuinely made. Feel free to scribble as much as you like. May I read the names as well? I might see something you don't."

She tried to speak, but what was she to say? *Nay, you fool, you certainly shall not read any list,* especially given that she had no intentions of making a list. What she was making was a missive to send to her *grandmère* to let her know details that she surely wouldn't have any other way.

"I see I have intruded," he said stiffly.

She looked at him in surprise. "Well, of course you haven't. I was just thinking about what to say."

He grunted at her. "You might consider that the next time you're tempted to tell me how to run my hall." He shot her a look. "What would your father have said if you had done the like to him?"

She supposed it was best not to answer that. "He preferred that I stay inside."

"That wasn't an answer."

"Nay, my lord, I believe it wasn't."

He pursed his lips, then started back for the door. "Thank you for the help with my brothers. Their studies aren't what they should be."

"I was happy to aid them in what small way I could."

He looked over his shoulder at her. "One wonders where a serving girl could possibly have learned so much Latin."

"Perhaps one shouldn't," she said easily.

He turned and leaned back against the wall. "One wonders what else a simple serving girl can do."

"Perhaps one should go to bed before his curiosity overwhelms him."

He smiled.

She decided abruptly that too much speech with the lord of the hall was a very bad idea, indeed. She took a deep breath. "I daresay I should be abed."

His smile faded, then he turned and walked out the door, pulling it closed behind him.

"Bolt it," came his voice, low but clear through the door.

She crossed the chamber and threw the bolt home. She put her hands on the door and forced herself to take deep, even breaths. Even if she had been looking for a husband, she wouldn't have chosen Gervase de Seger. He had secrets, he was ill-humored, he was exceptionally bossy to women he was in the midst of protecting. She suspected, after she'd considered that list to her satisfaction, that his worst flaw was his handsomeness when he scowled.

She didn't want to think about how he looked when he smiled.

She shook herself, hoping to restore some small bit of good sense. She had a quest to be about, obviously, but the first thing to do was determine the lay of the land outside Monsaert. The fastest and easiest way to do that was to communicate without delay with her grandmother so her family wouldn't think she was dead.

She walked across to Gervase's desk, putting all thoughts of that desk's owner behind her.

Not very successfully, but perhaps she could hope for nothing more.

Chapter 8

Gervase slipped into the back of the village hall, less gracefully than he might have wished, but only a few turned to look at him. To those, he shot a quick, reassuring smile. For the rest, he simply hoped that when they noticed him they wouldn't start shrieking about his having come to carry off their children to cook them up for supper.

He leaned back against the rearmost corner of the building and forced himself to pay heed to the dispensing of lower justice that was going on in front of him. It wasn't anything his father would have come to listen to, which had bothered Gervase on more than one occasion.

'Tis what they do and leave them to it, Gaspard de Seger had instructed. *They'll bring their most pressing concerns to me in good time.*

Gervase had disagreed at the time, though he'd kept his mouth shut. After his father was gone, he had decided that he would be a different sort of master. It was a bit difficult to quell an uprising if a man had no idea what was happening half a league from his front gates.

The concerns were of the usual sort: water, food, and shelter and how to keep ruffians from the forest from making off with all three. Given that those numbered amongst his concerns as well, he was happy to see what sorts of solutions his villagers could hit upon.

He listened for most of the meeting until he knew that if he didn't move, he wasn't going to be able to walk without either an embarrassing display or a great deal of aid, which would have been embarrassing enough. He slipped back out the back door, grimacing as he continued on with muscles that vigorously protested the work. He supposed the pain would have been far worse if he'd spent the night on the floor in his solar. Of course he wasn't going to admit that to the woman back at the keep, she of the mouth that ran too freely at his expense.

Where had a serving wench learned to play the lute that well? Or to speak Latin easily as well as he could? The saints only knew what else she could do. He had the feeling he was going to have to start admitting things to himself very soon that he didn't want to admit.

She was obviously not a servant.

The daughter of a minor noble, perhaps, or a well-educated freeman. Surely naught but a man he could intimidate with a look and avoid any patriarchal displeasure. Her presence in his hall could be deemed merely a little misunderstanding, one that could be resolved very simply with an apology and a smile. No need for bloodshed.

He walked about the village green, grateful for even the smallest bit of freedom to think. It wasn't that he couldn't think at the keep. There was simply too much there that required his immediate and full attention. He hardly had time to even let his mind rest from one problem before he generally found himself assaulted by yet another that needed to be solved before he could do anything else.

He walked with his hands clasped behind his back, watching at times what lay before his feet so he didn't trip and land on his face, at other times watching the sky and his surroundings lest he not be taken unawares. And while he was about that happy task, he allowed himself to think about what he had been. Before the fire. It was something he rarely did, because it was simply too depressing.

He supposed what he missed the most about his former life was the freedom to simply stride about the world, sure in his ability to face anything that came his way and emerge the victor. There was something to be said for having women throw themselves in his path and insist on attention, knights throw themselves at his feet and plead for mercy, nobles spend time devising a way to have him grace them with his presence.

It was entirely possible he might have been slightly arrogant about it all.

The one thing he was particularly sure of was that no fool would have plowed him over without having marked him beforehand—such as the fool who had come close to knocking him off his feet. He caught himself on his right leg and almost had it buckle underneath him. As it was, the pain almost brought him to his knees.

He regained control of both his leg and his temper and looked at the man in front of him who was babbling frantically about something Gervase couldn't quite make out. The fool was some sort of nobleman, obviously, but a very rumpled one.

"Cease," Gervase said in annoyance, "unless you've something useful to say."

The man looked at him, then, blessedly, held his tongue until he seemingly had control over himself. "I've lost her," he managed.

"Lost who?"

"My fiancée," the man said hoarsely.

Gervase didn't want to say the first thing that came to mind, which was that the wench in question had obviously found sense and fled before having to wed the tall, gangly youth standing in front of him. He dredged up a bit more patience.

"Where did you lose her?"

"On board a ship—"

"Impossible," Gervase said. "How can you possibly lose someone aboard a ship?"

"It sank!"

Gervase put his hand on the man's shoulder. "Perhaps," he said slowly, "she drowned. How were you able to escape?"

"I took a different ship—and paid handsomely for the privilege, I'll tell you that. There was a terrible storm and her ship was lost to it." He clutched Gervase's arm. "Her father will kill me!"

As well the man should. Gervase frowned and shook off the man's hand. He folded his arms over his chest, wincing as he did so. "Did you have charge of this girl?"

He closed his eyes briefly. "Aye."

"What is your name, lad?"

"Arthur of Harwych."

An Englishman, of course. Gervase was only surprised the fool had managed to find a ship, much less find a captain able to get him onto proper French soil.

"And your lady's name—"

"My lord Gervase!"

Gervase left off his conversation with the frantic man in front of him and turned to the village alderman who wanted his attention. "Aye?"

"About the planting, my lord. Perhaps you would care to see what we have stored here in the village to compare with what you have at the castle."

Gervase did care, so he went with the man to see what sorts of things the villagers had laid by. Of course he had enough stored at the keep to feed his own people plus those belonging to the abbey and Beauvois over the hills to the west, but there was no sense in dampening the man's enthusiasm. He spared a brief bit of envy for Nicholas de Piaget's view of the sea before he shrugged it aside. Beauvois was a lovely keep, true, but Monsaert was not only beautiful, it was intimidating as hell. There was much to be said for a place easily defended.

Not that he'd managed that very well of late.

The morning wore on and he felt his body begin to ache in familiar ways that he didn't enjoy at all. If he didn't at least sit for half an hour, he wouldn't manage to get on his horse and return to the keep. He excused himself from the discussion, then walked outside. He limped along a path for a bit, then made himself at home on the back edge of an obliging farmer's wagon. Its locale had the added benefit of giving him a good view of what was happening in the town square.

That daft Englishman was still wandering about, spewing his nonsense. Gervase shook his head. He could scarce believe that anyone would have let his daughter go off in the company of that one, much less hazard a journey with him from England to France. An irresponsible father and a very foolish girl. He had no doubt that the silly wench had been caught in a storm, shipwrecked, then drowned. His only surprise was that her body hadn't washed up on shore, but perhaps Master Arthur hadn't considered that.

Arthur finally gave up trying to enlist aid and instead settled for simply shuffling along, looking dejected. Gervase couldn't help a small—a very small—bit of pity for the lad. He flipped his page a coin, asked for two cups of ale, then offered one to Arthur when he managed to drag himself over to that side of the square and collapse alongside Gervase on the back of the wagon.

"Thank you," Arthur said numbly, accepting the cup and then looking at it as if he hadn't a clue what to do with it.

"Drink," Gervase suggested.

Arthur drank, then dragged his sleeve across his mouth. "Her father will kill me."

Gervase simply held on to his cup. "Why would he?"

"Because she asked me to accompany her on a quest to France," Arthur said glumly. "I agreed, of course, to further win her favor. She claimed it was so she could visit her grandmother, unbeknownst to her father."

That would be enough to inspire a father to entertain thoughts of murder, Gervase supposed. Best not to say as much, though, lest the man beside him become too terrified by the thought to continue his tale.

"There was some urgency to her journey, even though I think her grandmother is hale yet."

Gervase frowned. "Is your fiancée English?"

"Of course."

"Yet she had a French grandmother."

"Her grandmother is the abbess at Caours."

Gervase spewed out what he'd managed to get into his mouth. He looked at Arthur in shock. "Abbess Mary?"

Arthur looked at him in surprise. "Do you know her?"

"Well, of course I know her," Gervase said. "We're three bloody leagues from where she prays." He looked at the man next to him. "This poor wench's *grandmère* is the abbess?"

Arthur looked at him nervously, then nodded.

"But Abbess Mary has a son . . . "

His words ground to a halt right along with his wits, apparently. Mary of Caours was an interesting case, to be sure. She had been made the abbess of Caours a score of years ago, at least. Rumor had it her ill-fated marriage to Etienne de Piaget had been brief, producing a single son, a son she had apparently left in the care of others as she'd been forced to flee to France to save both her life and her son's. Gervase was a bit hazy on the details of how that had all come about, but he was clear on one thing: Mary's son was the very intimidating and protective Rhys de Piaget who just happened to be the father of the exceedingly lethal lord of Beauvois, Nicholas de Piaget. Robin de Piaget as well, damn that one to the fires of Hell. Gervase thought there might have been an older sister somewhere in that litter, but what he was sure of was that there was a youngest daughter whose beauty was rumored to cause otherwise reasonable grown men to fall to their knees in amazement.

A daughter named Isabelle.

He grasped for any last shreds of composure and examined the details in a cold, calculating fashion that perhaps even Aubert wouldn't have matched on his best day. There was nothing odd about Lord Rhys having a youngest daughter. There was especially nothing odd about the fact that Rhys de Piaget should have a gloriously lovely daughter named Isabelle while he himself should have a new servant—who couldn't possibly be a servant—who was also gloriously lovely but happened not to remember her name.

He looked at Arthur and found a new reason to scarce believe what his eyes were telling him. Isabelle de Piaget was betrothed to that irritating scab of a man?

He had never seen her, of course, because he had never been a guest at Beauvois when she'd been there and he had avoided England like the plague when she'd been at home. But he'd heard the tales. 'Twas rumored her goodness alone qualified her for sainthood, but her face inspired lays sung with reverence.

Joscelin hadn't seen Isabelle herself, though he had reputedly seen her elder sister, Amanda, because he knew Isabelle's older brother Miles fairly well and he didn't quite have Gervase's undeserved reputation for being a ravisher of noblemen's daughters, a lack of reputation that had allowed him places Gervase hadn't dared go.

Was there a reason beyond brotherly amusement for Joscelin to have been smirking at him for the past fortnight?

Gervase looked at Arthur. "Are you telling me," he said, trying to temper his surprise, "that you are betrothed to Isabelle de Piaget?"

The man shifted. Gervase had lost many things, but his ability to spot a liar at fifty paces hadn't been affected.

"Almost," Arthur said.

"Almost," Gervase echoed. "How betrothed does that make you?"

Arthur shifted. "Perhaps not as betrothed as I would like to be, if we're discussing something quite formal and archaic."

"Which means you haven't managed to speak to her father yet," Gervase noted.

"Not yet," Arthur admitted. "I'm hoping being of service to her will endear me to her sire and then he will agree to allow me in the front gates."

"I imagine not, now that you've lost her," Gervase said with a snort. He shifted to look at the man beside him. "What proof do you have that the ship was lost at sea? How long ago was it?"

"It was sighted coming hard up against the coast near here," Arthur said weakly, "almost a fortnight ago. I've found several of the crew who survived washing up ashore. I'm convinced she did as well."

"And why is that?" Gervase asked, having another sip of strengthening ale. He thought he just might have to have another cup very soon.

"I found one of her boots."

Damn it, if he didn't stop hearing things like that, he wasn't going to manage a decent drink of *anything*. He dragged his sleeve across his own mouth, ignored the ale he'd spewed all over his own bloody boots, and looked at Arthur.

"What?" he said in astonishment.

"She apparently lost one of her boots at sea. It was washed up onto the shore."

"And how could you possibly know what boots she was wearing?"

"Because they were mine," Arthur said sadly. "I loaned them to her. My father's cobbler has his mark, of course. They were of a particular color, a dark russet to match my horse—"

Gervase had the feeling he knew exactly the color of Arthur of Harwych's horse. He didn't want to think on why that was.

"She intended to travel in disguise," Arthur said wearily, "as a lad. I didn't see her, to be sure, but I know she had plans to cut off her hair—"

Gervase realized the man's mouth was still moving, but he could no longer hear anything he was saying.

His servant had been wearing one boot when he'd rescued her.

He shook his head, because that helped him to cling to the

surety that this was all a terribly amusing coincidence. The boy he'd rescued who had turned out to be a girl without a name hadn't been . . . well, she hadn't been in disguise. She had been garbed as a lad because that was a comfortable way for a woman of her beauty to travel alone along ruffian-infested roads. Her hair was shorn because, ah, because she no doubt feared the summer would be hot and less hair would be more comfortable for her. After all, it wasn't as if when he'd first seen her she'd looked half drowned. Or traumatized. Or sporting any sort of wounds that could have come from washing up ashore, such as a large bump on her head, which had rendered her without critical memories of who she was.

It definitely wasn't that she was so damned beautiful, he could hardly look at her.

And her name was likely Hildegard. He couldn't see himself calling out the name Hildegard in dulcet tones for the rest of his days—

"I think I should go to Beauvois."

Gervase looked at Arthur, then shook his head. "I wouldn't advise it," he said promptly. By the saints, that was all he needed, to have the fool next to him possibly spouting things he should have been keeping to himself. "Lord Nicholas will kill you. Go back to England."

"But Lord Rhys will kill me there!" Arthur wailed.

"Then head south to Italy. Good food, lovely women." He nodded. "That's the place for you."

Arthur looked as if he were ready to weep. Gervase had to admit he sympathized. If he thought he would have to soon face the full brunt of Rhys de Piaget's wrath, he might have been tempted to weep as well. Not a year ago, of course, but now? Aye, he would have scurried home, lowered the portcullis with alacrity, and bolted himself into his hall. He might have even gone so far as to hide under his bed.

In fact, all but the last was sounding better all the time. Perhaps he could command his new serving wench to come and play for him whilst he cowered. If she was reluctant, perhaps instead of plying his lute, he could have her translate all the ways possible to say *when your father finds out what I've done to you he will pull out my entrails, wrap them around my neck seven times, and then watch as I slowly and quite painfully smother until I'm dead* into all the languages she knew.

He patted Arthur absently on the shoulder, then heaved himself to his feet and handed his cup to his page to run back to the tavern. He walked to the stables with perhaps more energy than he might have another time. There was no time like the present to try to make it so when a furious father arrived on his front stoop, he wouldn't find Gervase unable to even heft a sword in his own defense.

He rode home, dismounted in front of his stables, then limped back to the great hall. He found Joscelin and Guy inside, standing in front of the fire no doubt discussing the few inane thoughts that were rattling around in their empty heads. He strode over to them—

Very well, he shuffled over to them, but it was done with a fair bit of enthusiasm given that he had suddenly discovered a new level of anxiety. It was nothing short of amazing how that sort of thing could spur a man on to feats of strength and agility heretofore unexperienced.

He stopped in front of his half brothers.

"Where is she?"

Guy looked at him in surprise. "Who?"

"The wench!"

Joscelin put his hand on Gervase's arm, no doubt to soothe him. "She's in your solar, of course, where you commanded she stay."

Gervase shook off his brother's arm. "And you aren't there watching over her?"

"Ger, she's perfectly capable—"

"I commanded that someone stay with her!"

Guy looked at him as if he'd never seen him before. "But Lucien is there—"

"Lucien is a useless child!" Gervase bellowed. He shoved his finger in his next youngest brother's face. "Go stand guard in front of that door and do not move. Joscelin, you come with me."

"I don't know that I want to," Joscelin began.

"And I don't give a damn what you want. Bring your sword!"

Joscelin trotted along after him. Well, Joscelin walked alongside him at a pace better suited to a stately promenade that would have suited the queen mother's vanity, but at least he had come along.

Gervase dismissed his guardsmen along the way, sending them to the proper lists, then gained his private garden. He waited until he had a modicum of privacy before he whirled on his younger brother.

"Do you know?"

Joscelin blinked. "Know what?"

"Who she is!" Gervase hissed.

Joscelin clasped his hands behind his back. "Ger, I'm not sure I understand—"

"Of course you understand, you cretin," Gervase snarled.

Joscelin looked at him coolly. "I can outrun you, you know, in your current state. If you would like me to prove the like, by all means continue to speak to me in that manner."

Gervase drew his sword. Unfortunately, it was damned heavy, his right hand was useless, and his leg like a jelly beneath him. The only reason he didn't go down to his knees in the lavender was because Joscelin caught him and steadied him.

Which he didn't deserve.

Joscelin took his sword, stabbed it into a flower bed, then slung his arm around Gervase's shoulders and led him over to a bench in front of a small pond full of fish Gervase was convinced Cook kept only for the cats. He sat because he simply couldn't stand any longer. He rubbed his good hand over his face, sighed deeply, then looked at his brother.

"I apologize."

"Of course you do," Joscelin said with a faint smile.

"Why you endure me, I don't know."

"Oh, nay," Joscelin said with a half laugh. "You'll not wring any maudlin sentiments out of me today. I tolerate your foul humors and sorry self because you taught me everything I know about chivalry, pretending to drink while not imbibing, and protecting my poor virtue while appearing to bed every eligible miss in any given place."

"And the ones beyond your reach as well."

"Aye, that, too," Joscelin agreed. He leaned forward with his elbows on his knees, then shot Gervase a look. "You'll recover your former strength."

"I wish I had your hope."

"You didn't puke when you came home today. That's progress."

"I didn't puke because terror has lodged in my belly and insisted on my full attention."

"Terror? You?" Joscelin smiled. "Surely not."

Gervase sighed deeply. "Who is she?"

"Who do you think she is?"

"Isabelle de Piaget."

Joscelin's smile deepened. "Did you divine that all on your own, or did you have help?"

Gervase would have tossed off a casual remark, but the truth was, he was afraid if he opened his mouth, he might just puke up what he'd managed to get down earlier in the day. "I met a lad in the village who claimed to be her fiancé—or, rather, wished he could claim to be her fiancé. He informed me in trembling tones that she had been traveling to France in the disguise of a lad when she had been caught in a storm and lost at sea."

"Interesting."

"Isn't it, though?" Gervase asked sourly. "And how odd that I should find not a fortnight ago a bedraggled lad who turned out to be a woman with no memories and no name."

"Odd, indeed."

Gervase shivered in spite of himself. "I'm afraid to even think her name, much less say it aloud, lest I draw her father's attention my way from his perch on that damned coast in England's barren north."

"What a coward you are, brother," Joscelin said with a twinkle in his eye. "It isn't as if Lord Rhys will be examining the blisters on her hands, or ask where you've been having her sleep, or wonder why it was you were too stupid to recognize a woman of breeding when you saw her."

"And you did?"

"Oh, I knew the moment I clapped eyes on her, but I also saw her sister at Beauvois several years ago. Isabelle wasn't with her, though I'm not sure why not. She and Amanda are mirrors of each other, though Amanda's tongue is much sharper."

"I don't suppose you would go to Beauvois and give them the tidings, would you?"

"Are you daft?" Joscelin said, wide-eyed. "And have Lord Nicholas run me through? Nay, brother, I'll leave you that pleasure."

"Hell."

"Probably."

Gervase stared grimly out over his garden, noting the first hints of green amongst the ruin winter had brought. He contemplated where he might like to be buried, though he found the thought less appealing than he might have at another time. What he wanted to do was to go inside, find that stunning Isabelle de Piaget, go down on his knees, and beg her to stay a bit longer until at least the blisters on her hands had disappeared.

Or until she might be able to look at him with something besides disdain and irritation.

Perhaps even until she regained her memories . . .

He looked at his brother and found himself experiencing a surge of good cheer. "I can't send her home yet."

Joscelin blinked in surprise. "Why not?"

"Because she's still missing her memories. The shock would be too great. She might return home and find her family nothing but strangers. Ask yourself what kind of man would leave a rare flower of that sort in a spot exposed to too much wind and rain."

"You're hopeless," Joscelin said with a smile.

"Chivalrous," Gervase corrected him. "I have no choice but to keep her here until she knows who she is."

"Hemming your sheets while she bides her time?"

"I'm not having her scrub my floors," Gervase pointed out.

"Ger—"

"Of course not hemming my sheets!" He took a deep breath. "I will shower her with luxuries, speak to her in dulcet tones, ply the lute with my crippled fingers until she begs me to stop. What else?"

"You could tell her you know who she is."

Gervase shook his head. "Again, too much shock to a woman's delicate humors is never good."

"Lord Rhys is going to murder you," Joscelin said thoughtfully. "But if I murder Guy at the same time, then I inherit the title. If I'm exceptionally clever, I might convince our lovely guest to look at me instead of you." He smiled happily. "Life has a way of rewarding lads with good hearts, don't you think?"

Gervase pointed back to the hall. "Go."

Joscelin rose, rubbing his hands together. "I'm off to plot your demise—nay, that's already seen to. I'll go plot Guy's demise—"

"Go!"

Joscelin went. Unfortunately, cheerful thoughts went with him until Gervase found himself with only his own black thoughts to contemplate—and they were very dark thoughts indeed. The end of his life was obviously rapidly approaching, so perhaps the best thing he could do was make an attempt at hoisting a sword so he might stave it off a bit longer.

He pushed himself to his feet, deposited his cloak on the bench where he'd been sitting, then fetched his sword. He walked farther out into the garden, as far away from the house as he could manage while there was still a path. If his private lists sported a bit of a hedge that shielded him from most prying eyes, could he help that?

Unfortunately, what he was faced with was not a pleasant afternoon spent sharpening his sword skill, it was a miserable few minutes wondering why he'd even bothered to get out of bed that morning. He had prided himself on being able to fight with either hand, but now all that holding his sword in his left did was throw him off balance. Holding his sword in his right was agony. He could only grasp his sword hilt, not heft the sword itself, and even closing his hand around the hilt cramped his palm and fingers so badly, he could scarce shake the hilt free. He stabbed the sword into the dirt at his feet, coming perilously close to skewering his toes, and looked heavenward and suppressed the urge to swear.

Weeping was simply beyond him. He'd wept enough already.

He supposed things wouldn't improve with his standing out in what was promising to be a good bit of rain in a quarter hour. He took his sword, tried to resheath it half a dozen times before he gave up, unbuckled his sword belt, then resheathed his sword with his left hand. He turned, then froze.

Isabelle de Piaget was standing twenty paces away, watching him.

The grief on her face was almost enough to do him in.

He put his shoulders back and glared at her. So he was no longer her brother's equal. At the moment, he expected that he wasn't her *grandmère*'s equal, which stung so badly that he stalked over to her, fueled by a fury that a little voice in the back of his head warned him to temper.

He didn't listen.

"What are you doing out here?" he snarled.

She looked rather unimpressed. "Gathering herbs."

"What the hell for?"

"I thought you might try a soak in a tub of very hot water," she said evenly. She held out the basket. "Put these in the water with you."

"I am not bathing with weeds!"

She looked at him narrowly. "You are excessively rude."

He growled at her. He couldn't help himself.

Obviously the wench was accustomed to the ways of impossible men. He supposed that didn't bode well for him, for it spoke eloquently of her father's potentially mercurial temper. He wondered absently if it were even possible to get his sorry arse under his bed or if he might have to fold himself in two and squeeze into his trunk—

"I'll leave these *healing herbs* near the hall," Isabelle said evenly. "Use them or not, as it pleases you."

Gervase watched her go, cursing her thoroughly. A man did that, he told himself, when he'd just made a complete arse of himself by insulting a woman who was simply trying to aid him.

He would have stomped back to the hall but he could scarce walk, much less stomp. Worse still, he only made it around the edge of the hedge before he almost walked into Isabelle. She looked at him as he came to a stumbling halt in front of her, then she reached out and took his sword away from him.

He opened his mouth to protest, then shut it at the look on her face.

By the saints, she was angry.

"You do not deserve this," she said distinctly, "but since I see you have no squire to attend to your gear, I will do it for you."

"I can carry—"

"So can I. I've done it often enough for my father."

After her father had spent a full day of doing in men foolish enough to mistake his beloved youngest daughter for a servant, no doubt.

She put her basket over her arm, propped up his sword against her shoulder as she'd done with the wooden sword she'd been using to fight with Yves—and if nothing should have alerted him to the fact that she was not what he'd thought, it should have been that—then looked up at him.

"Put your arm around my shoulders."

"Woman, you . . . you . . . "

"You talk too much."

"And you have absolutely no sense of your peril."

She looked up at him, again apparently completely unimpressed with his snarling. "I'm trusting in your chivalry. Let's go back to the house."

He put his arm around her shoulders, but he didn't dare lean on her. He was simply humoring her. He might have managed to humor her all the way back to the house if he hadn't caught his toe on a flat bit of stone that wasn't as flat as it should have been.

"I'll have that seen to," she said.

She said that, he had to concede, after she'd gasped at having to bear most of his weight. He wanted to snap at her, or shout at her, or somehow save his pride, but the truth was he had no pride left. All he could do was lean as gingerly as possible on a woman who was far stronger than she looked and wish he didn't require the aid.

And damn his brother Guy if he didn't simply stand in the doorway to the hall and watch their progress.

His brother took his sword from Isabelle, then took her place at Gervase's side. Gervase leaned on him more heavily than he would have liked, but there was nothing else to be done.

"I'll put my weeds in the kitchens, Your Grace," Isabelle said seriously. "Should you at some point think them useful."

Gervase watched her go until he couldn't bear to watch her any longer. Then he stood there and fought with himself. It would have been simple to draw his sword, wedge it in a useful spot, then fall upon it.

Simple, but cowardly.

He stood at the crossroads of what he could see was now his life. In one direction was what he had been for the past four months: broken, surly, hopeless.

In the other direction was a woman who had paused at the far end of his hall and was looking back at him. She had found things to aid him if he was willing to leave his pride behind and attempt to use them.

Fortunately for him, he wasn't going to have to decide on a direction, nor was he going to have to fall upon his own sword. His life that remained him was already counted in days, not years, because when Nicholas de Piaget found out Gervase had been forcing his beloved youngest sister to work as a scullery maid, Nicholas was going to murder him.

He patted Guy on the shoulder. "Send Cyon to me—oh,

there he is. Lad, go fetch me clean clothing. I think I'm having a bath."

"As you say, my lord," his page said, looking horrified.

"Are you unwell?" Guy asked doubtfully.

"I'm fine," Gervase said. "Remarkably fine."

Guy looked at him as if he'd lost all his wits, but Gervase ignored him. He tossed his sword to Aubert, refused to speculate on how much of the spectacle in the garden his captain had witnessed, and whistled as he limped across his great hall. If he was going to die soon, there was no reason not to enjoy the time that remained him.

Even if that meant bathing with weeds.

Chapter 9

Isabelle sat at the table under a window in the great hall and tried to concentrate on the lads' lessons. She had been happily attending to that labor for the past hour, but the passage of time chafed. What she needed to do was find a way to have her message carried to her grandmother before her family became convinced she was dead.

She'd had a very interesting conversation the afternoon before with Joscelin as Gervase had been soaking in a bath with her weeds. Apparently Gervase was convinced she had been shipwrecked and thereafter washed up ashore. There had been a terrible tempest and he had found her wandering along a road, missing one of her boots, and sporting an enormous bump on her head.

She supposed that was why she had lost her memory. It was rather inconvenient, that. She closed her eyes, stretching her mind back into shadows that seemed to fade in and out of a mist she couldn't sweep away. She sighed and opened her eyes to look up at Gervase's ceiling above her. She didn't even remember cutting her hair, much less getting on any ship. The last thing she remembered was standing at the edge of her father's great hall, watching her family. How she had gone from that to sitting on the edge of Gervase's great hall, watching nothing at all, was a mystery she had no way to solve.

What she needed to do was talk to Miles. She couldn't imagine she would have left Artane without having at least discussed her plans with him.

She jumped a little at the sight of Guy striding across the great hall. She patted Pierre on the shoulder.

"Please take your brothers and go find herbs suitable for use on the battlefield," she said. "Before it rains."

"But the sun is shining—"

She shot him a look that had him biting back whatever protest he'd been planning on offering. He rose and motioned for his brothers to come with him.

"Let's go, lads. The master has spoken and we must obey."

"Do we have to look for herbs?" Yves complained. "I'd rather train with the sword."

Fabien snorted. "A sword won't do you any good if you bleed to death, will it? Let's go look for herbs as she says. *Then* we'll train with the sword."

Isabelle waited impatiently until they had tumbled out of the hall, trying not to look as if she were waiting impatiently for them to leave so she could be about some sort of nefarious business. Guy had already disappeared outside before she managed to bolt across the floor and wrench the door open.

"Lord Guy!"

He turned and looked at her. "Aye, lady?"

"Might I ask a favor?"

"Name it, especially if it includes teaching my older brother manners."

She walked out down the stairs and out into the courtyard, making certain that her guardsmen were a discreet distance behind her. She smiled. "Your brother is in pain and I've found that men in pain can be quite spirited in their conversation. But nay, this is for myself." She slipped her missive down from her sleeve. She had managed to find wax to use to seal it and had done her best imitation of a mark she hoped her grandmother would recognize, poorly done as it was. "Would it be too much to ask you to find someone trustworthy to carry something for me to Caours Abbey?"

"Caours Abbey," he echoed in surprise. "For you?"

She had spent the whole of the previous day working out what she would say to any possible question even though the subterfuge didn't set well with her. She put on her best smile.

"I felt moved to pen a note to the abbess there," she said, which was actually quite true. She felt moved because she had no idea whether or not her parents were expecting to hear from her and she feared that if she didn't get word to them, they would be sick with worry. She held the sheaf of parchment out to him, trying to keep it hidden from prying eyes. "Nothing important, of course."

"Are you thinking to become a nun?" Guy asked in surprise.

She shook her head. "Nothing so dire. I thought perhaps she might know my family and have a way for me to, ah, regain my, um, memories."

He took the missive and tucked it down the side of his boot. "Consider it done." He made her a slight bow, then continued on his way to the stables.

She let out a shaky breath. That much was done. Now all she had to do was decide what to do with the time she had remaining before her father descended on Monsaert in a fury. She wasn't sure who he would be angrier with: Gervase for putting her to work in his kitchen or she herself for daring to leave England without half his guard in tow.

Assuming she had left England on her own.

She went back inside the hall, nodded to her guardsmen, then walked over to a bench set in an alcove. She sank down onto it with a sigh. Whatever else could be said about Gervase and his terrible reputation, the man's hall was spectacular. Beauvois was luxurious, to be sure, but she was forced to admit that it paled in comparison to Monsaert. Then again, her brother was not a duke, so perhaps with money and power came finer furnishings, painted motifs on the ceilings, and hearths and fireplaces that were more elegant than anything she had ever seen in England. She leaned her head back against the stone and turned to look out over the countryside below her. The soil was rich and the forest in the distance lush. Gervase was fortunate to call such a place his own.

Perhaps whoever had tried to kill him had thought the same thing.

She pushed aside that mystery as one she couldn't possibly solve. Her most pressing problem was trying to determine what her future should hold. She suspected that her grandmother would insist that she present herself at the abbey, which meant she would have to tell Gervase who she was. Better that, she supposed, than having her father discover that she was loitering in a keep not full of her brothers or cousins. Perhaps it said more about her character than she wanted it to that it was so refreshing to be alone for a bit.

Or, rather, not so much alone, but in a place where no one knew who she was and there wasn't a clutch of brothers hanging about to tell her what to do.

She certainly wasn't remaining at Monsaert because of Gervase de Seger. Not only was he thoroughly incapable of dredging up a consistent amount of courtesy, he was French. She wanted the rough and tumble of her brothers, not mincing steps and noses turned up at hearty English fare. She didn't want to be in a household of lads who were scarcely civilized, she wanted to be . . . well, she wasn't sure where she wanted to be.

She supposed thinking on what she could do was the easier task. She would stay where she was until she had heard back from her grandmother and until she had helped the lads a bit longer with their studies. It was the charitable thing to do. Her mother would approve. Even, she suspected, her father might approve. After all, of what use were all those years of study and contemplation if she couldn't apply them somewhere? Where better than with a collection of lads who'd lost their mother?

Besides, now that her grandmother would know she was safe, no one would worry about her. She was free to see to tidying up Monsaert. Once that was done, she would go on to Beauvois where she would—

Where she would return to a life of being the nameless, less-desirable daughter of Rhys de Piaget.

She could hardly bear the thought of it.

She realized she was no longer sitting, but instead pacing through the great hall. When that no longer provided her any comfort, she found herself continuing on to the kitchens. She came to the edge of the chamber and watched the quiet there. The men of the keep had broken their fast long ago and a midday supper was already prepared and simmering over the fire. Cook looked up from her chopping of vegetables and actually smiled.

"Mistress," she said, waving her in with her spoon. "Come and sit. Adele, fetch her a stool for the worktable!"

The appropriate seat was fetched and Isabelle sat. Cook pushed aside her veg and joined her there, barking for a pair of mugs to be filled with ale and brought immediately. Isabelle couldn't help but admit that she far preferred being on the less taxing side of the mug.

"The herbs did the master good yestereve."

Isabelle smiled. "Did they? I'm actually still a little surprised he used them."

"Aye, well, he can be a bit stubborn, that one."

Now, here were details she could listen to without argument. "Have you known him his whole life?"

Cook had a hearty swig of her ale. "Nay. I came with the second duchess as part of her household, so he was almost three, perhaps four winters. His mother had been dead but a month or so by then. He missed her terribly, I daresay."

"Poor lad," Isabelle murmured.

"Aye, and worse still, his stepmother wasn't a particularly maternal sort," Cook said, her lip curling. She shook her head. "And then six more to come from her, of all people. But in spite of that, Lord Gervase was a cheerful, pleasing lad."

"Lord Gervase?" Isabelle echoed in surprise. "Truly?"

Cook looked at her shrewdly. "Know you nothing of him?"

My brothers complained about the annoyance of tourneying against the oldest lad from Monsaert was almost out of her mouth before she managed to bite her tongue. She hadn't thought about that before, but it was the truth. She wasn't entirely sure that that particular lad—and she had to assume that was Gervase—hadn't been the subject of more than one evening's discussion. Evidently she'd been lost in thought through most of those discussions for she remembered little about them save her brothers' grumbles.

"I'm afraid I don't know much at all," Isabelle admitted.

"You were a sheltered miss, then."

"You could say that," Isabelle agreed. "I would be happy to be enlightened."

And apparently Cook was more than happy to enlighten her.

"He was sent off to foster at court when a lad, as is custom," Cook said. "I think it did him good to be away from—" She paused, then took a deep breath. "I'll just say that it was good for him to be away from here."

"You don't need to explain."

Cook nodded. "I imagine I don't. Being away is, I daresay, what saved him. The other lads—" She shrugged. "It was harder on them, of course, until they were sent away as well. Master Gervase returned as he was able, because he was the heir and took his responsibilities seriously, though I don't think it was done gladly. He felt some responsibility toward his brothers, true, but there was little he could do to improve their lots. His father was a good master, but he preferred to sit inside by the fire and hold grand councils rather than . . . " She shook her head. "He was a good master. I'll leave it at that, as well. But once Lord Gervase had his spurs, he fetched Lord Joscelin from court and took him under his wing. A pity he couldn't have taken the other lads, but they were too young. Lord Guy was content to come back home and be petted by his dam."

"Interesting," Isabelle murmured. She supposed it was a terrible thing to be gossiping with servants, but given that Gervase thought her nothing more than a servant, perhaps there was no shame in it. "Lord Guy seems happy to sit in the lord's chair."

"He is his father's son," Cook conceded, "and has more patience for that sort of thing than my lord. To each his own."

"What did Lord Gervase do away from home?" Isabelle asked.

"Tourneyed, for the most part," Cook said. "I think the only one who bested him with the lance was some foul Englishman—de Piaget, I think was his name—but given that they traded victories evenly, I suppose neither lad's pride was wounded overmuch."

Isabelle could only imagine. Obviously there were a few things she was going to have to discuss with her brothers at some point.

"Lord Joscelin benefitted greatly from his brother's company. Lord Gervase saw him knighted and outfitted in lavish fashion, then they spent several years traveling wherever they were welcome and many places where they weren't at first but left crowned with laurels."

"And the accident?" Isabelle asked carefully.

Cook shrugged. "I was away at the time, so I've little knowledge of the particulars. You might ask Lord Gervase. I can say that the damage was to more than his body. He was the most sought-after lad in France, endlessly invited to court where he was allowed to cross over even into the king's bedchamber for parleys. And then . . . "

Isabelle didn't have to hear more. She was tempted to weep as it was.

"It took him three months before his leg healed well enough for him to stand," Cook finished. "I don't think it healed very well, but what do I know? It isn't as if it can be broken again and remended. I'm not sure he'll ever be the same, though." She shook her head. "It cost him much."

Isabelle finished her ale and looked at Cook. "Thank you," she said quietly. "I appreciate the tale."

"You'll take care of him, won't you?" Cook asked.

"I'll do what I can."

Cook studied her for a moment or two. "You aren't a servant, are you?"

"What else would I be?"

Cook only smiled.

Isabelle smiled in return. "I still don't know why I'm here, but I suppose that will come to me in time."

"I imagine so. Until then, it looks as if Lord Gervase at least intends to keep you safe—Adele, the stew's burning!"

Isabelle left the cook to her business and left the kitchens with an entirely different impression of things than she'd had before.

She paused in the great hall and considered again her plans. The lads were obviously still outside, no doubt diligently hunting for useful leaves. Her family would soon know where she was and what she was doing. That left her free for the morning to see if she might be of some use to the lord of the hall.

She walked toward the front door only to find that she had her two accustomed shadows trailing after her. Obviously they had been released from their duties in the cesspit. She left the hall, stopped, then turned and looked at them.

"I'm so sorry," she said quietly.

They shook their heads as one.

"Was it terrible?"

Sir Denis cleared his throat. "Sir Aubert is a very skilled warrior."

"How long were you in the lists with him?"

"All day," Sir Lucas admitted.

"Did he hurt you?"

"No more than we deserved."

She supposed a pair of black eyes, what looked to be one

broken nose, and stiffness in them both was answer enough to that.

"I won't leave you behind again," she promised.

"Nay, lady, you won't," Sir Denis said firmly. Then he made her a little bow. "Begging your pardon, of course, for speaking freely."

She smiled. "No need." She paused. "I was thinking to visit His Grace's healer."

"We'll escort you there."

She had the feeling they would. She found herself flanked by them, which was actually quite convenient given that she wasn't entirely sure where she was going. They came to a stop in front of a building not far from the stables. She realized as she stood there that she did indeed recognize the place, though the particulars were still shrouded in a bit of a fog. Perhaps that was for the best. Given how long it had taken for her head to stop paining her, not having any memories of her first days at Monsaert was probably a blessing.

She knocked briskly and waited for quite a while before the door was finally opened. A very irritated-looking man with wispy white hair stood there.

"What do *you* want?" he demanded. "Er, no need for swords, lads."

Isabelle smiled at her guardsmen, then looked at the healer standing in front of her. She had vague memories of his having cursed her more than once whilst she was abed in his infirmary. She supposed it wouldn't aid her to remind him of that, so she put on her best smile and hoped that would be enough to distract him. "I was hoping I might trouble you for a few herbs."

"I don't keep useless flowers here," he said shortly.

"I'm not here for flowers," she said carefully, "I'm here for herbs."

"And what would a silly wench such as yourself know—"

"Paquier," a voice said from behind her, "give her what she wants."

"But, my lord!"

Isabelle turned to find Gervase standing behind her wearing a look that she was rather glad was being directed at the healer and not her. He looked at her, lifted his eyebrows briefly, then returned to glaring at the man in front of her.

"Let her in and give her what she wants," Gervase said. "Now."

Master Paquier hesitated, then apparently thought better of it. He retreated back inside his house, grumbling as he did so. Gervase looked at her guardsmen.

"Stay out here, lads. I think I can see to her for the next half hour."

"Of course, my lord!"

Isabelle would have smiled at their enthusiasm, but her nose hurt just looking at them. She walked into the healer's quarters, then paused and looked at Gervase.

"I appreciate the aid," she said. "I don't think your healer would have allowed me over the threshold on my own merits."

"He scarce allows me the same," Gervase said, "but you're welcome just the same. 'Tis the least I can do given that I *almost* slept last night for the first time in months."

"Perhaps we should shout at each other in the garden more often."

He snorted at her. "It wasn't the shouting that provided me with such a pleasant night, which I imagine you already know." He nodded toward his healer. "Go make your demands. I'll see they are fulfilled."

She wasn't about to argue with that. She nodded, then walked as boldly as possible into Master Paquier's domain. He was obviously not pleased to have her there.

"I can't imagine you know anything," he said, looking at her stiffly. "You, a mere serving wench." He lifted his chin and looked at Gervase. "I have tried everything possible, Your Grace. The body can only heal so much when the injuries are this grave."

"I am surely not questioning your knowledge," Isabelle said carefully. "I am only wondering if it might be possible to try a few things I've heard about."

Master Paquier sniffed. "I'll give you what you want because I obviously have no say in the matter, but don't expect me to tell you what I've already done."

"I'm sure I wouldn't understand it even if you did," Isabelle said. She supposed there was no point in saying that Robin's wife, Anne, had had her leg crushed by a stallion when she was young and she herself had often been the one to fetch Robin what herbs he'd needed from their healer to attempt to relieve Anne's pain, even years after the fact. If it could work for Anne, why not for Gervase?

"And don't blame me if the duke's time is wasted with your foolishness."

Isabelle decided that perhaps the first thing that could do with a bit of tidying up was the manners of the men in Gervase's keep. Then again, as far as they knew, she was nothing more than a servant. Perhaps this was how servants were always treated and she simply hadn't noticed before. It made her rather grateful that she'd been born to Rhys de Piaget. Then again, her father wasn't rude to women, no matter their station.

She glanced at Gervase, but he was simply standing next to the hearth built into one wall of the little house, leaning back against that wall, watching silently. She gave Master Paquier a list of things she wanted, ignored his dire warnings about their lack of efficacy, then turned and looked at Gervase when her basket was filled.

"I'm finished."

He pushed away from the wall and walked over to open the door for her. She left the house and heard him close the door behind her. She looked up at him. "You slept more easily?"

He nodded solemnly.

"Are you willing to try other things?"

He pursed his lips, but nodded just the same.

"Are you going to say anything today?"

"Not if I have any sense."

She smiled to herself. Obviously his night of almost sleeping had done him good. She watched him out of the corner of her eye as he walked and supposed he did so with more ease, but what did she know? It had taken Anne years to regain her strength and even now she still suffered when the weather turned foul. Perhaps Gervase would never be entirely whole.

Though for his sake, she hoped he would be.

She walked back with him to the keep and on to his solar. She set the basket of herbs down on his table, paused, then turned to look at him as he sat with a sigh in front of the fire. He was watching her with an expression she couldn't identify, then he suddenly leapt to his feet. It startled her so badly, she whirled around, wondering what it was he'd seen behind her. But there was nothing. She frowned, then turned back around and looked at him.

"What is it?"

He gestured toward the chair across from him. "You should sit first."

She blinked. "Why?"

"Because you are a woman."

At least he had noticed. "Why does that matter when I am a mere serving wench?"

"It matters," he said with a small bow. "Chivalry is always called for."

She imagined it wouldn't serve her to look at him as if he'd lost all his wits, though she was hard pressed not to. Obviously there were things going on that she was missing, but she supposed she might as well sit whilst she was about discovering them. Gervase sat with a wince, straightened his leg out with another flinch, then looked at her.

"How do you fare?"

She wasn't sure she'd heard him aright. "Did you eat something foul this morning?"

He pursed his lips. "Nay, I most certainly did not. I am attempting to be polite for a change." He paused, then seemed to gather himself together for another go. "Would you care for a walk in the garden later?"

"A walk," she said.

"In the garden," he repeated.

"Why?"

He blew his hair out of his eyes. "Because, again, it seemed like a polite thing to ask," he said impatiently.

"And you're feeling polite today?"

He glared at her. "Actually, I was thinking that walking with you in the garden might be a pleasant way to pass the day, but I'm beginning to wonder about the advisability of such an activity." He pushed himself to his feet, glared at her again, then limped across his chamber. "Sort your weeds, woman," he threw over his shoulder. "I'm going to go soak my head."

"If it pleases you, my lord."

"'Tis simply Gervase," he said as he wrenched open his solar door, "not *my lord*."

He pulled the solar door shut behind him with a bang. Isabelle stared at the door for a moment or two in silence, considered, then shook her head. The man was impossible. Perhaps if she'd been able to successfully compare him to one of her brothers, she could have predicted with some accuracy what he was going to do, but the truth was, he was like none of them. He seemed torn between wanting to be kind to her and wanting to snarl at her.

Frenchmen. What reasonable English lass could fathom their depths?

She rose, then stood with her back against his fire. It felt familiar, that sort of standing. She realized that she could bring to mind scores of times where she had either done the same thing herself or watched her siblings monopolize the fire that way whilst having themselves a goodly think.

That was comforting, somehow.

The door opened suddenly and Gervase poked his head inside. "Are you purposely provoking me?"

"I haven't been," she said honestly, "though I could attempt it, if you like."

"The saints preserve me," he said with feeling. He hesitated, then looked at her seriously. "I do have business to see to for the next hour or so. Please stay here where I know you're safe."

She supposed there was no point in trying to argue with that given her experiences in his hall to that point, so she nodded. He drew his hand back and banged it smartly against the edge of the door, which obviously pained him. She crossed the chamber and caught his hand before he'd finished with a rather impressive string of curses.

The scars on the back of his hand were fierce, that much was true. She ran her finger lightly over them and felt him shiver. She looked at him quickly.

"Hurt?"

"Ah," he said slowly, "not exactly."

She smiled. "Surely the touch of a cheeky wench is not so troubling."

"And yet it is." He slid her a look. "Have you always been this impertinent?"

"Actually, nay," she said honestly. "I've spent the whole of my life standing in the shadows, saying nothing at all."

"I can scarce believe that," he said.

"'Tis the absolute truth. I have several siblings, which makes it difficult to get a word in edgewise in my house."

He leaned slightly against the doorframe. "Are you going to tell me which house that is? Or how many siblings you have?"

She shrugged. "I can't remember."

"Lying is a sin."

"So is grumbling overmuch."

"I don't grumble. I express my opinions in stately, measured tones."

She turned his hand over and looked at the palm. There were no scars there, but she could see where his muscles were withered. She tried to stretch them out with the gentlest of pressure, but even that set him to swearing. She glanced at him.

"Was that a measured tone?"

"I don't think so."

She didn't think so either. She gave him a quick smile, then turned back to his hand. She worked on it a bit longer, then handed it back to him. "A poultice might help that. You should let me make you one."

"You are a bossy slip of a girl."

She pursed her lips. "I'm not afraid of you. I also don't believe you're a warlock."

"Well, there's a mercy, isn't there?"

And then he smiled, a grave, self-deprecating sort of smile that left her understanding rather abruptly how it was the female population of France might have been tempted to fall at his feet wherever he went.

She quickly reminded herself that he was rude and bossy and unafraid to lock her in his solar to keep her safe. He was, she realized suddenly, a great deal like her brother Robin only without any of Robin's, ah, charm. In fact, he was entirely too aggressive and warrior-like. Worse still, all that chivalry was wrapped up in a great deal of Frenchness she was just sure she didn't care for at all and would only continue to like less and less as time wore on.

She looked up at him to find that he was now scowling at her, which left her wondering if her thoughts had shown on her face. He muttered a curse or two under his breath—in stately, measured tones, it had to be said—then pulled something out of a purse attached to his belt and handed it to her.

It was several rather wilted, pale purple flowers.

"From the garden," he said grimly. "I don't think they're weeds."

Would the man never cease to leave her off balance? She looked at him in surprise. "What are they called?"

"The villagers call them *forget-me-nots*."

Then he backed out into the passageway, frowned at her again, then pulled the door shut in her face.

Isabelle stared at the door for another moment or two, then walked across his solar and set her flowers on the edge of his table. She sat down and stared at it for much longer than she likely should have.

She had never had anyone not of her family give her anything before.

She looked about her with a fair amount of desperation for a distraction. Her herbs were there, sitting innocently in their basket, waiting to be used. She sorted them, but that took far less time than she'd hoped, leaving her with nothing to do but wonder if she might find somewhere else to linger besides Gervase's solar.

She walked to the door and opened it slightly, wondering who she might find outside.

She could see two men standing several paces away, speaking in low tones. One she didn't recognize, but the other was definitely Gervase. She knew that because she recognized his voice.

"Want her?" he said shortly. "Are you daft? I want nothing to do with her!"

"But—"

"She'll regain her memory, then I'll help her back to her family without hesitation. Anything else is madness."

Isabelle blinked, then shut the door very quietly. Well, there was no question about how the lord of the castle felt about her, was there? She wasn't one to indulge in self-pity, but she was growing heartily sick of men who couldn't remember her name. She was even more tired of men who hadn't a clue as to who she was but apparently didn't want her just the same.

No matter what sorts of simple gifts they had just given her.

She ignored the way her feelings were smarting, cursing herself for being pained in the first place. Perhaps her grandmother had a place for her at the abbey. Amanda had considered it, even going so far as to boldly travel to Seakirk Abbey and commit to taking her vows.

Only then, Jackson Kilchurn had come to rescue her.

Isabelle had the feeling Gervase de Seger wouldn't make the same effort for her.

Chapter 10

Gervase walked up the way from the lists, humming a pleasant melody. The words that usually accompanied that were limited to bloodshed and mayhem, but he chose new, more cheerful words to accompany his tune as he continued on his way. It had been that sort of morning so far.

His leg was so much better, he could scarce believe it. There hadn't been a moment in the past four months that he hadn't been aware of it paining him on some level, yet the night before he'd had a moment or two when he'd almost forgotten it had been so abused. Of course, the slightest movement had reminded him abruptly of what he'd endured, but when he remained still, things had been much better.

And he had Isabelle de Piaget to thank for that.

He hadn't had any idea how to even speak to her the afternoon before. How exactly did a man go about being polite to a noblewoman he had first had scrubbing his filthy, grease-strewn floors under the watchful spoon of his ruthless cook, then left at the mercy of the saints only knew what sort of vermin on the floor in that kitchen until he'd regained his wits long enough to know she couldn't possibly be what he'd thought her to be? *Forgive me, Lady Isabelle, for treating you worse than my low-liest stable lad and would you be so kind as to forebear enlight-ening your sire about the same* had seemed an awkward way to begin a conversation. He supposed asking her if she wanted to have a brief stroll in his garden, then snapping at her because she'd looked at him as if he'd been daft hadn't been any better.

Perhaps he needed another trip to the kitchens where he would indeed soak not only his body but his head.

He was quite frankly amazed at how much good the former had done him. Once he'd gotten past all the scowling necessary to keep his kitchen help in line, that was. The first cheeky ser-vant who had dared say anything to him about it had been told that said bathing was in preparation for the sacrificing of brazen serving lads later on in the fortnight. It was the last he heard about it, thankfully. Now, if he could only keep himself from saying any more inane things to his former scullery maid, he might make a success of the day.

He walked down the passageway to the kitchens, then ran bodily into his younger brother before he realized Joscelin was standing there.

Joscelin looked over his shoulder, then put his finger to his lips. Gervase frowned.

"Another pitched battle?"

"Something much more interesting. Look carefully."

Gervase looked around his brother's fat head to find Rhys de Piaget's youngest daughter standing over a tub, washing pots.

"What in the hell—"

Joscelin elbowed him so hard, he lost his breath.

"Damn you," Gervase wheezed. "And damn her. What is she doing?"

"She is trading her labor for money."

"And just why in the hell would she need any gold?"

"She doesn't care to live on your charity," Joscelin said, "or she's preparing to make a journey. It depends on who you ask."

Gervase frowned. Neither of those things boded well for him, actually. He rested his elbow on Joscelin's shoulder and had himself a think. It wasn't comfortable for him to do so, but his elbow in his brother's flesh was causing that brother to flinch, which was definitely worth whatever discomfort he himself was feeling. He considered, then removed his elbow.

"Have Cook get her out of the bloody kitchen," he whispered in disgust.

"Where are you off to?"

"I was going to have something to eat, but I've lost my appetite. I believe I'll go consult with Sir Aubert about the state of the garrison."

"Sounds diverting."

Gervase glared at him, then walked back up the passageway. The rest of his brothers were lazing about uselessly, pretending to study. He glared at them as well out of habit, then continued on his way. He needed to be outside where men wielded swords and comported themselves in ways he could understand. He wasn't sure if Isabelle baffled him because she was an English-woman or because she was simply a woman. He'd known his share of women before, to be sure, but never one who left him scratching his head as she did.

Earning gold. Refusing to live on his charity. Just what species of creature was Rhys de Piaget spawning these days?

He spent a very unsatisfying hour in the lists watching his men and damning himself that he couldn't hoist a sword with equal ease, much less wield it. It left him with very foul humors he wasn't sure even a good soak could possibly balance. Perhaps a robust clouting over the head was what he required, but he wasn't sure he trusted any of his household to administer that.

He walked toward the stables for no other reason than he liked the smell of horses and the way they wickered at him when he approached. At least they behaved as he expected them to.

He had scarce entered the bloody place before he was forced to skid to an ungainly halt. He pulled back behind a wall and blew out his breath. The woman was going to be the death of him, in truth. He leaned his head against the post because that was preferable to taking his head and banging it against said piece of unmoving wood.

"But, Master Simon," Isabelle protested, "I am perfectly capable of mucking out a stall!"

The stablemaster made the noises of a man who had very recently been assaulted by half the king's army and was lying, winded, in the mud. "B-b-but—"

"Here, lad, give me that pitchfork," Isabelle demanded.

"But, mistress!" a lad squeaked.

"Aye," Simon managed, in tones not much more firm, "I cannot allow a woman to muck out my stalls."

"But I am in great need of gold," Isabelle said. "Do you mean to deny me an honest day's labor?"

"Ah—"

"Then a horse to exercise," she said. "Look you there, *there* is a horse who looks to need a bit of work."

Simon made a noise of disbelief. "That is His Grace's favorite warhorse!"

"Then His Grace has a very fine eye. Let me put him through his paces."

"I'll go speak to him," the stablemaster said, sighing heavily. "If he says aye—"

"I'll saddle him—"

"I'll see him saddled *for* you," Simon corrected, "but only *if* Lord Gervase approves. You may go find a curry comb, if you like, and we'll see if you have any skill with beasts."

"And if I do an acceptable job?"

"You'll earn accolades."

"I'd prefer coins."

Simon blew out his breath and walked away. Gervase waited until his stablemaster was within arm's reach before he reached out and snagged the man by the sleeve. Simon looked over his shoulder, then ducked behind the wall as well.

"Your Grace?"

"Give her a horse to ride."

"But, Your Grace!"

"I have every reason to believe she will filch one and ride it anyway, just to show the both of us what she can do. We may as well humor her while we may."

Simon hesitated, then sighed. "As you will, my lord. Do you have a preference?"

"Something that won't kill her," Gervase said.

Simon leaned back to look around the post, then looked back at Gervase with wide eyes. "She has saddled Diablo—"

"Not him," Gervase said firmly. "Absolutely not."

Simon hesitated. "I don't believe we're going to have anything to say in the matter, my lord."

Gervase dragged his good hand through his hair, then

realized it was his right he had just used and it seemed to be functioning as it should. He was surprised enough by that to look at his hand. Withered still, aye, but not quite as withered as usual . . . unless he was going mad and imagining things, which he supposed was quite possible. He looked at his stablemaster.

"I want her off him at a walk if she can't manage him."

Simon took a deep breath. "A serving maid?"

Gervase supposed that the worst damage his accident had done was not to his leg but to his ability to school his features. Simon only smiled faintly.

"I didn't suppose she was."

"And that, my friend, is what makes you such a good judge of horseflesh."

Simon made him a low bow, then walked off to see to his charge. The only thing Gervase could say, as he pulled back into the shadows and hid behind a handful of blankets hung on the wall, was that Simon had not been given his position out of pity. He was not only an excellent horseman, he had an eye for horses that Gervase had never seen matched in all his travels. There had been more than once that Gervase had purchased a beast, brought it home, and watched Simon consider it for less than a quarter hour before shaking his head slightly. He had never been wrong, fortunately or not, depending on one's perspective, and Gervase considered himself fairly discriminating when it came to his steeds.

The only thing he could say at the moment was he was fairly certain that Isabelle would be safe enough if Simon thought her so.

He waited until he'd heard her pass by before he waited a bit longer, then made his way out to the lists. It was easy enough to lurk behind the crowd gathered there to watch that daft wench to exercise a horse she surely didn't belong on—

He folded his arms over his chest and attempted a stern frown. Better that than gaping, which was precisely what all the rest of the men there were doing.

Well, hell. Perhaps many things could be said about Lord Rhys, but that he hadn't taught his daughters to ride as well as his sons was definitely not one of them. He closed his eyes briefly, shook his head, then laughed. He couldn't help himself. He looked about himself to find that a handful of the men standing there had turned to look at him as if *he* were the one who was daft.

He shrugged. What was he to say? The woman was spec-tacular. How he could have mistaken her for anything but what she was, he surely didn't know. He supposed that eventually his household would recover from the shock of seeing her rid-ing in trousers and a tunic, though he wasn't so sure about himself.

He allowed himself another quarter hour of watching a woman he was fully convinced would spell his doom, take his favorite horse, and work him very methodically, no doubt as she'd seen her father do with his own mounts countless times. For all he knew, she had her own collection of very fine steeds and this was how she filled her mornings.

By the saints, she was . . . well, she was not a woman he ever would have thought might run off into the world, dressed as a lad. What in the hell had possessed her to leave the comforts of her home? He'd had more than a pair of encounters with her brothers Robin and Nicholas and knew how they outfitted them-selves and their men. Isabelle likely enjoyed a quality of life and possessions that he suspected even he might lift an eyebrow at. Why would she have left all that behind?

She was, he had to admit, completely out of his experience.

She cooled his mount down just enough to be able to hop down out of the saddle and toss the reins to a stable lad who rushed forward to catch them. She strode over to Simon.

"Another," she said firmly. "If you please."

"One more, but *only* one," he said, just as firmly, "lest you leave my lads with nothing to do today."

"Perhaps one of Lord Gervase's particular favorites, that I might show him my services are worth his gold."

"As I said, you just worked his favorite jousting horse."

"Then let me see the second favorite, aye?"

Gervase walked away while he still could. He found himself caught up to by Simon, who was obviously on his way back to the stables. Gervase looked at his stablemaster, then reached into his purse and pulled out two silver deniers.

"Best pay her something."

"Very generous, my lord," Simon said in surprise.

"I know, and I'm not sure why I'm finding myself with the impulse," Gervase said frankly. The last thing he wanted was for Isabelle to feel as if she could hire away half his garrison to take her wherever she seemed to want to go.

He frowned. It wasn't possible that she had regained her memories and knew who she was, was it?

The thought was surprisingly distressing. In fact, it was so distressing that he determined he wouldn't spend any time at all considering it. He made his way back up to the hall, then continued on to his solar. Isabelle's guardsmen had quite obviously been in the crowd and there was certainly no lack of others to look after her, so she would be safe enough for the moment. That left him free to completely ignore questions about her that bothered him and concentrate on other more useful subjects.

He attempted to look at his accounts, to tally figures that instead swam before his eyes in meaningless waves. He was heartily tempted to put his head down on his hands and simply fall asleep.

A knock on the door made him jump so badly, he wasn't entirely sure he hadn't fallen asleep sitting straight up in his chair.

"Enter," he called, more feebly than he would have liked. He spared the effort to rub his hands over his face before he looked at his guest.

Damnation, it was the master of hounds. The man was a new one, retained by Guy while Gervase had been almost senseless in his chamber. That didn't matter so much except that he found himself completely incapable of bringing the man's name to mind.

"Aye?" Gervase asked, supposing they could forgo any pleasantries.

"My lord, the young mistress approached me with a proposition."

Gervase sighed. He didn't have to ask who the young mistress was. "Accompanied, I'm assuming, by her two guardsmen."

"Aye, my lord."

"What did she want?"

"To feed the hounds in return for the occasional coin."

Unsurprising. The woman was fiendishly determined. "And you said her nay?"

"My lord, I didn't dare!"

Gervase supposed he could understand that. "Send her to me."

"As you will, my lord."

The man—Henri, he thought his name might have been—bowed, then left the chamber. Gervase sighed, then rose and began to pace. No sense in not trying to recapture his wits before he was forced to argue with a woman whose ability to influence others to her way of thinking was apparently only matched by her skill not only with horses but a pot of hot, soapy water as well. He paced until he heard the door open behind him. He turned and stood with his back to the fire, wishing he had instead chosen to sit in a chair.

He had forgotten in the past half hour how fair she was. He supposed he might have been able to dismiss that if he hadn't watched her do things every other woman of his acquaintance would have turned her nose up at.

She shut the door behind her rather more firmly than necessary. "My lord," she said briskly. "You sent for me?"

Gervase frowned in surprise. He had expected several things, but anger hadn't been on that list.

"Ah," he managed.

"How many I serve you?" she demanded.

The truth was, she sounded as if she would have sooner stuck a knife in his chest than do anything useful for him.

"Well," he began slowly, "I was wondering where you were."

She lifted her chin. "I was attempting to earn a few coins."

Ah, now he would hear the reason from her own lips. "Why do you need coins?"

"Because I cannot forever live on your charity," she said stiffly. "And I have a journey to make."

So he'd heard. "You're not taking food out of my mouth," he said, which he considered to be an extremely reasonable thing to say. "Nor my brothers'. My peasants are equally well fed. Why not you?"

"Because I cannot live on your charity."

"You said that before."

"I meant it twice."

He could only stare at her, utterly baffled. Perhaps that was how all de Piaget women conducted their business. She wasn't pointing a sword at him, so he supposed things could have been worse.

"Why," he asked slowly, "do you need means that I cannot provide for you?"

She shifted. It was just a slight shift, but to his mind, it spoke volumes. There were realizations going on inside her head, things he supposed he might not want to know but knew he had to find out. He clasped his hands behind his back, had a slight moment of pleasure that he could actually manage the like, then turned back to his particular problem.

"I could help you more successfully," he added, "if you could tell me exactly why you need something to put in your purse. Perhaps you're regaining a few of your memories . . . "

She shook her head. "Still in a bit of a fog there."

She was a terrible liar. It was thoroughly refreshing, that lack of ability. He couldn't say that every woman he had known had been a liar, but he knew far too many for his taste. It was tempting to ask her for her opinion of him, but perhaps there were limits to how much truth he cared to hear at the moment.

"What do you think of my brothers' studies?" came out of his mouth instead.

"They are neglecting them," she said without hesitation.

That, at least, was a decent bit of truth. "Could you inspire them to greater heights of commitment?"

"Perhaps."

"Then I'll employ you to do that." Because that was preferable to having her clean out the cesspit, which he imagined she would do if she thought someone would hand her gold for the deed. Lord Rhys might only hurt him, not slay him, for having used his daughter thus.

"How much?"

He considered, then named a sum that no tutor would have taken on his most desperate day. Isabelle's mouth fell open a little, then she looked down her nose at him.

"Surely you jest, *monseigneur le duc*. I, however, am not jesting."

Damnation, that's what he was afraid of. He sighed. "I'll pay you whatever you ask."

"I'll have a gold sovereign at the end of every se'nnight."

He choked. It was involuntary at first, but he found that once he had started with it, there was no sense in stopping. He accepted a cup of something he hoped was drinkable from Isabelle but stopped her from pounding on his back. He held up his hand, caught his breath, then looked at her.

"You *mercenary*."

She only lifted an eyebrow in challenge.

He shook his head, suppressing the urge to laugh. He attempted to frown fiercely at her, but the best he could manage was an anemic sort of something that he was certain was not anywhere as intimidating as he might have wished it to be.

"Every fortnight," he said, "*if* they can prove some proficiency at anything but eating through my larder."

"Every *se'nnight*, and they will be proficient in whatever you demand."

He wondered, absently, if he would have the chance to tell Lord Rhys what a delightful daughter he had raised before the man ran him through.

She waved him on. He frowned.

"What?"

"Make your list of demands. I'll begin tomorrow."

He walked over to his table and sat down, then looked up at her thoughtfully. "'Tis miraculous, is it not," he said slowly, "that you can remember your Latin but not your name?"

"It is," she agreed.

He leaned his elbows on the wood and looked at her seriously. "Did you run from your home?" he asked. "Did your father use you ill?"

She looked as shocked as he would have expected her to. "Of course not."

Sit down, Isabelle was almost out of his mouth before he managed to bite the words back. He rose, fetched a chair from before the fire, then set it down around the corner from him and waved her down into it. "Take your ease, lady, while I attempt to make a reasonable list of demands."

She looked primed to balk, but perhaps she'd had enough of scrubbing and riding and attempting to breed insurrections in his keep that weariness had finally caught her up. She sank down onto the edge of the chair, but she didn't relax. She was still scowling at him slightly, but, again, he had no idea why. He resumed his seat and attempted to look as harmless as possible.

"Why did you run from your home?" he asked, because it was the first thing that came to mind.

"Why do you assume I ran?"

He made chopping motions near his ears.

She ran her hand self-consciously over her hair. "I don't remember how this happened."

"Lying is still a sin, you know."

"I'm hedging."

"Is that what you call it?" he said with a snort. "I daresay I had best see you down on your knees in chapel tomorrow morning, determining the difference between the two." He declined to add that he should likely be right next to her there praying for his own poor soul that would no doubt find itself on its journey in one direction or other sooner than he would like courtesy of one of her kinsmen.

"One does what one must when circumstances demand it," she said seriously.

He studied her for a moment or two. "Those sound like the words of a body on a quest."

Her mouth fell open. "How did you know?"

"I recognize the symptoms," he said dryly.

"If you tell me you've garbed yourself as a woman, I will not believe it."

He smiled in spite of himself. "Nothing so dire, I assure you. I understand what it is, though, to feel called to do something beyond the norm." He shrugged. "I'm just curious what it was in your case."

"Honestly, I'm not entirely sure," she said.

"Ah, honesty," he said with a nod. "Care to enlighten me about other things while you're wallowing in truth?"

She shifted. "Aren't you making a list of things you want me to see to with your brothers?"

"I'd rather discuss your quest and leave off for a bit facing things that will beggar me."

She froze. "Will I beggar you?"

He snorted. "Of course not, but I can't allow you to think anything else, can I?"

"I suppose not," she said. Then she smiled.

He was profoundly glad he was sitting down. Actually, he would have been happier if he'd had some sort of shield to hide behind. All he could do was sit there and wonder how it was that she hadn't been wed years ago.

"How old are you?" he asked, before he thought better of it.

"A gentleman wouldn't ask."

"Why do you think I'm a gentleman?"

She only smiled again. "I recognize the symptoms." She nodded toward his inkwell. "Your list, if you please. I'll need to plan my lessons for the morrow."

He reached for a quill, but winced at the pull of his hand. Before he could stop her, she had reached for his hand and taken it in both her own. She might have been gentle with his brothers, but she was absolutely ruthless when it came to tormenting his poor flesh. He supposed he might have uttered an impolite word or two.

She lifted an eyebrow. "Was that gentlemanly?"

"Considering what I wanted to say, I thought so."

She laughed softly, then bent again to her work.

The saints pity his poor miserable self, he thought that he might just throw himself at Rhys de Piaget's feet and ask him for mercy so he might . . . well, he had no idea what he wanted to do with the man's daughter, but he was fairly sure there might be polite words involved.

She put his hand back on his table and patted it. "I'll return for your list."

"Where are you off to, you heartless wench?"

"I'm going to go find more weeds for your bath."

He didn't bother to comment. He was too busy trying to catch his breath not only from the pain in his hand but the thought of potentially having anything at all to do with that astonishing woman pulling his door shut behind her.

He shuffled sheaves of paper about uselessly in an effort to feel as if he were accomplishing *anything* at all useful—

He froze.

He pulled a small piece of parchment out from the stack Isabelle had been using a pair of days before for—ah, in truth, he couldn't remember why she'd wanted anything to write with or write on. He looked at what he held in his hands, read the words there, and felt something sweep through him that wasn't at all pleasurable.

If you think this is over, Monsaert, think again.

He dropped the sheaf on his table as if it had been a live thing. He stared at the words in horror, cursing himself for the feeling but unable to initially master it. He drew his hand over his eyes, swore viciously, then took a deep breath and got hold of himself. He stood, put his hands on the table—curling his right hand into a fist to spare himself any undue discomfort—and looked down at the scrap of parchment with as much disinterest as he could manage.

That was a woman's hand. There was no doubt about it.

He could scarce believe it, but he couldn't reasonably believe anything else. He considered the words for several minutes, allowing his emotions to retreat back to where they belonged. The first thing to decide was who had written the damned thing. It could have been anyone, anyone with access to his solar, anyone with a mind to cause him grief—

But not Isabelle. He couldn't imagine it of her.

What he did know, however, was that it wasn't written in jest and that perhaps his troubles were indeed not over. And if that were the case, he was still in a fair bit of peril.

Which meant Isabelle might be exposed to that peril.

He shoved the sheaf back under the stack lying there, then walked quickly to the door and wrenched it open. Aubert wasn't there, but three other guardsmen were. Fortunately for everyone involved, none of those three belonged to Isabelle. He motioned to one of them.

"Go find the lady—er, I mean, go find the woman who just left my solar."

"I know the one, Your Grace."

"Good," Gervase said shortly. "Find her, then guard her with your life. Ignore her protests."

"Of course, Your Grace."

Gervase shut the door, then stood there with his left hand on the wood, bowing his head. He was going to have to send her home, obviously. It was one thing to humor her when he thought he was in no danger. That someone could have gained his solar without his knowledge was something he simply couldn't ignore.

Perhaps not on the morrow, though. The sky had been threatening some species of weather all day. Nay, the day after was soon enough. And until that time, he could surround Rhys's youngest daughter with half a dozen of his fiercest lads with unquestionable loyalty. He would perhaps even sit in on her lessons with his brothers on the pretext of wanting to make sure she did them aright. She didn't have to know that he wanted a few more hours of looking at her before he sent her away.

Because he couldn't involve her in the hell that was his life.

Especially given that his hell was apparently not over yet.

Chapter 11

Isabelle sat at Gervase's table in his solar, surrounded by his brothers in various states of Latin verbal conjugations. Gervase hadn't given her his list yet, and she hadn't pressed him for it. He'd been terribly grave the evening before which had led her to believe he was contemplating things she perhaps didn't want to hear about. All the reasons why he could wait to be rid of her, no doubt. Well, no matter. She was in his hall still because she had no means of getting anywhere else. The price of her journey was the education of his brothers and she could see well enough for herself what needed to be done.

She had nothing to say to Joscelin or Lucien. Joscelin was obviously as educated as she was, though he seemed to have less interest in helping his brothers with their sums as he did sharpening his wits with Lucien over the chessboard. That left her with Pierre, who had told her earlier he preferred swords to sums, and the little lads, Fabien and Yves. They were all three in truly dreadful shape. Their experience with logic was less than she would have expected and they all three struggled with their sums. Obviously no one had yet taken the time to light any fires of scholarly enthusiasm in them.

They were willing students, though, which she supposed was a boon. She could have been saddled with lads such as her own brothers who had been too intelligent by half, learning what they needed rapidly enough to spend more of their time combining ways to escape their lessons than actually sitting through them.

"You should have a name."

Isabelle looked up from her stitching to find Yves watching her closely. She smiled. "Should I?"

"We cannot go about forever calling you nothing," he said reasonably. "Can we?"

"I'll remember my name in time, I'm sure."

"And you're not going anywhere, are you?" he asked.

She found herself with not one, but five pairs of eyes on her. She swept all the lads with the best smile she could manage, was very grateful that neither Guy nor Gervase was there to accuse her of lying, and shook her head.

"Not that I know of," she said. "Where would I go?"

"Let's go read," Yves said, bounding up from his brother's table. "Ger has a trunk full of things, you know."

"Why don't you read to me?" Isabelle suggested.

Yves skidded to a halt. "Perhaps we should go to Mass first."

"I've already been this morning," she said, and she had, suffering under pointed looks from not only the priest but the lord of the manor himself. "You could go, though, if you can talk your brother's priest into humoring you."

Lads piled out of the solar. Joscelin was the last to leave, lingering by the door and looking at her with a smile.

"You'll be safe enough here, I suppose," he said. "What with your ever-increasing number of guardsmen outside."

"They are very fierce," she agreed.

"They don't dare not be," Joscelin said. "I think Gervase has threatened all of them with death should they fail to protect you."

She took a deep breath. "He is kind."

"I'm not sure that's the word I would use to describe him," Joscelin said with a bit of a laugh, "but you can credit him with all sorts of altruistic qualities, if you like."

She smiled. "You love him well enough, I daresay."

"I suppose I do," he agreed. He smiled, then left the solar, pulling the door shut quietly behind him.

Isabelle stood in the middle of the chamber and let silence

descend. It was comfortingly difficult to have peace for thinking with a collection of lads making a ruckus around her, but now that they were gone, she found she had more peace than she cared to have.

She walked over to stand in front of Gervase's fire, then rubbed her arms to ward off a chill she likely shouldn't have been feeling. There was no reason for it, of course. She was as safe at Monsaert as she had been at Artane, what with the guards Gervase seemed to think she needed. No one had been unkind to her save the Duke of Coucy's lad who she could only assume was either still loitering in the dungeon or had been sent back on his way, accompanied by a reminder or two of Gervase's displeasure.

Yet still she was unsettled.

She supposed the blame for some of it could have been laid at the lord of the hall's feet. He'd given her flowers, then not a quarter hour later insisted that he wanted nothing to do with her. The following day, he had agreed to pay her a ridiculous sum to tutor his brothers, then spent the rest of the day being gravely polite to her. He couldn't seem to decide if he liked her or loathed her, but perhaps she couldn't have expected anything else.

Unfortunately, it wasn't simply the changeable nature of the lord of Monsaert that troubled her. The very fact that she was in France and not at home was baffling. She couldn't imagine that she had simply decided on an adventure and trotted off without telling anyone. It was possible that she had discussed her plans with Miles, but her plans to do what? She had surely planned to come to France eventually with her mother to be there for the birth of Nicholas and Jennifer's second child, but if that were the case, why had she cut her hair?

She couldn't bring herself to think that perhaps her mother had been on the ship that had obviously gone down in the storm.

The door opened suddenly and she reached for the first thing that came to hand. Gervase froze, looked at the fire iron she held, then slowly held up his hands.

"I am unarmed."

"Is that reassuring?" she asked briskly.

He moved inside, then closed the door behind him. "I dare-say it should be."

"You still have a sword."

"And you look as if you might do a terrible bit of business with that weapon you have there."

She turned away to put the fire iron down because she didn't want to look at him. It was obvious that the man couldn't decide what to do with her past paying her to school his brothers—something she'd forced him to agree to—which was all good and fine with her. If she had been desirous of a husband, she certainly wouldn't have picked the man standing near his doorway, watching her gravely.

Certainly not.

"Where are the lads?" he asked.

She nodded to herself over that. He was interested in what she could do for his brothers, no more.

"In the chapel," she said. "It doesn't serve them to keep them longer at their tasks than they can bear."

"Of course," he said. "As you say."

She busied herself tidying up the table the boys had been using for their lessons, then sat down in front of the fire and tried to do a bit of stitching. It was difficult to ignore the man who had come to sit across from her, but she was made of very stern stuff, indeed. She also reminded herself with every stitch that he had said he didn't want to have anything to do with her.

Which was no doubt why he was simply sitting there, watching her.

She finally put her stitching aside and frowned at him. "What do you want?"

He looked at her gravely. "I was thinking perhaps you might enjoy a game of chess. Do you play?"

Why did he care what she might enjoy? "Occasionally," she said shortly.

Actually, that was a terrible understatement. The only one of her family who didn't look at the board with the same level of commitment they might have a pitched battle with was her mother—well, and Anne, too. Their mother spent too much time trying to keep them from killing each other whilst about their sport and Anne was too tenderhearted for that sort of ruthlessness. At least when it came to the game, Isabelle had never suffered from either of those impediments.

"Would you indulge me, then?"

She had the feeling her look was one of suspicion, but she couldn't seem to help herself. "Why?"

"I'm trying to distract you from inventing any more schemes to rid me of my gold."

She wasn't sure if he was teasing her or not, and she was actually rather alarmed at his faint, wry smile, so she nodded quickly before he found some other way to baffle her.

He rose and walked over to fetch the little table sporting his pieces. Isabelle put away her stitching to go stop him before he could. She had the feeling dropping those finely made pieces wouldn't do anything to encourage him to have a good afternoon. Considering what she planned to do to him over the board, she supposed it would be best that he cling to whatever happiness he might have at his disposal.

"I daresay we'll be more comfortable over here," she said quickly. "Lest the fire prove to be too much for our humors."

"As you will, of course."

He waited for her to sit, then took his own chair. He began to sort pieces on the board, carefully, as if he weren't quite sure how much aid to offer her. She didn't stop him. She hadn't learned to play at Rhys de Piaget's mighty knee without learning a few less savoury tactics, one of which was always to be underestimated. She frowned over a couple of pieces, blinking owlishly until Gervase sighed lightly and reached over to help her. She waited until he had set up almost the entire board before she looked at him.

"Does black go first?" she asked.

He frowned. "Don't you know?"

"I've forgotten."

"No matter," he said quickly, as if he were truly determined to save her pride. "I'll aid you as you require, of course. And white goes first, if my memory hasn't failed me."

"How lovely." She made a great production of studying her side of the board until he sighed lightly, then she looked at him. "Should we play for something?"

"Play for something?" he echoed.

"Isn't that what people generally do?" she asked. She almost felt a small bit of regret over using him so ill, but the man had declared quite enthusiastically that he wanted nothing to do with her not a quarter hour after having given her a wilted flower.

Perhaps he needed help in clarifying his thinking. Who was she not to offer a trouncing in chess to encourage that?

"I suppose some do," he conceded. "What would you care to play for?"

"Well, gold seems so . . . what's the word I'm looking for?"

"Pedestrian?" he suggested.

"Aye," she said with a smile. "Pedestrian. Wouldn't you agree?"

He studied her for a moment or two as if he were contemplating things he hadn't thought to before. "What I would agree with," he said slowly, "is that you have mercenary tendencies that I'm sure your father wouldn't approve of. "

"A girl does what she must to survive," she said with a shrug. She looked around his solar thoughtfully. "Your keep would be too much trouble, I think," she mused. "Perhaps something less substantial, but far more troublesome for you personally."

His eyes narrowed. "Shall I act as a lady's maid, then?"

"Could you manage that, I wonder."

The look he shot her almost made her smile.

"Very well," she said cheerfully, "I'll have that, then."

"And what shall I have when I win?" he asked evenly.

"Well, since I'm sure you will win handily, why don't you suggest something? "

His expression changed to something quite a bit more serious. "I believe, lady," he said, "that I would like your forgiveness for having made you scrub my kitchen floors."

She reminded herself that she did indeed not like him at all. He was going to help her regain her memories, then send her back to her family because he wanted nothing to do with her.

It was hard to remember that when he was looking at her in such a grave, serious way.

"Forgiveness doesn't sound very interesting," she managed.

He shrugged. "I thought it best not to frighten you away from the board by revealing my true, unpalatable self. If I told you what I truly wanted, you might tip your king right off."

She smiled. "Rogue."

"So I'm told, though the tales are greatly exaggerated." He nodded toward the board. "Your move."

She put her finger on her pawn, fourth in from her left. "This one moves forward, does he not?"

"I believe, *demoiselle*, that he does."

"Then let's move him forward a couple of these squares here and see how he fares."

He considered, then put one of his knights on the front lines.

"Oh, a horse," she said brightly. "I have one, too. I believe I'll move one of mine out to join yours." She smiled. "Is that right?"

"I believe it might be," he said dryly.

"And you moved one of your—what are these called again?"

"Pawns," he said with a sigh.

"I like them," she said. "I'll move another of mine. And another horse. This *is* an amusing game."

He looked at the battlefield she had staked out, then pursed his lips as if he had recently sucked on something that hadn't tasted particularly good. He shot her a look. "I believe, my lady, that you haven't been entirely forthright with me about your abilities."

"Do you think so?" she said smoothly. "Why don't you carry on with the game and let us see, my lad, if you know the movements of the rest of those things cluttering up your side of the board."

"'My lad,'" he echoed with a snort. "You, lady, have an appalling lack of respect for those who have only allowed you to march yourself out so far onto the field that you will find it difficult indeed to defend your major pieces."

She suppressed the urge to flex her fingers. "Have I? Do show me where I'm failing then."

He looked at her, then shook his head. And damn him if he didn't smile as if he knew he had just encountered a battle from which he would not emerge entirely unscathed.

It was a rather quick game, all things considered. She had taken him unawares, which left him scrambling to make up for it and left her with the time to compare him to the men of her family. He was definitely not as deliberate as her sire, who played the game as if every moment had the potential for ending his life, nor was he as rash as Robin, who threw himself into every encounter with either a chortle or an evil grin. She supposed if he reminded her of anyone, it was Nicholas, lethal and elegant about the damage he did. There was, however, something else about Gervase she couldn't quite lay her finger on. He stared at his king for several long moments, then shook his head before he tipped him over and laughed ruefully.

She wondered if he had laughed every time he'd taken yet another knight for ransom.

"You will not take me by surprise again," he warned.

"How embarrassing for you that you were taken by surprise in the first place," she said sweetly.

"I was exercising chivalry, a mistake I will obviously not be making again with you." He began to push pieces toward her. "Again."

"*After* you've polished my tack and seen to my wine, I imagine."

He shot her a look. "We'll keep a list."

"I suppose 'tis the least I can do to assuage your badly damaged pride," she conceded. "What shall we play for this time?"

"Why don't you play first and find out later?"

"Are you daft?" she asked with a laugh. "I'm not about to give you free rein."

"Afraid you'll lose?"

Actually, she was afraid of quite a few things, namely that she might forget that she didn't care for him at all.

"I am never afraid," she said. She looked at him quickly. "Not at the board, rather. And aye, I understand very well that you will be showing me exactly as much mercy as I've shown you. Fortunately, your black heart is very tender."

He rolled his eyes. "If you only knew." He collected her pieces and set them up on his side of the board. "I'll take white."

"'Tis more chivalrous to allow the lady to go first."

"You dare to speak to me of chivalry, you heartless wench?" he asked darkly. "I'll take white and you'll have to see what you can do to survive."

"I suppose 'tis the least I can do to give you the advantage of the first move," she said thoughtfully. She looked at him. "Wouldn't you agree? Oh, look. You've moved your steed out in front of those . . . what were they called again?"

He opened his mouth to speak, then shut it and glared at her. "Pawns," he said crisply, "which I can see I've been in your hands so far. Don't assume I'll allow myself to be put in that position again."

She smiled, poor fool that she was, because she knew he wasn't serious with those looks.

She heard his brothers tumble into the solar at one point, but her king was in jeopardy so she didn't pay them any heed. One thing she could say for Gervase de Seger, he was absolutely relentless. She led him on a merry chase, but in the end he gave her no choice but to surrender. She said a rather foul word, then tipped her king. Joscelin, who had apparently been standing behind her chair, laughed.

"I suppose that's one way to put it."

"I'm ahead by one game," she said, because she thought it needed to be said.

"Aye, because I exercised too much chivalry and allowed you an extra turn at white," Gervase said loudly.

"You absolutely did not," she said with a snort. "You allowed me to go first, as you should have. I can't be responsible for the results of that miscalculation on your part." She looked up at Joscelin. "He's rather good, you know."

"He's better against flesh and blood," Joscelin said with a smile. "And perhaps he feared to trample upon your delicate feelings."

"You weren't here to witness his snarling at me. There was a distinct lack of chivalry on display during the heat of battle."

Gervase smiled and rose. "Then allow me to remedy that by escorting you as you go collect my weedy winnings. The garden is likely particularly lovely right now."

"Since you'll spend the evening tending my wine," she said easily, rising as well, "I suppose the least I can do is make it comfortable for you."

He pursed his lips, then offered her his arm. She took it before she could remind herself that he was neither charming nor pleasant nor anything but a Frenchman who was very full of his own huffings and puffings.

"We'll come as well," Yves offered, dashing over and taking her free hand. He looked up at his brother. "It would be the chivalrous thing to do, wouldn't it, Ger?"

Gervase sighed and nodded. Isabelle considered that as she walked with him down the passageway, through the great hall and out into the back garden. She had recaptured her hands by the time they reached the garden, partly because Yves had deserted her to chase after a brother who had insulted him and it seemed a handy excuse to allow Gervase to have his arm returned to him.

"Yves is a good lad," she said. She looked up at Gervase. "They are all fine lads."

"They all could have benefitted from a mother, especially Yves." He sighed. "I have not been here as often as I should have been. I suppose some of that wasn't my fault, for I was sent away to foster at court when I was young."

"At court," she murmured. "Not a very wholesome environment for a lad, I imagine."

He laughed a little, but there was no humor in it. "Nay, it wasn't, and I suppose it was only stupidity that kept me from acquiring the most vulgar and depraved of habits. I was allowed to return home periodically, that I might not forget what my duty was, but once I earned my spurs, I found that I was less . . . ," He seemed to consider his words for quite some time before he finally shrugged. "They were accustomed to having me gone, I daresay."

Isabelle would have flinched, but she didn't dare. Her father had sent his sons off to foster, but only for a year or so, and he had always welcomed them home with tears of joy. When Robin and Nicholas had gone away to war, the entire family had mourned their absence daily. She couldn't imagine not wanting to have her family about her.

"Their loss," she said without thinking.

He smiled faintly. "You didn't know me then."

"How terrible could you have been?"

"I was arrogant."

"Skilled knights generally are," she said with a shrug.

"And you would know?"

"I've spent more than a maid's allotment of time listening to tales," she said without hesitation. "One hears things, you know."

He snorted. "I imagine one does. As for being home, I daresay it was impossible for me to have pleased my stepmother. She was furious when I took Joscelin with me as my squire."

"I'm sure he worshipped you."

Gervase lifted an eyebrow. "I think he was happy to be out in the world."

"And I suspect you took very good care of him," she said, "which seems to be a terrible habit you have. So, you gathered up your brother, took him with you to raze the countryside, then what? Vats of gold, scores of women, countless accolades?"

"Aye to the gold, to my surprise aye to the last, but tales of my prowess in the bedchamber are greatly exaggerated."

"But mine aren't!" Joscelin called from across the garden.

Gervase shot him a look, then leaned closer. "Don't believe him. I would hazard a guess he's still a—"

"Shut up, Ger," Joscelin warned.

Isabelle smiled in spite of herself. "And you, my lord?"

He pursed his lips. "We'll not discuss my adventures out in the world and what I want to know is, who was it who was daft enough to begin this conversation?"

"I believe it was you."

"I'm afraid you're right." He clasped his hands behind his back and walked along pathways with her for quite some time until he seemed to come to some sort of decision. He stopped and looked at her. "I need to go on a journey tomorrow."

She looked at him in surprise. "You don't sound pleased about it."

He seemed to be considering his words, which seemed very much unlike him. "I wouldn't say that," he said very slowly. He started to speak, then shook his head. "I'm not sure what to say about it."

"Do you need me to do something whilst you're away?"

"Nay, I need you to come with me."

"Do you?" she asked. "Where are we going?"

"I think it best to avoid saying."

She frowned. "Are you going to toss me into the sea?"

He shook his head solemnly. "Nothing so dire. Just a little ride through the countryside."

"As you wish, then," she said, wishing that perhaps she had been a bit more forthcoming when she'd had the chance. It would be just recompense for all her hedging if he carried her off to Caours where her grandmother would immediately identify her. But at the moment, it wasn't as if she could ask him where exactly he was intending to go because then she would be forced to tell him who she was.

And she simply couldn't bring herself to do that.

It was madness, but she wanted for one last day not to be who she was. She didn't want Gervase to look at her and see the nameless youngest daughter of Rhys de Piaget. She wanted him to see her, a woman whose hand he had just taken and tucked again in the crook of his elbow.

Just for one more day.

Chapter 12

Gervase was grateful for the rain in a way he wasn't usually grateful for it. It gave him an excuse to keep the hood of his cloak pulled around his face where he didn't have to look at the woman riding next to him. The truth was, he couldn't bear to see her expression when she realized where he was taking her.

Though he supposed there was no mystery to it. If she'd been to her brother's keep before, she would have known at least an hour ago where they were going. At the very least, she would have been able to see Beauvois in the distance.

Unless she genuinely had no idea who she was.

He wasn't sure which would have been worse, having her know or having her not know which would make him the one responsible for introducing her to her very intimidating brother Nicholas.

He'd had more pleasant rides, to be sure.

Unfortunately, there was nothing else to be done. He had attempted two nights previous to invent any sort of way to keep her near him and have it seem reasonable. He'd come to the inescapable conclusion that keeping her near him, no matter how much he might have wanted to, was madness. He'd been a fool to believe that whoever had tried to murder him four months ago had given up on the idea. To knowingly put Isabelle in that sort of danger was something he certainly would have killed a man for had his own daughter been in that man's care.

But because that thought didn't comfort him at present, he turned his mind to admiring Nicholas de Piaget's seaside holding. The keep was lovely, the surroundings productive, and the smell of the sea intoxicating. He wasn't unhappy with Monsaert simply for the sheer magnitude of the resources he could command and the truly lovely countryside. When it didn't sport scorch marks, it was quite a lovely place. But he couldn't help but admit he loved the sea and envied Nicholas his view of it.

He noticed a detachment of garrison knights riding his way and supposed there was no time like the present to assess the extent of the damage. He pushed his hood off his head and looked at the woman riding on his right.

She was watching the guardsmen coming toward them from the privacy of her hood. She didn't seem to be terribly unsettled by the sight, but what did he know? She finally turned her head toward him, though he could only see a shadow of her expression.

"Here for a visit, are we?" she asked mildly.

He wasn't in the habit of needing bracing breaths, but he supposed indulging in one at the moment wasn't unreasonable. He took a very deep one, then shifted in the saddle to look at her more fully.

"Nay, my lady Isabelle," he said quietly, "we're not."

She looked at him in surprise, then closed her eyes briefly. "I see."

"Do you?"

She considered her words for far longer than he was comfortable with, actually. "My father always taught us," she said seriously, "that if we found ourselves in dire straits to never give anything away."

He nodded, because he supposed he would have told his own children the same thing. "And you were in a strange place—"

"I should have told you sooner."

He shot her a look. "How long have you known?"

"I remembered my name as I was being assaulted by Coucy's man and you rescued me. The rest followed quickly."

He wasn't sure if he should have been offended or not that

she had felt unsafe enough at his hall to want to keep her particulars to herself. What he did know was that he would be damned before he made mention of it.

Damn her anyway.

He soothed himself with a handful of silent curses. He had known from the start that she was not for him. Discovering how long she had known who she was but had chosen to say nothing to him could mean nothing but that she had been looking for a reason to . . . well, he had no idea what it meant. He was simply glad that he was almost rid of her.

Lovely, sparkling thing that she was.

"Shall we continue?" he asked roughly.

She only nodded. "We likely should."

His mood soured with each mile they rode, but perhaps he could have expected nothing else. The riders reached them far sooner than he would have liked, but there was nothing to be done about that, either. He started to ride forward to speak with them, but Isabelle put out her hand.

"Let me," she said quietly.

In that, he supposed she might have a point. Better that she invent some reasonable-sounding excuse for why she found herself unchaperoned in his company than leave it to him. The saints only knew what sort of idiocy would come tumbling out of his mouth. Perhaps he would pattern the rest of his day after Sir Aubert's usual manner of comporting himself and remain safely silent.

He listened to Isabelle greet Nicholas's men by name, which led him to believe that perhaps the good Count of Beauvois had brought a few of his English lads with him. He supposed he should have paid more attention to the conversation, but all he could do was listen to her speak and wonder how he could have been so profoundly stupid not to have realized what she was the moment she had first opened her mouth on that muddy road that led to the sea.

"My lord Gervase was good enough to rescue me from ruffians and shelter me whilst I recovered my memories," she was saying. "But we'll ride with you, if you don't mind, and provide my brother with a pleasant surprise. I'm not sure he even knows I'm in France."

Gervase frowned thoughtfully. That was a mystery he would have happily investigated, to take his mind off his impending death if nothing else. How was it possible that the youngest daughter of a powerful lord could possibly escape not only her father's keep but the whole of bloody England and find her way to France? Surely Rhys de Piaget couldn't be so dense as to not recognize that that had been his child riding off into the sunrise, even with her hair shorn.

He would have given that a great deal of thought, but he found himself continually distracted by the woman riding next to him. She was impossibly grave. Gone was the feisty competitor he'd faced over a chessboard in his solar the day before; in her place was a young woman who obviously knew that what lay in front of her wouldn't be pleasant.

"Isabelle?"

She looked at him, an expression of surprise on her face. Then she smiled gravely. "I forgot you knew my name."

"It is unforgettable," he said frankly. He wondered how to phrase his question delicately, then gave up and plunged right into it. "Do you remember why you left Artane?"

She looked at him with an expression that he couldn't help but believe was wonder. "You know whence I hail?"

"Of course," he said. "Your reputation extends to France, to be sure."

"Reputation?"

"For goodness and beauty," he said quietly. "I fear, however, that the tellers of tales have neglected to mention your unwholesome skill at the chessboard."

She looked away, then bowed her head. "Very kind, my lord."

"Are you afraid to go to Beauvois?" he asked bluntly. "We can turn around, if that's the case."

She looked at him as if she'd never seen him before. He wasn't entirely sure that her eyes hadn't watered a bit, but it was, after all, raining and she had pushed her hood back off her face at least a quarter hour ago. She took a deep breath, then shook her head.

"Nay, I'm not afraid."

"Your brother won't strike you, will he? I will stand between you if you fear that."

She took a deep breath, then pulled her hood back over her face. "Nay, my lord," she said quietly, almost too quietly for her to hear him. "He will not harm me."

Gervase wasn't sure if what bothered him more was that she looked to be on the verge of weeping or that when Nicholas de Piaget shoved a sword through his belly, she likely wouldn't weep over him. He drew his hand over his eyes and swore viciously—but silently. No reason to trouble the rest of the company with his personal demons.

The rest of the journey couldn't have taken more than an hour, but it felt as if it took all day. Gervase didn't dare look at Isabelle, not, he imagined, that she would have been looking at him. He didn't want to know what she was thinking lest it include desires to see him burning endlessly in the unquenchable fires of Hell.

The gates were reached far sooner than he cared for, but there was nothing to be done about that, either. He rode inside those imposing gates, wishing he hadn't felt so trapped, then dismounted and looked up at Isabelle.

Whatever she was thinking, she wasn't going to allow it to show on her visage.

He held up his arms for her and helped her off her horse, almost managing not to flinch at her weight resting even slightly on his right hand.

"Oh, sorry," she said, taking his hand and holding it in both her own.

It almost killed him to do so, but he pulled his hand away from hers before Nicholas could open his front door and see things that would only increase his ire. He muttered a strengthening curse or two under his breath, reminded himself he was a score and eight and not a whelp of twelve summers, then looked at the woman he thought he just might be much too fond of for his peace of mind. He clasped his hands behind his back and looked at her, but could find not a single useful thing to say.

He knew he shouldn't have been surprised.

"When did *you* know?" she asked quietly.

"I saw Arthur of Harwych in the village a handful of days ago."

"Oh," she said, nonplussed. "I'd forgotten about him."

"Well, he hasn't forgotten about you. Or, it happens, the boots you seem to have borrowed from him."

She smiled faintly. "I suppose I'll have to send a new pair to him."

"I imagine he would appreciate that," Gervase agreed. "He

was, as you might imagine, exceptionally worried about you."
He lifted an eyebrow. "I believe his most pressing concern was
that your father not slay him before he could present his suit."
And given that he shared that concern, he thought he might have
recently acquired a bit more compassion for the gangly though
earnest master from Harwych.

"Did he know I was at Monsaert?"

"Nay, I didn't think I should tell—"

He would have finished his thought but the door was
wrenched open suddenly. Gervase looked up and found a very
agitated Count of Beauvois standing there. He gaped at his sister, then stumbled down the stairs and came to an ungainly halt
in front of her. He looked as if he'd seen a ghost.

"Isabelle," he said hoarsely. "You're alive."

She nodded slowly.

He dragged both hands through his hair. It looked, as it happened, as if he'd been doing the same sort of thing for quite
some time. "Where in the *hell* have you been?" he managed.

She pushed her hood back off her head. "I was on a quest,"
she said carefully.

Nicholas blinked stupidly. "You cut your hair."

"Well, aye, I did—"

Gervase was unsurprised by the turn of events from that
point on. Nicholas caught sight of him and his mouth fell open.
He pointed with a finger that unfortunately didn't tremble as
much as Gervase might have hoped for.

"You," he said in garbled tones. "What are *you* doing here?"

Gervase inclined his head as politely as possible. "Bringing
your sister to you, as you can see."

Nicholas's change in mood was swift and ruthless. Indeed,
his newly acquired temper burned with the exact amount of
brightness Gervase had suspected it might.

"What were you doing with her in the first place?" Nicholas
demanded incredulously.

"I found her wandering on the side of the road," Gervase
began carefully, "and—"

"And you stole her!"

"Nay, he rescued me," Isabelle said loudly.

"So he could ravish you at his leisure, no doubt," Nicholas
said furiously.

"Don't be ridiculous," Isabelle said with a snort.

"I'm not asking you for your opinion," Nicholas snarled at her. "I know his reputation!"

"He didn't ravish me."

"Then where have you been?" Nicholas spat. "In his stables? In his bed—"

Gervase supposed, in hindsight, that his first mistake was thinking that his right hand would work as it should have. His second mistake was taking that right fist and plowing it into Nicholas of Beauvois's damned mouth.

The only thing that saved him from being slain immediately thereafter was that Nicholas wasn't wearing a sword. He was, however, wearing knives down his boots. Once he'd picked himself up off the ground, those knives came from their sheaths with a speed Gervase might have admired at another time. At the moment, he was too busy trying to keep an avenging woman who had most definitely not passed the previous three se'nnights in his bed from lying somewhere else, namely her grave. She seemed to have no sense of her peril as she stood between him and her knife-wielding brother. He tried to move her aside, but she fought him, then turned herself about and gave her brother and his deadly knives a hearty shove.

"Stop it," she commanded. "I was in his hall, not his bed."

"For a *fortnight*?" Nicholas exclaimed.

"Nigh onto three se'nnights, I daresay," she said, "though I don't remember the first one. I think I was unconscious in bed—"

"What!"

"In the *healer's house*, you fool!" She looked at him with disgust. "Put your blades away before you do damage to someone with them. I daresay that someone will not be the man behind me."

Nicholas's fury had turned into something so cold, Gervase would have shivered if he'd been the sort of lad to shiver, which he wasn't. He watched Isabelle's older brother very deliberately resheath his blades, then straighten. He folded his arms over his chest.

"Very well, he is now safe. Given that he had you in his hall for so long, would you be so good as to tell me what he *did* do with you?"

Damn her if she didn't hesitate. "That's a bit complicated."

Nicholas shot him a murderous look. "It shouldn't have been. The good Duke of Monsaert sees a lady of breeding and rank and accords her the respect due her. Very simple, indeed." He turned to his sister. "Where were you lodged after the healer's house or did you remain there?"

Isabelle squirmed. "I remember being in the kitchens—"

Gervase wondered if it would be rude to simply put his hand over her mouth. He supposed that wouldn't be any more helpful than simply standing there and attempting to look innocent, but it was honestly all he could do not to elbow her in the ribs and tell her to stop trying to help.

"And then?" Nicholas asked in clipped tones.

"I scrubbed the floors first, then swept—"

Nicholas swore.

Gervase found himself with the youngest, fairest, most perfect daughter of Rhys de Piaget standing in front of him as if she sought to protect him. He wasn't sure how he felt about that, actually, but he didn't dare interrupt her.

"He rescued me not once but twice—"

"Which he wouldn't have had to do if you'd stayed at home where you belonged!"

"He rescued me from a particular lad with designs upon my person," Isabelle continued relentlessly, "showing a most admirable amount of chivalry. He has since then been nothing but an honorable, fairly polite, mostly reasonable—"

"Idiot who will be sporting my sword in his gut as soon as I can get you out of the way and send someone to fetch my blade for me," Nicholas snarled. "Isabelle, *move*."

"I will not—"

Gervase put his hands on her shoulders. He was almost tempted beyond what he could bear to turn her around and hug her until she couldn't breathe, but he supposed that wouldn't do anything to improve Nicholas's opinion of him. So instead he very gently held her in place while he stepped to her left.

And then, as he had expected, all hell broke loose.

The lord of Beauvois apparently didn't feel inclined to bother with his sword, which Gervase supposed he might have to protest later when he had the breath for it. At the moment, he was far too busy trying to keep Nicholas's clutching fingers from gaining any purchase around his own bloody throat.

It was a brief battle, made all the briefer by his own rather ignominious collapse in the mud. He would have cursed his right leg for continually deserting him when he needed it the most, but he was too busy trying to ignore the blinding pain in that leg. He knelt there in the muck and wondered how he was going to regain his feet before Nicholas simply kicked him to death.

"Isabelle, do not touch him!" Nicholas bellowed.

Isabelle shoved her brother, then reached out toward Gervase.

Gervase then did something he thought he might regret for quite some time to come.

He turned away from her.

Aubert hauled him to his feet, which he appreciated. He didn't dare look at Isabelle, who had been yanked over to stand next to her brother. He instead looked at Nicholas as coolly as he could manage. It was nothing, he supposed, compared to the look Nicholas was giving him.

"I will not kill you now," Nicholas said.

"Good of you," Gervase managed.

"I'll give you a month to regain your strength," Nicholas said. "Is that enough time, do you think?"

"So you can kill me?"

"Why else would I waste any time with you?"

Why, indeed. "Three fortnights, then," Gervase said. "Wouldn't want to rob you of any sport."

Nicholas's look was not at all friendly. "If you think that infamous charm of yours will keep me from repaying you for my sister's distress, you're sadly mistaken."

"I don't think I could reasonably expect anything else," Gervase said.

"Get off my land," Nicholas said in a low, rather unpleasant tone. "If I find you on it again, uninvited, I will kill you without hesitation. Is that clear?"

Gervase had definitely not expected anything else, so he simply nodded. He supposed there was even less reason to expect to have any opportunity to speak to Isabelle. He imagined if he tried, Nicholas would kill him right there with his bare hands.

He refused to allow himself the weakness of a sigh, but instead simply turned and walked away. He heaved himself back up onto his horse with as much grace as possible. He supposed his second mistake—or it might have been several mistakes farther down the list of disastrous decisions he'd recently made, actually—was not looking at Isabelle at that point.

He couldn't. He didn't want to see what she was thinking

written on her face. He rode out of the bailey before Nicholas decided that a month and a fortnight was too generous an offer.

There was nothing else to do.

Several hours later, he walked into his own hall. His leg ached as if it had been freshly broken. That was, unfortunately, nothing compared to the fiery agony that seemed to linger in the vicinity of his heart.

He knew he shouldn't have been surprised by the events of the day. He should have at least bid Isabelle good-bye, or told her that he was happy to know she would be safe, or that he loved her—

He rolled his eyes and snorted as best he could past the lump in his throat. Of course he didn't love her. He hardly knew her. She was not the sort of woman for him, obviously. She was . . . well, she most certainly didn't . . . and no one could reasonably deny that . . .

He cursed. It was all that was left him in his poor, mindless state.

The only bright spot in the gloom had been the opportunity to shut Nicholas de Piaget up before he had made a bigger ass of himself than usual by accusing his sister of—

He took a deep breath. What he needed was a very large, very strong drink. He wasn't one to indulge in the like, but he had a bottle of some sort of rot that Joscelin had found for him while he'd been out of his head with pain from his leg. Perhaps a very large glass of that would serve him at the moment.

He walked into his solar to find it full of younger brothers. He ignored their questions and cast himself down into his chair. His cloak almost strangled him, which he supposed he should have suspected before he sat. He pushed himself to his feet, pulled off his cloak, then threw it to Lucien, who apparently thought it was best to do something with it besides dump it onto the floor. Gervase sat again with a deep sigh and closed his eyes.

A throat cleared itself in front of him. He opened one eye, then realized he had no choice but to open both eyes.

Yves stood there, quivering with righteous indignation.

Gervase sighed. "What?"

"Where is she?"

Gervase considered, then lifted his brother up and set him

on his knee. Yves was not placated by it, though he did do Gervase the favor of glaring at him from less of a distance. Gervase stared at him in consternation. What now?

"Why'd you take her away?" Yves asked plaintively.

"Because she needed to go home."

"I wanted to keep her!"

And then Yves burst into tears.

Gervase looked for aid, but the rest of his brothers, damn them all to an eternity of roasting their arses against the fires of Hell, found other things to look at. He tamped down his own instinct to fling Yves across the chamber and flee for safer ground, then put his arms around his sobbing brother and drew him close. And he had to admit, as he proceeded to be drenched by a lad who sounded as if his heart had just been ripped out of his chest by bare hands alone, that he completely understood the feeling.

He patted, he made soothing noises, he sighed deeply a time or two, then simply waited for the storm to pass. What he eventually found himself with was a small lad curled up on his lap, chewing on his thumb. At least he was chewing, not sucking, which was a relief. Gervase was just certain that knights, no matter their age, did not suck their thumbs.

"Go get her back," Yves commanded at one point.

"I'd like to."

"Then do it."

"Aren't you the brave one," Joscelin said, collapsing into the chair opposite them, "to order such a fierce lord about that way."

"He'll go," Yves said confidently. He looked at Gervase. "Do you know her name yet?"

Gervase sighed. "Isabelle," he said. "Isabelle de Piaget."

Yves's mouth fell open. "Is she Lord Nicholas's sister?"

"Indeed she is."

Yves considered. "He's fairly fierce, though not invincible," he said, as if he merely discussed the merits of worms to take fishing with him. He looked at Gervase with an utterly serious expression on his tear-stained face. "We'd best consider our strategy well if we're to have her back as quickly as possible."

Gervase looked at Joscelin for aid, but Joscelin only smiled.

"He has a point. Pierre, why don't you take Yves and see what Cook has on the fire still. Then we'll make plans on what of your Latin to ignore. Best to give Lord Nicholas a reason to let the Lady Isabelle come back."

"We can do that," Yves said. He patted Gervase on the shoulder, then hopped off his lap. "Let's go, Pierre. There is much to do."

Gervase listened to the younger lads leave, then looked at Joscelin. "Any other spectacular suggestions?"

"I'm thinking."

Gervase imagined he was. He looked at Guy who had moved to stand with his back to the fire. "Are you now going to tell me you knew who she was?"

"Who, me?" Guy asked in surprise. "I'm the one who told you to put her to work scrubbing the floors. Why would I have known who she was?"

Gervase supposed it was better not to offer the opinion that Guy was obviously as dull as he was when it came to recognizing noblewomen going about in disguise.

"How did Lord Nicholas react?" Joscelin asked politely.

Gervase rubbed his hands over his face. "Let's just say that the only reason I'm still breathing is because he'd left his sword inside his hall."

"What are you going to do now?" Guy asked. "Send gifts? Apologies? Wine?"

Gervase sighed deeply. "I'm going to eat, soak my sorry leg, then make a measured retreat to my bedchamber where I will give the matter thought and hope that tomorrow the sun will rise on a new day. It can't be any worse than today."

"If you say so," Guy said doubtfully. "I'm not sure gifts will be enough to restore Lord Nicholas's good humors."

"Do you have any suggestions on what might?" Gervase asked sourly.

"Your head on a pike?" Guy asked seriously.

Gervase scowled at his brother and congratulated himself yet again for having chosen Joscelin to tourney with. He left his solar with a choice curse or two trailing along in his wake. Guy was probably right, but that didn't mean he had to agree.

He limped to the kitchens and made himself at home on a stool while Cook prepared his bath. He looked over the events of the day and examined them from all sides. He could have wished for a different outcome, but the truth was there had been nothing else to expect. He could hardly blame Nicholas for his anger, though he supposed he might be spending a bit of extra time in the lists on the off chance he was able to repay Isabelle's brother a bit more thoroughly for the insult to her honor. But as for anything else, what could he have expected? The most he could hope for was that Nicholas's guard might provide him with enough sport to take a bit of the edge off his fury.

But where Isabelle was concerned, perhaps there was a goodly labor to be done there. Gifts sent along at the appropriate time. What could possibly go wrong with that?

Cook stopped next to him with a basket. "Any preference with these, my lord?"

Gervase looked at the basket of fragrant things, then shrugged. "Toss them all in, I suppose. I can't tell any of them apart."

"As you will," she said, tossing the entire collection of things into a tub of steaming water.

Gervase began to pull off his boots, then froze. While it was true he had no idea what rot Isabelle had put in that basket, he could identify the odd herb and flower. And if even he could manage that, how much more would she be able to recognize? He could send her a message that even her reprehensible brother wouldn't be able to decipher.

He smiled for the first time that day.

Perhaps all was not yet lost where she was concerned.

Chapter 13

Isabelle left her chamber, which was yet another in a large list of guest chambers her brother possessed in his French castle on the edge of the sea. That castle was, she had to admit, a spectacular place. She had been there before, of course, so she wasn't surprised by the opulence. She was simply surprised to find herself enjoying it so abruptly.

She pulled the door shut behind her and steeled herself for the conversation she'd avoided having the day before by pleading a sudden and quite severe headache. Convincing her almost eldest brother that her head pained her from her tortures at Monsaert had been pitifully easy. He had immediately sent her off to lie down with wine and food hard on her heels. It had given her a chance to look out the window and breathe in the sea air, but it hadn't eased her heart any.

Gervase hadn't gone so far as to look at her as he'd ridden off through the gates.

She walked along the passageway and tried not to let the memory of that sting. After all, what could she have expected? Her brother had humiliated him in front of her, his men, and those of Beauvois who had cared to watch. She was only surprised that instead of simply turning away from her, Gervase hadn't snarled curses at her before he'd gone.

She supposed she would never see him again.

She walked out into the great hall and sighed a little in spite of herself. Her brother had many faults—being almost as pig-headed as Robin was the first one she latched on to—but stinting on luxurious surroundings was not one of them. She supposed he did it to please his wife, Jennifer, but she was happy to be the beneficiary of it at the moment. The hall was of pleasing dimensions, the ceiling painted in a particularly Gallic way, and the furniture sumptuous even in a locale that saw so much coming and going of servants and strangers.

Nicholas was standing in front of the fire, looking far too grave for her peace of mind. He caught sight of her and immediately crossed the hall to fetch her. He took her by the hand and drew her over to the fire, saw her seated, then took a deep breath as if he prepared for a very long, stern lecture.

"Don't trouble yourself," she said shortly.

He looked at her as if he'd never seen her before. She lifted her chin.

"What?"

"What?" he echoed. "*What?* Isabelle, what in the *hell* are you doing in France? By yourself? Missing very sensible *accoutrements* such as a heavy guard with very sharp swords?"

"I'm not entirely sure. As I said yesterday, I think I'm on a quest."

His mouth worked, but not a sound came from him. During that bit of spluttering, they were joined by another who collapsed happily in the other chair drawn up close to the fire.

"Go away," Nicholas said shortly.

Miles only propped his booted ankle up on his opposite knee. "Why?"

"Because I don't want you here."

"Afraid I'll hamper all the shouting you want to do?"

"Something like that," Nicholas said. "Now, go away."

Miles only put his hand over his mouth. "See," he said, his words muffled, "I can hold my tongue."

"You won't *have* a tongue if you use it in the next half hour," Nicholas said, in clipped tones. "Isabelle, what in the *hell* were you thinking?"

She sighed gustily. "I believe I already answered that."

"You were being held captive by *Gervase de Seger*," Nicholas bellowed. "Do you have *no* idea of your peril?"

She shrugged. "He seemed fairly harmless to me. Slightly cross, but that can be readily explained by the pain he still suffers in his leg."

Nicholas ground his teeth. "He has ravished half the virgins in France!"

Isabelle looked at Miles. "Is that true?"

"Rumor," Miles said dismissively. "Not that he isn't a handsome-looking man, of course, full of pleasing courtly manners—"

"We thought you were dead!" Nicholas interrupted with a shout.

Isabelle looked at her brother standing there in a towering rage and sighed. She had considered fleeing her father's keep numerous times, but what had kept her from it had been the thought of leaving her family, her brothers especially, in exactly the sort of state Nicholas currently found himself in. De Piaget lads were nothing if not protective of the women in their care.

She rose and went to put her arms around her brother's waist. She held on to him until he finally relented and returned the embrace, so tightly that she squeaked involuntarily.

"You witless chit," he said hoarsely, "we thought you were *dead*."

"So you've said," she noted. "Repeatedly." She pulled back to look up at him. "I'm sorry. I lost my memory—"

"I imagine your escort in a particular coastal village you would be wise never to name aloud wishes he had lost his," Nicholas muttered.

She pulled away. "Montgomery?"

"The very same. I understand even mentioning that port sends Father into absolute fits of fury. Montgomery, I imagine, has removed the word from his vocabulary altogether." He shot her a look. "What you may not remember is that you left the poor lad in an inn, unconscious and clutching not only a gown but apparently the hair you seem to be missing."

"Clever me," she managed.

"When will you gels stop cutting off your hair?" Nicholas complained. "You all seem to do it save Jenner, who is the only one with sense among you."

"It is a long and glorious tradition."

"Please allow it to stop with you," he pleaded.

She ran her hand over what was left of her hair and spared a regret for its loss. She resumed her seat and looked up at her brother. "Did I clout Montgomery over the head with something or did he simply volunteer to stay behind?"

"Ask Miles later," Nicholas said. "He has answers I don't. All I know is that Father will be absolutely livid when he learns where you were."

"But—"

"At Monsaert, of all places! With that damned Gervase de Seger—" Words seemed to fail him for a moment or two, then he took a deep breath and seemed to find his tongue. "He's a rogue of the worst sort."

"So you claim," she said calmly, "but all I've heard is that he has humiliated you more than once with the sword and unhorsed you at least thrice that his brother Joscelin remembers. Your pride has been stung."

"Nay, I don't want my youngest sister associating with a man possessing no redeeming qualities."

"I think you're misjudging him."

"And I think you've never watched him at court," Nicholas growled.

"And you have?" she asked with a snort. "You, an Englishman?"

"Bearing a French title?" he said pointedly. "Aye, I have."

"Jealous?"

"Hardly," Nicholas said contemptuously. He chewed on his words for a moment or two, then rolled his eyes. "I will allow that there are things about him that another might find acceptable. He is—or *was*, rather—a fair swordsman and marginally skilled in the joust."

"Nick, be honest," Miles said lazily.

"Very well, he was terrifying," Nicholas snarled at him. "He's also a ferocious bargainer, ruthless to enemies, and unfailingly loyal to friends as well as the one half brother I met. He was *also* continually trailed after by an endless collection of beautiful women. He took full advantage of their charms."

"Has he any bastards?" Isabelle asked.

"Rumor has it—"

"Not rumor, Nicky, demonstrable fact. How many bastards has he claimed?"

"Why would he claim any?"

She shot him a look.

He swore. "Very well, why wouldn't he, I suppose. And nay, damn you, I've seen no proof. Fortunately for us all he has provided ample evidence of his stupidity. That's seen easily enough by the fact that he put you to work in his kitchens."

"I'm not saying he can't be an idiot," she said easily. "He is a man, after all."

Isabelle realized she was talking to emptiness at the same time she realized her brother was no longer standing in front of the fire. She looked after him as he trotted across the great hall and disappeared up the stairs, then looked at her next oldest brother.

"He's excitable."

"Nervous rather," Miles said, smiling, "though I'm not sure why. Jennifer has at least another fortnight before the babe arrives, or so she believes. Her mother and grandmother will be here well before the birth."

Isabelle would have commented on that, but she had to admit she shared her eldest brother Robin's opinion of things that were . . . odd. The fact that Jennifer's mother didn't seem to have a hall in England and that her grandmother was likely as old as Queen Eleanor herself—a woman rumored to have her own pact with unwholesome sources that kept her living long past when she should have lowered herself into her grave—was something that Isabelle didn't think on often.

Paranormal oddities made her nervous.

And cold. She rose and stood with her back to the fire. "Let's speak of something else."

"Very well. Are the tunic and trousers yours?"

"I filched them from one of Gervase's brothers," Isabelle said.

"You have a terrible habit of that, you know."

"I learned it from Amanda."

Miles smiled. "I imagine you did." He rose and stood next to her, warming his own backside against the roaring fire. "You look to be plotting something."

"Your demise, no doubt," she said absently. She looked out over the hall and shivered. "I feel like we've done this before."

"How many times *haven't* we done this before? For as much of our lives as I can remember. Me, exhausting myself trying to convince you to see reason—"

"Ha," she said crossly. "It was generally you plotting mischief and me trying to talk you out of it."

"I suppose you have that aright," he conceded. "Only this time, it looks to have been you off combining mischief."

"It wasn't mischief," she said, "it was an adventure."

"Well, you did tell me you planned on one."

She turned to face him. "Did I? When?"

"Before you left Artane. You plotted and I listened, then offered my very sensible advice. You were extremely grateful to yours truly when I instructed you to stay at Artane whilst I saw to a bit of business for Nick at Wyckham. Indeed, you promised me that you would wait for me to return after which we would both don trousers and have ourselves an adventure by traipsing off to France in disguise."

She wished for a wall to lean against, but supposed she would just have to rely on her own two feet. "Very generous of you," she noted. "I'm assuming I agreed to this very generous offer."

"You did," he said easily. "And then you didn't, if you know what I mean. I returned home to find you gone, then filched a horse and rode like a demon south to try to find you. By the time I reached the inn where you had laid your youngest brother low, you'd been gone at least four days." He looked at her seriously. "I learned from lads on the dock that your ship had been lost at sea."

She shivered. "I'm sorry."

"You should be. I almost shed a tear or two."

She elbowed him companionably in the ribs. "You always were a maudlin thing."

He smiled wryly. "And so I am." He reached out and ruffled what was left of her hair. "And to answer the question I can see you're preparing to ask, aye, I found a ship and sailed to France myself to see if perhaps you might have miraculously survived. I'll give you the details of that later. What I will tell you now is that I sent a message off to Mother and Father yesterday to let them know you're alive and they can stop looking for you."

"Thank you," she murmured.

"My pleasure." He slid her a look. "You know, your demon lord from Monsaert didn't show all that well yesterday. I imagine he wasn't too pleased about that."

"Were you spying on him?" she demanded.

"Thought I'd be useful." He smiled. "Wasn't that useful?"

"Not very," she said. She pulled a chair closer to the fire, then sat down with a sigh. "What still eludes me is why in the world I would have ever wanted to come to France on my own. Outside of the usual desire to be off and having an adventure. I imagine that if I'd suggested the like, you would have told me to venture to the shore or some other rot."

He laughed and pulled up a chair to face herself. "As it happens, you did and I did. But that isn't the reason you left England."

She felt something slide down her spine, a finger of chill she hadn't expected. "Can I assume you know the reason?"

"You can," he said carefully. He glanced about them, no doubt to make certain they were relatively alone, then he looked at her seriously. "I found your diary."

"You are reprehensible," she breathed. "What did it say?"

"You assume I read it."

"Of course I assume you read it! What did you find there?"

He looked at his hands for a moment, then at her. "I think we should back up a bit. I'll tell the tale and you stop me when I've told you something you don't already know."

"Fair enough," she agreed.

"Very well. You made it very clear that you wanted to come to France sooner than with Mother, though you wouldn't tell me why you were so hell-bent on the idea." He looked at her, then shook his head. "There was something fey about you, Izzy, something I'd never seen in you before. I wouldn't have left you to your own devices if Nick hadn't been relying on me to see to his business for him. Believe me when I say I looked for every way possible to shove it off onto someone else. I couldn't, though, which left me leaving you behind and praying you wouldn't run off on your own."

"Which I apparently did."

"You had your reasons." He paused, then shrugged. "Suffice it to say that by the time I caught up to you in Alnmouth, you were gone and Montgomery was quite reasonably fearing for his life. I sailed to France, as I said, and after a bit of searching found your captain half dead in a small fishing village. He confirmed that you had been aboard his ship when it had been swept away."

"But you didn't find me," she said slowly.

"Nay, but we found one of your boots washed up on shore,"

he said, "and I found Arthur of Harwych wandering from place to place, wringing his hands and searching for you."

"He's useless."

"He's worse than useless," Miles said in disgust, "but rather useful for small bits of information. I questioned him until he wept, sent him on his way, then spent a se'nnight searching the shore where we thought you might have come to ground. I saw nothing of you, heard nothing of you, found no sign of you save that boot on the strand." He looked at her seriously. "I had feared you might meet your end in France, but I hadn't imagined it would come because of your journey here."

She looked at him in surprise. "What do you mean?"

"Because I know why you came here."

She felt still descend. It was a profoundly disquieting sensation, one she hoped she would be long in enduring again. "Do you?" she asked, finding that there was hardly any sound to her voice. "Say on, brother."

"I found a missive in your chamber," he said, sounding rather unsettled himself. "It instructed you to come to France or the lives of your entire family would be the forfeit. Why you were wanted here is something the missive didn't say, but I can't imagine it was for a pleasant purpose."

She felt the floor rock beneath her feet. The next thing she knew, Miles was squatting in front of her with his hands on her shoulders, holding her upright. She waved him away.

"Air," she wheezed.

"You fainted."

"Of course I didn't faint. I swayed."

"You almost fell out of your chair."

"Coincidence," she said, though the word sounded very garbled to her ears.

She put her hands over her face and simply breathed in and out for several moments in silence before she thought she could manage a decent breath without, well, without fainting. She clutched the arms of her chair to keep herself upright.

"So," she managed, "this sorry bit of scribbling didn't say why my presence was requested in France?"

He shifted. "Not in so many words. You were simply ordered to come. If you did not, there were the aforementioned consequences of death at Artane. And elsewhere."

She started to nod, then realized what he'd said. "Elsewhere?"

"You were told that our grandmother and grandfather here would pay a price, as well."

She felt the chamber begin to weave again, but waved Miles off before he reached for her. She pulled her legs up into the chair with her and made herself as comfortable as possible. "We have no grandsire living," she began slowly.

"Your correspondent seems to think so."

"But Joanna—"

"Wrong country, Iz. Here in *France*."

She shook her head, looked at him, then shook her head again. "But Miles, you know as well as I that only Grandmère Mary lives in France."

"I'll admit it baffled me," he said. "And you were instructed to come see her at Caours. Or both her life and our grandfather's would be in peril."

She shook her head, because she could hardly believe what she'd heard. "What do I do now?"

"Well, you're in France. Perhaps you simply wait until this lad who has such interest in your progenitors makes his presence known again."

She rubbed her arms suddenly. "I don't consider myself uncourageous," she said honestly, "but the thought of that is unsettling."

"Which is the first sensible thing I've heard you say in years," he said without hesitation. "As for the other, I believe I'll be shadowing you for a bit, if you don't mind."

"I can't think of anything I would mind less," she said faintly. "I think I would like to see that missive, actually. Perhaps I might recognize the hand. And I have to be honest and say I would like to see it for myself."

"I'll fetch it later. For the moment, why don't you go keep Jennifer company? I believe she has most of Nick's guard within shouting distance."

She looked at Miles in surprise. "Is he concerned about her safety?"

"He's concerned about everything," Miles said wryly. "This is nothing he can control, so he controls what he can. Which is, I imagine, why not knowing if you were dead or alive was so troubling to him." He glanced at her. "You couldn't have sent word from Monsaert?"

She had been halfway to her feet, but she found herself sitting again, quite abruptly. "But I did send word," she said. "I sent a missive to Grandmère a pair of days ago, telling her I was alive. Gervase's brother Guy promised to have it taken to her."

Miles shrugged. "Messages go awry. It would have been a useful thing for her to have known, but I wouldn't worry about it. I'll have one of Nick's lads go—"

"Don't," Isabelle said suddenly.

He blinked. "Don't do what?"

"Don't say anything," she said. "I'll go tell her myself."

His mouth fell open slightly. "Of course you won't."

"Don't turn into your brother."

"Brothers," Miles clarified. "Brothers and your father. And I certainly will turn into them because you absolutely won't go outside the gates."

She waved her hand dismissively. "You worry overmuch."

"Isabelle!"

"What else can I do?" she asked quietly. "Miles, I need to go because that's what I was told to do. The reason I left England—apparently—was to save my family from the fury of some unknown lad with as yet unstated reasons to want to harm them. Why would I want to remain here and possibly put Jennifer and her new child in danger?"

"Well—"

"Besides, we could go by way of Monsaert. I obviously can't abandon the boys now. Who will teach them their Latin?"

"The priest?" Miles said pointedly.

"Who will teach them their sums?"

"Lord Gervase?"

"He's very busy."

He rose and pulled her to her feet. "I'll think on it. For the morning, go keep Jennifer company. I'll find the missive, then show it to you without a score of nosey souls about. And do not disappear out the front gates without me."

"I wouldn't leave without you," she said pleasantly.

"Ha," he said with a snort. "Don't think I won't know exactly where you are at all times." He shot her a look. "I'm in earnest, Iz. Don't go without me. If you're determined to make a little journey to Caours, I will come with you."

"Very kind."

"Self-serving," he corrected. "I will look as if I tried to save you from yourself and thereby escape scrutiny whilst Father focuses all his ire on you."

She smiled, then linked arms with him as they walked across the great hall. She let him escort her to her sister-in-law's chamber and was unsurprised to find half a dozen very fierce lads standing guard outside the door. She was allowed entrance, then scooped up her nephew as he ran over to throw himself at her.

She stood there with young James de Piaget in her arms, then leaned against the doorframe and watched the scene before her with a smile.

Nicholas was kneeling in front of his wife, holding her hands in his, concern etched into every line of his face. As irritating and overbearing as he could be, she had to admit that he comported himself very well as a husband. Jennifer looked serenely happy.

She wondered if she would ever have anything like that for herself.

She let Jamie slide down to the floor when he grew weary of her simply standing there, then she slipped along the wall and went to sit on a seat in front of an open window. She looked out over the sea and forced herself to think about what she'd learned that morning.

Someone had wanted her in France badly enough to make terrible threats to have her there. If the missive was to be believed, she was intended to go to Caours and wait until some nefarious sort deigned to give her more details about what he wanted from her.

She didn't consider herself devoid of all courage, but she had to admit that the thought of someone demanding her presence somewhere was very unsettling. The irony was heavy and rather difficult to ignore. All those years when she'd complained about no one knowing her name and now to find that the one person who knew her name was quite potentially the last person she wanted to meet . . .

She turned away from that thought before it robbed her of any hope of a decent breath anytime soon. She would go to Caours, but first she would make a slight detour and see how Gervase's brothers fared. It was nothing short of irresponsible to leave them without a tutor. The very least she could do was give them a few lessons to work on so they would have something to do until Gervase could find another solution.

And for all she knew, the lord of the hall had run out of herbs. What else could she do but seek out sufficient supply for him?

Of course, it would have perhaps been a bit more seemly if he'd invited her, but perhaps he had listened too closely to her brother and been frightened off. She wasn't sure she would have returned to Beauvois anytime soon if she'd been the target of Nicholas's ire.

She didn't want to think about the possibility that he had no intention of ever returning to Beauvois to meet Nicholas on the field.

She pushed aside that thought and concentrated on what she could control which was getting herself to Caours as quickly as possible. If she found herself there by way of Monsaert, who could blame her? She would arrange for someone suitable to take over her duties with Gervase's brothers, then go to Caours and arrange for her family to live more than just the next fortnight.

It was all she could do.

Chapter 14

Gervase dismounted in the stable, handed his reins to a stable boy who only smiled and led his mount off, and marveled that he was still standing and not looking for the nearest place to sit down.

It was progress.

Of course, that progress was with his body only. His humors were so foul, he could scarce bear to be in the same chamber with himself. He supposed there was at least one benefit to that, for his own vileness had driven him outside almost constantly for the whole of the day before and since sunrise during the current sojourn in the hell that was his life.

"Ger?"

He looked up to find Joscelin loitering uselessly in the courtyard. He scowled at his brother.

"What do you want?" he snapped.

Joscelin only looked at him mildly. "I thought to see if you might want to train. We could repair to the garden where you could humiliate me without witnesses. Perhaps that means nothing to you, but I would surely appreciate it."

Gervase closed his eyes briefly, then nodded and walked

with his brother back to what had suddenly become a very gloomy place indeed.

A miserable hour later, he was beginning to suspect that the garden would be better used as a place for someone to bury him. It was a certainty that he wished he could simply lie down and make an end to the agony of using muscles that had lain fallow for far too long.

"How terrible was it?"

Gervase realized his brother had stopped forcing him to defend himself and was simply leaning on his sword and breathing easily, not gasping as if he'd been running for the whole of the morning.

"How terrible was it?" Gervase wheezed. "Must I describe it for you?"

"Since you didn't seem inclined to divulge details yestereve nor did you allow me to come along to witness the events for myself, I thought you might want to."

"You thought amiss," Gervase said, though he supposed the least he could do was entertain his sibling who had taken the time to spar with him that morning. He nodded toward the closest bench. "Let me hobble over there, then I'll tell all."

Joscelin followed him, then sat with the ease of a man who hadn't spent a trio of months in bed, reflecting on the sight of his thigh bone protruding through his flesh. "Do tell."

Gervase blew out his breath and glanced heavenward. "I suppose the only mercy was that the front door was shut when he left me in the dirt."

"No windows, then?"

"Oh, several," Gervase said, shooting him a cross look, "which I imagine you already know. I suspect the entire household was standing with noses pressed up against the glass, breathlessly privy to the spectacle."

"No doubt," Joscelin said cheerfully. "Was there spirited speech involved?"

"Aye, when he accused his sister of potentially spending her time languishing in my bed," Gervase said grimly.

Joscelin's smile disappeared abruptly. "Surely not. What did you do?"

"I attempted to knock most of his teeth out of his damned head."

"Well," Joscelin said, "there is that. Then what? How long did you keep hold of your sword?"

"Sword?" Gervase asked sourly.

"Hmmm," Joscelin said, rubbing his hand over his mouth as if he strove not to give vent to several supportive curses. "How long did you keep your feet, then?"

"Is it possible to measure such a brief space of time?"

Joscelin winced. "There is no denying that he is formidable."

"And I am not."

"Perhaps you forget the outcome of the last time you faced him over blades."

"I haven't," Gervase said, "nor, I suspect, has he. That no doubt led him to feeling a keener need to exact revenge than he might have otherwise. Or it could be simply that he's a complete ass."

Joscelin smiled. "There is that."

Only Gervase knew that at least when it came to the matter of his sister, Nicholas de Piaget had acted in exactly the way he himself would have behaved in similar straits. Indeed, he would have been surprised by anything else. They had thought Isabelle had perished. To have her resurface after having spent three se'nnights in the castle of a man with a less-than-pristine reputation . . . well, Nicholas's reaction was completely understandable.

Of course, it wasn't unthinkable that when Nicholas had clapped eyes on him, he had been immediately reminded of a former humiliation or two. Gervase supposed it was unkind to savour the memory of Nicholas de Piaget on his knees in the mud before him, but given that he'd recently been there himself, perhaps a bit of savouring was called for.

He enjoyed those happy memories for a bit before he realized he had no choice but to face the truth. He looked at his brother. "Her sire will never give her to me."

"Then give up."

Gervase blinked, then felt something stir within him. It might have been porridge from earlier—Cook had been particularly full of scowls for him over the past two days—or it might have been something else entirely. He frowned.

"Do you think she finds me—"

Joscelin held up his hand. "If you ask me to list your desirable qualities for potential consumption by the incomparable Lady

Isabelle of Artane, I will kill myself to spare my poor stomach the ache it would otherwise suffer. *I* wouldn't want you—"

"Thank heavens—"

"But I'm also not a wench. How she finds you, I wouldn't begin to speculate. Perhaps she's seen all your bad habits and is overjoyed to be rid of your grumbling self."

"I have no bad habits."

"Besides a terrible propensity to want everyone around you to be happy with their lot in life and an utter inability to endure insufferable noblemen bent on filling your ears with gossip, nay I suppose you don't."

Gervase dragged his sleeve across his forehead. "I have no patience for things our Father delighted in. I would much rather be on the field, allowing my sword to do my talking for me."

"Then why don't you do that?"

"And leave the running of the castle to whom?" Gervase asked wearily. "You?"

Joscelin laughed. "Of course not. The thought boggles the mind. I wasn't suggesting you relinquish the title. I'm merely suggesting that you make it yours instead of endlessly fretting over the fact that you are not Father. Thankfully."

"I do not endlessly fret."

"Is that why you're wringing your hands now?"

Gervase realized he was rubbing his right hand with his left, but it hardly had anything to do with fretting. He glared at his brother who only rose and walked away, laughing with more enthusiasm than Gervase appreciated.

He did not fret.

He paced, when necessary, and he wasn't above drawing back, examining the battlefield, when prudent, but he most certainly didn't wring his hands like a fretful alewife. Isabelle de Piaget would be fortunate to have a man such as he—

He muttered several strengthening curses under his breath. Isabelle de Piaget was perfection embodied and he would be damned fortunate if she deigned to look at him again.

Which was all the more reason to be about the business of seeing if she couldn't be convinced to do just that.

He rose, resheathed his sword almost without flinching, then strode back to the house for all of a dozen paces before he had to slow down to catch his breath. Damnation, he was more weary than he should have been. But, as Joscelin would have pointed out, he wasn't puking from the simple exertion of rising from his bed, so perhaps he would take what victories were his and be grateful for them. He would also be grateful for a hot fire and a decently comfortable chair in front of that fire in which to plan his strategy.

He shut himself inside his solar, happy to see there were no others with the same idea. He then paced—not fretfully—because that's what he did when about a hearty think.

He found himself standing over his chessboard without really knowing how long he'd been there. The pieces were all in their proper places for the start of battle, but he could see clearly enough the ending of several games from a pair of days before. If Isabelle had learned to play from her father, that didn't bode particularly well for him unless he took the time and trouble to think two moves ahead of her at all times.

He continued on his path about the chamber and paused by his table. The stack of sheaves was still there, but he had removed and locked in his trunk the offending sheet that had sent him careening into Nicholas of Beauvois's muddy court-yard. He continued to pace restlessly. He should have been at peace knowing that Isabelle was safe and that he had time and means to determine who it was who wanted him dead, but he found himself less satisfied with the situation than he suspected he would be.

Would that damned Nicholas de Piaget keep her safe?

He cursed himself and paced a bit more before he found himself sitting at his table, quill in hand. He penned a brief missive to the lord of Beauvois, digging deep for polite phrases that made his teeth ache to write down. He supposed that if he ever wanted to see the delightful Lady Isabelle of Artane again, he had to flatter her brother. What he wanted to do was flatten her brother, but he didn't think that would aid him any in his desires to have the man look on him with favor.

His hand ached from placing it ungently against Nicholas's face. His only regret was that he hadn't heard anything break. The whoreson deserved it for what he'd said to his sister—

Gervase took a deep breath, blew on the ink to dry it, then searched for sealing wax. It took him a moment or two to find it, jumbled as it was in the bottom of his trunk. He pulled it out, then cursed. Someone—Fabien, no doubt—had obviously been nosing about in things that didn't belong to him. His brother was actually quite clever, but if he colored one more damn thing that should have remained untouched, Gervase was going to take a switch to him. He looked for other uncolored wax, but could find nothing. Red would unfortunately have to do. He rolled his eyes, affixed his seal to the missive, then shoved the tools of composition back into his trunk. Then all that was left was for him to pace a bit more and fret—er, consider in a measured and sensible way his own tangle.

He almost paced into the edge of his open door before he realized his brother Joscelin was standing there, watching him.

"May I come in?" Joscelin asked politely.

"Well, you're halfway inside as it is," Gervase said with a curse. "You may as well come fully inside and torment me a bit more."

Joscelin entered, then shut the door quietly behind him. Gervase would have ignored him, but he had an expression on his face that bespoke serious thought indeed. He waited until his brother had made himself comfortable in front of the fire before he put his hands on the back of his own chair and looked at him.

"What?"

Joscelin looked at him seriously. "What do you remember of the day?"

It took Gervase a moment or two to determine which day Joscelin was talking about. "The day I was wounded?"

"Aye."

"Nothing but the usual. Why do you ask?"

"Just curious."

"Curiosity is a dangerous indulgence," Gervase said. He paced for a moment or two, then found himself back behind his chair. He looked at Joscelin and felt as if he'd never seen him before. Joscelin had a fair hand, didn't he? What if—

He looked at his brother sharply.

"Why are you asking that now?" he demanded.

Joscelin looked at him in surprise. "Why not?"

"Because 'tis a rather curious thing to wonder, don't you think?"

Joscelin returned his look for a moment or two blankly, then his mouth fell open. "You can't believe I did this to you."

"I'm not sure what to believe."

Joscelin looked neither offended nor incensed. He looked as

if Gervase had taken a blade and stabbed him in the heart. "You cannot believe that. Not in truth."

Gervase rubbed his hands over his face, prayed for a return of good sense, then walked around to collapse in his chair. "Of course I don't think you're responsible." He sighed deeply. "Why do you ask?"

"I've been thinking about Isabelle."

"Don't."

A smile played around Joscelin's mouth. "Possessive, aren't you?"

"Actually, I am," Gervase said shortly. "But go on. You were thinking about Isabelle in a purely brotherly, platonic, safe-for-your-sweet-neck sort of way. And?"

"I wondered if since her memory was so damaged, you might be missing a few things in yours, as well. That led me to wonder just what you might be missing. What's the last thing you remember?"

Gervase looked off into the fire. The whole thing was shrouded in a bit of fog, actually, with only brief glimpses of events being visible. It had been as the harvest was hard upon them and he had been meeting with his *prévôt* to assess the state of his fields. He remembered standing there in the crisp autumn chill at sunrise, calculating how much of his winter crop he could possibly get planted before the weather turned nasty. The next thing he remembered was standing at the door of his hall, watching the smoke curl up into the sky from the direction of his stables. He also remembered turning back into a smoke-filled great hall, thinking only that he had to get his people out of the bloody place before it turned into an inferno . . .

He remembered waking in his bed with Master Paquier standing over him, prepared to clout him again to apparently render him senseless so they could splint his leg. He wasn't entirely sure he hadn't begged Guy to do the deed to make certain 'twas done properly.

He shrugged. "I remember the same things as before. Fires. Hearing the hall collapse only to realize that was my leg snapping in two."

Joscelin considered his hands for a moment or two, then looked up. "I wonder, Ger, who it was that shot that bolt at you."

"And I haven't?" Gervase asked sharply. "I've watched every

bloody soul in the keep for the past four months, trying to determine who might want me dead. The list is long. The list that encompasses the rest of France is much longer."

Joscelin leaned his head back against his chair. "No doubt."

"Do *you* want me dead?"

Joscelin smiled. "Occasionally."

"I was too kind to you in your youth," Gervase muttered.

"Actually, Ger," Joscelin said mildly, "you were in truth the only thing that saved me from a life spent endlessly seeking to suck the closest ale spigot dry. 'Tis for damned sure both my mother and our father came close to driving me to it."

"Flatterer," Gervase managed.

Joscelin leaned forward with his elbows on his knees. "I'm in earnest about the other. The oddities surrounding your brush with death, I mean. You aren't the only one who's been watching the comings and goings inside the hall. Who set the stables on fire? Or the hall? Who was such a poor shot with a bow that he hit your leg instead of your heart? I should have thought you would have attracted a more skilled sort of assassin."

Gervase looked at his brother darkly. "Your humor is misplaced."

"But my ability to smell unpleasant stenches is something you continue to appreciate." His expression was very serious. "I've thought about what you said this morning, that Lord Rhys will not give Isabelle to you. It occurred to me that such might be a boon—perhaps he would consider me a less objectionable match for her than you—but then I realized that he won't give her to either of us if there is a murderer still walking about freely."

Gervase shut his mouth when he realized it was hanging open. "She doesn't love you."

"Perhaps with enough time—nay, stop looking at me that way." Joscelin laughed a little. "I'm merely provoking you for the sport of it. As for the other, I was just thinking. But that's what I do too much of, probably."

Gervase looked at his brother for several minutes in silence, then sighed and rose. He fetched a particular sheaf of parchment out of his trunk, handed it to Joscelin, then resumed his seat. He watched Joscelin read it, then waited for his brother to look at him.

"Well."

Gervase shrugged lightly. "Apparently that I continue to breathe still annoys someone."

Joscelin let out a low whistle. "I think perhaps it was worth the trouble to take your lady back to her brother's hall."

"I have to agree."

Joscelin studied the brief missive for another moment or two, then handed it back. "Where did you find this?"

"Amongst the accounts."

"Here in your solar?" Joscelin asked incredulously.

"So it would seem. A very fair hand, isn't it?"

Joscelin looked at him sharply. "You don't think Isabelle wrote this."

"The thought did cross my mind," Gervase said slowly, "but it continued on just as quickly. I can imagine her brother having written it, but not her."

"I think Lord Nicholas would prefer to murder you out in the open where everyone can watch," Joscelin said easily. "But since I'm not convinced our mystery lad shares that sentiment, perhaps you shouldn't be off anywhere by yourself."

"Aye, more than likely," Gervase said wearily.

"Perhaps the little lads should have a guard as well."

Gervase found himself slightly more winded than he should have been. "That hadn't occurred to me."

"You have other things to think on. I'll see to the lads."

Gervase closed his eyes briefly, then looked at his brother. He wasn't sure when it was that he'd known that that man sitting there was worthy of his trust. A hundred different things over more years than he wanted to count. He took a deep breath.

"Thank you, Joscelin. For more than just this."

Joscelin smiled. "Don't be daft. You rescued me at twelve and made me into a man. 'Tis I who am grateful."

Gervase nodded, because to say anything else would have left him sobbing onto his brother's neck, maudlin fool that he was. He cleared his throat roughly.

"I'll solve this quickly."

"Have plans for a certain miss, do you?"

"Assuredly."

"Her father will never let you have her," Joscelin said, stretching lazily. "As I suggested before, I'm a much better choice."

"You could only hope to aspire to such as she," Gervase said with a snort. He rubbed his hands together purposefully. "My plan is to first woo her brother with my undeniably charming self, then I'll turn to the girl herself."

"Impossible," Joscelin said.

"My favorite sort of thing."

"The idea is more impossible than your usual sort of thing."

Gervase smiled. "Hence my boundless enthusiasm for the thought."

"I don't think she likes you at all."

"I can be irresistible."

Joscelin laughed a little. "I won't list the women who would disagree. I'd hate to be the reason you crawled back in your bed and pulled the blankets over your head."

Gervase would have thrown something at his younger brother, but he had nothing to hand save a missive he supposed would be foolhardy to consign to the fire. He rose, locked it back in his trunk, then resumed his seat. He was fully prepared to close his eyes and have a nap but he was interrupted by a knock on the door. Hoping it wasn't anyone plotting his death, he called for them to enter. His brother Guy presented himself to him in front of the fire.

"Brother," he said gravely.

Gervase looked up at Guy who stood there, eminently capable and always willing to do what Gervase hadn't been able to, for whatever reason. "Joining us for the pleasure of it?" he asked politely.

"I thought I would," Guy said, just as politely. "Anything interesting on the verbal fire?"

"Nothing much," Joscelin said, yawning. "Just discussing Gervase's unsavoury reputation amongst the ladies of the court. What are you about?"

Gervase watched his brothers discussing matters of the estate and wondered about the two of them. It was no secret that Joscelin didn't care for Guy, but Gervase had never wanted to know the details. He had assumed it was simply the usual animosity that sometimes developed between brothers so close in age. He'd never suffered overmuch from that simply because he'd never truly felt a part of his father's second family. His stepmother had seen to that—

He rose because his leg was starting to stiffen, not because he wanted to escape thoughts that didn't serve him. He walked over to his desk and retrieved the missive he'd written to Nicholas of Beauvois. He considered, then walked over and sat back down. He looked up at Guy.

"Would you be interested in a bit of a ride tomorrow?"

"To where?" Guy asked.

"Beauvois."

Guy raised an eyebrow. "Interesting destination."

"I'm trying to make certain Nicholas doesn't send a small army after me for putting his sister to work scrubbing my floors," Gervase said.

"Which was *your* idea, Guy," Joscelin said pointedly, "if I remember it aright."

"How was I to know who she was?" Guy asked with a shrug. "Terribly pretty for a scullery maid, but not particularly memorable. Besides, we were preparing for Coucy's arrival. I was distracted." He held out his hand. "I'll happily take it for you, brother. I hear Lord Nicholas sets a very fine table."

"May you have great success in finding yourself seated at it," Gervase said. "The saints know I'll never manage it."

"I might leave now," Guy said thoughtfully. "There are a few decent inns along the route, I believe."

Gervase imagined there were and suspected that Guy knew them all. For all his ill-hidden desires to be lord of the manor, he spent an appalling amount of time roaming the countryside. Then again, what else was he to do? He wasn't particularly fond of the sword and wasn't interested in tourneying. That left him either loitering at noble tables or loitering at less noble tables. Gervase had little use for either, but he couldn't expect everyone to have his sensibilities.

He watched Guy leave the solar, then looked at Joscelin. His younger brother was simply regarding him steadily.

"I don't think I like what you're thinking."

Joscelin smiled very faintly. "And what am I thinking?"

"Whatever it is, I don't like it."

"Don't like it, then. But I believe I'll spend more time guarding your back than usual. And perhaps 'tis best that you leave your Isabelle safely tucked away at her brother's keep—"

"Damn it," Gervase said, pushing himself to his feet. "I mean to send something for her."

Joscelin laughed. "What? A sword to use on you the next time she sees you?"

"Something useful," Gervase said pointedly. "Something she'll enjoy."

"Do you know her well enough to know what she'll enjoy?"

Gervase slammed the door shut on his brother's laughter, then supposed Joscelin had a point. He had an idea what he would send, but he had to admit he had no idea whether or not she would enjoy it. He stood in the passageway and dithered, then realized his guardsmen were looking at him as if he'd lost his wits.

"I'm thinking," he explained.

They said nothing, but he supposed they didn't have to. He fretted a bit longer about his choice, then sent one of the lads after Guy.

He chose a different direction, but made equal haste.

Chapter 15

Isabelle paced restlessly through the courtyard, trying to ignore the half dozen guardsmen who trailed along behind her. She had had her share of lads looking after her at Artane, of course, but she had never chafed at the sight as Amanda had, endlessly. She supposed she could safely say that for the first time, she understood why her sister had complained so bitterly. It was difficult to think with a handful of men at one's heels, swords clanking, gear creaking, mouths muttering about her choice of paths. But she could no longer sit inside and worry. Miles knew she needed to be on her way, but damn Nicholas if he hadn't kept her brother so busy with foolish things that Miles had been helpless to do anything but acquiesce.

That enforced waiting had unfortunately given her too much time to contemplate what Gervase might or might not be doing. She had neither seen nor heard from him in the past pair of days, but perhaps she couldn't have expected anything else. He had likely trotted homeward, thrilled to be rid of her and her annoying relations. She couldn't say she blamed him. She would have happily been rid of an annoying relation or two herself.

She paused and looked at the steps leading up to the hall

door where her primary annoyance stood, looking as if he planned to insist that she come back inside. She scowled at him, lest he think she was interested in any conversation with him, then looked about for an escape. She found it in the commotion at the front gates.

A group of lads wearing Monsaert's colors were being allowed inside.

She started forward only to find herself thwarted in her desire by her guardsmen who closed in around her and prevented her from moving. She was tempted to relieve one of them of his blade and use it to prod the whole lot of them out of her way, but thought better of it almost immediately. It wouldn't do to look as if she had been breathlessly awaiting Gervase's return to her brother's keep.

She instead took a pair of cleansing breaths, then leaned up on her toes and peered between the shoulders of the men standing in front of her. She was fully prepared to see Gervase wearing a look of determination or sporting an intimidating frown.

Only it wasn't Gervase who was currently dismounting.

It was Guy.

She was surprised enough by the sight that she drew back behind her guardsmen to consider what it might mean. The first thing that occurred to her was that something had happened to Gervase. She looked again, but there was no indication on Guy's face that anything was amiss. He was simply handing off his reins to a stable lad and calmly taking off his gloves. Monsaert was obviously not under siege. But if that were the case, why was Guy in her brother's courtyard?

It took some effort, but she managed to leave her guardsmen with no choice but to inch their way toward the stairs as well. She supposed they must have looked absolutely ridiculous, six men surrounding one woman, moving along in a herd, but what else was she to do? If she relied on her brother to repeat the conversation accurately, she would never know details she most definitely wanted. Nicholas sauntered down the stairs and waited for Guy to approach.

"Why are you here?" Nicholas asked bluntly.

Guy made him a very low bow. "A pleasant visit, my lord, nothing more."

"Ah, well," Nicholas said, thawing slightly. "I suppose I have no reason not to allow it."

"Very gracious, my lord. I understand very well how fortunate I am to be allowed inside your very fine gates."

Isabelle ignored the pointed look her brother sent her way and concentrated on the nauseating conversation that continued on in front of her. She wondered if Guy could possibly be in earnest with all those flowery sentiments or if he were merely dredging them up to repair Gervase's relationship with her brother. She had to concede that he was very good at flattery.

She suspected Gervase would have plowed his fist into Nicholas's nose before he said anything polite to him.

"My brother?" Guy indulged in a small shrug. "He has a different way of seeing to his affairs. I'm not being critical, of course. We just don't see our responsibilities in the same way."

She blinked. What in the hell was Guy of Monsaert doing? Attempting to flatter Nicholas into allowing Gervase back inside his gates or stabbing his brother in the back? She listened to him continue to praise her brother's fine qualities whilst denigrating his own brother's and found herself reminded sharply of every single father who had come to Artane attempting to have a glance at Artane's fairest daughter, Amanda.

She pursed her lips. Obviously Guy was no less susceptible to the lure of rank than anyone else she knew. At least her brothers didn't seem to suffer overmuch from that sort of envy. Then again, her father had ample to share with his sons and made no secret of his intention to gift them everything possible, so perhaps they were more fortunate than other lads in their straits. She honestly had no idea what Gervase intended to do with his legacy. Perhaps Guy feared he would never manage to have anything for himself unless he fought for it.

"Come inside, Lord Guy," Nicholas said expansively. "We were just sitting down to a meal. Surely you'll stay."

"I hesitate to impose," Guy said, with a small bow, "but I cannot refuse such a gracious offer. I won't make it a long visit, though. I am unfortunately only here on my way to see to other things."

Which made Isabelle wonder where he had spent the night in order to have such an early arrival at Beauvois.

"Diligent, aren't you?" Nicholas asked.

"One does what one must," Guy said humbly.

More nauseating pleasantries ensued as they made their way up the stairs and into the hall. Isabelle had thought she had no opinion of Guy past knowing he was Gervase's brother, but she found herself forming one rather quickly. If the fawning went on much longer, she might take a sword to both him and Nicholas sooner rather than later.

She was allowed out of the encircling presence of her brother's men, finally. She climbed a pair of steps, then turned and looked at the lads who had kept her safe—if it could be looked at in the right way—that morning.

"Thank you," she said simply. "I'm grateful for your care."

And then she tried one of Amanda's smiles.

A pair of the men stumbled backward. She was pleased to see that all but one of them looked as if they'd taken a friendly fist to their ribs. She supposed the lad who remained unaffected would be the one to report most thoroughly on her activities, so she took note of his identity and promised herself a good think on how she might win him to her side eventually. Then she turned to trudge up the rest of the stairs into the great hall.

What she wanted to do was get close enough to Guy to find out what Gervase was doing, but she was obviously not going to manage that. Nicholas put her as far away from Guy as the number of diners allowed. Obviously she was going to have to count on Miles to tell her later what had been said. She managed to catch Guy's eye once or twice, but he only smiled and went back to his conversation with her brother.

"Are you certain you won't stay the day, at least?" Nicholas asked politely.

Guy shook his head and rose with Nicholas. "'Tis with great regret that I must forgo that delight," he said, making Nicholas a low bow. "Perhaps another time?"

"Of course," Nicholas said, sounding as if he contemplated that loss with great regret.

She had the feeling he wouldn't be so generous to anyone else from Monsaert who might find himself inside the hall.

"I assume your elder brother is still breathing?" Nicholas asked, sounding as if he would have been thrilled to have heard that such was not the case.

"When last I saw him." Guy started across the hall with Nicholas, then paused suddenly. "I almost forgot. I have a small token for your sister, if that isn't too forward. From those at Monsaert."

"From Monsaert's lord?" Nicholas asked sharply.

"Nay, my lord Nicholas," Guy said carefully. "Not precisely."

"Oh," Nicholas said, relaxing. "I see. Very well, then."

Isabelle looked at Guy as he walked toward her. His mother must have had light hair for he was almost as blond as Nicholas was. Perhaps if she had seen him first, she might have thought him very handsome, indeed. He resembled Gervase enough that she might have wondered if they were brothers, but she had to acknowledge that he simply wasn't as handsome as his elder brother.

She could see he was speaking, but she was having a difficult time hearing what he was saying. It was some long-winded tale about a missive that had somehow been stolen as he'd been overcome by ruffians along the road—

"Ruffians?" she asked in surprise.

Guy shrugged. "Not much trouble to anything but my purse. I did manage to save the most important part of what you were to have." He held out a little sachet fashioned of linen, then made her a small bow. "For your garden, my lady."

She took it, though not particularly willingly.

"I know how herbs please you," he said with another smile. "I thought perhaps a small token of our esteem and regard might be called for."

Isabelle sniffed. "What is it?"

"Lavender, I believe." He smiled deprecatingly. "For all I know about it, yes?"

"Very kind," Isabelle said.

He took her hand and bent low over it, then straightened and walked with Nicholas to the door. Isabelle stood next to Miles and fought the urge to scrub her hand on the back of her skirts. She glanced at her brother, but he was merely watching Guy with a pleasant expression on his face. She frowned. Perhaps she was overreacting.

Perhaps she was suffering disappointment that it had been Guy to come through her brother's gates and not someone else.

She wished, quite abruptly, that Nicholas would stop talking and escort Guy out the door. She fixed a smile to her face until the door was shut and she could turn her back on the spectacle.

She blew out her breath. "That's over, thankfully."

Miles looked at her in surprise. "What do you mean?"

She rubbed her hands, realizing as she did so that it wasn't going to do anything to erase the memory of having Guy touch her. "I'm not sure," she said uncomfortably. She looked at her brother. "Things bother me."

"What sorts of things?"

"I'm not sure where to begin."

"I'm all ears and no mouth, if that eases you."

"As always." She smiled up at him. "How would I survive without you?"

He smiled. "Poorly, I'm sure. So, tell me what troubles you."

She considered, then supposed there was no reason not to speak freely. Heaven knew she'd never minced words with him before. She blew out her breath. "He bothers me."

"Lord Guy?" Miles asked in surprise. "Why?"

She shrugged helplessly. "I don't trust him."

"Iz, far be it from me to gainsay you or disagree with your womanly instincts," Miles said slowly, "but you should know that Guy de Seger is above reproach. He has a reputation for honesty and fairness that is unmatched in all of France and half of England. I understand that he kept Monsaert running for Gervase without drawing attention to himself and has stepped back just as readily as Gervase has been able to resume his duties. He is without peer."

"Then why does my skin crawl when he touches my hand?"

"You're in love with his brother?"

She decided to ignore that. "Why did he bring me a gift?"

Miles started to speak, then shut his mouth for a moment or two. "I don't know," he said finally. "Perhaps it was from all of them—didn't he say as much?"

"He said he brought greetings from them, not gifts."

"Well," he said slowly, "it isn't as if Gervase could send you anything, now, is it?"

"Are you being helpful?"

Miles smiled faintly. "Iz, the good Duke of Monsaert isn't going to attempt to ingratiate himself with you until he's managed to soothe your brother's murderous rage. He certainly would have done himself no favors by sending you a gift without having first sent all manner of things to Nicholas. Fawning missives, rare foodstuffs, perhaps even a horse or two. That sort of thing."

She started to ask why Gervase hadn't done just that, but it occurred to her that perhaps he hadn't wanted to do just that.

Perhaps he had no intention of ingratiating himself with her brother because he had no desire to see her again.

She supposed her thoughts must have been readily apparent to Miles because he hugged her briefly, then ran his hand over her hair instead of making a mess of it.

"Gervase is biding his time," he offered. "I'm sure of it."

She wasn't, but there was no point in saying as much.

"Lavender is an interesting choice."

"Considering we're surrounded by fields of it," she said darkly, "perhaps not so unique."

"You can put it in a trunk and have your gear smell pretty. I even don't mind the smell. See?" He took the sachet from her, breathed deeply, then froze.

"Is it poisoned?" she asked grimly.

He considered what he held in his hand, then held it out to her. "I'm not sure I would call it poisoned. You take a whiff and tell me what you think."

She took the seeds and sniffed cautiously, then felt the same sort of stillness descend on her that had recently taken Miles in its grip. She looked at what she held in her hand for another moment or two before she looked at her brother.

"Perhaps our noses are deceiving us."

"Perhaps they aren't."

She took him by the arm and pulled him toward the hall door. "There's one way to know for sure."

He stopped her before she walked out into the morning mist. He opened the door slightly, peered out, and was still for quite some time before he nodded.

"He's gone."

"I thought you liked him."

Miles shot her a look, then opened the door for her. She supposed that was answer enough. She walked outside and into Nicholas who was looking as if he might be tempted to make a long list of Guy's virtues.

"What a lovely visit—wait." Isabelle cocked an ear toward the hall. "I think I hear Jennifer calling."

"What!"

Isabelle stepped aside as her brother bolted into his hall, then smiled pleasantly at her next oldest brother. "One annoyance seen to. Let's discover the truth about another one."

Miles tsk-tsked her. "That was unkind."

"So was making me sit through a meal with Guy de Seger."

"You don't like him at all, do you?" Miles asked, sounding amused. "The poor man has done nothing but bring you something he no doubt thought you would like merely as a gesture of friendship. Why that bothers you so much, I don't know."

She didn't know, either, but there was little point in saying as much. Perhaps perfection bothered her. She preferred men who laughed heartily, swore with enthusiasm, and appreciated irony. She considered that all the way across the courtyard before she had her answer. She looked up at her brother.

"When he smiles, his smile doesn't reach his eyes."

Miles opened his mouth to speak, then apparently thought better of it. "You're right."

She was, and she enjoyed that until she was standing in front of Nicholas's surgeon. She had little familiarity with the man, to be sure, but his small house was filled with wholesome scents and he had bunches of herbs hanging from the beams in his ceiling. Something else was simmering over his fire. She wasn't entirely sure that he didn't have bits of herbs in his hair as well. Obviously here was a man who knew his business. She greeted him politely, then held out Guy's sachet.

"Can you tell me, good sir, what these are?"

He sniffed, then spilled a few of the seeds out into his hand. He poked at them, sniffed again, then tasted a pair of them. He handed her back the sachet. "I believe, my lady, that they are *myosotis*."

"I'm unfamiliar with that," she admitted. "Has it any use besides adorning a garden?"

"I understand that Abbess Hildegard used it as the means of curing pains in the head," he offered.

"But does it have a common name?" she pressed. "Perhaps what the peasants here might call it?"

"I've heard it called *ne-m'oubliez–pas,* my lady. It is a very common flower, to be sure, and apart from its properties in curing pains in the head, I know of no great use for it." He considered the seeds, then smiled. "I suppose one must admit the name is quite charming."

Isabelle closed her eyes briefly. *Forget-me-not.*

She thanked the healer, then took her brother by the arm and pulled him from the house. He came without protest, or at least he did until he had pulled the door shut behind them.

"Care to enlighten me?"

She smiled. "These are forget-me-nots."

He continued to look at her as if she'd lost what few wits remained her. "So?"

"Lord Miles! Lord Miles!"

Miles shot her a look. "Don't move."

She wasn't sure she could. She watched him walk off to speak with the breathless master of the hounds who had come running their way. She considered eavesdropping, but she was too distracted. All she could do was look at the seeds in her hand and think about what they were.

Forget-me-nots.

Common flowers, true, but the memory of when she'd first been given a handful of them was very clear. Gervase had come close to flinging them at her, true, but a man did not give a woman a fistful of flowers without some thought having gone into the plucking of them, did he? And no man with any sense would simply gather up a fistful of seeds, shove them into a linen bag, and hand that to a woman without having at least an inkling of what he was handing over, would he?

He wouldn't, which was why it made no sense for Guy to have given her seeds for herbs that were in truth flowers that he obviously knew nothing of as opposed to his brother who obviously knew quite a bit about what was growing in his garden.

Miles was suddenly standing in front of her, which made her jump a little in spite of herself. He was wearing absolutely no expression on his face, which she supposed said much about what he was thinking. He took her by the arm and drew her away from prying eyes. She couldn't imagine the midst of Nicholas's courtyard was a very private place to hold a parley, but they had certainly plotted together in less private places.

"I found the missive."

She frowned. "What missive?"

"*Your* missive," he said. "Well, parts of it, at least."

"I didn't know you had lost it," she said in surprise. "When were you going to tell me that?"

"After I found it. Here." He held out something that looked to her as if it had been thoroughly gnawed on by something, hopefully not by him.

"'Tis wet," she said, taking it gingerly. "That's disgusting, Miles."

"'Twas mauled by a hound."

She shot him a dark look. "I won't ask what it was doing in a place where that was possible."

"Very wise. Just read it."

She attempted to unfold the sheaf of parchment, but it was almost impossible. The seal was mostly intact, though it was sporting teeth marks as well. She pulled the seal free of the soggy parchment, then examined what of the paper was still unchewed.

Grandmère was all she could see.

She looked at her brother. "I suppose I'll need to rely on your memory for the words. I'm not sure the seal serves us, though, does it? What ruffian would be fool enough to identify his foul missive with his own mark?"

"Hopefully a very careless one, but perhaps we don't dare hope for that." He took the wax from her and frowned as he examined it. "'Tis a most unpleasant shade of red. I would say that it looks a little like blood, but I've no doubt been thinking too much."

Blood. She looked off into the courtyard for several minutes in silence, ignoring her brother's repeated clearing of his throat, and realized what had seemed so strange to her earlier. She was a little surprised she hadn't latched onto it immediately, but the truth was, she hadn't been herself. She turned to look at Miles. "He didn't look particularly assaulted, did he?"

Miles blinked. "Who?"

"Guy. He said he'd been overcome by ruffians this morning on his way here. But he had his sword, his boots, his gloves, and his horse."

"Perhaps he fought them off."

"He didn't look rumpled."

He studied her for a moment or two, then shook his head. "Izzy, he is beyond reproach."

"So you keep telling me, but I find it very curious that a man who was supposedly robbed earlier arrives with not only all his gear, but two guardsmen in tow—guardsmen I'll admit I had forgotten about until this very moment. I find it also strange that he should gift me seeds for a particular flower that his brother had thrown at me whilst I was at Monsaert, seeds that Guy thought were lavender."

Miles smiled faintly. "You must bother Gervase a great deal."

"I don't think he likes me."

"And you don't care for him, either."

She shook her head. "Too bossy. Unpleasant. Possessing a very stale and obviously unused chivalry."

"Which is why he planted his fist down Nick's throat for insulting you."

"Exactly." She patted his cheek. "If we made haste, we could be off in half an hour."

"Isabelle," he said with a sigh.

"You promised you would take me to Caours and you've made me wait two days to be on my way. I'm already packed."

"So am I," he admitted. "I'll see to the horses."

She walked inside the hall and saw Nicholas standing by the fire. Just the sight of him left her trotting off to her right with a bit more enthusiasm than she might have used otherwise.

"Where are you going?" Nicholas called.

"To fetch my saddlebag and make a journey," she said.

"I am not giving you permission to go anywhere!"

That didn't merit so much as a snort, so she didn't spare him the effort of a reply. She gained her bedchamber and began the hunt for a pair of hose she had filched from the mending pile at Monsaert. She ignored the pointed clearing of a brotherly throat from the vicinity of her doorway. It was more difficult to ignore him when he walked into her chamber and sat down wearily on her trunk. She folded her arms over her chest and prepared to tell him to go be about some sort of useful labor, but he looked so contemplative that she couldn't bring herself to say anything.

He studied his hands clasped between his knees for a moment or two, then looked up at her. "I realize you are no longer a child."

"The saints be praised for that."

He smiled faintly. "Izzy, I simply want you to have a husband worthy of you."

"I'm not looking for a husband," she said, motioning for him to get up off her trunk so she could rummage about inside it. "I'm going to visit Grandmère."

Why she had to visit her grandmother was something she was absolutely not going to discuss with him. The truth was, it was best that she be as far away from Beauvois as possible. Knowing that she might be the one to possibly put Jennifer in danger was something she just couldn't bring herself to think about.

"Why do I have this nagging feeling that you'll go to Caours by way of Monsaert?"

"My route is none of your business," she said. She shot him a look. "Besides, he doesn't want me."

"Oh, he wants you," Nicholas said grimly, leaning back against the wall. "Guy didn't make that journey this morning because it was his idea."

"Perhaps Guy was simply out for a pleasant ride."

Nicholas pursed his lips. "Believe that if you want to, but I know better. Gervase is going out of his way to earn my favor and he no doubt sent his least objectionable brother to do the dastardly deed for him. Trust me, Iz, he's not sending gifts and flatteries here because he's fond of me."

She stopped looking for lad's clothes in her trunk because she realized that she'd already put them in her saddlebag. She shut the lid and looked up at her brother. "Then you aren't opposed to him."

Nicholas scowled. "I didn't say that—"

"Your feelings just smart because he bested you with the sword."

"And the lance," Miles said from the doorway. "I shudder to think about other possibilities."

Nicholas glared at his younger brother. "I shudder to think of what will be left of you after I see you in the lists." He pushed away from the wall. "Let's go."

"Can't," Miles said cheerfully. "I have other things to do."

"Nay, you do not."

"He does," Isabelle said. "He's coming with me."

Nicholas shot her a look. "Nay, he is not and neither are you. Going anywhere, that is."

"You, Nicholas, are not my father."

"I am the oldest male relative in the vicinity and 'tis my responsibility to help you. I will help you now by telling you that you cannot simply arrive at a man's hall without a reason."

"She did before and look how well it went for her," Miles noted.

"Aye, he put her to work as a scullery maid!" He frowned fiercely. "You both continue to deny it, but that sinking feeling in my gut tells me you intend something untoward once you leave my gates. And heaven knows I have enough experience with watching you put your wee heads together to combine mischief to know when my gut is telling me the truth."

Miles only returned Nicholas's look steadily. Isabelle rose, then hugged her almost oldest brother before she pulled away and gave him what she hoped would be a reassuring smile.

"I want to see Grandmère, to assure her that I'm safe and sound. Miles is coming along to guard my back. That seems reasonable, doesn't it?"

"I'm not sure you want to know what I think about your ability to be reasonable," Nicholas said seriously. "I don't like this."

"I have my reasons," she assured him.

"I think I would like those even less, did I know what they were," he said grimly. He kissed her on both cheeks, then walked to her door. "I'll arrange a guard."

"Thank you, Nicky," she said quietly.

He paused, sighed, then shook his head and continued on. Isabelle waited until he had disappeared around the corner before she looked at Miles.

"Thank you for coming with me."

"I wouldn't think to do otherwise," he said. "Besides, I love a good mystery."

"I just wish it didn't involve people I love."

"Aye," he said quietly, "I know. I feel the same way." He picked up her saddlebags and started toward the door. "Say your good-byes to Jennifer, then meet me in the stables. I'll see to the rest."

She nodded, sat back down on her bed, and looked at the piece of sealing wax she still held in her hand. She supposed she would be wise to put it somewhere safe lest she lose it and lose any proof she might have had as to the identity of her correspondent.

It was odd, wasn't it, that someone would seal a missive with something that could have potentially identified him? She wasn't sure if it spoke more to that shadowy figure's arrogance or his willingness to take ridiculous chances. At the moment, she wasn't sure which would have been worse.

Well, the only thing she could do was present herself at

Caours and see what happened then. She had the feeling, knowing Miles as she did, that her brother would find a way to guard her without being seen. She would be safe enough.

She had to believe that. Anything else was simply too terrifying to contemplate.

She rose, then walked over to the window and looked out over the sea. Perhaps she was a fool to even consider going to Monsaert. She didn't want to admit Nicholas might have had it aright and Gervase would be appalled.

Then again, the man had sent her seeds for a particular sort of flower that he had once thrust in her face. It had been a message of some sort, of that she was certain.

She put her shoulders back and went to look for her cloak. She would stop at Monsaert because it wasn't completely out of the way. She would make sure that Gervase's brothers were attending to their studies and she would thank him for the gift of seeds he had obviously sent her way.

One last afternoon of pleasure before she went to her doom. Perhaps not even her enemy could begrudge her that.

Chapter 16

Gervase stood in his private garden and wished for nothing more than a good disaster to concentrate on. He was shaking with weariness, but had only his own form to blame for it. He supposed it could have been much worse. He could have been abed, wondering if he would ever walk again. That he was actually standing out in the mud instead of wallowing in it was perhaps the best he could hope for at present.

A pity there was no one there to see it. Guy had left for Beauvois well before dawn—indeed, Gervase wasn't certain he hadn't left in the middle of the night. As long as Nicholas de Piaget had that fawning missive in his hands before sunset, Gervase was content. Perhaps fortune would smile on him and he would manage to gain an audience with the man before the year had waned. He didn't suppose he would be fortunate enough to have Isabelle remain unwed until then, but there was always the consolation of battle to take refuge in.

Battle defined as his identifying whoever might have the cheek to seek Isabelle de Piaget's hand in marriage and doing the pestilence in.

The rest of his brothers were the saints only knew where.

Joscelin would have been useful to him as a sparring partner, but he had decamped for less unpleasant pastures earlier that day. His other brothers were being kept far away from the garden by Lucien, that canny lad with a nose for staying out of trouble. He had considered inviting one of his guardsmen into his private lair with him, but wasn't sure he could bear the looks of pity they wouldn't be able to hide. Nay, 'twas best that he do what he could to regain his strength while no one was watching.

He took a firmer grip, such as it was, on his sword and put himself again through exercises he would have used with a page. The mind-numbing boredom of it soon got the better of him and he resorted to feigning battle against the fiercest opponent he could imagine up for himself.

That lasted fairly well until he stepped backward, slipped, then caught himself heavily on his right leg. The pain was blinding—

He paused, then frowned. Actually, that was quite a bit less pain than he'd expected. He couldn't move, of course, and his leg quivered as fiercely as a score of bowstrings fluttering in tandem, but he wasn't on his knees. He leaned on his sword and forced himself to simply breathe in and out until his leg steadied beneath him.

"My lord?"

He almost fell over in surprise. He turned to look at his squire and almost went down in truth as his leg gave way beneath him. Of course, that could have been because it wasn't just his squire standing there, peering at him from around the hedge, looking as if he expected Gervase to take his sword and heave it through his chest. Isabelle de Piaget stood there as well, watching him with absolutely no expression on her face.

Her perfect, stunning face.

"Isabelle!"

She turned suddenly and was almost knocked over by Yves who threw himself at her. She caught him, pulled him up into her arms and suffered a pair of small arms wrapped around her neck, no doubt cutting off any hope of breath anytime soon. Gervase would have walked over to rescue her, but that was beyond him. It was all he could do to stand there and not swear viciously at the unstable nature of his right leg.

He suddenly had a shoulder within convenient reach. He was too damned grateful for the saving of what was left of his pride to even snarl at his savior. He simply put his hand on someone's shoulder—he realized it was Miles de Piaget standing there after he'd already clutched the man's cloak—then watched as a woman he'd never thought to see again gathered up his brothers and shepherded them back to the house.

She didn't look back at him.

He decided he would think about that later. He took refuge in a choice curse or two, then looked at Miles.

"What are you doing here?" he demanded.

Miles only looked at him as if not a damned thing in the world could disturb his tranquillity. "We're on our way to Caours and thought it might be wise to rest for a bit. I believe your page was preparing to tell you that we were at your gates. As you can see, your men were good enough to permit us entrance."

Gervase grunted, then looked at his page. "Cyon, I'll not shout at you for their cheek. You're safe enough."

Cyon only made him a low bow, then strode over and looked boldly at the whelp from Artane.

"I can see to my lord," he said firmly. "If you wish to retreat to the house and refresh yourself with a bit of wine."

Miles only inclined his head. "You do your lord credit," he said seriously, "and I am sure he appreciates your loyalty. I was thinking that perhaps since the day is so fine, I might see if he would ply a bit of his famous swordplay on me, though I am surely a much lesser swordsman."

Cyon put his shoulders back, looking particularly fierce. He shot Miles a warning look, then turned to Gervase. "Does that suit you, Your Grace, or shall I remain?"

Gervase had to fight a smile, which was a rare enough occurrence of late that he had to savor it for a moment or two. "I think, Cyon, that I might manage to see to this one for a few minutes. Perhaps we will require a bit of wine out here, if you would be willing to fetch it. No doubt Lord Miles will need something strengthening after his humiliation at my hands."

"As you will, my lord."

Gervase watched his page turn and walk briskly back to the hall, then looked at his crutch. Miles was only watching him with a faintly amused smile.

"Instilling their arrogance early?" he asked.

"It seems prudent," Gervase agreed. "Now, what are you doing here in truth?"

"We're on our way to our grandmother's abbey," he said, "and Isabelle thought it looked like rain. It seemed reasonable to seek a bit of shelter, don't you think?"

Gervase didn't have to look up to note that there wasn't a cloud in the bloody sky. He also tried not to notice that Miles didn't move even though they were standing there like two statues and he was gasping every time he even attempted to take a step. Miles put his hand finally on Gervase's shoulder, conveniently around his back, and nodded toward the closest bench.

"Long journey here," he said, "and I'm exhausted. Let's go sit."

Gervase couldn't do anything but nod. He managed to gain the bench, then stretch his leg out without howling. He tried not to notice, again, that Miles had fetched his sword for him and impaled it in the nearest flower bed. Gervase couldn't bring himself to speak. It took all his strength to rub his leg and attempt to work out the cramping there.

"I faced you once," Miles said without preamble. "Or tried to, rather. I doubt you remember it, considering I was just another in a very long line of young lads wanting to cross swords with you. I believe you said something to the effect of 'come back, whelp, when you know which end of your sword to grasp.'"

"That sounds like something I would have said," Gervase agreed. "Arrogant whoreson that I was."

"Oh, I wouldn't slight your current incarnation of yourself," Miles said. "I believe there's ample arrogance still inside you just biding its time."

Gervase shook his head. "I daren't hope for it." He continued to work on his leg until the cramping had subsided into simply feeling as if he'd torn his muscles afresh. He looked at Miles. "Why did you come?"

"It is as I said," Miles said with a shrug. "We're on our way to Caours."

"And Lord Nicholas allowed you to leave?"

"Isabelle can be very persuasive under the right circumstances," Miles said. "Which is actually rather unusual. She's accustomed to simply standing and being unobtrusive."

"So she said to me, though I don't believe it."

Miles smiled. "Was she not unobtrusive in your hall?"

"Let's just say she's hard to ignore."

"These are tales I must hear, but perhaps later after we've worked a bit more."

Gervase didn't want to admit that the thought of it left him wanting to make a hasty trip back to bed, so he simply shook his head. "In another minute or two, if you please. So, tell me, did your brother enjoy the missive I sent him or is he still planning my demise?"

Miles studied him for a moment or two. "Nick might have," he said slowly, "but your brother was apparently robbed of it on the way to Beauvois, so all my brother had to enjoy was Lord Guy's sparkling wit and unwholesome ability to spew out endless flatteries. And I say that in the gentlest way possible. Your brother's reputation for having honor beyond reproach extends endlessly in all directions."

"He is a paragon of all virtues," Gervase said, almost easily. Guy could scarce wield a sword to save his life, but considering that he himself was having trouble with the same thing, he thought it might be wise not to point that out. There was no reason to dislike his brother. That he sometimes had less than warm feelings for him said more about him than it did Guy, no doubt.

"My sister enjoyed the seeds Lord Guy brought for her."

"But—" Gervase shut his mouth around the protest. He looked at Miles carefully. "Guy brought her seeds?"

"Lavender, apparently, that turned out to be not lavender but some common flower called forget-me-not." Miles looked at him innocently. "I don't think your brother can tell the difference."

What Gervase thought was that Guy couldn't tell the difference between quite a few things, which began and ended with knowing when he should and shouldn't flatter a woman he was most certainly never going to—

He had to take a deep breath. He found that he was taking an appalling number of them when he thought about Isabelle de Piaget.

"Isabelle thought the seeds might have been from you instead and Guy merely misspoke."

"Why would I send her seeds?" Gervase said shortly.

Miles only studied him for a moment or two in silence, then pushed himself to his feet. "Let's go work for a bit."

"Are you daft?" Gervase said sharply. "I can scarce stand."

"It will be worse if you simply sit."

"And just what in the hell would *you* know about it?" Gervase snapped before he thought better of his tone.

"My brother's wife had her leg crushed by a stallion standing on it when she was a youth. I wasn't too stupid to take note of what was done to allow her to walk."

Gervase suppressed the urge to roll his eyes. "And what was that?"

"Bathing with herbs, then as much walking as she could bear. If it eases you any, I won't force you to put any sudden weight on that leg of yours. Consider it my gift for your not having killed me when I was a cheeky youth."

"And what are you now?"

"A lad who loves his sister and wants to see her happy. I think she might indulge in a brief sigh of regret if your sorry self were to be slain by my elder brother because you put his youngest sister to work in your kitchens."

Gervase considered. "Brief?"

"Very brief," Miles said. "You would miss it completely, I imagine, if you weren't listening intently for it."

"Well, let's not cause her any undue distress, however brief that distress might be."

Miles smiled. "I think my brother might actually like you if he weren't so determined to slay you." He nodded toward the bare patch of garden Gervase had already trampled. "Let's go, shall we?"

Gervase supposed when the invitation was extended so politely, he couldn't in good conscience refuse. He pushed himself to his feet and followed Miles to his makeshift training ground.

He hoped that excessive show of politeness wouldn't leave him unable to walk off the field.

An hour later, he was ready for a bath and a hasty trip to his bed. He limped back to the house with Miles, but didn't see either his brothers or their lovely keeper. He supposed he shouldn't have been surprised by that. The lads were no doubt wallowing in the sheer delightfulness of her presence and she had no doubt been more than happy to leave him to her brother's foul ministrations.

"Isabelle said you were paying her a gold sovereign per se'nnight for teaching your brothers their Latin," Miles remarked.

"She will beggar me," Gervase said wearily. "She's a ferocious bargainer."

"She intends to collect, I believe."

Gervase resheathed his sword, grateful that his hand only set up a brief protest, not an outright mutiny. "Are you here long enough for her to do that, do you suppose?"

There. That was just the right amount of disinterest in his tone. He didn't give a damn how long they stayed, of course, but if Isabelle was going to have her hand so fully in his purse, she might as well do something in return for the privilege. He supposed it didn't serve him to even entertain the thought that if gold was what it took to keep her in his hall, he was willing to part with a great amount of it.

"Just until the storm passes, I believe."

Gervase squinted up at the blue sky, then at his sparring partner. "That might take a day or two."

Miles didn't smile. "If you hurt her, I'll kill you and rob my brother of his sport."

Gervase closed his eyes briefly. "She deserves better than I can give her."

"Nick has already said as much."

"I'm unsurprised." He looked at Miles. "And you?"

"I'm withholding judgment. She seems to find you not completely without redeeming qualities. She also doesn't believe the tales of your conquests in the bedchamber."

"I think I should be offended," Gervase managed. "What of my conquests on the field?"

Miles clapped him on the shoulder. "Those, I believe, were never in dispute. If it gives you pleasure, know that my elder brother snarls about both." He smiled. "He doesn't like you at all."

"I called him names while he was on his knees in the mud in front of me," Gervase said. He paused. "Not very nice names, if memory serves."

Miles laughed a little. "I should hope not. He would have been terribly disappointed otherwise."

Gervase walked back to the hall with Isabelle's twin brother— unwholesome demon spawn that he was—and wondered where he might find that gel who had no doubt come to wring a bit of gold out of him while she was on her way to see her grandmère.

He had scarce gained the great hall before he was assaulted by several catastrophes all in an orderly line.

First was his steward telling him that despite their best efforts, the oats would not be as plentiful as hoped because some of their seed was missing. Gervase took a deep breath, prayed his horses would survive, and tried to get across the hall only to be intercepted by Sir Aubert with tidings about the garrison Gervase didn't want. He left his captain to sort things out, was momentarily placated by learning that Isabelle's guardsmen were back at their previous posts, then turned to servants who seemed to be making a bit of a commotion near the hearth. That, added to the collection of most of his brothers making an equal ruckus, left him leaving his patience behind him as he strode across the stone with as much enthusiasm as he could muster.

He realized Isabelle was in the midst of the chaos, obviously trying to keep his brothers at bay while about the task of ordering his servants about.

"His Grace will need a tub of hot water," she said to one of the kitchen lads, "as quick as may be. Aye, Yves, I will come and see to your sums in a moment. Cook, are there any healing herbs remaining, or shall I gather more?"

Gervase folded his arms over his chest and waited for someone to notice him. He knew he shouldn't have cared. 'Twas for damned sure he could not possibly have cared less about the running of his hall as long as he had food on the table and a marginally clean place to sleep. He had happily left all that rot to Guy. Who was this slip of a girl who thought to come into his hall and take over?

And why the hell wouldn't she look at him?

He cleared his throat but had exactly the reaction he'd been having all along, which was none at all. He had the feeling that opening his mouth was a very bad idea indeed, but apparently there was nothing left in his half-empty head but bad ideas because he couldn't seem to keep his thoughts to himself.

"I don't want a bath," he said curtly.

"But, Your Grace," Cook began slowly, "the lady Isabelle—"

"Isn't here to tell me when to bathe," he said.

It was possible he might have shouted it. He suspected that he had used a tone akin to what Yves favored when asked to do something his six-year-old self didn't particularly care to do. Very mature and reasonable. Gervase nodded to himself over that. Just the sort of way a man of a score and eight should speak when trying to impress a woman who was simply trying to care for him.

Silence descended. Well, silence save for the buzzing in his ears and what he was quite certain had been the whisper of Miles de Piaget's sword coming from its sheath. He glanced over his shoulder and found that that last bit at least had been nothing more than his imagination. Miles was simply watching him with the look a man wears when he's watching another man make a colossal ass of himself. Gervase felt fingers tangle in the neck of his tunic before he looked to see to whom those fingers might belong.

Isabelle tugged until he was leaning down where she could put her mouth against his ear.

It would have served him right, he supposed, if she'd bellowed at him loudly enough to deafen him. Instead, she merely whispered.

"If you have any sense at all," she murmured, "you will not make me look weak in front of your servants."

Make her look weak? It was all he could do not to leave her looking thoroughly kissed. He took a careful breath, then reached up and put his hand over hers.

By the saints, he was not at all himself.

"Of course," he said, just as quietly. "I apologize."

"Perhaps you should say that again," she said, her voice sending shivers down his spine. "More loudly this time."

She stepped back and waited. He cleared his throat and looked at the company gathered there, all watching him with assessing gazes. Well, save Cook who was watching him with a smirk.

"I spoke out of turn," he announced. "It shall of course be as the lady Isabelle wishes. The household is hers for as long as she graces us with her incomparable self."

Isabelle nodded regally to him, then proceeded to ignore him again.

He found a chair, found himself joined by her brother in the seat adjacent, and decided that perhaps the best way to pass the rest of the day was to simply sit and enjoy the sight of Rhys de Piaget's youngest daughter. Silently.

"She can't wield a sword, you know."

He looked at Miles. "Do you think not?"

"I'm not saying she wouldn't try," Miles said. "On you, as the case might be. But if she does, you might want to stay out of her way."

"Oh, I've already seen her try," Gervase said, then realized that perhaps the most dangerous thing about Miles de Piaget wasn't his swordplay, it was his ability to put a body at ease. He sighed. There was obviously no point in not being honest. Miles would find out the truth eventually anyway, no doubt through the same sort of nefarious means he was using at present. "She was defending herself against a man belonging to the Duke of Coucy. And before you ask, aye, she was laboring as a scullery maid because I was too stupid to realize who she was."

"Have you never seen my older sister or mother?"

"Neither, nor Isabelle. And I thought she was a lad."

"Any other confessions?"

"None that are fit for your ears."

Miles only lifted an eyebrow. "Then they obviously involve your poor heart, for which I pity you. My father will do serious damage to you, you know."

"Before or after your brother has a go?"

"Oh, I imagine both Robin and Nicholas will want a turn," Miles said with a lazy smile. "How much you have to look forward to. Ready to flee?"

Gervase would have answered, but he found himself distracted by the prize who was deep in discussion with Cook over what he supposed would be a perfectly edible supper. It would be a welcome change from the slop he'd been eating for the past three days.

Nay, he wasn't ready to flee.

Not at all.

Several hours later, he sat in his solar and for the first time in years—or ever, truth be told—enjoyed the sensation of being amongst family. Guy wasn't there, which for some reason left him feeling slightly guilty over enjoying his absence, but there it was. Too much perfection could be trying, to be sure.

Joscelin was there, as were all his other younger brothers. Miles de Piaget sat to his right, engaged in a spirited conversation with Fabien about whether it was more desirable to humiliate an opponent in chess quickly or with painful slowness.

Gervase couldn't bring himself to join any of the conversations. He was far too busy ignoring the woman sitting across from him who was just as busy ignoring him.

Yves, however, seemed not to have that problem. He was sitting in Isabelle's lap, wrapped in her arms that he'd pulled around himself. She was resting her cheek against his dark hair, a look of such peace on her face that Gervase felt his eyes begin to burn.

And then she opened her eyes and looked at him.

He wished he could have smiled. He was far too busy trying not to weep.

What his brothers had missed in not having a woman in the house. What they had missed by not having *that* woman in the hall, gracing it with her beauty, her smiles, her complete disregard for men with swords who could do her harm.

Though who would have ever considered such a thing, he couldn't imagine.

Miles had spent an hour during the afternoon entertaining him with tales of his sister and her brushes with would-be suitors who had come looking for Amanda. Gervase couldn't imagine it, but what did he know of Englishmen save he took particular satisfaction in humiliating those cheeky enough to challenge him at tourney? He'd been tempted to ask Miles for a list of those who had vexed Isabelle, but he supposed that list wouldn't have served him. It wasn't as if he could have seen to them properly at present.

Though for the first time in months, he felt some small bit of hope that he might manage it in the future. Perhaps it was the cumulative effects of Isabelle's weeds or perhaps the knowledge that winning her favor was the least of the thorns lying before him—the others being her father and brothers who would no doubt be salivating at the thought of taking a bit out of him. No man with any sense at all would give a beloved daughter to a man who couldn't protect her.

He thought he might have to double her guard and perhaps that with lads who were slightly less clean-scrubbed than the two who trailed after her at present.

"Isabelle?"

"Aye, Yves?"

"You're staying, aren't you?"

The chamber fell silent. Gervase didn't dare look at Isabelle to see her expression, so he made a serious study of the flames in the hearth.

"Well, I must go see my grandmother," Isabelle said slowly.

"But after that," Yves pressed. "You'll come home, won't you?"

It took her a ridiculously long time to answer, damn her anyway. And when she did, Gervase wanted to swear.

"I don't know, Yves," she said, as easily as if stabbing the lord of the hall directly in the heart was something she did half a dozen times each morning before she broke her fast. "I suppose someone has to teach you your sums, aye?"

"If I refuse to learn them, will you stay longer?"

Isabelle laughed, the heartless shrew. "We'll see, love."

Love. Gervase glanced at her because he was a bloody fool. He supposed he shouldn't have been surprised to find she was not looking at him but rather at his damned youngest brother who couldn't possibly realize what a treasure he was being embraced by. It was wicked to loathe a lad who was simply soaking up the love of an angel. Gervase was fairly convinced of that.

"You should be abed," Isabelle said, kissing Yves on the cheek. "As should I, which means I'll need to find somewhere to sleep."

Gervase cleared his throat. "She's right, lads. Off to bed." He looked at her and was appalled to find that actually meeting her eyes left him feeling as nervous as a cat in a stable of restless horses. "You'll take my chamber."

She considered, looking as if she were fully prepared to protest. Perhaps she thought she had pushed him as far as she dared that day. Perhaps she was simply weary from a long journey and too tired to argue. Whatever the reason, she simply nodded, put Yves off her lap, and then rose.

"We'll see you safely there," Lucien said. "Let's be off, lads."

Gervase caught Isabelle's hand as she passed him. He supposed it was the height of foolishness, but he had touched her before he thought better of it. He looked up at her.

"Thank you," he said quietly.

"For what?" she asked, tilting her head slightly.

"The list is long."

She squeezed his hand gently, then pulled away from him and herded his brothers out the door.

Silence fell. He resumed his study of the fire in the hearth until he thought he could look at the men who had remained in the chamber with him. He looked first at his brother Joscelin, then at Isabelle's brother Miles. They were both watching him with slight smiles. He glared at them both.

"What?" he demanded.

Joscelin looked at Miles. "Pitiful."

"Hopeless," Miles offered.

Gervase pushed himself to his feet. "I don't need the opinions of two lads without the wit to offer anything useful."

"Where are you off to?" Joscelin asked politely.

"To combine mischief of one sort or another," Gervase muttered. "I would suggest the both of you not be here when I return."

He walked to the door more steadily than he would have dared hope a month earlier. Perhaps those herbs had done him some good.

"Will your father allow him to have her, Miles, do you think?"

"You know, Joscelin, it won't matter. Your brother will be too dead to wed her after he's met my sire in the lists—"

Gervase pulled the door shut with a fair amount of enthusiasm so he didn't have to listen to their speculation any longer. It was likely less speculation than it was prediction, but he didn't care for that, either, so he tromped off down the passageway, looking for mischief to make.

Perhaps if he looked hard enough, he might find something to distract himself from the feel of Isabelle de Piaget's hand in his.

Poor fool that he was.

Chapter 17

Isabelle rose and wrapped a dressing gown around herself to ward off the bone-chilling cold in Gervase's chamber. She went to bring her fire back to life, but found there was no more wood to throw on it. She supposed if she'd had any sense, she would have gone back to bed, but she was cold. She also supposed it wouldn't hurt to admit that she was restless as well.

She wasn't sure what she'd expected at Monsaert when she'd arrived unannounced and uninvited. Watching Gervase train by himself in the garden had been heartbreaking. Surely he could have found someone to face him if he'd cared to. His former glory had been readily apparent and she couldn't help but grieve a bit for that. Not for herself, of course, but for him.

His brothers and convincing Cook to prepare something edible had taken up a good part of her afternoon, but during the evening she'd had nothing to do but hold his youngest brother and attempt to keep her heart from breaking over his unwillingness to let her go. She hadn't asked any of them about their mother, but it was obvious to her that she should be on her knees every day in gratitude for her own mother who had loved her so deeply.

She rubbed her arms and wished for something more substantial to wear. Even something more to toss on the fire would have been very welcome. Well, she could perhaps retreat safely to Gervase's solar and warm herself against his fire. Miles had delivered her gear to her and informed her that he would be bedding down in the solar that night so it wasn't as if she would be disturbing anyone important. No doubt her ever-present guardsmen would be standing outside her door, waiting to escort her wherever she wanted to go.

She opened the door, then froze. Well, there was someone there standing guard, but it wasn't one of her usual lads. The man standing against the opposite wall, his arms folded over his chest, happened to be the lord of the castle.

She would have popped right back in his bedchamber, but she'd already been spotted. She could have attempted to ignore him—she had, after all, done a damned fine job of it the day before—but that seemed a little silly given that they were the only ones in the passageway. Besides, she didn't suppose she wanted to ignore him. He was, after all, the reason she'd come to Monsaert. Even she couldn't lie to herself well enough to believe that she'd only come to conjugate Latin verbs.

She cleared her throat. "My lord."

Gervase inclined his head. "My lady."

She pulled her robe more closely around herself, not for any fears over her modesty but because she was cold. Or too warm. At the moment, she honestly couldn't tell which it was. She had forgotten, somehow, in that short time she'd been at Beauvois just how appallingly handsome Monsaert's lord was. Perhaps Nicholas had it aright and the man had ravished every woman he'd ever clapped eyes on. All she could say was she could see how it was possible. She settled for simply leaning against her doorframe and looking at him.

Rogue that he was.

She thought she might have a bit of sympathy for the women he'd been roguish with.

"Did you need something out of your bedchamber?" she asked.

He shook his head.

She waited, but he seemed disinclined to volunteer anything. She frowned. "Then why are you here?"

"I thought you needed to have your door guarded."

"My door?"

He smiled faintly. "You, Isabelle," he clarified, "not your door. I thought you needed to have yourself guarded."

'Twas ridiculous, of course, to be so affected by the sound of her name from a handsome man's lips, but she found herself profoundly grateful just the same for a doorframe to lean against. Perhaps she should have taken Nicholas's advice and stayed at Beauvois. She realized at that moment that she wasn't looking at a callow youth such as the ones who had come, floundering in their fathers' wakes, to see if there might be a bride available at Artane. She was facing a man who . . . well, she had the feeling he had never been a callow youth.

"You should be abed."

She shook her head. "I'm not sleepy. And I was cold."

He looked at her seriously. "We've been careful with leaving too much wood lying about, especially in my bedchamber. I should have made certain you had enough."

"I think it might have been less the chill than too much on my mind."

"So you thought to roam the passageways looking for a distraction?"

"It seemed reasonable."

He pushed away from the wall and pulled her gently out into the passageway. "Wait here," he said. "And do not move."

She wasn't sure she could have managed that even if she had wanted to. She leaned against the passageway wall and waited until Gervase came back out of his bedchamber. He pulled the door to, then put a cloak around her shoulders. He looked at her with an expression on his face she couldn't quite identify.

"Let's go sit by the fire in my solar," he said. "Perhaps that will be distraction enough for you without leaving you catching the ague. We'll play draughts or something equally as undemanding."

"For money?"

"For money," he echoed with a snort. "Would your father approve of these mercenary tendencies you display?"

"I'm not sure my father would approve of anything I'm doing at the moment," she said with a sigh.

"And just what have you done of late that is so terrible?"

"Besides forcing my youngest brother into skirts and the remains of my hair, scampering off to France, then arriving on your doorstep this afternoon uninvited?"

He clasped his hands behind his back. "You've had quite a busy spring, haven't you?"

She managed a smile. "So far, it seems so."

"I would have invited you here, of course, had I but known you were able to escape your foul brother's clutches. Or that you might care to."

She supposed it wasn't cowardly to avoid meeting his eyes. After all, she'd done it for the whole of the day thus far.

He took her hand and tucked it under his arm, then nodded down the passageway. "Let us repair to my solar where you can confess all your darkest secrets to me. They'll give me something to distract your father with as he takes me out to the lists and beats me to death with the hilt of his sword for forcing you to be a servant. For all you know, it might save my sorry life."

"You didn't know who I was."

"Isabelle, I thought you were a *lad*. I deserve to be disemboweled for that spectacular piece of stupidity alone."

She smiled at him. "Perhaps you were under duress."

"You can spend all night attempting to excuse me, but the truth is I was just an idiot," he said. "Though I will say that you were doubtless the most beautiful boy I'd ever seen. My heart went out to you for it."

She looked up at him in surprise. "Was that a compliment?"

He started to speak, then closed his mouth and shook his head. "It might surprise you," he said finally, "to learn that I can be polite when the need arises."

"At least you know my name," she said. "Most men don't remember it."

"Then most men are fools," he said.

She smiled. "Thank you."

"A pity you seem to have forgotten *my* name."

"I wasn't sure if you wished me to use it. Considering how you've ignored me all day today, it seemed prudent to be, well, prudent."

He stopped, then turned to look at her. "I couldn't look at you. I was afraid I would do something I would regret."

"What?" she asked lightly. "Tell me to go home?"

"Oh, nay," he said seriously. "I don't think that would have been it at all."

She smiled at him, then felt something shift. And that had everything to do with the way he was looking at her. The truth was, the lads who had come seeking her hands were, well, lads. If there was one thing Gervase de Seger was not, it was a lad.

She realized at that moment that he was going to kiss her. And she had the feeling that she wasn't simply going to allow it, she was going to bloody his nose if he didn't.

"You're scowling at me," he said softly. "Isabelle."

"You keep saying my name," she managed.

"'Tis a very lovely name for an exceptionally lovely woman. And 'tis *your* name."

She closed her eyes briefly. "My lord—"

"Gervase."

She sighed. "Gervase, then."

"See how easy that was?"

She looked up into his eyes, though she couldn't quite tell their color. Blue perhaps, or green. She would have to ask him to look at her in the daytime so she might make a note in her diary that she didn't have at the moment. She wondered if he would come to Artane to see her when she went home. Perhaps she would ask him that as well, after. At the moment, she was too busy being completely overcome by the feel of his taking her face in his hands. He bent his head toward hers—

Or he might have if he hadn't been frozen in place by a very pointed clearing of a male throat from a few paces away. Isabelle looked at him and wondered if her eyes were as wide as his.

"You could kill him, if you liked."

"It might grieve your mother."

Isabelle looked to her left to find her brother standing not five paces away.

"Go away," she said.

"Are you daft?" Miles asked incredulously. "Iz, you are in the middle of a passageway in the middle of the night, unchaperoned!"

"We're not unchaperoned," she said. "Unfortunately."

"Too much time in trousers has rotted your wits," Miles said, striding into the light of a torch. He took her by the hand and pulled her away from Gervase. "I don't think you want to know what Father will do if he finds out that that one has ravished you in his passageway."

"I wasn't going to ravish her," Gervase protested.

Isabelle watched them exchange a look she wasn't quite sure she knew how to identify. A conversation was definitely going on, but one that seemed to require no words. Gervase conceded the battle first.

"Very well, I was going to *kiss* her," he said. "A very brief, very chaste kiss."

Miles pursed his lips. "Try her hand first."

Gervase started to speak, then sighed and said nothing.

"In plain sight," Miles added.

"Am I allowed to at least *hold* her hand in private?"

"I don't think you need worry about privacy now that I'm here to help you be sensible. Let's retreat to the lord's solar, shall we? I'm sure the fire can be built up and my sister warmed by that instead of those scorching looks you were sending her."

Isabelle would have kicked her brother but he seemed to sense that and moved out of her way before she could. She scowled at him instead. "He wasn't sending me scorching looks."

"Iz, you were too busy smoldering to know what he was doing." He looked over her head at Gervase. "My lord?"

"Very well," Gervase said heavily, taking Isabelle's hand and tucking it under his arm. "We'll play cards and I'll empty your purse."

"My purse," Miles said with a snort. "Rather you should be looking in a different direction for the lightening of *your* purse."

"By your sister? Surely not."

"The quiet ones are always the most trouble."

Isabelle cleared her throat. "Are you going to spend all night discussing me as if I weren't here?"

"I thought giving him a fair warning was prudent," Miles said. "And whether or not we discuss you all night won't trouble you because you will be having one turn at cards, then returning speedily to your bed. Your lord needs his sleep as well if he's to face me in the lists on the morrow."

Isabelle decided she would argue with him later. She was too distracted at the moment by the feeling of Gervase's hand covering hers that was folded over his arm. She had been escorted many places over the course of her life, to be sure, but never by a man who had fair set her afire not five minutes earlier with looks she had never once had from anyone.

She had to admit she was relieved to soon be sitting in a chair close to a fire he built up for her in his solar. He brought over the small table that served as a chessboard, then sat down across from her. He looked at Miles.

"I suppose you can provide yourself with a chair."

Miles fetched one, then sat down between them with a pleasant smile. "Isn't this nice?"

"Lovely," Gervase grumbled. "Very well, what shall we play?"

"Cards," Miles said. "Where are yours?"

"A better question is, do I want you to find them?"

"I could escort my sister back to her chamber," Miles pointed out.

Isabelle watched Gervase sigh, rise, and fetch cards out of his trunk. She looked at Miles to find him watching her with a small smile. She attempted a scowl in return, but found she couldn't truly put any enthusiasm behind it. So, instead, she returned his smile, because she knew he loved her, and she was grateful that he was kind to someone she thought she just might love.

An hour later, her brother was sitting across from her and Gervase had moved Miles's recently relinquished chair closer to hers so she could work on his hand. Miles was making noises of disapproval that she had ignored with varying degrees of success. She finally glared at him.

"It helps him," she said, exasperated.

"And it's painful," Gervase added.

"Well, as long as it hurts," Miles said, stretching his legs out and yawning, "I'll allow it. Behave, you two."

"Go to sleep," Gervase suggested.

"Hands in plain sight."

Isabelle took off one of her shoes and threw it at her brother. "Shut up."

Miles only smiled lazily and tossed the shoe to Gervase. "She is, as you can see, dangerous with a slipper in her hands. And just so you know, there is an unwholesome bond between us. I can always tell when there's something amiss with her. Or, more particularly, when she's annoyed with me."

"Which only proves you aren't an imbecile," Gervase said with a snort. "Close your eyes and rest, little lad. I will keep your sister safe."

"Well," Miles said with a yawn Isabelle could hear, "you have so far. When she isn't in your kitchens, that is."

Isabelle worked on Gervase's hand, ignoring the continued

banter between her brother and her . . . *victim* was, she supposed, the only word that seemed appropriate. She didn't dare look at him. He hadn't looked at her earlier in the day, so perhaps turnabout was what he deserved. Well, he had looked at her out in the passageway earlier in the evening, that was true, but even thinking about that left her feeling unaccountably warm. Better that she concentrate on his hand and leave admiring his face for another time.

Only her willpower wasn't what it should have been. She finished, held his hand in both hers, then relented and looked at him. He was watching her with a grave expression on his face. Then he smiled, an equally grave smile that left her wondering when it had suddenly grown so bloody hot in his solar.

"Oh, my," Miles drawled. "I sense something afoot."

"Aye, my foot booting your sorry arse out of my solar," Gervase said, not looking at him.

"Do *not* kiss her," Miles warned.

"Miles!" Isabelle exclaimed. "Be silent."

Miles held up his hands. "I'm saving him a skewering. You may fall upon my neck, weep, and thank me later."

Gervase rose, fetched a blanket from off the back of a chair, then put it over her and tucked it around her feet. He sat down and reached for her hand, ignoring her brother's sounds of horror. Isabelle would have thrown another shoe at that brother, but she didn't want to draw any more attention to herself than was already there. It wasn't that she was nervous about holding hands with Gervase, it was, well, it was that she had never had a man take her hand and hold it between both of his in a way that indicated he might *want* to hold her hand.

"So," Gervase said, stroking the back of her hand with his fingers, "perhaps now would be a good time to apologize for not knowing who you were right away." He met her eyes. "You know when."

She shrugged lightly. "No one does."

"Oh, I should have," he said quickly, "because I knew *of* you. I just hadn't expected to find you wandering on the side of the road with your hair shorn, puking into the weeds."

"Charming," Miles said pleasantly.

Gervase shot Miles a glare, then looked back at her. "I should have known."

"I should have told you," she said with a smile. "The thing

is, you have a rather unsettling reputation amongst those with weak stomachs. Though I'll admit I never believed the rumors about you."

"I don't seem to remember you cowering," he agreed. "Ever," he added almost under his breath.

"Yet you had her scrubbing your floors anyway," Miles said.

"I would blame Guy for suggesting it—because he did—but I was stupid enough to pursue the course," Gervase said. He shrugged lightly. "I'll pay for it in the end, I'm sure."

"You don't have to face my father in the lists," Isabelle said.

A silence fell. She wasn't unused to silences, certainly. It was what happened when fathers were informed that Amanda was indeed wed with a child already in her arms. But this wasn't that same sort of silence. It was a sort of silence that Gervase seemed to be filling with chewing on his words and Miles seemed to be filling simply with his obvious waiting for something. She sent her brother a warning look because that seemed like a reasonable thing to do, then looked back at Gervase.

"Well," she said, "you don't."

"Oh, I think I do."

"Why?" she whispered.

He looked at her hand in his for a moment or two, then brought her hand up and kissed the back of it.

It was slightly more powerful than a scorching look, she had to admit.

"Warm in here, isn't it?" Miles drawled.

"Shut up, Miles," Gervase said absently.

"Aye," Isabelle managed, "be silent, Miles."

"Why does everyone tell me to be quiet?" Miles asked. "I'm baffled."

Isabelle looked at Gervase. Green, perhaps. His eyes, that was. She would have to look at them in the daytime to be sure, but they were surely a pale color. She thought, though, if she looked in them too long, she might do something she regretted.

"Time for bed," Miles announced loudly. "Iz, you look overcome by weariness."

Well, weariness wasn't exactly what she suspected she was being overcome by, but she couldn't exactly tell her brother the impulse she was fighting was to lean over and scandalize all of France by kissing Gervase de Seger herself.

Gervase had been smiling at her, but his smile deepened, as

if he knew exactly what she was thinking. She pursed her lips at him, retrieved her shoe from where it currently resided on the other side of him, then handed him her blanket. She put her shoe on, then rose.

"I'm tired," she announced imperiously.

Miles laughed and rose. "I'm sure you are. Let's see her to your bedchamber, my lord Gervase, then seek out our own rest. A busy day awaits us on the morrow, I daresay."

Isabelle ignored them as they escorted her from the solar and back to Gervase's bedchamber. She paused in front of the doorway and looked at Monsaert's lord.

"Thank you for the fire," she said quietly.

"And the gold," he added with a sigh.

She smiled. "I believe I earned that fairly."

"I told you so," Miles remarked. "If you're going to indulge in amusements with her, never involve your purse. The only one of us who hasn't learned that lesson thoroughly is Robin. He's convinced that Isabelle is a delicate, innocent thing of approximately ten-and-two. I'm a little surprised he hasn't made a more concerted effort to find her a husband before she rids him of all his funds, but with Robin you never know what he's thinking."

Isabelle found her hand taken by Gervase. He smiled, kissed the back of it, then opened his door for her.

"Go to bed, you ruthless wench," he said gravely. "We'll have a rematch tomorrow."

"You'll regret it," Miles said.

Gervase laughed, sounding slightly exasperated. "Does he ever stop talking?"

"Rarely," she said. She walked inside his bedchamber, turned to smile at him, then started to shut the door. "Thank you for the fire," she said. "Gervase."

Miles reached in and pulled the door shut. She was tempted to open it back up and clout her brother on the nose, but she didn't want to disturb anything about the hand Gervase had just kissed. It was odd, she supposed, how little desire she had to immediately find water and wash her skin.

She sighed and walked over to the bed to turn down the covers. What she needed to do was sleep before she thought too much and got herself into trouble she wouldn't easily extricate—

She froze.

There was a sheaf of parchment there, sticking out just far

enough from under her pillow that she saw it. Perhaps that wouldn't have mattered in a quarter hour for she would have surely felt it when she'd laid her head down. Convenient, that's what it was, that she should see it before she'd blown out her candle and put herself to bed.

She pulled it free and read it uneasily.

To the Lady Isabelle de Piaget,

I sent you to France for a particular purpose you neglect at your peril. Go to Caours as you were meant to. Know that I am everywhere and see everything.

Isabelle dropped the sheaf as if it had burned her, then stared in horror at it as it lay on the floor next to Gervase's bed. She jumped when she realized that someone was knocking on the door. She kicked the sheaf under the bed, then stumbled across the chamber to open the door. She realized as she did so that perhaps that had been one of the more foolish things she'd done over the course of her lifetime. What if the writer of that missive was standing there—

It wasn't. It was just Gervase, looking genuinely startled.

"What is it?" he asked.

She could hardly bring herself to speak. "Nothing," she said, her voice sounding thin and sharp. "Why do you ask?"

"You shrieked."

"Bad dream."

Gervase seemed to be considering something. She was also considering something, a possibility that she could hardly bring herself to entertain.

What if Gervase had written that missive?

She shook her head sharply. She couldn't imagine that Gervase had been the one to leave that missive where she could find it, but what else was she to think? And if he had sent her the second missive, was it not possible that he had sent the first? The thought of that almost sent her reeling. That would mean he had somehow found out things about her family or sent a spy to ferret out details or paid someone to discover things about ones she loved in order to use those things against them.

She shook her head, because she simply couldn't believe it.

It couldn't be him. Not that man standing there, looking at

her as if he thought she was about to indulge in some sort of feminine display of overwrought emotion.

"Isabelle, you're pale," he said slowly.

She would have smiled at his using her name, but she was, frankly, too unsettled to. It couldn't have been Gervase to write that, but how was she to know if it were or not? She'd never seen any of his handwriting to tell the difference. She was tempted to simply return to his solar and paw through his things there, but she supposed that might be a little obvious if he were the one who had written that truly vile note.

I am everywhere and see everything . . .

The impulse to simply curl up and weep lasted the space of a single heartbeat before she put her shoulders back and recaptured her good sense. She didn't have a sword, but she could find a dagger and wield it if she had to. Never mind that Robin had never taught her a damned thing, the lout. She had watched him endlessly and was fairly sure she could imitate his arrogant stance alone if she had to. She could defend herself. Perhaps she could even defend Gervase.

Assuming he was the one who needed defending.

"Miles, stay here with her," Gervase said. "I'll see that her fire is built up."

Isabelle realized that her brother was there in the passageway as well. She put on a smile that she didn't feel, then produced a yawn she definitely didn't feel. She didn't protest when Miles put his arms around her and held on to her.

"What is it?" he asked quietly.

"I'll tell you tomorrow."

He frowned at her. In time, both he and Gervase were frowning at her in tandem, as if they had planned their expressions when she hadn't been attending them. She bid them both a pleasant good night, then locked herself inside and leaned back against the door.

The sight of a brightly burning fire made her jump and reach for a nonexistent blade. She rolled her eyes. Gervase had told her he was building up the fire in his bedchamber, hadn't he? She took a deep breath, then deliberately looked about the chamber, in the trunks, under the bed, and behind the privy screen. There was nothing.

She dug the missive out from under the bed, stuck it under her pillow, then went to the door. Perhaps she would borrow a knife from Miles, who was no doubt standing guard outside her door. She opened the door, then felt something rush through her, but it wasn't anything pleasant.

She could hardly believe it was merely the sight of the lord of Monsaert standing there that gave her such a feeling of dread.

Gervase frowned at her. Was that because he waited for her to react to the missive she'd found or something more sinister?

"What is it, Isabelle?" he asked quietly.

She tried to swallow but couldn't manage it. "Nothing," she said hoarsely. She realized she was still wearing his cloak, so she took it off and handed it to him. "Thank you, my lord."

He took it and folded it over his arm, then looked at her. "Gervase," he said.

She nodded. "Of course. Gervase." She attempted another swallow. "You wouldn't have an extra knife, would you?"

He looked at her in surprise. "A knife?"

"In case I need to cut something." *Like a man's belly or other useful part of him,* she added silently.

He reached down and pulled a knife free of his boot, then handed it to her slowly. "Will that suit?"

The haft looked unsettlingly well used, as did the sheath. Obviously Gervase wasn't shy about doing what needed to be done. She looked at his knife, then at him.

"You don't mind?"

"As long as you don't intend to use it on me," he said seriously.

She attempted a careless laugh, then dropped his knife. She almost clacked heads with him bending down to retrieve it, then straightened and took it back from him. He frowned thoughtfully at her again, then took a step back.

"I'll keep watch," he said, inclining his head.

"You?" she squeaked. "Surely not all night."

He lifted one shoulder in a half shrug. "Perhaps not all night. I do have to face your brother in the lists in the morning."

She nodded and considered him. Why would he have waited until she was in his hall before he left her a note if all he'd wanted was for her to go to Caours? Surely he would have sent something instead to Beauvois—

Perhaps that was what he'd intended to do but the missive had been stolen.

"Isabelle?"

"I'm tired," she said without hesitation. She smiled politely.

"Thank you for the knife. I'll return it." Eventually, once she was certain he wouldn't use it on her.

She backed into her chamber, shut the door, then bolted it. She put her hand on the wood and let out a shaky breath. It wasn't possible . . .

She supposed the most sensible thing she could do was escape from the keep whilst she could and run for the abbey. She could garb herself as a nun perhaps before anyone was the wiser, then she could find out who it was who was hunting her.

Before anyone in her family paid the price.

She pulled a blanket off the bed, wrapped herself in it, and went to sit in a chair in front of the fire. She set Gervase's knife on the little table next to her. She would sit up for as long as she could, on the off chance that someone somehow found his way inside her chamber.

And then, assuming she lived to see the sunrise, she would run like hell to her grandmother's abbey and hope she survived the journey.

She would leave thinking on what would come after that for daylight.

Chapter 18

There was something to be said for bathing with weeds.

Gervase nodded to himself over that fact as he faced a de Piaget lad who had definitely learned which end of his sword to point away from himself. He supposed he had Isabelle's tender ministrations to thank for the fact that his hand wasn't cramping as it grasped the hilt of his own sword, but there was certainly no denying that it had been her herbs to give him such ease in his leg. That coupled with Miles taunting him to the point where he was willing to run around the outside of the lists—a bit at a time, it had to be admitted—in order to catch him and kill him and, well, he wasn't displeased with his progress that morning.

He looked past the yew hedge to make certain that Isabelle was where he'd left her, sitting in the sunshine and discussing some sort of scholarly business with his two youngest brothers. Actually, there looked to be less discussion of Latin and more instruction in the art of dance, but he couldn't complain. His brothers adored her.

He understood.

He jumped aside as he realized suddenly that Miles was

doing less adoring than he was plotting, apparently to rid his sister of a potentially vexatious suitor. He glared at Isabelle's brother who had come within a finger's width of shoving his sword through Gervase's arm. Miles only smiled pleasantly.

"Dozed off there, did you?"

"Not quite."

Joscelin clapped slowly from where he stood on the edge of the little field. "You're not on your knees," he noted. "Well done."

Gervase glanced at his brother. "Who? Me or this blight here?"

Joscelin only laughed, then walked away. Gervase cursed him, then leaned on his sword and allowed himself a brief respite to catch his breath. That he was having to catch his breath from hoisting a sword was somehow far more satisfying than having to catch his breath from merely staggering to the garderobe. Perhaps he would never be what he had been, but at least he might attain the level of a lesser swordsman such as the one in front of him who was looking too damned energetic for his taste.

He scowled at Miles. "Why are you doing this?"

"Because I am naturally generous."

Gervase suppressed the urge to swear. "The truth, with details."

Miles only smiled faintly. "Do I need to give those details?"

Gervase considered what Miles wasn't saying, then sighed deeply. "I suppose not. I'm also not sure, honestly, that any of this is worth the effort. Your father will slay me before I manage to begin to flatter him. And for all I know, your sister has no interest in me."

"If you cannot tell when a woman fancies you, Your Grace, then there is nothing I can do for you."

"Perhaps she hasn't seen what else is available."

"My lord Gervase, she has seen every eligible lad in England and a handful from France," Miles said dryly. "Of course, your own betrothal might be a bit of a stumbling block, but I imagine you can clear that up with enough effort."

"Coucy made it clear I'm no longer on the field, as it were."

"Are you sure?"

"Very," Gervase said. "I sent him on his way, then celebrated with a bottle of wine in my solar."

Miles shrugged lightly. "You might want to say something to my sister."

"What?" Gervase said with a snort. "That I was betrothed to a woman who decided I wasn't worthy of her?"

Miles shrugged. "A wench of little discernment, obviously. My sister is not so foolish. But let it be as you will. I'll say nothing of it."

"There is nothing to say," Gervase said, "so perhaps we can both let it languish in the past where it belongs." He looked at the woman in question and was faintly surprised to find Guy standing to the side, watching her teach their younger brothers dance steps that he recognized as the fashion in London.

How was it he could have gone to England half a dozen times in his life and never encountered that woman there?

He put up his sword and started toward her.

"Are we finished?"

"I believe so," he tossed over his shoulder without looking at Isabelle's brother.

He continued on his way until he was standing next to Guy, watching the spectacle. Brothers had been pressed into service as gels, which they seemed to accept with only a minor amount of resistance. Gervase understood. He thought he might have done the same thing—and more—if Isabelle had asked it of him.

"Interesting journey to Beauvois?" he asked, turning his head to look at Guy.

Guy pointed to a blackened eye. "Assaulted on my way there, I'm afraid."

"No permanent damage, I hope."

"Bruises to body and pride," Guy said deprecatingly. "I left my lads behind and rode on, leaving them to follow, but came to regret it." He shrugged. "You know how it is to wish for a bit of peace for thinking."

"I must admit I do," Gervase said with a sigh. He had occasionally left the keep without a guard simply because his arrogance had left him believing that he was invincible. He couldn't blame Guy for suffering from the same delusion. "But you delivered my missive, I assume."

"I lost it, along with my pride," Guy said. "But I delivered your seeds and your compliments to Lord Nicholas, as requested."

"Thank you," Gervase said.

"How fortunate that the lady Isabelle seems to have found her way back to our hall."

"She's on her way to Caours," he said, though once the words were out of his mouth, he regretted them.

He frowned to himself. That was, of course, ridiculous. His brother had never displayed anything but utter loyalty to first their father, then him. It would have been very easy for Guy to have protested when Gervase found himself back on his feet, but he had turned over the reins of Monsaert without so much as a breath of protest. Why would he not share his most private thoughts with a man who had never been anything but supportive during his darkest hours?

He shook his head. There was another answer, something that he was missing. Obviously someone still wanted him dead, but who? He supposed it could have been any number of souls to write a single sentence on a scrap of parchment. Surely there was an equal number of souls who might have had the opportunity to tuck that scrap into a stack of parchment pieces lying on his table. Any of his brothers. Any number of servants.

A woman who had drawn from that stack to aid his brothers with their studies.

He watched that same woman as she danced with Fabien. She was smiling, but there was something about her smile that looked less than peaceful.

As if she had something that troubled her.

He wondered if it was a guilty conscience that plagued her or something else—not enough sleep perhaps or lingering disgust over his having kissed her hand the night before. Was his appeal so lessened, then, that such a thing would cause a woman to look as if she were on the verge of bolting?

He unbuckled his sword belt and handed it to Miles without looking at him. "Keep that."

Miles made no comment, which was likely rather wise given the circumstances. Gervase walked out onto Isabelle's floor, such as it was, then removed Fabien from his place. He made Isabelle a bow, then looked at her gravely.

"May I?"

She seemed to be keeping her gorge down where it belonged through sheer willpower alone. He supposed even his brothers were too appalled by the sight to make any comment, for there was no snickering or ribald jesting about his effect on the lovely *demoiselle* from Artane.

"I was teaching them, ah, something my brothers saw at, um, court—"

"I recognized it," Gervase said, wondering if he would manage to dance even a single pattern with her before she ran. "Let us show my brothers how 'tis done."

She nodded uneasily, but followed him through an entire set. He would have pressed her for more, but he wasn't in the habit of forcing himself on unwilling women.

That and he had a question or two about what was going through the admittedly lovely head of Lady Isabelle de Piaget.

He noticed that Sir Aubert was standing just outside the door to the hall and supposed that was excuse enough to leave Isabelle to her work with his siblings. He made her a low bow, excused himself, then retrieved his sword from Miles before he went to speak to his captain.

Perhaps she was merely anxious to see her grandmother. He could understand that. He hoped she understood that she would not be going with just Miles and whatever guardsmen they had brought along with them.

As Guy had proved, the wilds of France were not safe for travelers.

Three hours later, he finished with a fairly long list of things he hadn't wanted to attend to and rewarded himself for his diligence by going to see how the morning of study and dancing had proceeded for his brothers. If he were fortunate enough to find their lovely tutor still sitting with them, he would count that as an added blessing. Perhaps he would challenge her to another afternoon of chess and see what he could add to the list of things she owed him.

His list being, he had to admit, a bit on the thin side.

He walked into the great hall to find his brothers clustered at a table pushed under the window. Isabelle, however, was not with them. He walked over to the group, then paused.

"How goes it, lads?" he asked.

Yves looked up at him. "Boring," he said without hesitation. "Isabelle had a headache, Ger, and went to lie down in your bedchamber. She left Fabien in charge and he doesn't know anything."

"Oh," Gervase said, nonplussed. "I see."

"She said she would return, but she hasn't yet," Yves said, sounding as if that had been a personal slight. "I wanted to go look for her, but Fabien said I shouldn't."

Gervase started to congratulate his second-youngest sibling for his good sense when the import of Yves's words seeped into what was left of his feeble brain. He looked at his brother. "How long ago?"

Yves shrugged, then looked at Fabien. "A little bit ago, yes?"

"An hour," Fabien said.

"Don't be daft," Pierre said. "'Twas at least a pair of hours. You've been dawdling ever since and Isabelle told you to have your sums done when she returned."

Gervase frowned thoughtfully and left his brothers to their undone work. He walked bodily into Joscelin before he realized his brother was in his way.

"Move," he said shortly.

Joscelin stepped aside, but unfortunately he wasn't the only impediment. Gervase didn't bother with Miles, he simply pushed him out of the way and strode out of his hall.

It took him a very brief time indeed to reach his bedchamber. He found Isabelle's two new guardsmen—the steely-eyed warriors he'd chosen that morning to guard her at all costs—standing there looking fierce. He nodded to them, then turned and rapped briskly on the door.

There was a muffled noise from inside that alarmed him so greatly, he set aside any hesitation he might have felt at entering a woman's bedchamber uninvited and simply flung the door open.

A lad sat in front of the fire, tied to a chair.

Gervase whirled on Isabelle's guardsmen. "Who left this chamber?"

The lad on the right made him a sharp bow. "No one, Your Grace. A serving lad emerged a pair of hours ago, to be sure, but—"

Gervase swore viciously and strode inside the chamber. He pulled the gag out of the lad's mouth and bent over to glare at him.

"Bested by a girl?" he said shortly.

"She's vicious!" the lad wailed.

Gervase threw up his hands in despair. Truly there were times he feared for the continuation of the species. "What did she say?"

"Nothing, Your Grace," the boy said, looking thoroughly

unsettled. "She simply clouted me over the head—with a very large rock, I'm sure—while I was adding wood to the fire. The next thing I knew, I was sitting here and she was smudging soot on her cheeks."

"Did you encourage her to stop?"

"My mouth was full of cloth, Your Grace. I shook my head quite vigorously, but she ignored me."

Gervase was unsurprised by that. He was surprised, however, by one thing and that was why the hell she had run. Was she suffering from a guilty conscience and had decided that fleeing was her only alternative? If that were the case, then why would she have come back to Monsaert to start with? Much easier to simply hire someone to slip inside his gates and slay him while he was napping.

He folded his arms over his chest and looked into his fire. It took a moment or two, but reason returned. It couldn't have been Isabelle to pen that missive simply because it made no sense. She hadn't been there for the first attack on his person, why would she be interested in a second? More to the point, why would she have spent all that time gathering herbs and enduring his snarls and disdain if she'd had any other end in mind but helping him heal?

He leaned over and looked at his serving lad with the most harmless expression he could muster. "Did she say anything," he began slowly, "anything that would indicate where she intended to go?"

"The stables, Your Grace," the boy said faintly.

Gervase straightened and cursed as he turned and left his bedchamber. He didn't bother to chastize the guardsmen standing there. He was stopped at one point in the passageway by Miles and Joscelin—to see them combining forces was truly appalling—but he parted them efficiently and continued on his way.

It occurred to him as he strode toward the stables that he was striding not limping, which he supposed was an almost miraculous improvement. It was a miracle he had Isabelle de Piaget to thank for.

Then why had she run?

"Ger, wait!"

He ignored his brother, collected his captain and another pair of lads on his way, and procured his fastest horse from Master Simon, who only nodded approvingly at the choice. Aubert lifted an eyebrow as they mounted in front of the stables.

"Caours Abbey," Gervase said.

"She took Philip, you know." Aubert looked at him knowingly. "The horse, not the young monarch."

His second-fastest horse. He supposed in that he could credit her with a bit of sense. She had bought herself at least a handful of minutes where he might not have suspected what she was about. That Simon had let her take anything at all was a mystery, but one he had no time to solve at present. Perhaps she had dazzled the man with her smile. The saints only knew he could understand that.

A quarter hour later, he was thundering away from his front gates, grateful that he was able to do it in some manner besides clinging to the saddle and hoping he didn't fall off.

Two hours, damn it to Hell.

Anything could have happened to her in two hours.

Chapter 19

Isabelle found herself exceptionally grateful for the quality of the steeds in her father's stables and the amount of time her sire had taken to teach her to ride. That had allowed her the freedom to take choice of the offerings in Monsaert's stables, though she had settled for a lesser animal than the one she'd brought from Nicholas's stables. The stable lad she'd flipped three coins to and pressed into secrecy had only sighed when she'd promised him that her brother was waiting for her in the village, so she would certainly be safe on her own. The stable-master had glanced at her, then made a serious study of the hayloft as she had snuck out right in front of him.

She could only hope that would be enough to keep the both of them from joining Coucy's man who still lingered in the dungeon.

She supposed she was fortunate to have escaped Monsaert at all without a score of men trailing after her. The truth was, she hadn't known what else to do. She had a knife and a very fast horse which meant she would at least gain the abbey in safety. What happened there was something she couldn't control. For all she knew, if she didn't arrive when summoned, something terrible would happen to her grandmother.

And her grandfather, whoever he might have been.

Whatever other failings her mount might have had, endurance was not one. He was willing to stay at a canter for long stretches and his trot was exceptionally enthusiastic. She had been forced to pause a time or two to catch her own breath— and that was something she would have to address at a future time—but supposed that merely a trio of hours had passed before she saw her grandmother's abbey rising up before her in the distance. She looked around her to make certain there was no one lurking about with evil intent, but there seemed to be no ruffians in the area.

There was, however, a man riding her way in a tearing hurry.

Gervase de Seger, as it happened.

She would have kicked her mount into a gallop, but the truth was she had ridden him too far already that day and couldn't bring herself to abuse him. Her only piece of good fortune was that the abbey was indeed close enough that she thought she might manage to at least gain the grounds before she was caught.

Gervase, on his own. That did not bode well for her.

She rode her horse for a bit longer, then she jumped down and ran.

"Isabelle, stop!" Gervase shouted.

She didn't take the time to snort, but she supposed that would have been the only useful reaction. As if she would simply give up and give in! She looked over her shoulder to find that he had almost reached her. He reined his horse in, then jumped down from the saddle himself. She winced at his curse, then turned and fled. She couldn't help his pain any more than she had already.

Either he had recovered almost instantly or he was impervious to nagging twinges in his form because she soon realized he was directly behind her.

"Isabelle," he gasped, *"stop."*

She whirled around, pulling his knife from her boot as she did so. She pointed the blade at him. "Don't come any closer to me."

He pulled up short and looked at her in such astonishment, she blinked. It crossed her mind that perhaps she had misjudged him, but nay, that wasn't possible. He was following her, so what else was she to think?

"Do you think *I* would harm you?" he asked, sounding stunned.

She took a firmer grip on her blade. Well, his blade, but perhaps he wouldn't notice. "You were following me."

"Aye, to *protect* you!"

She lifted her chin. "Or to do me in."

"Well," he said, looking as if the admission pained him, "I did consider that, but not perhaps for the reasons you might think."

"You will not find me an easy victim."

He said no more, but simply leaned over with his hands on his thighs and drew in a dozen very ragged breaths. She was tempted to clunk him over the head as he was otherwise occupied, but the truth was, whilst his knife might have been beautifully crafted, it wasn't enough to render him senseless. The best she could do was hold her ground.

He finally heaved himself upright, then put his hands on his hips. "You can't be serious."

"Why wouldn't I be serious?" she demanded. She looked at him standing there and felt her certainty fade a bit. He didn't look like a man who wished her ill; he looked like a man who had ridden a fair distance in great haste to execute a rescue. She frowned. "Actually, I don't know what to think."

He slowly held up his hands. "I have no weapon, lady, as you can see."

"You have a sword."

He stared at her for a moment or two without moving, then slowly unbuckled his sword belt and tossed his blade at her. She caught it thanks to long years of doing just that, then set it on the ground behind her, never taking her gaze off him.

"You're still very dangerous," she pointed out.

He was looking at her as if he'd never seen her before. "Isabelle, I was riding after you to keep you from doing something stupid and thereafter finding yourself dead in a ditch."

She ignored the pleasure of hearing her name from a man she wasn't related to. A handsome man, a very dangerous man, an extremely baffled man. She supposed that last bit gave her the upper hand, so there was no reason not to use that hand.

"Why does everyone think that when I'm riding off," she said crisply, "that I'm doing something stupid?"

"Because you're missing critical *accoutrements* necessary for the accomplishment of dastardly deeds."

"And what would those be?"

He held up one finger. "Sword skill."

She glared at him.

He held up two fingers. "Ruthless ability to kill when necessary."

"Shut up."

He laughed a little and reached out, presumably to pull her into his arms, then stopped. "Would you mind putting up your very fierce weapon there?"

She continued to point the blade at him. "How did you know where I'd gone?"

"I found that poor serving lad you tied up in your chamber," he said, "which you should feel a great amount of guilt over. I don't know that he'll recover from the trauma. He had very few answers for me, but as I was looking at him trussed up like a fine goose, I remembered that you were terribly anxious to come visit your grandmother."

She resheathed his knife down the side of her boot, then folded her arms over her chest and dredged up the sort of frown she thought might most closely resemble one of her father's.

"Don't think your charming smiles will win you my trust."

He looked so genuinely surprised that she shifted.

"Well," she said, "they won't."

"Isabelle," he said in disbelief, "you can't believe I would harm you."

"You might not," she said, then pointed behind him. "What of them? Are they yours?"

He looked over his shoulder and then turned. "Sword," he barked.

She picked it up and put it into his hand, then watched him shake off the scabbard before he reached behind her with his left hand and pulled her up close behind him.

"Do *not* attempt anything heroic," he said briskly over his shoulder.

"I have a knife—"

"Isabelle!"

"Well," she muttered, "I do."

He laughed, the lout. She would have poked him with his

knife, but that seemed rather unsporting when he was putting himself between her and potential danger.

She put her hands on his back and waited to see if the tension would seep out of him or not. She attempted a quick peek around his shoulder and had a curse in return. She shook her head. He was so much like her father, which she supposed wasn't a bad thing. Her father had a way of making the women in his care feel, well, cared for.

But that didn't mean she couldn't be useful. She lifted her foot up and pulled Gervase's knife free with an unfortunately quite audible hiss.

He only sighed. "Incorrigible."

"Just trying to be useful."

"How can I argue with that?"

She realized abruptly that not only was he not arguing, he was not concerned. She felt the muscles in his back relax a bit more and realized that he was standing there, perfectly at ease.

"You've misled me," she accused. "You weren't worried."

He turned around and smiled faintly. "Of course not. 'Tis simply my lads and your brother, Miles. Well, and Joscelin." He shrugged. "It seemed a convenient way to distract you from stabbing me with my own blade."

Isabelle scowled at him. "Rather unsporting of you, don't you think?"

"I'm not sure we should be discussing sporting. After all, I'm the one who's been chasing you for most of the morning, fearing with every hoofbeat that I would catch you up and find you dead. I believe I haven't begun to repay you for my feelings of terror."

She looked up at him seriously. "Is that what you were thinking?"

"Yes, Isabelle, that was what I was thinking. Why would I think anything else?"

She took a deep breath, but could say nothing.

"Why did you not wait for an escort?"

She wasn't sure what she dared tell him, or if she dared tell him anything.

"No particular reason."

The look he gave her was so reminiscent of something her father might have favored her with, she almost smiled. She would have, if she hadn't been so terrified. He stabbed his sword into the ground, then put his arms around her and drew her close.

"Oh, there'll be none of that," Miles called.

"Not now, Miles," Gervase said, glancing over his shoulder. "Purchase me a few minutes of peace and quiet with your sister, why don't you?"

Isabelle watched the company move off out of earshot, then considered her position. She stood in Gervase's arms and felt for the first time in weeks almost safe. She considered many things, not the least of which was that for someone who might want to kill everyone she loved, he didn't seem to be in a rush to see to it.

"Can I trust you, I wonder," she murmured.

"I haven't given you very many reasons, have I?" he asked with a sigh.

"You guarded my door."

"I guarded *you*."

"Aye, well, that's true," she agreed.

He continued to drag his fingers through what was left of her hair. "I believe we must have serious speech together, my lady, about several things that puzzle me."

"Must we?" she asked, attempting to sound as if she might not have time for such a thing.

"Why did you leave England, Isabelle?"

"I wanted an adventure."

He pulled back far enough to look at her. The skepticism on his face almost made her smile. "Try again."

She wasn't sure she wanted to give him the real reason, not yet. She pulled away from him. "I can't say," she said honestly.

"Why not?"

"There is a price attached to that sort of honesty," she said quietly. "Might we walk, instead?"

He frowned thoughtfully, then reached over and picked up his scabbard. He resheathed his sword, belted it around his hips, then took his knife out of her hands. He very carefully resheathed it down the side of her boot, then straightened and clicked to his horse who seemed to sigh with a bit of regret over tasty grasses left unsampled. He did, however, amble over obediently. Gervase offered her his elbow.

"Let's go."

She took his arm, then walked for a bit before she looked at him. "Have you ever stood in the shadows and simply watched?"

He looked very briefly as if she'd elbowed him in the gut. He blew out his breath, then laughed a little. "What a question."

She only continued to watch him. "Well?"

He glanced at her, then sighed. "I suppose I felt, on the occasional evening while my stepmother held court, that I wasn't exactly welcome to participate."

She'd heard the tale from his cook, so that didn't surprise her. "That must have been difficult."

He shrugged. "Cook was almost a score at that point, working under her father's flashing spoon, yet she didn't seem to mind an extra lad hanging about the kitchen."

Isabelle smiled. "She's inordinately fond of you, you know."

"Anyone supping at my table over the past several days might disbelieve that," he said with a snort. He shot her a look. "She was seriously displeased with your absence. I believe I am back in her good graces for the moment, but she has a fickle heart."

Isabelle doubted that quite seriously. She considered what he'd said and what she already knew and grieved for him. Her youth had been the stuff of legends in comparison.

"I'm sorry," she said, finally. "That your childhood was difficult."

He shrugged. "I put away childish traumas years ago. I regret that I have not aided my brothers as I could have, but that is a discussion for another time when you have perhaps plied me with strong drink for the whole of an evening. Let's turn to something more comfortable for me, which is examining your childhood more closely. What is this business of the shadows that drives you to take such terrible risks?"

"I love my family," she said simply. "Even my siblings."

"Who are pompous, overbearing, and far too impressed with themselves," he mused, "save your sister, who I am sure is almost as flawless as you are."

She smiled. "Flatterer."

"I am scrupulously honest."

"Save when you were pretending not to know who I was," she said.

"I also have a finely honed instinct for self-preservation and a sense of altruism that is rarely matched in all of France," he said with a smile.

"Which only means you feared my brother would slay you, but that doesn't explain anything else."

He slid his hand down her arm and laced his fingers with

hers. "I didn't want you to suffer a swoon from realizing too soon who you were. Again, very altruistic of me, wouldn't you say?"

"I believe, Your Grace, that you are telling a falsehood."

"Well, it isn't as if I can admit to wanting to keep you captive in my hall a few more days, is it?" he grumbled. "And just so you know, I can understand wanting to be out of the shadows."

"Unless you're a woman."

"There is that." He shot her a glance. "You de Piaget women have strange and unwholesome ideas of independence."

"Unlike your current queen regent who is with a fair amount of ruthlessness keeping a kingdom intact for her son."

His mouth fell open, then he shut it and smiled. "You have me there." He studied her for a handful of very uncomfortable moments. "Why do I have the feeling that this whole adventure was about more than simply escaping from the long shadows cast by your overbearing brothers?"

She looked around her to make certain there were no men within earshot. Miles, at least, was watching her whilst doing his best to seem as if he weren't watching her. The rest of the lads were watching the countryside, which she appreciated. She took a deep breath, then looked at Gervase.

Green. His eyes were a pale green. They were truly a lovely color. More to the point, they were full of something that she had to believe was disbelief.

"I'm unnerved," she admitted.

"That is, my lady, the first sensible thing I've heard you say. And in honor of that show of good sense, why don't you tell me the rest of the tale?"

She took a deep breath, then stopped and turned to face him. "I was told I must come to France."

He froze. "What?"

"A missive was delivered to me," she said, "which said that if I didn't come to France, my grandmother would die." She supposed there was no need to speak of a grandfather she was sure she didn't have. "I don't have the note, of course, because Miles lost it," she said. "Or, more particularly, dropped it and one of Nicky's hounds tried to have it for supper. But Miles had read it in England."

"A missive," Gervase said, his voice completely without inflection. "What else did it say?"

"Not much more than that."

He studied her. "And that is what sent you off on this ill-advised flight today?"

She hesitated, then pulled the rolled missive from her tunic. She supposed he would think what he would of it, so there was no sense in saying anything. She simply handed it to him and waited.

He took it carefully. "Where did you find this?"

"In your bed."

His mouth had fallen open. He gaped at her a bit longer, then unrolled the missive. He gaped at it, then at her.

"You found this in *my* bed?"

She only nodded.

He looked at the note with distaste. "This isn't in my hand."

"Do you recognize it?" she asked carefully.

He shook his head. He rolled it up again and handed it back to her, then rubbed his hands over his face. "Someone, then, is either having us on, or using my hall for foul deeds."

"Why do you say that?"

"Because I received something several days ago that warned me that I was most definitely still in the sights of someone who wished me ill."

She frowned, then felt her mouth fall open at the way he was watching her so steadily. She pulled away from him and stepped back so quickly that she almost tripped over her own two feet.

"You can't think *I* would be responsible."

"The hand was very fair," he said slowly, "but nay, I didn't suspect you."

"For very long," she finished.

"Well, it would seem we are both guilty of coming to hasty conclusions." He dragged his hand through his hair. "I believe we would do well to seek out a safe place, then have speech together."

"I'm not sure there is a safe place," she said honestly. "The missive told me my entire family would be harmed if I didn't come immediately to France. To Caours, if you want the entire truth."

He looked at her in surprise. "And you came?"

"What else was I to do?" she asked defensively. "Allow her to be slain?"

"Send one of your intimidating brothers to guard your grand-mother instead?" he suggested.

"The missive called for me to come."

He drew her into his arms. She went, because there was something unwholesomely pleasant about his embrace. She put her hands on his chest, then turned her head and rested her cheek against his shoulder. He was just the right height for it to be a comfortable place to lay her head. That and his dragging his fingers through what was left of her hair was more enjoyable than she thought she might care to admit.

"I assume Lord Nicholas knows nothing of this," he said finally.

"Of course not. He would have locked me in my bedchamber otherwise."

"A pity Miles does not have his good sense."

"I intimidate him."

He laughed a little. "Aye, I imagine you do."

"But I don't intimidate you."

He pulled back and gave her a look that had her cheeks beginning to burn. She couldn't say she was overly acquainted with the ways of men and women, but she did have siblings and they did have mates. She'd seen that look before. Of course, she'd never seen it on any of the lads who had come courting her, but perhaps that was because they'd been too busy looking around her to see if her older sister was still available.

"I'm not sure that finds itself on the list of things you do to me," he said solemnly, "which is probably a very good thing." He exchanged a look with his captain, then put his arm around her shoulders and nodded toward the abbey. "Let's get ourselves behind at least marginally sturdy walls, then we'll put our heads together and see if we can't unravel both these tangles."

She nodded and ignored the look Miles gave her as he took the reins of Gervase's horse along with his own. If Gervase wanted to keep her close whilst they walked, who was she to gainsay him?

At least they were safe enough for the moment with his guards and her brother fanning out around them. How much she had taken for granted, living in her father's lovely hall on the edge of the sea, always being surrounded by men who would have gone to battle to protect her.

"Just so you know," Gervase said casually, "that while I'm not in favor of your decision to come to France alone, I'm not opposed to the results of it, despite the blisters on your hands from your labors in my kitchens. And I understand why you did what you did. I hope you understand that from now on, I will be seeing to your problem."

"Bossy thing, aren't you?"

He smiled briefly. "Protective," he corrected. "Though I'm not sure this is exactly the sort of place I would choose to be protective in."

Isabelle had to admit that whilst the gates were not large, they did seem overly imposing for a locale supposedly unlikely to need a defense. She considered that for a moment or two, then realized Gervase was simply watching her. She looked at him and attempted a smile.

"Here we are," she managed.

"Please leave the sword work to me," he said very quietly.

"You're robbing me of my chance to step out of the shadows," she said lightly.

"You can investigate all you like—and I cannot believe I just heard myself say that—as long as you have a guardsman within sight. I would prefer that guardsman to be me."

"Would you?" she asked wistfully. "Why?"

"Why do you think?"

"You're overprotective of your brothers' language tutors?"

"I'll tell you what I'm protective of when your brother isn't staring at me as if he'd like to use me as an ornament for that very sharp sword he seems to be considering drawing," Gervase said dryly. He sobered. "Isabelle, I'm in earnest. I won't stifle this very unsettling independence you're displaying—" He paused, then rolled his eyes. "Very well, be as independent as you like. But please, please let me keep you safe."

"You know, you can be very charming, when you want to be."

"You haven't begun to see charming," he said grimly. "Here, in an abbey of all places." He shot her a look. "You, Isabelle de Piaget, have me so turned about, I scarce recognize myself."

"But you remember my name," she said with a smile.

"Always."

She walked with him up to the gates, listened to him talk their way inside, then continued on until they reached the abbey itself. She glanced at him as they paused to wait for his men to sort themselves.

"If you'd met me in another venue besides your kitchens, what would you have done?"

"I would have gaped at you from afar, miserable in the knowledge that I would never get closer to you than shouting distance, which would unfortunately mean that my bleating would be lost in the chorus of cries made by lads lauding your beauty and goodness."

She looked at him in surprise, then laughed. "You're not serious."

"Oh, I'm quite serious—"

"Her hand only!" Miles bellowed.

Gervase blew his hair out of his eyes. "I'm going to kill him before the day is over." He took her hand, merely bent over it without touching her, then straightened. His expression was very grave. "If I survive an interview with your sire, I would like to court you."

She wondered how it was the weather in France could be so changeable. One moment she was freezing, the other she was burning up.

"Would you?" she managed.

"If the idea suits you."

"I hadn't even considered it," she said frankly. "I was too busy wondering if you were the one trying to kill me."

He tilted his head and smiled faintly. "Would you consider it now, do you think?"

"Would you teach me swordplay?"

"Absolutely not."

She pursed her lips. "My brothers have taught their wives swordplay."

"Your brothers are daft," he said with a snort. He started to speak—no doubt to warm to his theme—then he looked at her and shut his mouth. He dragged his free hand through his hair. "I'll consider it."

"I've taken extensive notes over the years of my siblings' activities."

"I can only imagine," he muttered. He shot Miles a warning look, then gathered her into his arms briefly. "I will," he whispered against her ear, "consent to be led about however you will if you'll simply agree to look at me twice."

"You will not."

"You might be surprised."

"I might be convinced to look at you more than twice, then."

He pulled back at the pointed clearing of more than one throat. "We must elude them at our earliest opportunity."

"I'm fairly sure they have lists here."

His mouth worked for a moment or two, then he bent his head and laughed a little. "If that is the price to be paid, I'll pay it." He took her hand. "Let's find something to drink first and greet your grandmère, then we'll see what else the day brings."

She walked with him, though she couldn't help but hope the day brought nothing more than pleasant conversation in her grandmother's solar. No more missives, no more threats, no more reasons to look skeptically at those she loved. Unfortunately, that left her with a single question that she wasn't sure she was all that eager to have an answer to.

If Gervase hadn't written that missive and put it in his bed, who had?

Chapter 20

Gervase walked behind Isabelle and their brothers as they were led to the abbess's audience chamber. He had sent his men off to seek their fortunes in the buttery and hoped that his own journey wouldn't land him in whatever served for a dungeon in the place. It wasn't as if he hadn't paid his respects to Lady Mary before; it was that he hadn't visited her when his most pressing concern was how to woo her granddaughter before her son could do him in.

Actually, he supposed it was a bit simpler even than that. He had to determine who was stalking Isabelle and who had his death on his mind, then eliminate both threats so he could go on to a peaceful, lengthy life spent admiring a woman whom he was most definitely *not* going to be meeting in the lists, no matter what he might or might not have agreed to earlier. He told himself that several times, because every time he caught sight of her fetching self in hose and sporting shorn hair, he realized that she might be less amenable to being told what to do than she should have been.

Not that he would have wanted her to be tractable, he supposed.

Heaven knew he didn't care for being ordered about himself. Why should she be any different?

He had the feeling a very long conversation with Rhys de Piaget about the proper care and feeding of a de Piaget lass was going to be in order, assuming he was still breathing in order to have that conversation.

He looked next to him to find that his brother had dropped back to walk alongside him. His hands were clasped behind his back, his expression one of perfect calm. Gervase glared at him on principle.

Joscelin blinked. "What?"

"You look very comfortable."

"And why shouldn't I?" Joscelin asked, reaching up to scratch his head. "I'm not the one who put a lady of rank and breeding to work in my kitchens."

"Nay, you're the fool who knew who she was and allowed me to do the like."

"If it eases you," Joscelin said, "I did keep watch over her. Well, except for that moment when Coucy's man assaulted her, but one must take care of certain bodily functions now and again."

Gervase shook his head. "Would you have told me the truth about her eventually?"

"And miss the delight of watching you realize who you had with a broom in her hands? Of course not."

"So you could have her for yourself?" Gervase asked sourly, deciding there was no point in not testing those waters a final time.

"As you know, I've had the thought cross my mind. Unfortunately, she wants you. 'Tis a pity she has no unwed sisters, else I might throw myself on Lord Rhys's mercy and beg for her. Then again, perhaps there will be nothing left of you after he finishes and I might assist our fair flower in recovering from her grief—"

Gervase caught Joscelin by the sleeve before he trotted ahead to put his plan into action. "Let us see what Lord Rhys leaves of me before you start planning your nuptials."

"I'm provoking you," Joscelin said with a smile. "To take your mind off more troubling things."

Gervase didn't bother asking what his brother thought those more troubling things might be. He could make up that list easily enough himself.

He slowed as their guide stopped in front of a heavy set of wooden doors. He took a deep breath, shot his younger brother a warning look simply because he could, then dredged up a pleasant expression. He could do no more.

They were ushered inside the chamber. Lady Mary was standing in front of the fire, but she rushed over immediately and enveloped Isabelle in a ferocious embrace. A veritable storm of weeping ensued along with a volley of questions concerning exactly what Isabelle had been combining that had left her entire family without any idea where she was.

Isabelle finally pulled back from her grandmother, indulged in the mutual dabbing of eyes and cheeks, then looked at the abbess carefully. Gervase knew she was treading carefully because there was something about the set of her shoulders that said as much. He rested his elbow on Joscelin's shoulder and frowned thoughtfully.

"But, Grandmère, I sent you word," Isabelle said slowly. "Did you not receive it?"

"Nicholas had a messenger arriving with all due haste," the abbess said, "but until then—Isabelle, I thought you were dead!"

"Nay, I was well," Isabelle said, submitting to another embrace and patting her grandmother on the back. "His Grace saw to that personally."

Gervase frowned. When had Isabelle sent word to the abbess? He couldn't imagine that she was remembering things amiss, but what did he know? The entire time around his accident was nothing but a fog, still. Obviously, there were things he still needed to discuss with her. He suspected more details about the missive he'd seen not a half hour earlier would be first on the list.

"I see you've brought a friend."

He realized that Abbess Mary was talking about him. He supposed there was no time like the present to begin his wooing of the intimidating Rhys de Piaget. If that ingratiating could begin with the admittedly charming woman standing there with her arm around her granddaughter, so much the better. He walked forward and made the abbess a very low bow.

"My lady," he said politely. "It is a pleasure, as always."

"Lord Gervase," Mary said, extending her hand toward him. "I believe there is a tale here I would like to hear. I can only assume I have you to thank for rescuing my sweet Isabelle from perhaps an unsavoury fate?"

"He was the epitome of all knightly virtues," Isabelle said smoothly. "I believe we could spend the bulk of the afternoon discussing them and not reach the end of them."

Mary laughed a little. "Spoken like a girl who has been treated very well by a chivalrous man." She kissed Isabelle on the cheek. "Let's take our ease in front of the fire and you can begin your list. Lord Gervase, will you join us?"

Gervase made her another low bow. "I believe, my lady, that perhaps I would do better for the moment to stand and stretch my leg. I will gladly accept the invitation later."

And with that, he was summarily abandoned to his fate. He smiled briefly at Isabelle, then sought refuge against a spot of bare wall.

He supposed that said much about his life at present. A year ago, he would have been perfectly happy to sit in front of the fire in the midst of the chaos, but now he found himself far preferring to stand on the edge of things where he could see things approaching.

Ah, how things changed in an instant.

He sighed deeply, then distracted himself from the ache in his leg by considering the scene before him. The chamber was smallish but well appointed. Obviously someone—Lord Rhys, no doubt—had made certain that the abbess was comfortably housed. There was certainly no lack of security for the woman. There had been guardsmen attending the abbess at a discreet distance, to be sure. And that nun who was standing next to the door with her arms folded over her chest looked perfectly capable of seeing to any disturbance—

Gervase felt his mouth fall open. He shut it before he could make a complete ass of himself, but even so, his surprise was great.

The woman standing there was very tall, easily as tall as he was, with shoulders that stretched the confines of her garb in a way that left him thinking that engaging her in even a simple clasping of hands might not go so well for him. Her hands were tucked into the sleeves of her robe, which left him unable to ascertain their condition, but 'twas a certainty that her feet were large enough to do damage with, did she care to give a recalcitrant donor a boot in the arse.

He looked about the chamber to see if anyone else was finding the sight of that hulking brute—er, that fully fleshed sister of the cloth, rather—to be as odd as he was. Isabelle was too busy being fussed over by her grandmother to have the chance to notice anything. Miles, however, was watching not Isabelle and the lady Mary, but the woman standing post next to the door.

He jumped a little himself as he realized Joscelin was standing right next to him. "How long have you been there?" he said out of the side of his mouth.

"Longer than you noticed."

Gervase shivered. "Have you seen that sister there by the door?"

"She's hard to miss," Joscelin whispered.

He considered a bit longer, then looked at his brother. "Are my eyes failing me?"

"Um," Joscelin said uncomfortably, "I don't think so."

Gervase didn't think so, either. He looked at Miles who was still studying the nun with an intensity Gervase had rarely seen on his face before. Perhaps he was coming to his own conclusions about things that couldn't possibly be the case.

That was a woman standing there, wasn't it?

"Let's see if they have lists," he said under his breath. "I need some exercise to clear my head."

"Are we taking that one with us?"

"I don't want to cross blades with her," Gervase said honestly. "Do you?"

Joscelin shook his head, wide-eyed.

"Then we'll leave her here to guard the women and work off a bit of our energy." Gervase pushed away from the wall and walked over to lean down and speak to Miles. "Do they have lists here that we could trample for an hour or two?"

Miles looked up at him. "The question is, do you dare drag me out to them?"

"Oh, I think I dare."

Miles smiled. He pushed himself to his feet, then reached out and put his hand on Isabelle's head. "Grandmère, the lads and I are in need of a bit of fresh air. May we use your yard to seek the same?"

"Of course, love," the abbess said. "The good sister there will show you where to go."

Gervase hesitated. "But if we take her, my lady, will you be safe here?"

Lady Mary looked up at him in surprise. "But of course, my lord Monsaert. Why wouldn't we?"

"I wouldn't want to rob you of your protection there by the door." Actually, he didn't want to face that hulking wench in the lists, but he supposed he could go all day without admitting that. "I could send for my men to stand without. In fact, why don't we leave your good sister there with you and I'll send for my men. Then my mind will be at ease."

Mary smiled at him. "If that suits you, Your Grace."

"It does, my lady." He elbowed Miles out of the way and looked down at Isabelle. "I'm assuming you'll remain safely ensconced here."

She opened her mouth, no doubt to protest, but apparently good sense prevailed. She looked up at him, then nodded. "If you like."

"I like," he said. "I promise I'll escort you into every nook and cranny allowed when I return, but *please* stay here until I come to fetch you."

Lady Mary laughed a bit. "So says a man who has more than a passing acquaintance with my granddaughter. Has she been a great deal of trouble to you, Your Grace?"

"Aye," Gervase said, returning her smile, "but 'tis trouble I would happily entertain for as long as she sees fit to grace me with her unequaled self."

"Has she convinced you yet to meet her in the lists?"

Gervase suppressed the urge to sigh. "She has, and I'm assuming she knows that my willingness to do so rests entirely on her remaining safely here in your solar until I return."

Mary looked at Isabelle. "Protective."

"Bossy."

"Delightful."

Gervase thought it best to beat a hasty retreat while the words that were flying were still complimentary. He put his own hand on Isabelle's head, slid it down her hair with as much affection as he dared show with Miles de Piaget standing there, then turned and walked to the door. He nodded to the sister standing there, then left the chamber before she volunteered to come with them.

"Follow me," Miles said from behind him, "but you'll have to let me by first. If memory serves, the space is surprisingly large, which should give you ample choice of places to flee."

Gervase cursed him, had a laugh in return, then walked through the cloister with the two men he thought he might trust the most at the moment. Aubert's loyalty was beyond question, of course, and he trusted his captain to vouch for the loyalty of his men, but having trustworthy members of his family was a bit more unusual. He had trusted his grandfather, of course, without reservation. His father, much less. Perhaps that was why he had never been completely comfortable with Guy. They were too much alike, those two.

"Good hell, it's the manly sister," Joscelin squeaked suddenly. "She's following us to do the saints only know what." He looked at Gervase. "You don't think she's planning on engaging in any swordplay, do you?"

Miles cleared his throat. "I believe there is the tip of a sword hanging below her skirts, which perhaps tells us everything we need to know."

Gervase didn't particularly care for what he was being told, but short of stopping and confronting her, there was nothing to be done. "We'll gain the field, then see what unfolds. I see no other alternative."

"None besides scampering back to my grandmother's solar," Miles said uneasily, "but that would make us look like cowards, which we are not. Onward, lads, to our fate."

Gervase nodded, then continued to follow Miles until they were on the edge of what obviously served as some sort of training field. An odd thing to find in an abbey, perhaps, but the place was filled with vulnerable sisters. No sense in not having some sort of garrison there to keep them safe and a place for that garrison to hone their skills.

He stopped several paces into that rather muddy expanse with his companions, then waited for a handful of moments until he thought they might have been joined by Lady Mary's mysterious companion. Then he turned around abruptly and looked at the nun who had been following them. She had come to a stop a handful of paces away and merely folded her arms over her chest. Gervase returned her bold look, taking the opportunity to examine details he hadn't been able to inside.

Such as the fact that the nun had missed shaving quite a bit of her upper lip while about her ablutions that morning. He might have felt a bit of compassion for her, but the truth was, she looked as if she had removed hair from more than just most of her upper lip. Stranger still, *she* looked a damn sight like Miles de Piaget, only with a few wisps of silver hair escaping her wimple.

"Hmmm," Gervase said, because he could think of nothing else to say.

"Indeed," said the nun in a high, raspy voice.

Gervase was hardly an expert on the twists and turns of the de Piaget lineage, but he would have wagered a hefty bag of gold that standing before him was someone who belonged to that clan. He supposed all he could do at that point was throw himself on the mercy of the woman in front of him and hope she had more than a passing acquaintance with the truth.

"I don't suppose, my good, ah, woman, that you have any records of genealogies here at the Abbey, do you?"

"And why would you ask that, my son?"

"I'm curious by nature," Gervase admitted. "I'm particularly curious about the generations of de Piagets."

"Fond of the little one, are you?" the nun asked with a smile.

"Very," Gervase said. "I wouldn't want her to be—how shall I say it?—kept in the dark about potential relatives she might not realize she has."

The nun lifted her eyebrows briefly. "Speaking of relatives, I knew your grandfather, you know."

Gervase supposed he shouldn't have been surprised to be caught so off guard by that, but he was. "Did you indeed?" he managed.

"You're so much like him, I almost had a bit of a swoon when you walked in."

"How distressing for your delicate humors."

The nun laughed. "So it was, lad."

Gervase studied the soul in front of him and wondered if he might manage to pass a month in the company of any de Piaget lad or lass and guess from the start whether they were lass or lad, or if he would be continually presented with an endless procession of them masquerading as what they were not.

For he would have bet his hall that the creature before him was not a woman.

"Bad luck with that—what would you call what befell you?" the nun asked.

"An accident?" Gervase said slowly.

The nun snorted. "I believe you'll find, son, that when you wear the mantel of power and riches, there are no accidents."

"Would you know?"

"Who me?" he—um, *she* said, putting her hand to her throat and coughing delicately. "Assuredly not."

Gervase considered what he did and didn't know about the de Piaget family. The truth was, his family had had more to do with that family than he'd taken the trouble to think about very often. His grandfather, Abelard, had been a great friend of the abbess. He hadn't been particularly interested in how her place at the abbey had come about, but he did vaguely recall over-hearing a conversation between his grandfather and his father in which her calling had been discussed. There had been rumors that her husband—father of the intimidating and powerful Lord Rhys—had been about some secretive business that no one was comfortable discussing, but he'd been slain in an unfortunate accident. She had been settled at the abbey by the current king's father in gratitude for . . . well, Gervase couldn't bring to mind at the moment what act had earned her that gratitude, but he supposed it must have been something spectacular. Caours was, after all, a rather impressive place.

He looked at the nun in front of him and wondered just how familiar that one was with the mantel of power and riches.

"One merely observes," the good sister continued, "when one has no power of her own."

Gervase shot the nun a skeptical look. *"Merde,"* he said mildly.

The nun looked at him, then laughed. "Watch your mouth, boy, or Lady Mary will be taking a switch to your backside."

"Better her than you," Gervase said slowly. "My lord Etienne."

The nun went very still. "What do you think you know, little lad?"

"That you should likely polish up your sword a bit more before you use it as a mirror," Gervase answered. He pointed to his lip. "You missed a spot there. Several spots, actually."

The nun sighed deeply. "Hell," he said, pulling off his wimple. "Caught, I see."

Miles gasped. Gervase supposed that might have been worth all the aggravation Isabelle's brother had caused him up until that moment. He stood back and watched as the younger de Piaget stumbled over to the elder de Piaget and gaped at him.

"Grandfather?" he managed.

Etienne smiled, looking so much like Miles that Gervase

had to shake his head in wonder. The man pulled his grandson into his arms and engaged in a hearty round of manly back slapping and no small amount of dissembling. The number of *ums* and *ers* and *wells* that came out of the man's mouth was impressive, to say the least.

"Where have you been?" Miles demanded finally.

"Hiding in plain sight, whelp," Etienne said with a snort. "Where else?"

"But I've been here half a dozen times and never noticed you!"

"Which does not recommend your powers of observation," Etienne said pointedly, "something I daresay we should see to during this visit. Oh, damnation, here comes your sister."

A wimple was restored without delay, but the robes were still askew. Gervase supposed that was something Lord Etienne would have to discover on his own. He was going to be too busy reminding Isabelle that two guardsmen were simply not enough.

"Hasn't she grown up to be a beauty?" Etienne said proudly. "I imagine there's quite a line of eligible suitors beating a path to my son's door. I believe I'll need to look them all over before I offer an opinion on who might be an appropriate husband for her." He looked at Miles. "Where has she been hiding since she disappeared from Artane?"

"I'm not exactly sure," Miles lied. "I know she's been at Beauvois for the past few days, but those se'nnights before then? Perhaps our good duke can provide some insight." He looked at Gervase and blinked. "Your Grace?"

Gervase shot Miles a look of promise, then turned a pleasant expression on Isabelle's grandfather. "She was shipwrecked, my lord Etienne, then I found her wandering along the road near Monsaert. She was missing her memories, so I thought it best to bring her back to my hall and care for her there."

Etienne lifted an eyebrow. "Why do I have the feeling there's much more to the tale than that?"

"I have the same feeling," Miles said, moving to stand shoulder-to-shoulder with his grandfather. "Do tell, my lord Gervase."

Gervase took a moment to wiggle his jaw before he said something to Isabelle's twin he might later come to regret, then turned his attention fully to her grandfather. "This is, I believe, where things become a bit less comfortable to relate," he said carefully.

"If you tell me you have vanquished her," Etienne said without hesitation, "I will kill you."

"Why does everyone think vanquishment of maidens is the only thing I do?" Gervase asked in irritation. "I do have some small measure of control over myself."

"I don't think he's going to like what you *did* do any more than that," Joscelin said helpfully, "so perhaps you should tell him quickly while he's still irritated over the thought of the other."

Gervase looked at his supporters—if that's what they could be called. "I believe I will be seeing you both in the lists today. Don't expect it to be a pleasant experience for either of you." He turned to Etienne. "Here is the absolute truth. She spent a week in my healer's house, recovering from a bump on her head that rid her of certain important memories such as her identity. After that, I put her to work in my kitchens until I had the wit to realize she couldn't possibly be a servant, then I set her to educating my younger brothers. And before Joscelin tells you, she did have a brush or two with a particular ruffian, but he's still rotting in my dungeon for his cheek."

Etienne shook his head slowly. "Are you so dense that you couldn't recognize her right off?"

"I'd never seen her before," Gervase said. "Neither her, nor Amanda, nor even the lady Gwennelyn."

"Not popular at Beauvois, are you?" Etienne asked, seemingly fighting his smile.

"My reputation for seducing maidens is greatly exaggerated," Gervase grumbled.

Etienne reached out and clapped him companionably on the shoulder with perhaps a bit more enthusiasm than was necessary. "I know, lad. Just doing my part to make your life a misery. Don't think Rhys won't add to that when he arrives."

"I'm afraid of that," Gervase said honestly.

"You likely should be. So, you realized after an extended period of stupidity who you had in your hall, then I assume you returned her to Beauvois where Nicholas tried to kill you?"

Gervase looked at him in frustration. "Are you trying to be helpful?"

"Not particularly," Etienne said, "though I will do you a favor. There is a woman here, a healer of unusual and forward-thinking talents. Let's have her look at your leg and see if she can't see what's amiss with it."

"What's amiss with it is that it was broken with the bones coming through the skin," Gervase said pointedly. "I'm not sure there's any mystery about that."

"Nevertheless, it might be worth your time. Greet that sweet girl coming our way, then let's allow Sister Jeanne to have a look at you. If she doesn't rip your muscles to shreds, she might do you some good. She can also tell if your leg was set properly."

Gervase looked at him doubtfully. "But how can she feel—"

"She has hands like a blacksmith. You really don't want to know more than that before she starts to work on you. I can clip you under the jaw before she begins or give you a leather strap. You tell me how much you value your teeth. Or I can simply sit with you and hold your hand as you weep."

Gervase would have thanked the man for the suggestions, but he didn't have the chance before Etienne's granddaughter was standing in front of him, looking slightly annoyed. He looked at her in surprise.

"What?"

"You promised me time in the lists." She gestured behind him. "I think they're right there."

"Ah—"

"Even the sisters here have swords," Isabelle said. She gestured to the nun she didn't know was her grandfather. "See? She has a sword."

"But perhaps not the skill to use it," Miles offered.

Etienne delivered a brisk slap to the back of his grandson's head. "Of course I know how to use it," he said delicately. "One does what one must to keep the abbess safe."

Gervase could only imagine. He sighed over the pointed look Isabelle sent his way, then reached for her hand.

"Knife work," he conceded. "Perhaps."

"For a few minutes, my child," Etienne said in a remarkably high voice. "I believe there is a sister here who might do a goodly work on his leg if you can leave something of him for her to see to."

The look on Isabelle's face almost brought tears to Gervase's eyes, hard-hearted lout that he was.

"In truth?" she asked. "I've tried herbs, but there is only so much they can do."

"I'm sure you've aided him greatly," Etienne said. "By the time Sister Jeanne is finished with him, he'll be back to his former self. I understand he has a few challenges in the lists to look forward to, so we'd best put him back together as quickly as possible. Wouldn't want him failing now, would we?"

Isabelle blushed. Gervase suppressed the urge to sit down and wait until events rearranged themselves in a fashion he could be comfortable with. He was courting—and he used that term very advisedly—a woman who blushed at the thought of any of it, he was listening to that woman's grandfather begin to offer her all manner of advice on the proper way for a woman to wield her blade, and he was quite certain that what lay in store for him in the chambers of the woman with hands reputedly akin to a blacksmith's wasn't going to be at all pleasant.

If that weren't enough, the path to Isabelle de Piaget's hand was strewn with things he wasn't particularly comfortable with. Someone was vexing her, someone wanted to slay him, and her father was going to be absolutely livid when he discovered the extent of Isabelle's activities over the past pair of fortnights.

He only wished that was all he had to look forward to.

Unfortunately, he had the feeling there were many, far less pleasant things awaiting him.

Chapter 21

Isabelle walked toward the kitchens, trailed by a collection of guardsmen. She supposed she didn't need to see to any preparations, but she had needed some air. She also wasn't unhappy for the chance to have a look around, though she wasn't entirely sure what she thought she would see. She was, however, fairly sure of what she didn't want to see.

She wasn't one to purposely seek out corners to hide in, but she had to admit that she was tempted to try it for a change. The only reason for hiding she'd had in the past had been to avoid whatever fools had come to Artane, hunting for a bride. Her situation was quite a bit more perilous at the moment.

Worse still was not having any idea where to look. In the single day she'd been at Caours, she had started at shadows, looked askance at every soul she'd encountered, and even gone so far as to very briefly speculate on whether or not her brother might have had nefarious plans. The ridiculousness of that thought was, she had to admit, the only thing that had calmed her. No matter what she might have done to him over the years, she had no doubt that Miles loved her.

But there was obviously someone out there who didn't.

Isabelle shivered, then paused at the door to the kitchens. There was another door on the opposite side of the large chamber, true, but she didn't see anyone with evil intent lurking there. The kitchen staff seemed to be nothing out of the ordinary. Besides, she had a knife and had taken extensive notes on how to use it. Actually taking blade in hand and trying to spar with Gervase earlier in the afternoon had been something of a disaster, but could she be blamed if she had found the sight of his appallingly handsome face to be more of a distraction than she'd been able to overcome? She would have to make a more serious study of the art with someone she wasn't quite so fond of. Miles, perhaps, if he could be prevailed upon to venture into the lists with her.

She turned to her guardsmen and smiled. "I think I'm safe enough for the moment."

Sir Denis made her a sharp bow. "We'll wait without, Lady Isabelle, well within earshot."

She imagined they would. She nodded her thanks, then turned and walked into the chamber. She introduced herself to the cook, then simply kept herself out of the way. She would have, at one point, extended her compliments regarding the delicious smell of the stew on the fire, but it was easier to simply lean back against the wall and feel safe. Or it could have been that speech was suddenly beyond her. That happened, she supposed when one caught a glimpse of a man who she suspected had left more than one lass rather speechless.

Gervase had walked past the other door—on the path that lay there, apparently—then returned and leaned back into the kitchen. Isabelle couldn't imagine he had paused because he'd seen her, but there was no denying that he was looking at her at present.

He smiled.

She would have backed up, but the wall was already firmly behind her. That was handy enough, she supposed, simply because leaning against a substantial amount of sturdy stone seemed like a reasonable thing to do in order to regain her composure.

That one there, the man now leaning his shoulder against one side of the opposite doorway, watching her, was dangerous. She had noted to herself several times in recent memory that he was too handsome by half and fully too charming for the safe consumption of any female. She couldn't quite bring herself to believe the rumors of his seduction of most of the eligible maidens in France, but she could certainly see how they might have been true.

She realized at a certain point that he was simply watching her gape at him. She shut her mouth, considered, then pursed her lips at him, just so he would know that she was not going to endure being mocked by an extremely handsome man who was obviously well aware of his considerable charms.

He lifted an eyebrow.

She settled herself more comfortably against the wall behind her and with great ceremony folded her arms over her chest.

He smiled. She had to close her eyes in self-defense, but that ended her very fine view, so she decided that perhaps it was just best to keep an eye on him to see what he would do next.

Actually, she supposed there was no point in not being honest with herself. She wasn't watching him because she wanted to know what he would do next, she was watching him because he was beautiful. Beautiful and determined and possessing a smile that left her rather weak in the knees.

And he knew her name.

He pushed away from the wall and walked to the center of the kitchen. He stopped, then clasped his hands behind his back.

"I can wait," he said with a shrug. "All night, if necessary."

"As can I."

He looked as if he were fighting a smile. "I'll take you out in the lists first thing tomorrow."

"To do what?"

He did laugh then. "Not to look at flowers, surely."

"Specifics, Gervase."

"Well," he said, his breath catching a bit, "if you're going to use my name, I suppose I'll have to meet you over steel. Does that suit?"

She pushed away from the wall and walked over to him. She stopped a handsbreadth away and looked up at him. "Check," she said.

"Check*mate*," he said pointedly. He smiled. "I got you across the kitchen, didn't I?"

"Halfway, which is not all the way, and you promised me time in the lists for that halfway, which means I win."

He put his arms around her. "You are a feisty thing."

"'Tis a recent discovery, but I think I like me this way." She smiled at him. "How went your time with my grandmother's healer?"

He winced. "All I can say is I now know how wheat feels on its journey from grain to flour. Worse still, she wants to see me again tomorrow."

"She can hardly be blamed for that," Isabelle said. "You are a rather handsome man."

"She's old enough to be my mother."

"That doesn't mean her eyes don't function as they should."

He smiled at her. "Why, my lady Isabelle, I believe that was a compliment."

"I have an obsession with truth," she said primly.

"And I think I have an obsession with you."

She thought she just might share that, as it happened. "Are you suggesting that you aren't always this willing to go halfway across kitchens to be friendly with your former scullery maids?"

He smoothed her hair back from her face. "What I'm saying is that I would have come *all* the way across the kitchens tonight to fetch you if you'd asked it."

She smiled. "Would you?"

"Actually, I think if I hadn't been convinced your sire would have killed me outside his front gates for daring to show my face there, I would have made the journey to Artane, and then presented myself to your sire with a very pointed request to see the lady Isabelle. Not her sister, not any of her sisters-in-law, but the youngest daughter."

She felt her smile fade. "You wouldn't have," she said. "Not in truth."

He sighed. "Isabelle, the truth is, I was deep in the morass that was my own life, unhappily pulled from a life spent living simply to flatter my own ego in order to take over my father's place. But rest assured that I *definitely* knew who you were and had spent many unhappy moments in envious contemplation of the man who would eventually be fortunate enough to win your hand. I simply never considered that I might contend for that place myself."

She shook her head. "I can scarce believe that."

"I'll work on convincing you later," he said seriously. "And as for my father's very useful title, I believe I'll keep it gladly. I don't think your sire would allow me within a hundred paces of you otherwise."

She smiled. "I believe, Your Grace, that you're slightly closer than a hundred paces at the moment."

"So I am," he said. He looked at her, then took her face very gently in his hands. "But still too far away—"

"What in the *hell* is going on here?"

Isabelle wasn't sure who moved first or more quickly but she found herself standing a good five paces away from Gervase who looked easily as guilty as she felt. She turned to the source of that bellow only to see her eldest brother standing just inside the door, an expression of thunderous disapproval on his face.

Well, he was wearing a bit of a smirk as well, but it was Robin after all.

Robin pointed at her. "You," he said distinctly. "Come over here."

Isabelle would have suggested that he go to Hell—indeed the words were on the tip of her tongue—but before she could stop spluttering long enough to spew them out, Gervase had reached over and pulled her behind him.

"Do not," he said crisply, "speak to my lady that way."

Isabelle peeked over Gervase's shoulder to see if that had left any sort of impression on her brother. Robin's smirk had only grown more pronounced.

"And who, boy," he boomed, "are *you*?"

"Don't be an ass," Gervase said shortly. "You know exactly who I am."

Robin pursed his lips. "Unfortunately I do, which hardly leaves me any more at ease. Release my sister, you rogue."

Isabelle supposed there was no reason not to offer her own opinion. "We know each other."

"I'm unhappily a witness to that fact."

"Miles said Gervase could kiss my hand," she said.

Robin folded his arms over his chest. "I believe our little Gervase was intending to kiss quite a bit more than just your hand."

She leaned to the side and glared at her brother. "Then give him permission to do so."

"He'll have to earn it."

Isabelle patted Gervase on the back. "Well, go to, my lad."

Gervase turned and looked at her in surprise. "You're sending me off unprotected to face that ruthless bastard?"

"You don't want to be coddled."

He studied her for a moment or two in silence, then took her face in his hands and smiled. "I believe, my lady Isabelle, that I just might be inordinately fond of you."

Isabelle thought she just might feel the same way. And she realized at about the same time that he was going to kiss her—

"Oh, there'll be none of that," Robin said. "Release her, vile thing, and let's trot out to the lists and see if you're worthy of kissing anything but her boots."

Gervase looked over his shoulder. "'Tis dark outside. I'll see you in the morning."

"We'll bring torches."

Gervase sighed, took her face again in his hands, then very deliberately kissed her on first one cheek, then the other. He smoothed the hair back from her face. "I'll return."

"I'll come along and watch."

"It might be too much for your delicate humors."

"I've seen my brother humiliated before," she said airily. "It won't trouble me overmuch."

"Me?" Robin spluttered.

Isabelle watched as Gervase winked at her, then took off his cloak and put it around her. He put his arm around her shoulders and led her over to collect her brother.

"Let's go discuss past humiliations of yours, shall we?"

Robin swore. "I don't remember any humiliations."

"Langres," Gervase said distinctly. "Laon as well, I think. My memory begins to fail at that point. Didn't we meet at Guérande?"

"You bastard," Robin growled.

"You're one to talk, aren't you? Let's go."

"I will when you release my sister."

Isabelle ignored the pointed look her brother gave her as she slipped her hand into Gervase's, ignored with more vigor the strangled noises of horror he was indulging in, and wondered how it was Anne of Artane endured him.

"Where is your sainted wife?" Isabelle asked, suppressing the urge to insult her brother whilst she had the breath for it.

"I left her and the children with Mother and Father and the fiercest of my guardsmen," Robin said, "and rode ahead to see if I could be of some use. To Grandmère, if to no one else. I would suggest you make a measured retreat to her solar and join her before her fire, but perhaps you don't want to miss the humiliation I have in store for your would-be lover there." He shook his head. "I can scarce believe I just heard myself say that. Are you old enough to have a would-be anything?"

She shot her brother a warning look, which he received with a bland look before he turned to Gervase.

"Heard a rumor about your little troubles," Robin said as they walked away from the kitchens and along the cloister. "I'm surprised you didn't see it coming."

"My hall was full of smoke, as it happens, so I didn't see much of anything."

"I heard about that as well. At least you were left your visage, which I suppose my sister thinks she'll be appreciating as the future unwinds itself. Perhaps you might want to keep a few more guardsmen about yourself from now on."

"Thank you for that," Gervase said dryly.

Robin smiled wickedly. "I do what I can for the lesser men who seem to find themselves drawn into my sphere of influence."

"Lesser?" Gervase returned Robin's smile. "You *are* still smarting from that thrashing I gave you in—where was it again?"

Isabelle listened to them discuss just where that impossible event had never taken place as they made their way to the place of new torture, then finally found herself standing with her brother, waiting for Gervase to listen to a report from his garrison captain. Isabelle found herself hugged until she had to pound Robin on the back to let her go. He put his hands on her shoulders and looked at her seriously.

"We worried."

She sighed. "I had to come, Robby."

"Aye, so Miles told me not an hour ago. And just so you know, he told me everything." He started to speak, then finally shook his head. "Could you not have trusted me with the tidings, Iz? I could have taken this burden on for you."

"You have three children, Robin," she said seriously.

"And you are my youngest sister," he said, "which leaves me with the obligation to protect you as I would them." He pulled her back into his arms and hugged her again so tightly she squeaked. "Daft wench. What were you thinking? First you trot off to see to a possible murderer on your own, then you fall in love with Gervase de Seger, of all people."

"Do you dislike him so, then?"

Robin grunted, then stepped aside and slung his arm around her shoulders. "Speaking as a swordsman? I have grudging respect for his skill. As the brother of the woman he obviously loves? Can't stand him. I foresee many hours spent putting him in his place so he doesn't dare kiss your dung-encrusted boots." He smiled pleasantly. "Doesn't that sound lovely?"

Isabelle supposed it was best not to answer that. She leaned against her brother as she watched Gervase speak to Sir Aubert.

"Is he in danger, do you think?" she asked quietly.

Robin sighed. "I find myself singularly unable to make light of it, so I'll simply say aye. He's fortunate to be alive. Of course, I might manage to remedy that tonight, but I'm a hopeful sort of lad."

"Robin," she said with a sigh.

Robin laughed a little. "You know I'm preparing him for what he'll face with Father."

She looked up at him. "Was he formidable?" she asked. "Before?"

"Rather, which made him all the more loathsome. Just my sort of lad, of course. And just so we're clear, the vanquishing was spread about equally. I'm simply choosing not to remind him of his prior failures during this delicate spot in the negotiations between the two of you."

She watched Gervase for another moment or two until she thought she could ask what ate at her. "And," she began very slowly, "will he be formidable again, do you think?"

"Do you care?"

She met his gray eyes. "Not for myself, but for him?" She took a deep breath. "Aye, I care very much."

"You know," he said, smoothing her hair away from her face, "you are a woman without peer."

"Not even Amanda?" she asked wistfully.

He closed his eyes briefly. "Isabelle, your strengths lie in different areas."

"I wish mine lay with steel."

"Why?"

She nodded toward Gervase. "So I might guard his back if the need arose."

"You're too fond of him."

"Can you blame me?"

"Of course I can," Robin said promptly. "He's hopelessly

arrogant. No one ever wanted to sup with him when he was off raiding the countryside."

She smiled. "You're not serious."

"Well, no one ever wanted to sup with him because he was forever holding cheeky knights for ransom and pouring their gold into his coffers. I suppose there were women enough who invited him to grace their tables."

"Then perhaps he wouldn't want me," she said slowly.

Robin looked at her in surprise. "You forget who you are."

"I don't think that matters here."

"I think it matters to *him*, damn him anyway. And because of that, I daresay I'll be forced to train you a bit. It might be the only thing that saves you from that reprobate out there."

"I already have Gervase's knife in my boot."

"Give it back to him," Robin advised. "He might need it." He patted her and stepped back. "Go find a bit of wall to sit on. I'll find you a knife tomorrow and we'll work."

She looked at him seriously. "Why now?"

He pursed his lips. "Because I should have done it earlier but always thought there would be time enough. When did you stop being a child?"

She rolled her eyes and walked away from him. But she fully intended to hold him to his promise.

She found herself a spot for watching the madness, was grateful for a decent amount of moonlight, and supposed if there were ever a place to pray that her brother wouldn't kill the man she thought she just might love, it was her grandmother's abbey.

Chapter 22

G*ervase* stood outside the abbess's solar, looked at his love's eldest brother, and was tempted to thank him for a lovely evening. He supposed it said much about his life before his wounding that he never would have unbent far enough to thank someone for taking him out to the lists and beating the bloody hell out of him.

Things changed, indeed.

He leaned his shoulder against the stone because he was simply too damned tired to stand up all on his own any longer. He cursed to give himself a bit of courage, then looked at Robin.

"Thank you."

Robin grinned. "That had to have hurt almost as much as the thrashing I just gave you."

"I'm surprised to find it doesn't," Gervase said honestly.

Robin clapped him with unpleasant firmness on the shoulder. "Poor babe, you are in sad shape. I'll see what I can do over the next several days to remake you into a warrior who might someday hope to stand against my squire, but the task is daunting."

Gervase shook off Robin's hand because he knew Isabelle's brother would have expected nothing else. "Do you *ever* shut up?"

Robin only lifted an eyebrow. "'Tis all part of the regimen, my lad, to build your strength for both swordplay and insults. You would think you hadn't lost your resilience for the latter, at least, but I find I'm continually surprised by the condition of the lesser swordsmen I'm called on to better." He smiled. "Don't fret, little one. When you reach my august age with my number of full, rich years behind you, you'll understand."

"I'm not that much younger than you are, you fool."

"At least four years by my count," Robin said, "which leaves you wet behind the ears still."

Gervase was fairly certain that Robin waxed rhapsodic on that subject for quite some time, but he found he couldn't quite pay attention any longer—though he supposed he might come to regret that on the field at some point. He looked around him, frowned, then looked at Robin.

"Where's Isabelle?"

Robin left off with his babbling. "Surrounded by your guard and mine," he said with a shrug. "Why?"

"Because I haven't seen her in a quarter hour," Gervase said. He looked over Robin's shoulder but saw neither Isabelle nor her guard. "Move," he said, pushing past Isabelle's brother.

He found himself running. That was, he had to admit, excruciating. Worse still was that Robin was keeping pace with him without the slightest sign of exertion.

"You'll recover," Robin said mildly.

"And how the bloody hell would you know?" Gervase said with perhaps a bit more enthusiasm than he should have.

"I almost died of a fever in my youth," Robin said. "Took me half a year to be able to shuffle across the damned courtyard and that much time again to feel like myself. I'd suggest you find out sooner rather than later who wants you dead so you can heal. You don't want my sister endlessly coddling you, do you?"

Gervase most certainly did not, which he supposed he didn't need to say. He skidded to a halt, though, when he saw Isabelle walking toward him along one side of the cloister. Actually, he couldn't see her, but he could certainly see her cluster of guards well enough. He suppressed the urge to continue to run toward them all. Obviously, he was simply on edge. She was well.

He waited until they had stopped in front of him before he

parted Robin's men and his with equal ease, then looked at his lady. It took but a single glance to know that something was amiss. He thanked his men, reached for her hand, and pulled her out of their circle. He supposed taking liberties with her person was not going to endear him to her brother, but he didn't give a damn what Robin of Artane thought. He pulled her into his arms.

"What befell you?" he whispered against her ear.

"Nothing."

He might have believed that if she hadn't been so still. He considered that for a moment or two, then stepped back and cleared his throat. "Thank you, lads," he said in a cheerful tone. "My lord Robin and I can see his sister back to safety, so please seek your own rest by a warm fire."

The men nodded respectfully, even Robin's, and walked off to presumably the abbey's garrison hall. Gervase didn't have to put Isabelle between himself and her brother, he merely watched Robin take her far side. He also didn't have to look behind him to know that Sir Aubert had elected to ignore the order to decamp and was following them as they wasted no time walking back to Lady Mary's chamber. There was another lad walking alongside Aubert who wore Artane's colors and looked passing unpleasant, so Gervase assumed he was Robin's captain. Isabelle would be safe enough.

He reached for her hand and squeezed it. "The truth," he said quietly.

"The truth is I'm cold," Isabelle said. "Robin, stop crushing my fingers."

"Monsaert is holding your hand," Robin said. "I'm just keeping you balanced."

"*He's* not crushing my fingers!"

"I'm warming your fingers," Robin said. "You're cold."

"That's because I *am* cold."

Gervase considered interrupting to pry answers from her, but he supposed if anyone were going to be an annoyance to her, it was better that it be her brother and not him. He listened to them bicker in a relatively good-natured way until they were standing in front of Mary's solar. He jumped a little at the sight of his younger brother arriving at the same time from a different path.

"Lord Joscelin," Isabelle said faintly.

Gervase was surprised enough at her tone to look at her. She was as pale as if Yves had recently flattened her and she was having trouble catching her breath. He frowned, then looked at Joscelin and tried to pit his poor wits against the mystery of why Isabelle would look terrified and Joscelin baffled. Well, the latter was easier, surely. Joscelin was often overcome by the view of a lovely woman. But Isabelle? That she should look so unsettled was very odd, indeed.

"What ails you?" he asked carefully.

She was trembling, but she lifted her chin. She stepped away, toward Joscelin, and turned to put her back against his chest.

"Put your arm over my throat."

"What?" Joscelin asked in astonishment.

"Do it," she said harshly.

He looked as shocked as Gervase had ever seen him, but he gingerly complied. Isabelle patted his arm, then took him by that arm and spun out from underneath him. She shoved his sleeve up to his elbow, then closed her eyes briefly.

"It wasn't you."

"What," Joscelin said in a garbled tone, "are you talking about?"

"Nothing." She released him and patted him on the shoulder. "My apologies."

Gervase would have asked her what in the hell she was doing but found there was no need. She walked over to him, then pulled his head down toward hers. He sincerely wished she had been preparing to kiss him. He wished it with even greater fervor after he'd listened to her words.

"The lad we're looking for caught me in the garderobe," she murmured against his ear.

Gervase froze. "Are you hurt?"

"Nay, nor embarrassed, thankfully."

He ignored Robin's noises of protest as he put his arms around Isabelle. "What did you do to him?"

She laughed a little. "What faith you have in me."

He found he wasn't equal to even making a poor jest. All he could do was hold her tightly and hope that she mistook his trembling for something coming from her.

"I'm sorry to do that to your brother," she said quietly. "I just don't know who to trust."

"I think we're safe inside," he said. He lifted his head and looked down at her. "Only family there."

She nodded, but said nothing.

He let Robin open the door, then hung back until he saw everyone settled. Isabelle had saved a chair for him next to her, which he appreciated, but he didn't suppose it served him to sit quite yet. He shut the door, then joined Lord Etienne in standing by the solar's entrance.

"What news, son?" Etienne said, covering a feigned yawn with his hand.

"Betrayal," Gervase murmured. "Danger. An assault on my lady."

"Who is behind it?"

"I haven't determined that as yet."

"Best hurry then, hadn't you?"

Gervase looked at Isabelle's grandfather. "I'm not sure how to tell you this, but apparently you and your wife are in the lad's sights as well."

Etienne lifted a single silvery eyebrow. "That puts it in a different light."

"I believe, my lord, that it might be time for some honesty. About not only who you are, but what Isabelle knows. I imagine I'll contribute a thing or two, as well."

Etienne sighed deeply. "Why did I know you were the harbinger of doom?"

"Because I am the Griffin of Monsaert," Gervase said with a snort, "which tells you all you need to know, I suppose."

Etienne elbowed him companionably. "And your grandfather counted the days until you wore that title, my lad, so bear it proudly. I'll tell you about our more notable exploits over a bottle of wine after you've solved your little tangle here. You'll appreciate them, I daresay."

Gervase blinked. "You have exploits? With my grandfather?"

"Several," Etienne said cheerfully. "Very dangerous, very secretive. Abelard was an excellent swordsman, but he didn't make a particularly good nun. I'll tell you about that later, as well." He started to move, then hesitated. "What will my little Isabelle do, do you think? When I reveal my true self?"

"I wouldn't presume to guess," Gervase said. "*Rid her of all steel beforehand* would be my first suggestion. And stand between her and the fire irons."

"You would know?"

"I would know."

Etienne sighed, then pushed away from the wall and walked over to the company there in front of the fire. It occurred to Gervase as Etienne edged closer to the fire that perhaps he should have warned Robin about what was to come, but it was obvious by the lack of anything resembling surprise on the heir to Artane's face that he already knew that his grandfather was still alive.

Etienne looked at Mary for a moment or two, then went down on one knee in front of his granddaughter.

"There is no easy way to tell you this, Isabelle," he said quietly.

He pulled his wimple and veil from off his head. Gervase watched Isabelle's eyes widen. He supposed that she simply gaped for a handful of breaths before throwing her arms around her grandfather instead of pushing him into the fire was a good sign.

She recovered enough to notice that Robin didn't seem to be as surprised as perhaps he should have been, but obviously her brother was not going to fare as well. She looked at him in astonishment.

"Don't tell me you knew."

"Well, of course I knew," Robin said with a snort. "I met Grandfather before Artane was built. You don't think I've been crossing swords with a nun all these years here, do you?" He smiled at his grandfather. "You're looking well, my lord."

"I keep myself busy," Etienne said modestly. He rose to his feet, then sat down next to Isabelle. He looked over the company, his smile fading. "And I believe, children, that the time has come to discuss what's afoot before we allow ourselves the pleasure of other, simpler conversation. Since things seem to be revolving about our lovely Isabelle, why don't we allow her to begin?"

Gervase leaned back against a wall and listened to Isabelle describe what she remembered of the original missive—interrupted continually by Miles who apparently had seen the thing for himself. He couldn't say he was surprised by the details about her flight that were supplied by her brothers, but he certainly wished he could have somehow spared her what she'd endured. He allowed Joscelin and Isabelle both to describe her time at Monsaert which left him enduring looks of promise from an elder brother and a grandfather. He closed his eyes briefly and allowed the conversation to go on around him. To say he was weary didn't begin to describe how he felt. Then again, he was still on his feet. He certainly wouldn't have been a month ago.

"You suspected *me*?"

Gervase opened his eyes to find his brother gaping at Isabelle.

"If it eases you any," Isabelle said, looking at him seriously, "I suspected your brother as well."

Joscelin reached for her hand. "I'm sorry, Isabelle," he said quietly, lifting that hand.

Two throats cleared themselves pointedly. Gervase would have checked his own to see if the noise had come from him but he realized that both Robin and Etienne were frowning at his younger brother. Joscelin released her hand immediately, accompanied by a hasty apology.

Robin reached out to pat him on the head. "I can see you have no one of substance in your household to see to these sorts of matters for you. It leaves me, obviously, stepping forward to accept that heavy burden."

"Good of you," Miles drawled. He refilled Joscelin's cup, then his own. "Perhaps I'll stay on in France for a bit and accompany you on the search for a bride. And I won't admit 'tis for anything but purely selfish reasons."

That took the conversation in an entirely different direction, something for which Gervase found himself rather grateful. He looked about the chamber for a seat, but saw only a bench residing against the back wall. It looked serviceable enough, though, so he walked over and made himself at home on it, groaning a bit as he stretched his poor legs out in front of him. Memories of his afternoon with that brutal healer came back to him with unpleasant clarity. He didn't want to admit that an hour spent biting back the very vilest of curses and convincing himself that his eyes were simply watering—he hadn't wept, of course—had served him any, but he couldn't deny it. A pity he hadn't known to come look for her two months ago. Then again, considering the lack of enthusiasm he was feeling about the idea of having her anywhere near his poor flesh on the morrow, perhaps he would have avoided her just the same.

He realized, after a bit, that he had been joined on his bench. He looked to find that his companion just happened to be his favorite would-be shieldmaiden. She looked at him glumly.

"Robin promised me a lesson in knife work tomorrow. Perhaps I'll show better than I did earlier."

That wasn't what he'd expected her to be thinking about, but perhaps everything else was more than she could look at. He couldn't blame her. Heaven knew he'd felt the same way over the past several months.

"You were distracted with me today," he offered.

"I was distracted *by* you today."

He smiled in spite of himself. "Were you, indeed?"

She looked at him for so long, he would have squirmed if he'd been the sort to squirm. Instead, he went perfectly still as she put her arm around his neck, leaned over, and kissed him.

Not on the cheek.

She met his eyes. "Thank you, Gervase."

He found, to his horror, that he was blushing. He wasn't sure he'd ever blushed in the entirety of his life. And damn the woman if she didn't smile, kiss him full on the mouth again, then lean back against the wall and take his hand in both her own. She closed her eyes as if she hadn't anything better to do than to take a small rest.

For himself, he wasn't sure which was the best of all the courses of action laid out before him. He considered first rising and killing Robin de Piaget, who was plainly incapable of any sort of seriousness befitting an elder statesman. He dismissed Miles, who was burying his smiles in his cup, and vowed to remind Joscelin of his place in the family later. He immediately decided that taking Isabelle's chuckling grandparents to task wasn't in his best interest.

He also couldn't very well say anything to the woman who had left him blushing like a callow youth, so he squeezed her hand and leaned his head back against the stone of the wall. Perhaps in time the chill would render him blissfully numb from the neck up.

Isabelle leaned closer and put her head on his shoulder. "Are you blushing?" she whispered.

"You called me by my name," Gervase managed. "It was so startling, I had a bit of an attack."

She sighed happily. "You, Gervase de Seger, are very charming."

He pulled his hand, which was quite nicely attached by a sweet clasping to both her own, into his own lap where he felt a bit more in control. "And you are so full of goodness and beauty, I scarce know where to begin in listing your virtues."

"I tend to cut my hair and run when events require it."

He brought her hand to his mouth, kissed it, then shifted to look at her. "Could you, do you think," he said slowly, "allow me to perhaps see to events for you, that you need not cut your hair again out of desperation?"

She was watching him gravely. "Instead simply because the weather demands it?"

"I wouldn't argue with that," he said. "Well, not overmuch."

"If you like." She leaned her head back against the stone again and watched the conversation going on in front of the fire. "I wondered about him."

"Her."

She shot him a quick smile, then turned back to watching her grandfather. "Whatever he is at the moment. But it never occurred to me to ask." She rubbed her thumb over his absently for several minutes in silence before she spoke again. "Odd that our lad should know that Lord Etienne lives, isn't it?"

"There are many odd things about this," Gervase agreed.

"You said you received a missive as well?"

He shrugged. "Just a little note of love telling me I shouldn't be sleeping easily quite so soon."

"Did you recognize the hand?"

He shook his head. "Nay, but it looked as if it had been written by a woman."

"Which is why you suspected me."

"Aye, for the space of a single heartbeat before good sense returned."

She shifted to look at him. "I could want to do you in, you know."

"I promised you time in the lists, woman. You can't have that if I'm not still breathing."

"So you did." She glanced at him. "And there are other things I believe I would miss if you weren't still breathing."

He shifted uneasily. "I think you should leave off with that sort of talk before you leave me blushing again."

"And the sight of that, my lord, was worth the fact that I'll never live down my actions in my brothers' eyes. Then again, they've never had anything before with which to bedevil me, so I won't deny them their sport." She sighed, then smiled wearily. "What do we do now?"

"We sleep safely, then make plans on the morrow." He shook his head. "I can't say I'm particularly comfortable with the abbey as a battlefield. I suppose your grandparents have their own guards, but I would prefer to see them in a place where our mysterious lad can't move about as freely as he seems to here." He frowned. "Where is your brother's wife?"

"Robin left Anne and his children with my parents, from what he said."

"At least they're safe," he said slowly. "If I had any sense, I would send you off to join them."

"I think that would defeat the purpose."

He looked at her with a frown. "What do you mean?"

She took a deep breath. "I told you he caught me in the garderobe, but I didn't have a chance to tell you what he said. Or what he gave me," she added.

He felt something slither down his spine that he didn't care for in the least. He shifted and looked at her carefully.

"Isabelle," he said quietly, "what are you saying?"

She pulled one of her hands free of his. He supposed it said something about the year he'd had that his first instinct was to make sure she wasn't reaching for the knife down the side of his own boot. Instead, she fumbled at a purse hanging from her belt. Too small for a knife, which he also found more reassuring than he should have.

She drew out a very small bottle, sealed with wax.

"What's that?" he asked lightly.

"I believe 'tis poison."

"Were you given any suggestions as to who might benefit the most from a few doses of it?"

She nodded again.

He closed his eyes, then released her hand to put his arm around her shoulders. He put his right hand, the hand that already bore the scars of his most recent encounter with death, over her hand that held yet more death intended for him. Then he pulled her as close to him as he dared and held her while she shook.

"There are those who always want me dead," he said finally in as casual a tone as he could manage.

She pulled back and met his eyes. Her eyes were very red.

"I believe the difference this time is, Gervase, that there is someone who wants me to do the deed."

Chapter 23

Isabelle rode inside Monsaert's gates and wondered if she were riding into certain death. She supposed it was somewhat reassuring to find that, at least based on first glance, all she was riding into was certain chaos.

The courtyard was full of wagons and wains and men-at-arms and their gear, all wearing colors that resembled Gervase's but weren't quite the same. Isabelle looked at Robin who was leaning on the pommel of his saddle and watching the goings-on with an assessing glance.

"Well?" she asked.

He straightened, then shrugged. "Don't ask me. I'm just the guardsman."

"Who are you guarding?"

"You or Gervase," he said. "Depends on who needs me more at the moment, though your lord isn't fond of the idea. He doesn't believe that there's nothing I like more than stomping about as a lowly garrison knight and appearing where I'm not looked for."

"Or wanted," she said, unable to resist the barb.

He laughed a little. "You know me too well, which means

you also know *I* know you don't mean that. Kings have salivated over the thought of having me to guard their sorry arses and look you here how I'm doing the like for you and Monsaert without demanding gold in return." He smiled pleasantly. "I can hardly begin to describe how truly remarkable I am."

"Don't hurt anything in the attempt," Isabelle said.

"You're starting to sound a little like Amanda, if that pleases you, though I don't suppose you'll ever manage to stay with that unpleasantness for long." He nodded toward the commotion in front of them. "Have any idea what that's all about?"

"None," she said honestly, "though Gervase doesn't look happy, does he?"

"Too many souls milling about for his comfort," Robin said, "which is why you'll notice he's divided our forces into two groups to better keep the rabble controlled."

"Has he?"

Robin rolled his eyes. "Iz, you will never make a soldier, so don't bother trying. Of *course* he has. See you there how he has most of his men going about their normal business, the sort of business you would expect from them? The ones with less delicate humors—or more ruthlessness, depending on how you see it—aren't quite as busy—nay, don't look."

"You told me to look."

"Well, don't be so obvious about it."

"I want to see where something might be coming from," she said, finding the conversation not at all to her liking. She looked at her eldest brother and had to admit that she was vastly relieved to have him there. "I can't believe I agreed to any of this."

Robin's expression was rather serious, for Robin. "I doubt Father would be pleased by the idea, but in this I must admit I agree with your lord there. Your mystery murderer is obviously much more interested in Gervase's death than yours. Gervase's mystery murderer has obviously not given up on the plan to see him in his grave. It makes perfect sense to see if you can't bring the two lads together in a place where Gervase knows all the bolt holes."

Isabelle watched the goings-on around her as casually as possible whilst trying not to look as if she were watching those same happenings. Gervase was going out of his way to play the part of lord of the manor, loudly commanding servant, and

guardsman alike. If he were trying to linger near an escape, he
gave no sign of it. She considered him a bit longer, then looked
at her brother.

"I wonder things."

"Do you?"

She was past shivering, so she simply sat there in the drizzle
and didn't even spare a thought for the warmth of a goodly bit
of morning sun. "It would be interesting if the lad who had sent
for me and the lad who had tried to kill Gervase in the fall happened to be one in the same, wouldn't it?"

Robin smiled in a particularly unpleasant way. "It would be
interesting."

She looked at him in surprise, then felt her mouth go slack.
"Is that what you think—nay, is that what he thinks?"

"Well, you don't imagine he's as disgustingly rich as he is
because he can't keep at least a pair of steps in front of opponents he'd intended to fleece at tourney, do you?" He leaned
closer to her. "Of course that's what he thinks. We chewed on it
all the way here."

"I thought you were discussing horses!"

Robin rolled his eyes. "Really, Iz. After all the studying of
my admittedly superior reasoning skills you've done for the past
score of years and that's the best you can do?"

"Why didn't he tell me?"

"I believe he thinks you have enough to think on for the
morning," Robin said with a shrug. "You're supposed to be poisoning him by degrees, remember? He didn't want to take your
mind off that happy task with these trivial details."

She tried to swallow, but it was difficult. "I don't know how
you can make light of this."

"'Tis either that or weep, isn't it?" he said cheerfully, then he
swung down. "Watch your back."

She had absolutely no answer for that. She watched her
brother blend almost immediately into the press of men-at-arms.
Robin, amusing himself.

She caught Gervase exchanging a brief look with Miles who
took over where Robin had left off. No doubt he was fully
informed of Gervase's thoughts as well. Obviously she was
going to have to have speech with a certain lad very soon to let
him know she did not appreciate being kept in the dark. She had
help out of her saddle, then found herself surrounded not by her

usual guardsmen but by a handful of steely-eyed, rough-looking men made up equally of Gervase's and Robin's guardsmen. Her brother was leading the charge, as it were, dressed in less-than-pristine gear and happily wallowing in his obscurity.

She sighed. She supposed she'd been fortunate in that she'd even been allowed to come back to Monsaert. Her grandparents had been banished to the safety of Beauvois. Gervase had been on the verge of sending her along with them until she'd pointed out to him that it would be a little hard for her to kill him if she wasn't close enough to his supper to poison it. He had agreed, reluctantly, and she had been warned that her ability to move about freely would be reduced to nothing.

"Wonder who's here?" Miles murmured.

"I don't want to speculate," she said.

"Those are Monsaert's colors," he mused, "though slightly altered. This should be entertaining." He lifted his eyebrows briefly, then walked with her through the courtyard and up the way to the great hall.

She watched the people around her, not recognizing half of them, as she followed Miles into the great hall. It was then that she realized *entertaining* wasn't going to be the half of it.

A woman was there, holding court. There could be no other way to describe it. Isabelle would have turned around and gone to hide in the stables, but Miles had a hold of her so she couldn't move.

"Who," she managed, "is that?"

"I believe, sister, that Mother Monsaert has returned to the fold."

The one thing she had always disliked about her brother was his strength. She supposed the only way she would manage to be free of him would be to pull a dagger from her boot, only she hadn't managed to get to the abbey's armory that morning to procure one, leaving her singularly unable to stab Miles in the gut with it. Obviously, she needed to attend to her weaponry sooner rather than later. *Sooner* seemed a good option at the moment, but again, Miles seemed to have a death grip on the back of her tunic.

"I think we should go meet her," Miles murmured.

"Are you daft?" she whispered furiously. "I'm wearing hose."

"Why do you care?"

She shot him a murderous look that he only smiled at, damn him anyway. She pulled her cloak closer around her, but supposed that would do nothing to hide her lack of gown. Then again, perhaps she would manage to simply remain in the background. If Robin could blend into the garrison, then so could she. She edged behind her twin, fully intending to use him as a shield if necessary. She pitied Gervase that he didn't have the same option open to him. The hall was full of his men, true, but he was the one left standing alone in front of them all.

The lady of Monsaert didn't bother to rise from her place before the fire to greet him. She simply waved a languid hand.

"Gervase," she said, her voice slicing through the air like a painfully sharp sword, "do come over and do me the honor due me. Then perhaps you can explain why you weren't here to welcome me when I arrived."

Isabelle found herself joined on her other side by Joscelin who seemed just as determined as Miles to keep her from fleeing. How they managed to both have hold of bits of her clothing whilst she was standing mostly behind them, she didn't know, but they did. She glared at Gervase's brother, just so he wouldn't mistake her lack of movement for acquiescence. Joscelin only shook his head.

"You know you'll have to meet her eventually."

"Perhaps when I'm dressed properly?" she said pointedly.

"Don't know why you'd care," Joscelin said with a shrug.

"Would you go into battle on a goat?"

He opened his mouth, then shut it and smiled. "I suppose not. Very well, we'll try to keep you out of sight as much as possible, though I don't think you'll escape scrutiny altogether." His smile faded. "I'm sorry for that, Isabelle. She's not a pleasant woman."

Isabelle could hear that from where she was standing. It had to have been an art, she was fairly sure, to be able to speak that distinctly yet in tones that were barely above a whisper. Isabelle strove to keep a pleasant smile on her face whilst the dowager duchess of Monsaert pointed out, kindly of course, her stepson's failings in being prepared to entertain her in style. That Gervase listened to it all without saying anything said much about his self-control. Then again, Isabelle could tell he was coldly furious. She couldn't fault him for it. Lady Margaret was fortunate he didn't pick her up and throw her bodily from his hall.

"And who do we have over there?" Margaret said with a yawn. "Joscelin, drag him out from behind you and let me see what sorts of servants we're employing at present."

Isabelle took a deep breath, then stepped forward and inclined her head. "Your Grace," she said quietly.

"A girl," Margaret said, with a tinkling laugh that contained nothing but sharp edges. "And who might you be, my dear, dressed in lads' clothes?"

"She's Isabelle," Yves blurted out defensively, "and she's very kind."

The look his mother shot him had the poor lad backing up quickly behind an older brother. Isabelle returned Margaret's look because whilst she was not Gervase's stepmother's equal in rank, her father was also not a kitchen lad.

"But why are you here?" Margaret asked, her perfect brow creasing slightly. "Surely not as a guest."

Miles stepped forward and made Margaret a sweeping bow. He straightened and smiled at her. Isabelle had to admit her brother could be very charming when he wanted to be. It was undeniable that he was at the height of his prowess and the sheer beauty of his face had left lesser women fanning themselves. Then again, Margaret was old enough to be his mother and she was apparently made of sterner stuff than most for she merely looked him over, then pursed her lips.

"A de Piaget son, obviously."

"Miles, my lady Margaret."

"And that bedraggled urchin next to you?"

Isabelle found that neither she nor Miles had a chance to speak because they were interrupted by a quiet, but undeniably cold voice.

"That, my lady mother," Gervase said, "is my lady, Isabelle de Piaget. She is here as my personal guest."

Margaret looked at him, then laughed. "Surely you jest."

Isabelle realized that with all the looks she'd had from the young lord of Monsaert, she had never, ever had him bestow on her a look of utter disdain. Decades of breeding and a healthy dose of his own confidence had obviously done a goodly work in helping him master that. She would have wilted on the spot.

Lady Margaret, however, was obviously made of much sterner stuff. She only returned Gervase's look with one of her own.

"I don't suppose, my boy, that you saw fit to tell her that you are already betrothed?"

Isabelle felt Miles shift beside her almost imperceptibly, though she could have told him he didn't need to bother. She would have put her own eyes out before she gave the woman in front of her the satisfaction of seeing any reaction on her face.

"I believe," Isabelle said smoothly, "that such is common knowledge, isn't it?"

"Then what, you common tramp, are you thinking to do with him?" Margaret snapped.

Isabelle smiled. "I don't know that I've indicated any wishes to have anything to do with him, Your Grace." She started to move away, then she stopped. She supposed she should have thought better of the words on the tip of her tongue, but at least she was merely planning on speaking. Amanda likely would have slapped the woman in front of her. "I can't imagine you don't already know this, but I've found that most often when one uses a slur against another—common tramp, for example—that the words are ones the speaker tends to apply to herself when no one is looking." She smiled. "Don't you agree?"

The stillness in the hall was palpable. Isabelle inclined her head and moved off. No sense in giving the lady Margaret the opportunity to filch a blade and use it. She glanced over her shoulder as she left and paused. Perhaps it was the closeness of that immediate circle by the fire that afforded her such a fine view of Gervase drawing his hand over his face, or perhaps 'twas a bit of happy fortune. He shot her a look that she couldn't quite decipher, then shook his head, looking as if he might be fighting a smile. Isabelle shrugged and started for the kitchens.

Somehow, that seemed particularly appropriate.

"Well played," Miles managed under his breath.

Isabelle said nothing until she had her brother all the way to the kitchens. Once she was certain they were out of sight of anyone who might have been loitering at the top of the passageway, she whirled on him.

"Is he betrothed?" she demanded.

"Ah—" Miles said.

"Is that all you can say?" she exclaimed. "Tell me what you

know and tell me now before I cause you a great amount of pain."

"Um—"

That was as far as he got because he was suddenly shoved out of the way by the lord of the hall who had apparently wasted no time in coming after her so he could make a full confession of his hedging. Isabelle put her hands on her hips and glared at him instead.

"Is it true?" she demanded. "Are you betrothed to someone? And who in the bloody hell might that be?"

His eyes were rather wide. "Is that language ladylike?"

She looked around for something sharp to use on him but realized that all she had to hand was her tongue. Unfortunately, the unpleasant amount of surprise she was laboring under seemed to be robbing her of anything useful to say. "I don't give a damn," she said finally, "what my language is at the moment."

He looked as if he might be fighting a smile. "Would I be courting you if I were engaged to Evelyne of Coucy?"

"Courting?" she echoed. "Is *that* what you call it? This bossing of me, chasing me—"

"Luring you into semi-darkened corners and kissing you?"

"You haven't lured me anywhere," she said shortly. "And if you think I have any intention of ever again kiss—"

Well, apparently, that was indeed what he was thinking. She found herself in his arms in the middle of his kitchens being thoroughly kissed. She closed her eyes because she decided that there was no sense in not giving her full attentions to a man who obviously knew how to kiss a maid so she thought she might like him to keep on with his labors.

He finally allowed her to breathe and instead kissed her once on the end of her nose. "Does that answer your question?"

She managed to pry her eyes open. "What question?"

He smiled. "Isabelle, I love you."

"I'm not sure that is a decent answer to the question I can't remember at the moment, but so be it. When did you decide this?"

He bent his head and kissed her again, softly. "I think I knew it when I first looked at you and fell off my horse."

She was eventually going to have to tell him to leave off with that or she wasn't going to be able to attend to the task of poisoning him by degrees, but perhaps later when she could think clearly again. "Did it hurt, that falling?" she managed.

"I landed on you."

"No wonder I lost my memories," she said, reaching up to tuck a stray lock of hair behind his ear. "And I think you're avoiding my question."

"Do you remember your question?" he asked politely.

She scowled at him. "Details, Gervase. Don't make me draw my blade on you."

"You don't have a blade," he said, sounding far more relaxed about that than he should have. "And aye, I *was* betrothed. The woman in question's sire came through the hall several se'nnights ago and made it quite clear she had no more interest in wedding me."

"Then she's daft," she said.

He smiled and bent his head to kiss her again. "I love you," he whispered against her mouth. "And before you shower me with all manner of sentiments in return, I will commend you to your brother's care and return to the viper's nest in the great hall. Please stay out of her way."

"I tried to improve her character," Isabelle pointed out. "Did she not appreciate that?"

He laughed uneasily. "She may not have, but you have earned the undying loyalty of her sons. But because she does not offend well, *please* stay behind your brother and leave her to me."

"And just what are you going to do with her?"

"I'm going to try to have her come to court with us—"

"We're going where?" she asked in utter surprise. "And when did you decide this?"

"Robin and I discussed the possibility on the way here," he said with a shrug, "but seeing our guests half an hour ago made the decision for me." He smiled. "I thought you might like to meet the king and his mother."

She knew she was gaping at him, but she couldn't do anything else. "Court?" she wheezed.

He kissed her cheek, then smiled. "If we don't remove Margaret from the hall, we won't have a hall to return to because I'm quite sure she'll burn it to the ground out of spite. Besides, there is safety in a crowd." He looked over her head. "Watch over her well, Miles. I'll try to find her later."

"Oh, I think not," Miles said, pulling her over to stand next to him. "She's fair to swooning now as it is."

"That's because I haven't anything to wear to court," Isabelle said through gritted teeth, "and that makes me nervous."

Gervase only smiled pleasantly, then turned and strode from the kitchens. She watched him go, then looked at her brother.

"What is he thinking?"

"That his stepmother won't kill you if the queen mother is watching?"

Isabelle shivered. "I don't suppose I made a friend in her today, did I?"

"Even Amanda would have hesitated to speak to her so bluntly," Miles said hesitantly. "I believe you have surpassed even her cheekiest comments. If I were you, however, I would take your love's advice quite seriously. Don't let her catch you alone."

She nodded slowly, though it occurred to her that that sage piece of advice could apply to more souls than the dowager countess of Monsaert.

Evening shadows had fallen when Isabelle stood in the great hall, taking up space against the wall next to Miles. She was leaning against his shoulder partly because he made a handy pillar and partly because she had the strangest feeling that they wouldn't have all that many more opportunities to do the like. She looked at him finally.

"I have the feeling our days of lingering on the edge of the hall are almost over."

He bumped her companionably with his shoulder. "It depends upon how often your future husband allows me inside here, I suppose."

She couldn't smile. "You're assuming he'll want to have anything to do with me once he's seen what's available at court."

"Iz, he's already seen what's available at court," Miles said dryly. "Repeatedly. Unclad, if rumor has it aright."

She scowled at him. "That is rumor only."

"I'm not saying he partook of what was offered," Miles said with a shrug, "just that he's seen more of what's available than might be considered polite. He's had his choice of women, which I believe we've discussed before. He knows what he wants and apparently what he wants is you."

She sighed. "Is Evelyne of Coucy beautiful?"

"Oh, I'm not sure that word does her justice," Miles said, with more reverence in his voice than perhaps was necessary. "She's almost too beautiful to look at."

"Are you being helpful?"

He winked at her. "I'm trying to help you see how useless it is to discuss her. She's beautiful, true, but no man with sense could possibly endure her longer than a handful of minutes without looking for other company. I've only met her once and I wanted to run the other way."

Isabelle took a deep breath, then nodded, because she could do nothing else. She wasn't anticipating a journey to the French court with any relish at all. One, she was English and she had the feeling that no matter whom she arrived with, she would not be a popular addition to the company. Two, she did not care at all for the niceties that were required to move successfully in court circles. Her mother didn't care for it either, though she was willing to do what was required of her. Amanda enjoyed the game, but she was also in the enviable position of not giving a damn what anyone thought of her.

The one who had turned out to be the most deft hand with things of a political nature had been Robin's wife, Anne. Her shyness was taken as a proper and appropriate amount of reserve and her words, always chosen with utmost care, were looked upon as gifts when offered.

Isabelle had to admit that there had been times when she'd been with Anne that she'd felt as if she were tromping about in boots better suited to working in the stables.

She sighed as she looked out over the company, then she froze as she realized she was being watched. It wasn't by Margaret the viper, nor by any of Gervase's brothers. Not even the servants or guardsmen were paying her any heed. But that man, the lord of the hall sitting in his great chair in front of the fire, was watching her as if the sight of her pleased him.

"Evelyne is not your worry," Miles murmured.

"What is?" she asked.

"Having that man ever let you out of his arms."

She looked up at her brother, then smiled. "He's kind."

"Oh, I wouldn't say that," Miles said, "but he does love you.

As do his brothers, apparently." He smiled. "Are you prepared to be a mother to them?"

"I think Guy and Joscelin are past needing mothering," she said. "But as for the others, aye, I think I can manage them."

"Well, 'tis for damned sure they want nothing to do with their dam. I've never seen a collection of lads beg for more time in the chapel the way these have today, righteous souls that they are."

Isabelle nodded because he had it aright. Gervase's brothers seemed to want to have nothing to do with their mother. Then again, Margaret obviously had no interest in her sons. Surely the lads had to have felt that. She smiled very briefly at Gervase, then watched him turn away and put on a polite face for his stepmother.

Poor man.

At least he was alive to pretend to be polite. She rubbed her arms, then looked casually about the hall to see if there might be anything out of place. Robin was leaning against the opposite wall, obviously enjoying his anonymity greatly. Gervase's brothers were sitting as far away from their mother as possible—well, except for Guy, but perhaps he had a stronger stomach than the rest of them. Then again, he was Margaret's eldest son, so perhaps she had favored him with a regard she hadn't been willing to offer the others. Isabelle supposed that was her right, but she couldn't understand it. Guy certainly had the appearance of a useful sort of lad, but obviously he couldn't be trusted with anything of import.

"You're thinking hard," Miles remarked.

She shrugged. "Something troubles me."

"It sounds like a secret," he said with a faint smile. "My favorite sort of trouble."

She looked out over the hall and wished there weren't so many souls there. So many possibilities for things to happen she couldn't control. She didn't look at her brother because she didn't want to give anything away, but she leaned closer and spoke behind a smile that she knew from long experience wouldn't alert anyone to what she was saying.

"Remember the seeds Guy gifted me?"

"Aye."

"And that I told you I'd sent a missive to Grandmère?"

"That, too."

She glanced at him. "She told me last night that she never received it. I asked her specifically about it, but she had seen nothing, not even a messenger claiming to have been robbed of it."

"Perhaps she was distracted with all the goings-on," Miles said. "You know, us finding out that our grandfather lived and suppressing the urge we both felt to kill Robin for never having told us."

"We owe him for several things," she conceded, "but about the other? You can't believe that she simply overlooked my telling her I was alive. Besides, that was almost a se'nnight ago. We hadn't yet been to the abbey to distract her."

He sighed. "Have you asked Guy what he did with your missive? For all you know, he sent it with an unreliable messenger and is too embarrassed to admit it."

She shot him a look. "Do you think so?"

He turned toward her, leaning his shoulder against the wall. "A better question is, why would he purposely waylay your message?"

"So he could read it himself."

"But why?" Miles asked, looking genuinely puzzled.

"Because I hadn't revealed my identity at the time," she said, "and I was writing to the abbess of Caours. Perhaps he was curious."

"Perhaps he thought you were lovely and hoped that reading your correspondence might help him divine a way to make you look on him with favor."

She blew a stray hair out of her eyes. "He fails to deliver my message, then he fails to deliver Gervase's. Doesn't that seem slightly suspicious to you?"

"It seems annoying," Miles said, "but not suspicious. And haven't we had this conversation before?"

She sighed lightly. "Aye, but I wasn't satisfied with it."

"Because you don't care for the man is no reason to suspect him of nefarious doings," Miles said carefully. "But, if you like, I'll keep him in my sights."

"Or perhaps we'll run afoul of a decent piece of good fortune and he'll remain behind whilst we're about our business at court, then you won't need to keep him in your sights."

"I wouldn't hold out much hope for that," Miles said, watching the commotion near the fire that seemed to consist of Lady Margaret requiring attention. "He seems particularly attached to his mother, so I imagine if she comes, he'll come as well. But perhaps that's for the best. We won't need to worry about his filching Gervase's chair and thereafter refusing to relinquish it."

There was that, she supposed. She watched as Margaret left the hall, obviously off to seek her bed. The woman ignored everyone but Guy, but perhaps that was the usual sort of business. The hall door banged shut behind her and stillness descended.

And then everyone in the place seemed to take a decent breath.

Isabelle found herself encircled suddenly by Gervase's brothers. She dispensed embraces, pats, compliments, and spent a good half an hour listening to them tumble over themselves to tell her of the hell they had passed through that afternoon. She did her best to remind them that the lady Margaret was their mother and deserved respect. It was to their credit that they at least listened politely to her admonition before they inundated her again with their adventures.

"All right, lads, that's enough," Gervase said, coming up behind their little group. "Off to bed. The lady Isabelle and I have plans to make for the morrow."

Yves seemed less-than-eager to release her hand he was holding. "Where are you going now?"

"A brief journey to court," Gervase said, reaching out to ruffle Yves's hair.

"Are you bringing her back home?"

"If she'll agree to come."

Isabelle found herself the subject of scrutiny by several of Gervase's brothers. She felt herself beginning to blush a little.

"I believe he needs to propose first," she said, "if that's his intention."

"Come on, lads," Joscelin said wryly. "Let's leave Gervase to his wooing and you to your beds. Yves, let her go before you crush her fingers."

Isabelle braced for Yves throwing himself into her arms, hugged him tightly, then set him down and sent him on his way. He put his hand in Joscelin's.

"Who is that fierce lad over younder?" Yves whispered loudly. "Never seen him before, but he looks a great deal like Lord Miles, doesn't he? Much fiercer, of course, but that's all to the good."

"We'll find out in the morning," Joscelin promised. "But aye, he does look as if he might have some idea how to use a sword. If he needs aid in the morning, I'll see what I can do for him. Lucien, see these little ones to bed. I'll remain with Lord Miles and roam the passageways."

Isabelle smiled at the look of promise Robin was sending Joscelin, then smiled a bit more as Gervase took her hand.

"He doesn't have to do this," Gervase said quietly, "which I'm sure he realizes."

"Don't be too quick to credit Robin with altruism," Isabelle said. "He loves nothing more than to pretend he's an ordinary guardsman, then dazzle and befuddle those foolish enough to think so." She shrugged. "He's complicated."

"But he loves his sister, obviously," Gervase said, "which I understand." He drew her into his arms and held her close. "You'll take my chamber for the night. I'll stand guard and make certain you're safe."

"Nay," Miles said, "Robin and I can see to it. I think you would be wise to rest." He smiled briefly. "Perhaps you should feign a bit of sour stomach, just to move things along."

"And speaking of that," Isabelle said, pulling back to frown at him, "what is this new scheme you and my brother have discussed?"

Gervase looked at her seriously. "It occurred to me last night that while I might feel more comfortable at home, being at home wasn't going to help me discover anything new." He glanced about himself, then lowered his voice. "If you're being followed and I'm being followed, I thought that perhaps it might help us flush out those unsavoury types if we were all to be on unfamiliar ground. As it were."

"Did that unfamiliar ground need to be the queen mother's court?" she asked with a wince.

"I couldn't think of anywhere else," Gervase admitted. "I don't want to endanger your family or mine. This way, my guards and your brother's can lose themselves amongst others without drawing undue notice to themselves, we can have at least a modicum of safety in a crowd, and hopefully the lot of us being in a relatively strange locale might force our attackers to make a misstep."

"Attackers?" she echoed pointedly.

"At this point, whether they are two or one in the same, you and I are both in a fair bit of peril." He pulled her closer and wrapped his arms around her. "Short of locking you in my solar for the rest of your days, I'm left with very few moves on the board."

She held on to him tightly for a moment or two, then pulled away. "I understand your reasons. I just wish I had filched a gown from Nicholas's wife. I fear I will be a great embarrassment to you."

"Let's worry about that later," he said. He kissed her briefly, then looked at Miles. "I believe I would be wise to accept your offer of sleep, but be careful." He paused. "I hardly know whom to trust even in my own household."

Isabelle said nothing, and she didn't dare look at Miles, but she understood the sentiment completely. She walked with Gervase from the hall and was grateful for the escort of Miles, Joscelin, and, trailing along behind them all with a handful of unpleasant-looking lads, Robin as well. She had to admit she agreed with Gervase's plan. Losing themselves in a crowd at court might possibly be the only thing that drew their attackers out of the shadows.

Unfortunately, as she knew very well, it was difficult to be seen when one was standing in the shadows, never mind where that darkness found itself.

She only hoped that inability to see where danger lay wouldn't be what killed them both.

Chapter 24

Gervase spared a fond thought for all the years he'd been at court as a simple knight instead of the lord of an extensive holding. That anonymity would have perhaps left him less able to move about freely than he was at present, but at least he could have made an attempt to blend in. As it was, he was genuflected to by everyone he passed, he had servants following him at all hours, and women he hadn't seen in at least a year had suddenly found their way, individually and in some cases collectively, to his bedchamber to see if he might have a need for companionship.

The woman he wanted to spend time with was so far away from where he was currently pacing that she might as well have been in England. He supposed she was safe enough with a pair of her brothers and Joscelin guarding her at all hours. That left Aubert to look after him, a fact for which he was, as usual, grateful. Silently.

Their three-day sojourn at court had been a fruitless exercise so far. He had danced until his feet ached. He had made an obvious production of eating as much rich food as possible, which had invariably resulted in loud complaints about pains in his belly. He had gone to Mass every morning in order to ingratiate himself with Her Majesty's priests, then loitered about afterward to see if he could admire their copywork. He supposed they had found it slightly strange that he'd wanted to admire a few contracts as well, but he'd pled the excuse of looking for a fair hand to perhaps supplement his own men at Monsaert. He supposed the only reason they hadn't sent him away in irons was the strength of his grandfather's name that he ruthlessly used to get what he wanted.

He had seen nothing that had resembled either his missive or Isabelle's.

He had passed the rest of his time making a nuisance of himself in various salons, flattering every single bloody woman he saw with quill in hand so he might have a look at her scribbles on parchment. That had resulted in several rather personal notes being tucked into various parts of his clothing when he wasn't looking, leaving him feeling rather like a stuffed goose and looking like a dolt.

The only thing he regretted was not having retrieved the note of love he'd received in his own solar at home. That colossal piece of stupidity would, he feared, come back to haunt him at a future moment. In his defense, he'd been too busy spending all his time thinking about Isabelle de Piaget and her flawless face, but he supposed that was no defense at all.

He suppressed the urge to draw his hand over his eyes. Did he ever manage to wed the woman, he imagined he would never again do a decent day's labor.

He followed his nose into the great hall, which was a poor description for the place. Monsaert was grand, true, but he was the first to admit that Louis's palace was another level of spectacular entirely. He paused at the edge of the chaos and looked to see who might be there whom he could corner and force to show either the color of their sealing wax or an example of their handwriting.

Truly, he had to solve the mystery of who wanted him dead before he lost what was left of his wits.

He almost plowed over Robin, Miles, and Joscelin before he realized they were standing there in a little cluster, obviously watching something. He joined their group and looked for what they seemed to find so interesting.

"Oh," he managed.

"Aye, oh," Robin said, nodding knowingly. "Though I suppose you paid for the gown, didn't you?"

"A premium," Gervase managed, because it was the truth. He had sent his fleetest messenger ahead with instructions to bribe at whatever cost necessary the finest couturier at court to make Isabelle at least two gowns.

It would have been impossible, he had known, to match the color of her eyes, but he had to admit that the deep green silk had been a good choice. The price, he had learned upon arrival, was eye-watering, but he hadn't cared. He simply hadn't wanted her to feel inferior. Though he would have liked to have said he didn't care anything for clothes and baubles, the truth was, he knew their value in certain situations. Given the way Margaret had treated her at Monsaert, he supposed his gold had been very well spent indeed.

"Glorious," Robin said, "and that's my sister I'm speaking of, just so you know."

Gervase leaned his elbow on Robin's shoulder. "I will never, ever manage a decent day's labor." He looked at Isabelle's brother. "That was my thought earlier. It seemed prudent to give voice to it at some point, so when I don't manage the same ever again, I'll have a witness that I knew that before I wed her."

Robin smiled. "You'll have to give the poor girl a bit of relief from your vile presence now and again. Perhaps you could trot out to the lists and attend to your sword skill."

"Is this experience speaking?"

Robin sighed lightly. "Aye, lad, it is."

Gervase slapped Robin on the back of the head. "Stop calling me *lad*. And know that I realize the reason you continue to provoke me is to satisfy a desperate hope that I'll meet you in the lists. I can see why you would want to, what with what has to be your endless desire to pit yourself against a superior swordsman."

Robin laughed. "My endless desire is that your leg heal fully so I might not have to tiptoe about you in the lists." He nodded toward the middle of the chamber. "But until that happy day arrives, perhaps you might want to concern yourself with rescuing your lady. My eyes could be failing me, but that looks a bit like Evelyne of Coucy sweeping across the room with a purpose—"

Gervase left him talking to thin air as he made his way also across the chamber with a purpose. He caught Evelyne ten paces away from where Isabelle currently stood, looking profoundly uncomfortable. He made her a low bow.

"My lady Evelyne."

She was shaking with fury. "I understand you are sniffing at another's skirts, my lord Monsaert."

Gervase pursed his lips. "I don't sniff at skirts, my lady."

Evelyne pointed a shaking finger at Isabelle. "Then what are you doing with *that*?"

"I'm not sure why what I'm intending to do with anyone else is your concern," he said coolly. "Or perhaps I misunderstood your father's visit to my hall recently?"

"That was before I realized you could walk," Evelyne snapped.

And I am not in the habit of plighting my troth with women who find it within them to throw others away when they're no longer serviceable was almost out of his mouth before he bit the words back.

The truth was, he had never had any feeling but resignation where Evelyne of Coucy was concerned. He'd needed to wed, she had been the most beautiful woman at court, she had obviously wanted him for reasons he didn't suppose he wanted to contemplate overmuch, and the deed had been done.

How fortunate he had been to have been rescued from that.

He started to say the most innocuous thing that came to mind only to realize that Evelyne was no longer standing in front of him. She was now standing in front of Isabelle and her lips were moving.

Gervase cursed himself and strode over to the pair. He took Isabelle's hand in his, wincing a little at the coldness of her fingers, then looked at Evelyne.

"If you'll excuse us?" he said politely.

"So you can trot off to bed with this uncultured urchin from England's northern wasteland?" Evelyne spat. "Why you would choose her over me is something I simply cannot fathom. That and I will not allow it—"

Gervase pulled Isabelle with him out of the chamber, leaving Evelyne talking to no one.

"Gervase—"

He shot Isabelle a look and continued on. She jerked so hard on his hand, he almost tripped. He spun around to simply command her to stop fighting him, then he realized that her visage was almost white. He closed his eyes briefly, then pulled her into a quick, tight embrace.

"Please," he whispered against her ear, "*please* come with me."

"Well, that's better," she said briskly.

He smiled, then walked on with her. He opened several doors, interrupting at least one couple in the business of things they likely shouldn't have been engaging in, then found an empty chamber. He had no idea to whom it belonged, nor did he care. He shut the door, then pulled Isabelle into his arms.

She was trembling. "I don't like it here."

He slipped his hand under her hair, looked at her seriously, then kissed her.

He kissed her for quite some time, actually. It occurred to him at one point through the haze that had become his poor mind, that if he didn't find a priest and wed her soon, he would be apologizing to Rhys de Piaget for more than just putting his daughter to work in his scullery.

"You would not."

He blinked and looked at the woman in his arms. "What?"

"You would not bed me before you wed me," she said, looking as dazed as he felt.

"Did I say I would?"

She nodded solemnly.

He frowned. "Well, I wouldn't. Don't think it hasn't crossed my mind, especially at the moment, but I wouldn't think to." He paused. "Well, I would think to, but I wouldn't." He looked at her. "I think I should stop kissing you."

She laughed a little and threw her arms around his neck. She hugged him until he thought he might never breathe properly again, then pulled back far enough to kiss him until he thought he should ask her to stop.

"I love you," she whispered in his ear.

"I love you much more, I'm sure," he said, wondering if he would ever manage to let her out of his arms. He smiled at her when she sank back down to her heels. "Arthur of Harwych never kissed you, did he?"

Her mouth fell open. "Of course not. I've never kissed anyone before. Well, save my family, but that's different."

"Then allow me to present myself as someone on whom you might practice your skills. Repeatedly. At great length."

"You're very generous."

He laughed and kissed her again, because despite everything, there was something about Isabelle de Piaget that inspired happiness in his poor self. He pulled back and smiled at her.

"Have I told you today how lovely you look?"

"Uncultured urchin that I am?" she asked lightly.

"She's jealous," Gervase said dismissively, "and not because I can seemingly keep neither my eyes nor hands off your sweet self. You put every other woman here to shame."

"The gown is lovely," she said. "Thank you."

He shook his head. "Nay, Isabelle, *you* are lovely. The gown is simply a poor setting for the true jewel."

She looked at him as if she'd never seen him before. "What's come over you?"

Where to begin? He supposed there was no point in even attempting to tell her what she had done to him, not when he had to make certain he would be alive for the next fifty years to make a list for her each and every day, so he simply kissed her.

"You," he said simply. "You came over me." He wrapped his arms around her, held her close for several minutes in silence, then sighed deeply. "We have to go back out there."

"I'd rather go clean the kitchens."

"I daresay I would prefer to join you there, but that is unfortunately not our lot." He took her face in his hands, then kissed her softly. "I'll keep you safe."

"I should have found a blade in your armory," she said thoughtfully, "so I might keep you—"

"Iz, *nay*."

She looked up at him in surprise. "What did you call me?"

He opened his mouth to justify what he'd said, then decided he couldn't. He suppressed the urge to shift. "It just came out."

She smiled. "I'm not complaining," she said. She looked at him thoughtfully for a moment or two. "Coming from you, I daresay it was akin to a brief, sweet kiss."

He looked at her uneasily. "I think we should go before I beg you for kisses that are anything but brief." He took her hand. "Let's do what we must."

She only squeezed his hand and walked with him out of the chamber. He walked into his clutch of guardsmen before he realized they were there, which likely said more than it should have about his inability to concentrate on what was going on around him. Before he could protest, Miles and Joscelin put Isabelle between them and walked off with her. Gervase looked at his captain, but Aubert only shook his head slowly. *You poor fool* hung unspoken there in the air. Gervase turned to Robin.

"Well?"

"You were in there a long time, weren't you?"

"Kissing your sister, as it happens."

"I won't stick you for it because she's a grown woman," Robin said thoughtfully, "but I will tell you that I have a hard time thinking of her as such. The last time I noticed, she was approximately ten-and-two. What's happened since then, I just don't know." He glanced at Gervase. "You look distracted."

"I feel distracted."

"It would be better if you looked poisoned. Why don't you think about kissing Evelyne of Coucy and see if that doesn't produce the desired expression on your face?"

"You have that aright," Gervase agreed with a faint shudder. The thought was actually quite bracing, when looked at in the proper way. He looked at Robin. "I need to think."

"We could run the lists," Robin offered. "If they have lists here, which given the sorry state of French soldiers these days, I seriously doubt."

Gervase considered, then looked at Aubert. "Watch over my lady, will you? I think Lord Robin and I can manage ourselves for an hour."

Aubert made him a sharp bow, then trotted off after Isabelle and her keepers.

An hour later, he was unfortunately much closer to thoughts he hadn't wanted to think, all courtesy of running in circles about the lists with a madman who seemed to find the exercise absolutely delightful. He stopped on his way back to the palace and looked off over the gardens as things occurred to him that made him very uncomfortable.

Why would a lad who had for all intents and purposes forced Isabelle to come to France want *him* dead?

The truth was, while he had never seriously considered trotting to England to vie for Isabelle's hand, his father had actually mentioned it a time or two. He could remember sitting on the edge of several conversations between his father and grandfather where they had mentioned they were particularly fond of the de Piaget family. That was odd, wasn't it, how their families seemed to be connected but not connected?

He shook his head as he examined the truths he could no longer deny.

Someone wanted him dead. Someone had convinced Isabelle to come to France or her family would die as a result. And, most recently, someone had told her to kill him. It was true that he'd discussed all those things with Robin at length on the journey from Caours to Monsaert, but he had to admit that he'd considered how they fit together merely as a possibility of what he might be facing.

The very real probability that the person was the same was profoundly chilling.

He looked at Robin. "I'm having thoughts."

"'Tis the running," Robin said wisely. "Very dangerous business, that. Are you going to share these thoughts?"

"I might be using large words," Gervase said solemnly. "Are you up for that sort of thing?"

Robin slung his arm around Gervase's neck, slapped him so hard on the back of his head in the process that he saw stars, then started with him back to the hall.

"I like you. I'll advise my father not to kill you when he first claps eyes on you."

"Good of you," Gervase said faintly.

"Altruistic to the last. Now, come tell Uncle Robin your sorry tale and let's see if we can't make sense of these large words that I'm quite sure you don't know the meaning of."

Gervase did.

Chapter 25

I*sabelle* stood at the edge of a large chamber and forced herself to keep her mouth shut instead of gaping as she so desperately wanted to do. She had thought for the whole of her life that she had lived in incomparable luxury. She supposed in a certain sense that was true. Artane was majestic, secure, full of fine food, lovely music, and family.

But it paled in comparison to the absolute decadence of her current surroundings.

She had never seen walls painted in that fashion, candles everywhere, souls garbed in clothing so fine she wondered how they dared wear it without worrying they would spoil it beyond salvaging. The music was glorious, the food surely straight from a dream, and the souls there beautiful and elegant. What surprised her, though, was how cold everything seemed.

Or perhaps that was just her.

She rubbed her arms and wished desperately that she was back at Monsaert in Gervase's solar, surrounded by his brothers, sitting in front of a hot fire with Yves on her lap. The only thing that eased her any was that Miles and Joscelin couldn't have been flanking her any more closely if they'd been sewn into her clothes. She supposed that made her feel safer, but it didn't make her any happier. All she could do was stand against the wall and watch as every eligible maiden—and a few she was quite sure had to have been wed—tripped over themselves to attract the attention of one Gervase de Seger.

"Are you unwell?" Joscelin asked suddenly.

"Just flushed," Isabelle managed. "Is it hot?"

Miles laughed. Isabelle elbowed him so hard in the ribs that he gasped, but he only put his arm around her shoulders.

"You are going to be very happily wed," he predicted.

"How?" she asked plaintively. "Look you at all those women out there!"

"And who is the woman he can't stop looking at?" Joscelin ventured. "I believe, my lady, that 'tis you."

She supposed she couldn't deny that that was true. Whatever else he might have been doing, he was keeping an eye on her.

That didn't make her feel any better, but the reasons for that were almost too numerous to name. She didn't care for court, for the intrigues, the heavy gowns, and the ridiculous thing she was wearing on her head. She was hardly going to complain because just the thought of how much gold Gervase had seen spent to garb her properly left her with the overwhelming desire to go lie down. She leaned closer to Joscelin.

"Does he enjoy coming to court?"

Joscelin smiled at her. "He enjoys—or *enjoyed*, rather—tourneying because it allowed him a reason to strut about and be the braggart he is, but court? Nay, he doesn't care for it. He's very good at navigating its shoals, but I daresay he would put his feet up at home in front of his fire and never leave it if he had the choice."

"Do you think so?" she asked seriously.

Joscelin opened his mouth to speak, then shut it. He sighed. "The truth is, he will be forced to be at court regularly whether he wills it or not. I would imagine that when you two are wed, he will make it so he is either by your side constantly or you are left in the care of those who will protect you from more unsavoury elements."

"It isn't nice to call Evelyne of Coucy *unsavoury*," Miles said placidly.

"And what would you call her?"

"Damned beautiful," Miles said. He glanced at Isabelle. "I

introduced myself to her. She said I smelled rather strongly of rustic stable lad."

Isabelle smiled. "You don't and she's a fool."

Miles winked at Joscelin. "This is my sister who loves me."

"So I see," Joscelin agreed. He looked out over the company, then froze. "My mother is closing in on Gervase. I wonder what she wants."

Isabelle had no idea what the woman wanted, but she couldn't imagine it was anything good. She watched Margaret speak to Gervase, then watched him go very still. Gervase considered for a moment or two, then nodded slowly. Isabelle started forward but found herself caught by both Miles and Joscelin. She glared at them.

"Let me go."

Joscelin shook his head sharply. "I don't trust her."

"So you'll leave your brother alone with her?" she asked incredulously.

"Robin is there," Miles said, "and Sir Aubert is lurking in the shadows."

"But he might need the both of *you*," she insisted. "We can't leave him unprotected."

They exchanged a look over her head that she didn't bother to interrupt. She'd been ignoring looks cast over her head for as long as her brothers had been taller than she. They seemed to come to some mutual decision that required no words.

"We'll have to bring her with us."

"For the moment, at least."

She ignored them both as they walked with her toward a side door. She had anticipated that they might try to lock her into a chamber for her safety and refused to go inside any doors until she saw that Gervase and Margaret were already inside a fairly large chamber that looked as if it might have been a royal solar of some sort. She found herself pulled behind Miles and Joscelin and the ranks closed before she had a good look at the proceedings, but she was accustomed to that as well. She considered who might most easily be eluded and chose Joscelin because he was likely less accustomed to protecting sisters than Miles. She eased around the side of him where she could actually see what was going on.

"Well," Gervase said flatly, "you have me here. What do you want?"

"What do I want?" Margaret echoed in disbelief. "You stupid boy, what do you think I want?"

Gervase folded his arms over his chest. "Well, what you might want, my lady, is exactly what you cannot have." He shrugged. "Not my fault you weren't born a man—"

Margaret slapped him so quickly, he obviously couldn't avoid it. He stuck his tongue in his cheek, as if he tested the flesh there for undue damage, then looked at his stepmother coolly.

"What would you like me to do about your desires to have my hall?" he asked. "Shall I die this time?"

Margaret drew herself up. "What are you suggesting?"

"Spare me the outrage," Gervase said curtly. "I saw the missive in my solar warning me this wasn't over. It took me a bit, but I realized that while at first I thought I didn't know the hand, I had certainly seen it before." He looked at her. "Did someone spell the words for you, Margaret, or have you been acquiring a bit of education while you've been exiled from Monsaert?"

She flung herself at him but perhaps he was past chivalry where she was concerned for he simply stepped aside and allowed her to stumble forward. She caught herself on a chair, straightened, then spun around and glared at him.

"Aye, I would like you to die this time," she spat. "Then *my* son will have the title that should rightly belong to him."

Gervase's expression looked as if it had been carved from stone. "If you tell me you slew my mother, I will kill you where you stand."

Margaret made a noise of disdain. "I wouldn't have bothered with her. She died in childbirth, which perhaps you're too stupid to have realized. I will say that I didn't mourn her passing." She nodded toward Isabelle. "She was a sickly sweet girl like that one there. Perhaps you'll lose her in childbirth as well."

Isabelle thought she should have been alarmed by that, but realized immediately that perhaps she had other things to worry about.

Guy was shutting the door quietly behind himself. He leaned back against the wall and seemed content to observe the conversation—if it could be called that—going on between his stepbrother and his mother. That seemed to only amuse him for so long before he looked about the chamber.

Isabelle caught his eye and flinched at the hate she saw blazing there. Very well, so she had suspected him of foul deeds.

She had never said as much to him, so why should he have any reason to look at her that way?

He reached up to brush aside a tassel dangling from a tapestry hanging over his head. Perhaps that wouldn't have been noteworthy if the sleeve of his tunic hadn't caught on part of his belt.

He had scratches down his forearm.

She could hardly believe her eyes, but there was no denying what she was seeing. She felt Joscelin pull her behind him, which she supposed she should have expected at some point. She moved to stand more or less between them where she could look over their shoulders that they seemed to be determined to keep pressed together. No matter. She needed time to think, though she supposed she wouldn't have all that much of it.

She had been taken unawares at Caours in the latrine, of all places. Fortunately her modesty hadn't yet been compromised, something that had actually been what had concerned her the most initially. Her mind had turned to other things once she'd felt her attacker's arm come across her throat. She had been too busy trying to breathe to pay attention to the sound of his voice, though she'd understood his words clearly enough.

Here is poison. Kill Gervase de Seger with it or your family dies.

In truth, how much clearer could it have been than that? She would have been happy to have nodded, but the truth was, she'd been finding it increasingly difficult to breathe. She'd half wondered at the time if the man would have let her go if she hadn't raked her fingernails down his forearm.

It was odd that Guy de Seger should be sporting wounds in approximately the same place on his arm, wasn't it?

Odder still that he should have sent her a look of such loathing. As if perhaps she had done something he hadn't approved of. It was possible, she supposed, that he disliked her simply because she loved his brother. She couldn't quite bring herself to believe he would have wanted her for himself and the disappointment of knowing he wouldn't realize his desire had left him so ill-humored, but it was a possibility. It was a certainty Guy's mother had no love for her.

Then again, she obviously had no love for her stepson, either.

Isabelle forced herself to listen to the bile Margaret was spewing at Gervase and was slightly shocked at the viciousness.

"Kill your father?" Margaret echoed with a laugh. "Are you mad? Of course I didn't kill your father."

"Didn't you?" Gervase asked calmly. "Then I don't suppose you know who did."

"Well," Margaret said with a small smile, "I do know that."

"Are you going to enlighten me?"

She shrugged. "Why not?" She gestured expansively to the blond standing against the wall, a man who had ended his fight with his tassel by pulling a small tapestry down off the wall and throwing it across the chamber. "There he is. Your father's killer. Yours too, if I'm not mistaken."

Isabelle felt her mouth fall open. Gervase, however, didn't look particularly surprised.

Margaret cleared her throat. "Guy?"

"What?" Guy said in annoyance. He looked at his mother. "What?"

"I told Gervase what you've done, darling. You don't mind, do you?"

Guy shrugged. "He'll be dead by the end of the day anyway, so I don't suppose it matters now."

"Will I?" Gervase asked politely. "How do you suppose that will happen?"

"I gave the lady Isabelle a bottle of poison and told her to give it to you or I would kill her family."

"Clever you," Gervase said, clapping slowly. He folded his arms back over his chest. "And what a remarkable coincidence that you should find her at Caours right when you needed her to be there. Or did you plan that as well?"

"Well, of course I planned that as well," Guy snarled. "How stupid do you think I am?"

Isabelle supposed she might have an opinion on that, but perhaps 'twas best not to offer it. She had seen a flash of Guy's mercurial change of mood a handful of moments earlier, but it was somehow quite a bit more alarming to see that flash of anger turned on Gervase. She poked Miles in the back, hoping he would understand her unspoken command that he go stand a bit closer to Gervase but he only elbowed her in return, catching her high up enough in her gut that she abruptly lost her breath.

She would have cursed him, but in her desperation to suck in air and the accompanying bit of looking for a place to sit for use in doing so, she noticed that there was perhaps a very good reason Miles wasn't as concerned about Gervase's safety as she would have liked.

She had no idea when he'd slipped inside the chamber, but there Robin was standing to Guy's right, so still that she might have thought him just another statue. Sir Aubert was standing next to him, still as a statue himself. That was reassuring, to be sure, but apparently those weren't the only two who had found their way inside Her Majesty's solar. Isabelle looked over in the corner that surely wasn't but ten paces behind Lady Margaret and saw none other than her grandfather leaning negligently against the wall. He was partially hidden by a painted screen.

He was also wearing hose and a tunic, not skirts.

"Of course I knew who she was!" Guy shouted without warning. "Who do you think got her to France in the first place?"

Isabelle dragged her attention back to the conversation at hand. Gervase was watching his brother grow increasingly angry as he spewed out details Isabelle supposed he might regret having admitted to.

"You?" Gervase asked, looking for the first slightly surprised. "How did you manage to bring Isabelle to France?"

"Well, I wrote the bloody missive that told her to come," Guy said, looking down his nose at Gervase. "How did you think I did it? And you can thank your sainted grandfather for that idea. I'd heard a great deal about those damned de Piagets from him as he chatted endlessly with Sir Etienne. And unlike you, I had at least seen her older sister at Beauvois so I knew what she looked like."

"You were fortunate, then," Gervase said mildly. "But why not go wed her in England? Why bring her to France?"

"To kill you, of course," Guy said with a snort. "It was a very simple plan. She would come to the abbey, I would instruct her to kill you, then I would wed her."

"I see," Gervase said slowly. "And you assumed that she would want to wed you after you'd forced her to become a murderess?"

Guy shrugged. "It wasn't as if she would have much choice. When you convince someone to kill for you, that body tends to feel a certain sort of desire for you not to tell everyone what he's done." He shot Margaret a dark look. "Wouldn't you agree, Mother?"

"What would I know of anything?" Margaret said coolly.

Isabelle watched realization dawn on Guy's face. He gaped at his mother.

"You can't be serious," he said incredulously. "It was your idea to start with!"

"Of course it wasn't—"

Guy's face turned a mottled shade of red. Isabelle realized with a start that the color reminded her a bit of the sealing wax she and Miles had examined. She supposed she didn't want to know what Guy had used to turn it that bloodred color, though she supposed there was clay enough somewhere near Monsaert to satisfy anyone with a penchant for red wax. The one thing she was certain of was that she wasn't going to be asking Guy the details anytime soon. What she wanted was for the men of her family to overpower him, take him to the queen mother, and be done with him.

Unfortunately, Fate seemed to have a far different idea of how things should proceed.

Chapter 26

Gervase realized with a sinking feeling that he didn't care at all for the way the game was playing out. He didn't like the feeling of being trapped, but he could see that he was coming perilously close to finding himself in just those straits. He considered the battlefield, then moved back until he had both Margaret and Guy in his sights, hopefully drawing them away from Isabelle and her guardsmen. He couldn't see her any longer, but he supposed that was because Miles and Joscelin were keeping her behind them.

He could see Aubert and Robin leaning negligently against the back wall of the solar and he wasn't entirely sure that wasn't Etienne de Piaget over there in the corner, but what did he know? He had assumed his stepmother was responsible for all his ills. At the same time, he had been trying to convince himself that his next youngest brother was a man of honor and virtue. Obviously, his intuition had failed him, and badly. He could only hope Isabelle didn't pay the price for that.

He listened to Margaret and Guy spend several minutes arguing over who had first had the idea to slay him before he cleared his throat.

"Have we decided yet?" he asked politely. "I'd like to have it out of the way, if you don't mind. Things to do, you know."

Guy's look of loathing was unsurprising but a little startling nonetheless. Gervase supposed that if he had the chance, he would spend a decent amount of time berating himself for his stupidity. If only he'd been a bit more skeptical, he might have spared himself the loss of his father.

Which would have meant the loss of his future with Isabelle, but perhaps that was something he could think about later, as well.

"Feeling poorly, brother?"

Gervase looked at him. "I'm in perfect health, actually. Why do you ask?"

"You look flushed."

"That comes with knowing that I am master of Monsaert, a vast and fertile holding, and that I will yet live many years to enjoy it all," Gervase said with a shrug. "'Tis enough to bring a rosy bloom to any lad's cheeks, wouldn't you say?"

Guy apparently didn't have anything else to say. Instead, he moved as quickly as a striking snake. Gervase drew his sword, fully prepared to bloody the floors with his stepbrother's innards only to realize too late that a sword fight was not what Guy was interested in.

Guy leaped forward and kicked him as hard as possible.

Exactly on the place where his leg had been broken.

His sword clattered to the polished stone under his feet. He was suddenly on his knees without knowing quite how he'd gotten there. The pain was absolutely blinding. He found himself hunched there on all fours, fighting a ferocious battle against a blacknesss that threatened to engulf him.

Guy laughed.

Or perhaps that had been Margaret. Gervase supposed that when listening to voices that belonged with the damned in Hell, perhaps it didn't matter how closely one identified them. He fumbled for the knife in his boot and managed to get it free in spite of the stars that swirled about his head. He looked up and knew immediately that his knife, no matter how well crafted, was going to be of absolutely no use against the sword he saw coming down toward his witless head.

And then events took a turn he hadn't expected.

Guy froze. The sword fell from his hands and rang out as it struck the stone, much as Gervase's blade had done. Gervase sat back on his heels and looked up in surprise at his half brother, then realized what seemed odd.

There was a blade sticking out of Guy's chest. Just the point, though, as if it hadn't been so much a sword as a knife.

Gervase could hardly see through the haze of agony that still surrounded him, but he was lucid enough to watch Guy sink to his knees. His brother gurgled something at him, then fell forward. Gervase managed to move out of the way, but that cost him another wave of pain crashing over him. He grasped a heavy chair and simply forced himself to breathe until the wave receded and he thought he could pay heed to what was going on in front of him without being ill.

Isabelle de Piaget was standing there, looking very green.

She looked at him, turned, and then puked.

Down the front of Margaret of Monsaert's very elegant silk gown.

All hell broke loose, which he supposed was something he should have expected given the day he'd had so far. His stepmother began to shriek, though she was taken in hand by a silver-haired man who invited her to sit down before she did something she would no doubt regret.

He found himself hauled to his feet by Miles and Joscelin. He used their sturdy shoulders to keep himself upright, then glared at Robin who was standing behind his heaving sister, simply watching the goings-on with interest. Gervase gestured toward Isabelle.

"You couldn't have helped her?" he asked, feeling something that ran quite a bit hotter than mere annoyance.

"Why?" Robin asked, scratching his head. "She had things well in hand. She poached Miles's knife and went to work. I thought it best to simply stay out of her way."

But then he lifted his elbow slightly. A long, wicked-looking dagger gleamed in the candlelight. Robin lifted an eyebrow briefly, then resheathed his knife before he knelt down to see if Guy still breathed. Gervase suspected the effort might prove futile.

He thanked his brother and future brother-in-law for their aid, then limped over to gather up his bride-to-be and move her out of Margaret's long reach. He barely managed to stop Margaret from hitting Isabelle, though he paid the price on his own jaw. Etienne used a bit more force to induce Margaret to resume her seat, which Gervase appreciated. He pulled Isabelle out of the way—behind Robin, thankfully—then realized they weren't quite as alone as he had thought.

The young king stood at the open doorway, his eyes wide with shock. His mother stood behind him, her hand on his shoulder. Gervase made his monarch and the queen regent a low bow, then realized that Isabelle had dropped a very lovely curtsey in spite of her weeping. He then straightened and exchanged a glance with the young king's mother.

The queen waved her guards inside. Gervase supposed it said something about his life at present that he found himself vastly relieved the men were simply there to remove Guy from the chamber and offer Margaret an escort out as well, not escort him to the dungeons.

He caught Margaret by the sleeve and stopped her. She looked at him, her visage white.

"I will settle you somewhere," he said in a low voice. "I suggest you stay there, comfortably out of sight. You won't enjoy your life otherwise."

She apparently couldn't muster even the slightest of replies. She simply pulled her sleeve away from him and followed her escort from the chamber. Gervase had the feeling that settling her wouldn't be anything he needed to concern himself with anytime soon. If she managed to avoid losing her head, she would be very fortunate, indeed.

He watched the queen exchange a brief word or two with Sir Etienne, which surprised him greatly, but it was over and done with so quickly that he wasn't sure he hadn't imagined the entire exchange. It had been that sort of day so far.

He found a chair, sat, and pulled Isabelle down onto his lap. Her weight on his leg almost sent him into oblivion, which had her trying to stand. He shook his head and pulled her back into his arms. He closed his eyes as she wrapped her arms around his neck and wept.

He understood, for a variety of reasons.

"I want to go home," she said finally.

He looked into her red eyes and felt his heart stop. "Artane?"

She blinked. "I was thinking Monsaert. Unless—"

He shook his head and pulled her close again. "Monsaert," he said quietly. "But perhaps we'll stop at the abbey so we can deposit your grandfather back where he belongs."

"My grandfather?"

"He was hiding behind a screen." He paused. "I'm not entirely sure he doesn't know the queen mother."

"I have questions for him."

"You aren't the only one, love," he said with a weary smile. He closed his eyes, let out a long, slow breath, then listened to her brothers, her grandfather, and his younger brother discuss the events of the day.

He had no stomach for the conversation. Perhaps he would manage to discuss the particulars with Isabelle's brothers and his at some point, but at the moment it was all he could do to simply think about what he'd learned that day.

Guy de Seger, of all people. The epitome of all knightly virtues, with the possible exception of decent sword skill. Gervase could hardly believe that his brother, his father's second son, could have been responsible for so much misery. His father's death, which, now that he thought about it, had reportedly come upon him after a very brief illness. Isabelle's terrifying journey to France. It was little wonder that Guy had suggested she be put to work in the kitchens. Perhaps he had thought to spirit her away when no one was looking and set her to her predetermined task.

Gervase supposed it would take him quite a while before he was able to think about that without feeling rather ill.

He supposed he could now credit his younger brother with his own wounding. Fortunately, as Joscelin had once pointed out, his would-be assassin hadn't been a very skilled shot, else he would have been dead, not left with a limp. Perhaps a few more visits to Sister Jeanne would remove even that reminder of what Guy had tried to do to him.

So much pain caused by a pair of souls fixated on things that, in the end, didn't matter. He shook his head, then pushed his thoughts aside. He closed his eyes, held his lady, and was grateful for the ability to do so.

One test down and only Rhys de Piaget left to face.

He hoped he wasn't breathing easily prematurely.

Chapter 27

Isabelle woke, then looked at the canopy of the bed she was lying in. She lay there for several minutes, trying to decide why it was she felt as if she had been to Hell and back. Then she remembered the truth of it. She *had* been to Hell and back.

In that moment, she realized that there was in life a great abyss between knowing something and actually doing the same. Take embarking on an adventure, for instance. 'Twas one thing to stand in the shadows and plan a grand journey full of peril and the unknown; it was another thing entirely to actually be off on the same, trying to keep one's feet aboard a heaving ship, trying to keep one's heart protected whilst in the care of a terrible rogue.

Shoving a knife into the back of that rogue's brother whilst he'd been about the nefarious business of attempting to kill the man she loved.

She would have heaved again, but she was past that somehow. All she could do was let the tears trickle down her temples and wonder if she would ever stop shaking. She closed her eyes and concentrated on simply breathing for quite a while until she thought she could perhaps look about her and see where she was without making any untoward noises. She looked to her left to find none other than her mother sitting there in a chair, watching her.

She crawled out of bed with a cry and threw herself into her mother's arms. Gwen laughed a little, then reached to her right and pulled a blanket over and around Isabelle.

"Poor lamb," she said, sounding pained. "You've had quite a time of it, I understand."

"Oh, Mama, you've no idea."

"Then tell me, love. Tell me everything."

Isabelle wasn't sure where to begin, so she began at the end and worked her way backward. She finished her tale with the last thing she remembered at home, which was standing at Artane's gates, having a hurried conversation with Arthur of Harwych. She wasn't entirely sure she also didn't remember riding away from Artane, looking at it over her shoulder, and feeling as though she would never see it again.

"Oh, Isabelle," Gwen said with a sigh, "what in the world drove you to such a course?"

Isabelle looked at her mother. "Did they not tell you?"

Gwen shook her head. "I've heard many things, but not that."

Well, there was surely no reason now not to be honest. "I received a missive," she said slowly, "one that said Grandmother and Grandfather would be slain if I didn't appear in France as quickly as possible. I feared to say anything to anyone."

Gwen rubbed her back soothingly. "I can't say that I blame you, love, or that I wouldn't have done the same thing in your place." She paused, then shivered. "The risk you took was great, however."

"I was fortunate that Gervase found me," Isabelle agreed.

"So you were." Gwen nodded behind her. "I believe he's managed the feat again, only this time with a companion. Robin, darling, how are you?"

"Acting as chaperon to this one there," Robin said with a snort. "Seems he already has a bodyguard in that wee thing you're holding, so I'm only here to make sure he behaves himself."

Isabelle looked over her shoulder to find Robin standing at the foot of her bed with Gervase standing behind him. She glared at her brother, because it felt like a normal and reasonable thing to do. Robin only laughed and leaned over to give her a loud kiss on the cheek.

"That was good work you did, Iz," he said cheerfully. "I don't suppose I need to give you any lessons in knife play now, but don't say I'm not willing to."

She supposed there were several things she could say, but the thought of any of them having anything to do with what she'd just been through was more than she could stomach. She shot her brother a weak glare, but he only laughed and stepped aside. Gervase went down on his good knee and inclined his head to her mother.

"My lady Artane," he said politely.

"My lord Monsaert," Gwen said with a smile. "Isabelle has been telling me a fascinating tale about her time spent tidying up your kitchens."

Gervase looked far more uncomfortable than he should have. Isabelle found it in her to smile.

"Mama, don't tease him. He was distracted."

"And determined to spend the rest of his life making up for the error," Gervase said solemnly. "If your husband will consider it, my lady."

Robin slapped Gervase affectionately on the back of the head. "He's outside sharpening his sword, my lad. What does that tell you?"

"It tells me that if you call me *lad* one more time, I'll stick you for it."

Robin bounced on the bed and chortled. "Ah, a brawl. I was robbed of my sport at Louis's hall, you know, so I must look for a replacement as soon as possible."

Isabelle looked at her mother in despair but Gwen only smiled.

"Pull up a stool, Your Grace," Gwen said, "and sit with us for a bit."

Isabelle was happy to sit wrapped in her mother's arms with Gervase's hand smoothing over her hair. She listened to her mother and her love speak of simple things and was content to leave them to it. They kept at it for longer than she'd dared hope before the conversation wound back around to things Isabelle was far less comfortable with.

"You know, Lord Gervase," Gwen said softly, "you could talk to Robin about the trials of a woman saving the life of the man she loves."

Isabelle watched Gervase look at Robin in surprise.

"In truth?" he asked.

Robin lifted his eyebrows briefly. "'Tis entirely possible that my lady might have known a bit more than I did about a lad who wished me ill—I'm not admitting anything, of course—and that I might have been looking in the wrong direction—again, not that I'm admitting anything but perfect awareness—"

"Robin?" Isabelle said with a sigh.

"Aye, sister?"

Isabelle thought of all the things she could say to her brother, but realized very quickly that Robin knew exactly how Gervase felt and Anne might be exactly who she needed to talk to. She looked at her brother.

"Say on," she whispered.

Robin shrugged. "I won't say that Anne didn't have terrors at night for quite some time. I would make light of it, but the truth is, it was my privilege to be there to hold her as she grieved." He smiled faintly. "I suppose my slobbering gratitude to her for my sorry life wasn't displeasing to her." He looked at Gervase. "Slobber, my *lad*. Often."

"I will," Gervase said seriously. He looked at Isabelle briefly, then rose. "I will leave you in peace, my lady."

Isabelle watched him collect Robin and go, then shivered in spite of herself. If she hadn't killed Guy . . .

She crawled off her mother's lap. Obviously she'd spent too much time already that day entertaining idle thoughts. She looked at her mother. "Where do you think they've gone?"

Gwen smiled. "To the lists, I imagine."

Isabelle felt her mouth fall open. "But Guy hurt Gervase's leg so badly yesterday."

"I don't think your father cares. Actually, I imagine Gervase doesn't care, either. I understand he was prevented from an early start in the lists only by a desire to assure himself that you were well."

"Who else is there?" Isabelle demanded.

"Robin, of course," Gwen said. "Miles, though he doesn't seem all that interested in the sport. He's too busy talking to Etienne about things I don't think I want him considering. John and Montgomery are waiting their turn, as you might expect. Montgomery has expressed a desire to meet you in the lists as well, which you might find surprising. Or not."

Isabelle looked at her mother with a fair bit of reluctance. "I understand I clunked him over the head with a shutter." She paused. "In a roundabout way."

Gwen rose. "I believe he's interested in discussing that with you in detail."

Isabelle threw her arms around her mother and hugged her. "I'm so happy."

"That your brother wants to meet you in the field or that your would-be lover is going to be confined to his bed for a fortnight?"

"Nay, Mama," she said, pulling back and looking at her mother seriously. "That Gervase knows my name."

Gwen laughed a little, then kissed her on both cheeks. "He certainly does, love. Best wear something warm if you're intending to spend the morning watching the battle. I'll see if someone can't be prevailed upon to bring you something to eat later."

Isabelle nodded, then took her mother's advice on clothing. Still, she shivered as she left the warmth of her chamber and hurried out to the field where the men of her family were gathered. She had the feeling that had less to do with the weather than she might have wished.

She paused in the cloister and hid behind a pillar where she could see where danger lay before she walked out directly into it. Gervase was in the middle of the field, such as it was, facing her father. He was on his feet, which she supposed was a good sign. The line of souls waiting to have their turn was, she supposed with less enthusiasm, not a good sign. She left the safety of her hiding place and sidled up to Miles, because that seemed a less dangerous proposition than hopping up onto the wall to sit next to Montgomery.

"How's he doing?" she whispered.

"I believe there's been some pointed conversation about his care of you," Miles said with a smile. "That's gone about as you might expect."

Isabelle didn't have to ask if Robin had had his turn yet. He was bouncing up and down on the balls of his feet, looking as fresh as if he'd just rolled out of bed. She eased forward and looked around Miles. John and Montgomery were there, leaning against the wall and watching with stony expressions on their faces. Isabelle took a deep breath, then walked around Miles to stand in front of her younger brothers. She looked first at John.

"Good to see you, brother," she said with a smile.

John pulled her into his arms, embraced her so tightly she squeaked, then set her away from him. He nodded briskly to his right where Montgomery was standing, scowling fiercely. Isabelle put her hands on his crossed arms.

"Montgomery."

He looked at her. His eyes were very red, as if he had tears to shed but couldn't. She put her arms around him and held on to him tightly.

"I'm sorry," she said.

He shook his head sharply. "You did what was needful."

"And when did you come to that conclusion?"

"An hour or two after I stopped wanting to find you and kill you."

She pulled back and smiled up at him. "And how long did that take you?"

He pursed his lips and unbent far enough to embrace her. "Several days after we learned you weren't dead, which means I decided an hour ago that I would let you live."

John snorted. "Tell the entire truth, Montgomery, you coward. You were fully prepared to do damage to her until you saw what's out there facing Father."

Isabelle moved to sit atop the wall between her youngest brothers. "He's doing well, isn't he?"

And with that, they were off. Isabelle settled herself more comfortably atop the flat rock and listened to her younger brothers and Miles discuss Gervase just as they'd discussed innumerable swordsmen over the course of her life. She found the discussion widened to include the opinion of Joscelin, who revealed himself to be a reasonably fair soul.

She wasn't sure she could be as objective. All she saw was a man who had been through hell over the past few days yet was still willing to do what was necessary to fight . . .

For her.

Her father wasn't showing Gervase any mercy. She hadn't expected him to, not truly. She supposed the one thing she could say for what was going on in front of her was that at least her father was talking to Gervase, not snarling at him.

The morning wore on. Isabelle supposed she might have suppressed a yawn or two. She eventually leaned against Montgomery's shoulder and closed her eyes.

She realized she had dozed only when she felt an elbow in

her side and almost fell off her perch as a result. Strong hands caught her before she went sprawling. She looked up to find Gervase standing there.

His hands were shaking.

She met his eyes. "How are you?"

"Still on my feet."

"Is the effort worth it?" she asked.

He smiled, then leaned forward and very carefully kissed her on the cheek. "The prize is worth it, Isabelle. The prize is worth countless mornings such as this."

"Come out from behind your lady's skirts, Monsaert," Robin bellowed. "Let's be about the true work of the day!"

Gervase looked at her, sighed lightly, then smiled. "I'll return."

She watched him go, then found herself enveloped in her father's embrace. He pulled away from her, took her face in his hands, and looked at her with tears in his eyes.

"Isabelle," he said with a sigh.

"Papa, I had to come."

"So I see now, but I warn you that if you ever do anything so foolish again, I will take my blade to you."

Miles leaned over and cleared his throat. "I believe, Papa, that you'll need to go through her husband to get to her."

Rhys scowled. "Aye, I suppose there is truth enough in that." He looked at Isabelle. "Don't give him gray hairs, daughter."

She smiled. "You like him, then?"

"I gave him permission to court you, didn't I?"

"I don't know," she said. "Did you?"

"I think he means to wed you, then court you, but I find that I can no longer control these new and incomprehensible ideas youth entertain these days. I suppose you may have him if you wish."

"I'm not finished with him," Montgomery said loudly. "And then I intend to see to her. I think perhaps speaking of a wedding is slightly premature, Father."

Isabelle smiled at her father, then rested her head on his shoulder whilst she watched the man she loved fight with her oldest brother and laugh as he did so.

Chapter 28

Gervase stood at the door to his chapel with his newly made wife at his side and watched the procession retreating to the great hall. He looked at Isabelle.

"They abandoned us," he said. "I wonder why?"

"Food," she said succinctly. "I have four brothers, you have five. Nicholas isn't here, but they just had their second son which leaves us, again, with more lads surrounding us."

He put his arm around her and pulled her close. He smiled, then bent his head and kissed her. "I suppose if their tromping off to the kitchens purchases us a bit of time alone, we can't complain."

She put her arms around his waist and rested her head against his shoulder. He closed his eyes and supposed there was little that could possibly disturb his happiness at present. Isabelle's family had decided he would, with enough time, be worthy of her, and her father and brothers had stopped threatening to kill him when Isabelle was out of earshot. He had received a grudging invitation to Beauvois, an invitation that had been extended following the birth of the youngest de Piaget lad. With any luck, he would manage to get himself in and out Nicholas's gates while remaining alive enough to care for his bride.

As far as his own family was concerned, he supposed there was much to celebrate there as well. Guy was dead and buried. That was a cold comfort, he supposed, but at least he could walk through his own hall without worrying about dying.

His stepmother had been banished to a remote little house attached to the estate of a minor noble desperately trying to curry favor with the queen regent. Gervase supposed it was only good taste that inspired him to refrain from commenting on whether or not he might or might not have had anything to do with offering that as a suggestion to Louis's mother. He had settled a generous sum on his stepmother, done the same to all her relatives, and suggested politely that if they didn't want to run afoul of his ire, they would not arrive at his doorstep asking for anything else.

His brothers had been overjoyed to finally have some measure of peace and security in their lives. The older lads were, he supposed, happy to know Monsaert would be a place where they were welcome and wanted. The little lads were simply beside themselves with the thought of having Isabelle to themselves.

He thought he might have to clarify a few things for Yves and Fabien, but perhaps later, when they had stopped weeping tears of joy.

"Oh, my."

Gervase opened his eyes and smiled at his bride. "What is it?"

She nodded toward the gates. "We have a visitor."

Gervase looked, then blinked. He considered, then turned his lady to him and put his arms around her. "I love you."

She smiled up at him. "And I love you."

"I believe that's Arthur of Harwych trotting up the way."

"I believe it is, my lord."

"Do we invite him in for supper?"

She laughed a little at him. "Aren't you the generous one today."

He slipped his hand under her hair, bent his head, then kissed her. He considered, then decided there was no reason not to do a proper job of it. He continued with his delightful labors until the gasping of a soul faced with things he couldn't begin to think about became so distracting that he had no choice but lift his head and look at the lad standing to his left.

"B-b-but," Arthur said, pointing at Isabelle.

Gervase felt compassion spring to life inside his breast. He reached out and clapped a hand gently on Arthur's shoulder.

"I wed her," he said simply. "So sorry."

"B-b-but," Arthur said, pointing at Gervase.

"I know," Gervase said gently. "A bit of a shock, I'm sure."

"Ahhh—"

"Your boots?" Gervase asked. "I'll replace them, of course." He smiled at Isabelle. "Shall we go inside for the feast?"

"Of course, my lord."

"Shall we invite this lad here?"

Isabelle nodded, then disentangled herself from his arms and turned to face Arthur. "You aided me when I needed it," she said seriously. "For that, I will be forever grateful."

Gervase leaned forward. "Not enough to name a son after you, of course, but grateful just the same."

Isabelle elbowed him in the ribs, then reached out and put her hand on Arthur's arm. "Come and sup with us, Arthur. My lord Monsaert has no sisters, to our sorrow, but I understand the Duke of Coucy has several very lovely daughters. Perhaps my husband can arrange an invitation for you."

"I saw the duke half an hour behind me," Arthur squeaked. He looked at Gervase. "Might I have an introduction today, do you think?"

"Why not?" Gervase muttered. He pointed toward the hall. "Go on up the way, my lad. We'll be along very soon."

Arthur trotted off, looking far happier than he likely should have looked. Perhaps he was anticipating enjoying his new boots.

Gervase realized that Isabelle was looking at him. He shifted, then looked at her reluctantly.

"Aye?"

"The Duke of Coucy?"

"Come to wish us hearty felicitations, no doubt."

She blinked, then laughed. "Gervase, if you are still engaged to that shrill harpy, I'm not quite sure what I'll do to you."

Gervase looked over his shoulder at his priest who was holding on to a particular sheaf of parchment. He nodded, then looked back at his wife.

"His Grace signed a contract the last time he was here. A

contract reversing a previous contract committing me to wed with his eldest, shrillest daughter."

"Does His Grace remember either?"

"I doubt it, though there were witnesses," Gervase said. He paused. "One of them was Guy, which I suppose might put us in a bit of a spot—"

"Gervase!"

He laughed, kissed her heartily, then took her hand and pulled her from the chapel. "Joscelin was there, as was the duke's wife, who was very happy to have her daughter released from any obligations to a beast such as I."

"Good," she said shortly. "I would hate to spoil the day by being forced to draw my blade on them."

He looked at her quickly, but she was only smiling faintly, not puking into the flower beds. He embraced her briefly, then kept his arm around her as he walked with her into his great hall. He released her into the cloud of women who came to fetch her, a cloud that included her sister, Amanda, her mother, and her sister-in-law, Anne. He supposed he would be allowed to sit next to her at table, then, with any luck, spirit her off without having to do damage to any of her male relations with ideas of traditions best left in the past. He leaned back against the wall and allowed himself the very great pleasure of simply watching his hall be full of family.

"You're fortunate to have her."

He looked to his left to find his now next youngest brother standing there. He smiled.

"And so I am."

Joscelin lifted an eyebrow. "I heard Coucy's on his way up from the gates."

Gervase patted his brother on the shoulder. "Why don't you go invite him in to supper. He can eat, then collect his guardsman, who I'm afraid is still languishing in our dungeon. I believe I'll go see to the more pleasant labor of rescuing my wife from the clutches of the women in her family." He shot Joscelin a look. "I wouldn't set my sights on any of Evelyne's sisters, were I you."

Joscelin shook his head. "I wouldn't dare. Besides, Robin says he has advice for me in matters matrimonial."

"The saints preserve you," Gervase muttered, but he supposed his brother would fare well enough. Then again, with Robin of Artane, one just never knew.

He walked over to the press of souls in front of the fire and realized that he might be farther away from having his bride to himself than he had first hoped. She was sitting in front of the fire, surrounded by her family and his, with Yves on her lap. Gervase leaned against the wall near the hearth where the fire was comfortably warm but not too hot and counted his blessings.

First was family, not only his but hers as well. His keep had been overrun with both sides for almost a se'nnight and he couldn't remember when he'd enjoyed chaos more. The laughter of children, the delightful company of women, and the continual ring of swords coming from his garden. It had been an unexpected pleasure.

Second was the hall he'd been blessed with, gifted to him in spirit by his grandfather and held for him in trust by his father. It was a beautiful place, lovely enough to please his need for beauty and intimidating enough to satisfy his need for security. It was a place perfectly designed to keep his family safe, and for that he was grateful.

Last but surely the most important was the woman who sat in the midst of souls who loved her, a woman who had brought them all a joy he'd never thought was possible. Her family loved her, his brothers adored her, and he . . . well, he hadn't taken a decent breath since he'd gone down on his good knee a pair of fortnights ago and begged her to be his.

He realized Isabelle was looking at him. He felt a little winded, but that was his usual state around her so he thought nothing of it. She smiled at him, as if she knew what he was thinking.

She was the stuff of dreams he'd hardly dared dream. She was surely more than he deserved, but he wasn't going to argue with Fate. He would take what he'd been blessed with and be grateful.

It was enough.

Turn the page for the
MacLeod and de Piaget family trees.

family lineage in the books of
LYNN KURLAND

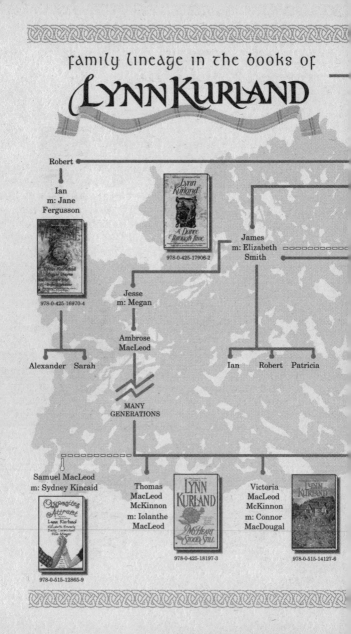

Robert

Ian
m: Jane
Fergusson

978-0-425-16970-4

Alexander   Sarah

A Dance Through Time
978-0-425-17906-2

James
m: Elizabeth
Smith

Jesse
m: Megan

Ambrose
MacLeod

Ian   Robert   Patricia

MANY
GENERATIONS

Samuel MacLeod
m: Sydney Kincaid

Opposites Attract
Lynn Kurland
978-0-515-12865-9

Thomas
MacLeod
McKinnon
m: Iolanthe
MacLeod

My Heart Stood Still
978-0-425-18197-3

Victoria
MacLeod
McKinnon
m: Connor
MacDougal

978-0-515-14127-6

MACLEOD

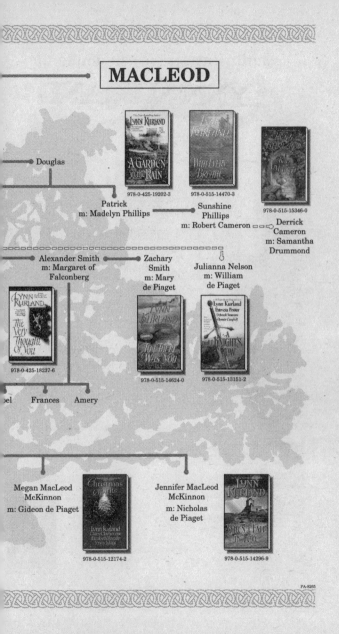

Douglas

Patrick
m: Madelyn Phillips

978-0-425-19202-3

978-0-515-14470-3

Sunshine
Phillips
m: Robert Cameron ▫▫▫ Derrick
Cameron
m: Samantha
Drummond

978-0-515-15346-0

Alexander Smith ◦◦◦ Zachary
m: Margaret of   Smith
Falconberg   m: Mary
de Piaget

Julianna Nelson
m: William
de Piaget

978-0-425-18237-6

978-0-515-14624-0

978-0-515-13151-2

bel   Frances   Amery

Megan MacLeod
McKinnon
m: Gideon de Piaget

Jennifer MacLeod
McKinnon
m: Nicholas
de Piaget

978-0-515-12174-2

978-0-515-14296-9

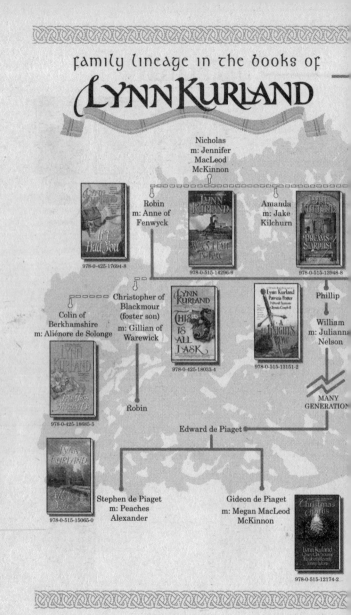

family lineage in the books of
LYNN KURLAND

Nicholas
m: Jennifer
MacLeod
McKinnon

Robin
m: Anne of
Fenwyck

978-0-425-17694-8

978-0-515-14296-9

Amanda
m: Jake
Kilchurn

978-0-515-13948-8

Colin of
Berkhamshire
m: Aliénore de Solonge

Christopher of
Blackmour
(foster son)
m: Gillian of
Warewick

978-0-425-18033-4

978-0-515-13151-2

Phillip

William
m: Julianna
Nelson

978-0-425-18685-5

Robin

978-0-515-15065-0

Edward de Piaget

MANY
GENERATION

Stephen de Piaget
m: Peaches
Alexander

Gideon de Piaget
m: Megan MacLeod
McKinnon

978-0-515-12174-2

DE PIAGET

Rhys de Piaget
m: Gwennelyn
of Segrave

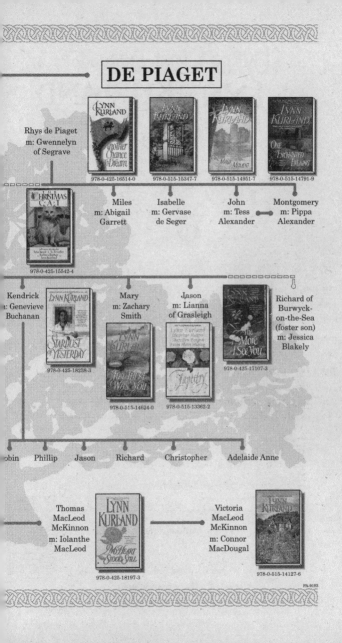

978-0-425-16514-0

978-0-515-15347-7

978-0-515-14951-7

978-0-515-14791-9

978-0-425-15542-4

Miles
m: Abigail
Garrett

Isabelle
m: Gervase
de Seger

John
m: Tess
Alexander

Montgomery
m: Pippa
Alexander

Kendrick
m: Genevieve
Buchanan

Mary
m: Zachary
Smith

Jason
m: Lianna
of Grasleigh

Richard of
Burwyck-
on-the-Sea
(foster son)
m: Jessica
Blakely

978-0-425-18238-3

978-0-515-14624-0

978-0-515-13362-2

978-0-425-17107-3

Robin   Phillip   Jason   Richard   Christopher   Adelaide Anne

Thomas
MacLeod
McKinnon
m: Iolanthe
MacLeod

Victoria
MacLeod
McKinnon
m: Connor
MacDougal

978-0-425-18197-3

978-0-515-14127-6

PA-9193

FROM *NEW YORK TIMES* BESTSELLING AUTHOR

LYNN KURLAND

Trapped first in Elizabethan England, then caught in a web of modern-day intrigues, a beautiful textile historian and an adventurous antiquities dealer are forced into an unlikely alliance by peril, never imagining that what they're forging is a timeless love...

PRAISE FOR THE NOVELS OF LYNN KURLAND

"Stepping into one of Lynn Kurland's time-travel novels is definitely one magic moment in itself."
—*All About Romance*

"Kurland is a skilled enchantress."
—*Night Owl Romance*

"One of romance's finest writers."
—*The Oakland Press*

lynnkurland.com
facebook.com/LoveAlwaysBooks
penguin.com

M1407T1113